PRAISE FOR *WHEN IT'S OVER*

"In extraordinary times, a single decision can mean the difference between life and death . . . *When It's Over* brings the forces of history to a very human level."

—*Booklist*

"Romantic without triteness and intelligent without laboriousness, seeing *When It's Over* appear as a BBC miniseries . . . wouldn't be a surprise. It's a sweet read, with thoughtful, touching storytelling to provide balm and resonance for our most human selves."

—*Foreword Clarion Review*

"A lively and compelling book which highlights many of the logistical and bureaucratic issues faced by refugees arriving in Britain, as well as the hardships of everyday life during WWII."

—*The Association of Jewish Refugees newsletter (UK)*

"Barbara Ridley has the rare ability to take the life of a real person— her mother, a Czech Jew who fled Prague for Paris and finally England—fictionalize it, and end up with a character so fully realized that we care not only about the bigger backdrop of history but about her daily life and the lives of those who surround her. Compelling and complex, with a strong female protagonist, *When It's Over* adds a much-needed fresh perspective to the canon of World War II literature. A first-rate first novel that makes you look forward to Ridley's second."

—**Lori Ostlund,** author of *After the Parade* and *The Bigness of the World,* winner of the Flannery O'Connor Award and the California Book Award

"A vividly realized story of wartime lives. This beautiful novel weaves an enchanting path through bravery, sadness, unexpected love, and sparkling hope. An involving story, utterly convincing in its historical detail. Barbara Ridley's heartfelt wartime novel *When It's Over,* will remind you of why you love reading."

—**Amanda Hodgkinson,** author of the NY Times Bestseller *22 Britannia Road*

"... a haunting story of love and loss, politics and prejudice."

—*East Bay Times*

"In Lena Kulkova, the reader finds an engaging, resilient character who comes of age amidst the turbulence, chaos, and devastation of 1930s and 40s Europe. [Her] intelligent and sensitive perspective exposes all the idealism and hope of young love and optimism, followed by the poignant realizations of human frailty and political reality as adulthood dawns ... Ridley's commanding sense of place and well-drawn supporting cast bring this intricate historical fiction vividly to life."

—**Barbara Stark-Nemon,** author of *Even inDarkness,* winner of the Sarton Literary Award for Historical Fiction

"... it was intriguing, yet heartbreaking, to read about the war from the perspective of those who are safe but whose families are trapped."

—*Historical Novel Society.*

"This fraught love story brings to life passionate, personal, and political struggles in the face of paranoia and prejudice in wartime England ... a story that resonates with the tensions and blindness all too apparent in the twenty-first century."

—**Desmond Barry,** author of *The Chivalry of Crime*

"With rich, sensuous details, Barbara Ridley captures the tumultuous 1940s in England, transporting you with a captivating story about love, loss and war."

—**Nina Schuyler,** author of *The Translator*

WHEN
IT'S
OVER

A NOVEL
{ BASED ON A TRUE STORY

BARBARA RIDLEY

SHE WRITES PRESS

Published 2017
Printed in the United States of America
Print ISBN: 978-1-63152-296-3
E-ISBN: 978-1-63152-297-0
Library of Congress Control Number: 2017936020

For information, address:
She Writes Press
1563 Solano Ave #546
Berkeley, CA 94707

Cover design © Julie Metz, Ltd./metzdesign.com
Interior design by Tabitha Lahr

She Writes Press is a division of SparkPoint Studio, LLC.

This is a work of fiction. Names, characters, places, and incidents portrayed in it, while at times based on historical events and figures, are the product of the author's imagination, or are used fictiously. Any resemblance to actual persons, living or dead, is entirely coincidental.

An excerpt, adapted from Chapters 14 and 15, was previously published in *The Copperfield Review,* as a short story, "Mapped Out"

Dedicated to the memory of my parents, Vera and Jasper

. . . and to the hundreds of thousands of courageous refugees
fleeing war and persecution in today's world

TIMELINE

SELECTED HISTORICAL EVENTS MENTIONED IN THE NOVEL

March 1933	Hitler comes to full power in Germany. Thousands of political opponents, mainly socialists and communists, arrested and sent to Dachau, one of the first concentration camps. Restrictions on Jews begin.
July 1936	Start of Spanish Civil War: Franco launches coup of Nationalists against the left-wing elected Republican government. Nationalists supported by Hitler. International Brigade of volunteers fight for Republican side.
March 1938	Hitler annexes Austria: the Anschluss.
May 1938	Reports of German troop movements towards the Czech border lead to full Czech Army mobilization, threat averted.
Sept. 1938	British and French governments sign Munich accord with Hitler; Germany granted right to annex the Sudetenland region of Czechoslovakia.
Oct. 1938	International Brigades withdraw from Spain.
March 1939	Franco declares victory, end of Spanish Civil War. Hitler invades Czechoslovakia.
Aug. 1939	Hitler and Stalin sign Non-aggression Pact.
Sept. 1939	Hitler invades Poland. Britain and France declare war on Germany. Followed by period of 'phony war' with very little action on Western Front until April 1940.
April 1940	Hitler invades Denmark and Norway.
May 1940	Hitler launches invasion of Belgium and France. Chamberlain resigns as British Prime Minister, succeeded by Churchill as head of Coalition Government.

June 1940	France falls to Germany.
	Internment of 'enemy aliens' begins in Britain.
July 1940	Arrival of Free Czech Army divisions in Britain.
Sept. 1940	German bombing of Britain, the 'blitz', begins.
June 1941	Germany invades Soviet Union, violating non-aggression pact: Soviet Union enters war on side of Allies.
Dec. 1941	Japanese bomb Pearl Harbor.
	U.S. and Japan enter the war.
Jan. 1942	Deportation of Czech Jews to ghetto of Terezín begins.
Nov. 1942	Publication of Beveridge Report in Britain advocates for post-war Welfare State.
Feb. 1943	Germans surrender to Russians at Stalingrad, their first major defeat of the war. Followed by significant Allied advances in the East, Africa and Italy—but no 'Second Front' in the West.
June 1944	D-Day landings on the northern coast of France.
	Start of V1 "Doodlebug' reprisal rocket attacks on Britain.
	Red Cross visit to Terezín, performance of Brundibár.
July 1944	Soviet troops liberate first concentration camp at Majdanek.
Aug. 1944	Paris liberated.
Oct. 1944	Siege of Dunkirk by Czech Brigade—continued until May 1945.
Oct –Nov. 1944	Sustained V1 and V2 rocket attacks on London.
Jan. 1945	Soviet troops liberate Auschwitz.
May 1945	Surrender of Germany to Allies, end of war in Europe.
July 1945	Churchill dissolves Coalition Government, calls General Election.
	Labour Party wins election in a landslide.

PART I

CHAPTER 1

PARIS, JANUARY 1940

Lena Kulkova stood at her tiny fifth-floor window, surveying the rooftops of the foreign city that she had come to love but was being urged to leave. She was wan and thin; her hair hung in limp strands to her earlobes, framing her broad cheekbones and sky-blue eyes. She crossed her arms to gather her nightgown tight against the early-morning chill. It was an inauspicious start to the day, but she focused on a streak of brightness piercing through the clouds. A puddle on the gray slate roof across the street reflected the shimmering image of a row of terra-cotta chimneystacks. Off to the left, a glimpse of her favorite landmark: the round balustrade atop the St. Sulpice tower, tinted with a spot of crimson.

Surely a good omen, she thought.

"You're up early," Marguerite said from the bed across the room. "*Ça va?* You all right?"

"I'm going back to the embassy," Lena said. "One more try." She straightened the eiderdown on her own bed and fluffed the pillow.

"If it doesn't work, you know you can stay here with me. Paris will be perfectly safe."

"I hope you're right."

Marguerite was her one true French friend; they had shared this small apartment for the past six months. She stood now and took Lena's hands in hers, holding her gaze. "They'll negotiate a peace treaty soon." She threw her dressing gown over her shoulders in an agile gesture, donning both sleeves simultaneously. "Then it will all be over."

Lena sighed. Yes, she heard that everywhere.

But not from Otto. For months he'd asserted that she must get out. That Paris would not be safe for a girl like her: Czech, Jewish, with known socialist connections.

The smell of the morning's fresh bread wafted up from the *boulangerie* on the corner. Usually, she bought a baguette every morning and nibbled it slowly throughout the day; sometimes this served as breakfast, lunch, and dinner. But today, she would wait. She still had an apple left over from the small bag Mme. Beaufils had thrust upon her, after her day of watching little Sophie. Tuesday nights at the Beaufils' was the only time she saw a full meal. She tried to eat with some restraint at these family dinners under the high chandeliers, but she felt Madame's gentle eyes upon her, couldn't hide the fact that she was ravenous.

"I'll be late tonight," Marguerite said, heading for the toilet on the landing. "Leave me a note. Let me know what happens."

"*Bien sûr.*"

"And I'll try to bring home some leftover pastries from the café."

"*Merci.*"

Lena dressed quickly, choosing the brown wool skirt, rather than the gray, and her new shoes. The soles of her old shoes were worn so thin they let in water, and she could not trust the rain to hold off. This new pair had cost 50 sous at the flea market the previous week. Tan, with a wide buckle, showing only slight wear on the heels, they had seemed a bargain. Now, she tried them on again and wiggled her toes; they should suffice for today's long walk.

In the kitchen annex, she sliced the apple and drank two cups of hot water to keep the hunger at bay, cradling the mug in her hands, inhaling the warmth. She retrieved Otto's letter from the bedside table, extracted her passport and the money from their hiding place among her undergarments, and placed them in her handbag. On second thought, she removed the crisp, peach-colored 1,000-franc note, folded it carefully into quarters, and plunged it deep into her skirt pocket for safekeeping.

Taking a final look around the room, she felt her eyes drawn to the watercolor tacked next to the window. Her little sister, Sasha, had painted it; Máma sent it last year, in a birthday package from Prague. Its colors were faded now, but you could still make out the eagle soaring high over the treetops, and the girl in the blue coat with her arms outstretched, as if trying to lift off the ground.

By the time Lena reached the British embassy, her feet ached, the sky was dark and overcast, and a cold wind whipped her face. She climbed the familiar stone steps and pushed through the heavy door. At least she would find a few hours of shelter inside.

Two dozen people already stood in the queue. The woman immediately ahead of her turned and smiled. She was in her thirties, older than Lena, with large gray eyes and a mass of auburn curls. In front of her, a tall man in a worn black coat looked nervously around the room, shifting his weight from one foot to another. A couple farther up spoke softly to each other in what sounded like Polish. Even farther ahead, a very young man, no more than a boy, really, read the newspaper. An older man, perhaps accompanying the boy, stared down at the tiles on the floor. The usual motley assortment.

The room looked drabber than Lena remembered. The war might have stalled on the battlefield, but here it was clearly taking its toll. More paint had chipped off the ceiling; a thick layer of grime coated the high windows, almost obscuring the bare branches of the trees outside as they swayed in the wind. Even the portrait of the King in the gilded frame behind the counter had lost some of its luster.

Only one station was open today. The clerk looked dour and inscrutable. A well-dressed woman with a large hat waved her hands excitedly, pleading her case, rummaging through her handbag for documents.

"I'm sorry, madame," the clerk said, loudly enough for all to hear. "We cannot continue with your application without the proper documentation."

The woman withdrew from the counter, avoiding eye contact with those behind her. The queue shuffled forward. Eva's boyfriend, Heinz, had a theory that the first fifteen applicants of the day were always denied, so perhaps it was just as well Lena had not arrived earlier, lining up for the doors to open at nine thirty. She didn't believe Heinz; the process seemed utterly random.

But her walk had taken longer than expected because the new shoes had rubbed her heels raw before she crossed the river. Now, she wiggled her left foot out of its shoe and shifted her weight to the right.

The boy and the elderly man moved up to the counter. The man spread a dossier of documents in front of him. The clerk looked at them with a cold, skeptical stare. Everyone in this queue wanted the same thing: the coveted visa for England.

Lena reached into her bag for Otto's letter. Apparently, her Czech friends Peter and Lotti had now arrived and were staying with him in the ancient cottage in the south of England.

Mein Schätzchen, he'd written, using his favorite term of endearment. They always wrote and conversed in German, his native tongue. *There are five of us now. It's like the Prague days. We've established a commune of sorts. You belong here with us.*

A second clerk appeared, opening up an additional window. *Things should move a bit faster now,* Lena thought—but then she recognized the man with square shoulders and the thin-rimmed spectacles. She had encountered him on three of her previous attempts, and he was sure to recognize her.

"Back so soon, Mademoiselle Kulkova?" he'd sneered the last time.

The problem on that occasion had been that she couldn't prove she had enough money to get herself to England. Lena touched her skirt, felt the outline of the pristine 1,000-franc note lying safely in her pocket. Tonight she would return it to Heinz so another expatriate could use it: to present to some bureaucrat, to prove solvency, as needed.

"You should forget about England," Heinz had said the night before, as they'd sat in Les Deux Magots, where all the Eastern European émigrés gathered. "The food will be terrible. They eat jam with their meat."

Lena didn't say that she rarely ate meat these days. Heinz obviously dabbled in the black market; he was always able to get his hands on things far beyond her reach. His arm draped around Eva's shoulders as he leaned back in his chair, blowing perfect smoke rings into the thick, noisy air. It was too wet to sit outside, as they usually preferred.

"She's not going for the food," Eva said. "She's going to be with Otto."

"You can do better than that, sweetheart." He winked at her. "Besides, you need to get out of Europe." He boasted that he would soon hear back from a second cousin in Chicago. "The New World: that's where the future lies."

Lena felt a tap on her shoulder. A dark-haired man with a pencil-thin mustache jerked his chin wordlessly to the space in front of her. She'd been daydreaming; the queue had moved ahead. Lena pushed her foot back into her shoe and edged forward, irritated, wincing in pain. Jamming together like the morning crowds on the Métro wasn't going to get them there any faster.

A younger man stood at the counter now, pleading his case loudly in very bad French with a thick Eastern European accent.

"L'autre homme promissons que si je revenir . . ."

The clerk raised his eyebrows and curled his upper lip in contempt. Lena's own French was fluent, perfected during her twenty months living in Paris. She read everything she could find: newspapers abandoned in cafés, cheap secondhand paperbacks from the green metal bins along the Seine: Proust, Verne, Zola. Especially now that she had so much time on her hands.

But she would speak English, she decided, when her turn came to face the clerk. It wasn't as polished as her French—but anything to make a good impression. She took a deep breath, trying to shake the nervous twitch in the pit of her stomach.

The Polish couple proceeded through quickly and left looking relieved, the woman hooking her hand through the man's crooked elbow, leaning into him as they made their exit. Lena watched their backs, remembering the pressure of Otto's arm against *her* breast, the coarse fabric of his jacket against her cheek.

She realized with a start that she was next. She pulled out Otto's letter again and removed the enclosed letter of invitation from . . . what was her name? A Mrs. William Courtney-Smithers had written in an elegant script on heavy, ivory-colored paper embossed with the family coat of arms. The address: The Grange, Upper Wolmingham, Sussex. Lena was to come and visit immediately. Spring was on its way, and the daffodils were sure to be spectacular. Mrs. Courtney-Smithers was anxious to show Lena all the delights of the English countryside.

Lena had no idea who this woman was. Obviously wealthy, but it didn't sound like Otto's landlady, based on what he had written in earlier letters. Yet somehow Otto had procured this invitation. He was clearly very impressed with her. *Just go back to the embassy and show them this letter*, he wrote; *she's very rich, almost an aristocrat.*

"Next!" The first clerk, not the man with the glasses, called her up to the counter.

"Please, I would wish to apply for a visitor visa," Lena said, in what she hoped was perfect English. She presented her passport. "I have been invited to stay with Mrs. Courtney-Smithers, an old friend of my parents, and I want very much to see her."

Lena handed the letter to the embassy clerk, trying to prevent her hands from shaking. The clerk glanced at the letter. "Where is the envelope this came in?" he asked.

"I think I threw it away." She concentrated on saying the *th* sound, placing her tongue behind her top front teeth and blowing gently, as she'd learned in school.

"Pity. I'm sure it was a fine envelope. Tell me, Miss, er, Miss Kulkova: What is the good lady Mrs. Courtney-Smithers . . . What is her Christian name?"

"Her Christian name?" *What does that mean?*

"Her first name. *Son prénom.*"

"I don't know, sir." Lena said. She knew enough not to suggest William; that must be her husband's name. "My parents always referred to her as Mrs. Courtney-Smithers. It would have been not respectful for me to address her as anything else."

"How did your parents make this lady's acquaintance, may I

ask?" He stared at her with piercing blue eyes. Lena was determined not to lower her gaze.

"Through my father's business. She and her husband came to Prague; I believe he was in the same line of business as my father," Lena said. "Carbon paper," she babbled on. "My mother and aunt showed Mrs. Courtney-Smithers all over Prague. She loved it."

The piercing stare again. Lena was sure LIAR must have been emblazoned on her forehead.

She remembered the 1,000 francs in her pocket. "I have money. I mean, I'm sure Mrs. Courtney-Smithers will be very generous, but I can pay my own way."

"I see. Well, Miss Koulkava"—butchering her name—"I'm afraid we are not issuing any visitor visas at the moment. We would only be able to issue a temporary visa for you to enter if you could prove you were in transit to another nation, such as the United States or Australia."

He looked again at the letter, before handing it back to Lena with a thin smile. "You will have to wait until the war is over before admiring the daffodils in England." He looked over her head and shouted, "Next!"

It took a moment for her to realize she had been dismissed. She stood with her mouth hanging open, as if waiting for the next question, until she felt the shoulder of the man with the mustache pressing against her, taking his place at the counter.

She walked back through the Jardin des Tuileries. She knew there would be little shelter from the wind along its wide, exposed paths, but she welcomed the open space to gather her thoughts. The statues stood serene, immutable, capable of withstanding the fiercest of storms.

She stopped at one of her favorites: three strong women, tall and proud, two facing forward, the other back, their fingertips gently touching, independent from each other yet interconnected. Soft and graceful and resilient.

Nearby, in the shelter of a tall hedge, Lena saw a bench, grimy and damp. She perched on the edge to take the weight off her feet, ease her heels out of her shoes. So she could not get a visa. *Otto was right: I should have left with him last year. Before the war started.* Now she had no idea when she would see him again.

She swallowed to fight back tears. She had to remain strong. Like these women of stone. Her left heel was bleeding now. Taking her handkerchief from her pocket, she folded it to create an improvised padding and squeezed her feet back into place. She had to go home and lie down for a while, get out of her wretched shoes.

As she entered her building and closed the front door behind her, blocking out the noise and bustle of the rue Cassette, she heard her name. It was Mme. Verbié, beckoning Lena into her inner sanctuary. This was unprecedented. Normally, the concierge conducted business firmly planted in the doorway, allowing only glimpses of the interior, with its rose-patterned wallpaper and cluttered counter. She liked to stand at her station, spreading the latest gossip about who was cheating on his wife, or which shopkeeper was charging exorbitant prices. But now Lena was being invited to enter and find a seat, while Mme. Verbié searched through one of the cabinets.

"I have something I want to give you, but you have to keep quiet about it now. Don't you go telling no one, especially not that young man I've seen your friend walking out with. I don't trust his sort."

She rummaged through piles of junk on the shelf while Lena tried to imagine what on earth would emerge from this search.

"I can't get one for everyone, *bien sûr*. But you're a decent young lady, and I don't like to see you go without. Ah, here it is."

She dropped into Lena's lap a heavy gray object: a gas mask. The government had issued these free to all French citizens three months earlier, but foreigners had been instructed to purchase their own. Lena couldn't afford one. Now, she looked down at the gaping eye sockets and the hideous, cylinder-shaped chin covering, which formed a grotesque grimace staring back at her.

She turned it over to inspect the head straps and felt a wave of nausea as the smell of the rubber filled her nostrils. She recognized the gift as a truly generous gesture, but she was afraid she might throw up right there on the carpet.

"*Merci beaucoup*, madame," she managed to mutter as she made her escape.

She was still shaking when she reached the fifth floor. The apartment was cold and empty. Kicking off her shoes, she threw the mask on the floor, collapsed on the bed, and curled onto her side, pulling the eiderdown around her back. The prospect of bombs and poison gas was suddenly real, imminent, and petrifying. How was she ever going to face such a threat alone?

She looked up and saw the watercolor on the wall. This time, her eyes focused on the eagle making his escape over the trees.

CHAPTER 2

PRAGUE, MARCH 1938

Lena waved from the steps of the Hus memorial as Eva emerged from the crowded corner of Celetná Street. She was easy to spot in her distinctive green coat with the sable collar and padded shoulders, a holdover from better times.

"Any luck?" Lena asked, as they hugged in the cold evening air.

Eva shook her head. "More than thirty girls applied. I didn't even get an interview."

"You'll find something." Lena tried to sound encouraging. But Eva had been looking for six weeks, and Lena's own job was as tenuous as a slippery eel. Another girl from the office had been let go the previous week. "We'll have fun tonight at Café Slavia," she said, linking her arm through Eva's.

"I think I'll stay home."

"Come with me, please. I want to go to the meeting, but I'm afraid Father won't let me. He's been in a terrible mood all week." The wind picked up as they approached the river. "My best chance is if he thinks I'm going out for a drink with you."

"Why are you so keen to go tonight?" Eva asked. "What's happening?"

"A volunteer from the International Brigade has just returned from Spain. He was wounded in the fighting at Teruel. He's going to give an update from the front lines."

"Doesn't look good, from what I've seen."

"But that's just it," Lena said. "We have to hear what's really happening. You can't trust what you read in the newspapers."

It had been two years now since the start of the war in Spain. Lena had been in her last year of school; three boys from Lena's class had left to join the fight. She was so caught up in the excitement it had been hard to focus on the *matura*, her final examinations.

"The Republican side will rebound," she said. "It has to."

They passed the queue waiting for the soup kitchen on Lilová Street. A woman with sunken black eyes pulled her shawl tight around her shoulders; the men stooped, shuffled forward past the boarded-up shop fronts.

"I had coffee with Peter this morning," Eva said. "Have you heard about the German political refugee who's just arrived from Vienna? He was high up in the Party in Berlin, apparently."

"Yes, I heard. He'll be there tonight, I'm sure. You'd better come see him yourself. They say he's a great speaker."

Eva laughed, tossing her auburn hair off her face. She always looked so pretty, with her high cheekbones, her perfect little nose, and the tiny mole on her upper lip—her "beauty spot," as she liked to call it. "I suppose you're going to tell me he's handsome, too."

"I'm sure he is!" Lena said, with a laugh.

"All right. Sold."

"I'll pick you up at seven thirty." They had reached the Charles Bridge. Lena paused to take in the view of the Vltava and the castle soaring high on the hill. She never tired of this vista. The branches of the chestnut trees stood stark and bare, no sign yet of their spring foliage. "Have you met Peter's new girlfriend?"

"I know her. Lotti Schurova," Eva said in a sneering tone. "It won't last."

"Why not?"

"She came with us last summer on that day trip to Cerné Lake. I told you about that. We got caught in a huge thunderstorm. Lotti became hysterical. I bet she's even too nervous to ride on the back of Peter's motorcycle."

"She's not, though. They rode out to Terezín last Sunday. He showed her the barracks where he did his military service."

"She's not his type," Eva insisted.

Lena poked her in the ribs. "You're jealous." Eva had been Peter's girlfriend for several months last year, but then she had grown tired of him. Peter probably seemed more interesting again now that he had someone else.

"I'm not. Peter and I are just good friends."

"If you say so." Lena laughed again. "Just promise me you'll come to the meeting."

Lena opened the door to her family's second-floor apartment and heard the piano in the front room: Sasha at her lesson, the notes of *Eine Kleine Nachtmusik* flowing easily from her little fingers. At eight, she was already far better than Lena had ever been. Lena crept down the hall to avoid another interrogation from Frau Grünbaum on why she was no longer playing.

Máma was in the kitchen, supervising Adele in the final stages of dinner preparation. Her parents complained they could no longer afford a maid, but Adele was still employed for all the cooking. Lena didn't criticize; it kept Adele in work, after all, and she was supporting her elderly mother.

"Hello, dear," Máma said. "How are you? How is Eva? Her mother told me she had an interview at a bookshop in Nové Město."

"She didn't get the job."

"Poor Eva." She waved a hand in Adele's direction. "Not too many Brussels sprouts, Adele; you know Ernst and Sasha won't eat them." She pulled Lena with her into the dining room. "Everything all right at your work, dear?"

"Fine." Her job was boring—typing all day in the office of a textile trader. But she didn't whine to her parents. She had taken the position over their objections and relished the modicum of independence it gave her.

Father was in the dining room, tuning the wireless, waiting for the evening news. Máma continued, "Your father says the Olšakovský place is closing next month. Wherever will those people find work?"

"Lena doesn't have to worry," Father said. "After all, she *was* offered a job working for me, but . . ." He spread his arms and left the *but* hanging in the air, a familiar gesture, irritating with its silent, implied criticism. "Thanks to your father's foresight and good planning, we are doing so much better than most. And carbon paper," he declared, "is very secure. The world is always going to need carbon paper."

The sound of Sasha's footsteps in the hall gave Lena the excuse to ignore this remark. Her sister ran toward her. Lena caressed the crown of her head, envying Sasha's pretty blond curls, so different from her own thin, straight hair, an indeterminate shade of brown. Máma ushered Frau Grünbaum to the front door while Sasha told Lena about her day at school.

"I have to write a report on *O Dvanacti Mesickach*!" she said.

Lena laughed. "That should be easy." It was one of Sasha's favorites; Lena had read it to her many times.

The front door of the apartment opened again and closed with a thud. Lena's brother, Ernst, threw his knapsack into the dining room, aiming for the chaise longue in the corner, but he missed and it crashed to the floor.

"Pick that up, young man," Father said, adjusting the wireless. He held up his hand to demand silence. "Shh. The news is coming on."

Lena helped her mother set the table. The broadcast was dominated by the latest developments in Austria. Chancellor Schuschnigg had called for a referendum on unification with Germany.

"Surely, Jakob, the Austrians won't vote for that, will they?" Máma asked over dinner. "To join the Third Reich?"

There was a new hint of fear in her voice. For years, Lena had watched her parents' stunned disbelief as the much-admired, sophisticated neighbor to the north had succumbed to the Führer. The land of Goethe, Beethoven, and Schiller? It was unthinkable. Hitler couldn't last. Six months had been the consensus. But the months had stretched to years, and the anti-Semitic decrees in Germany could not be ignored. Not that her family had ever identified as Jewish. They were patriotic Czechs. They rarely attended synagogue. They had a Christmas tree every year.

Now, Father shook his head. "Normally, I wouldn't think so. The Austrians value their independence as much as we Czechs do. It's all the fault of the Reds, you know." He raised his voice and waved his knife in the air, not quite pointing at Lena, but there could be no mistaking his intended target. "It's their troublemaking that has led to this. Strikes and riots. No wonder people crave law and order."

Not this argument again. As if the Left were responsible for the rise of the Nazis—so absurd. The socialists and communists were mounting the only effective opposition, while the conservative and social democratic parties hedged their bets, seeing the fascists as a bulwark against communism. But Lena would not take the bait. A full-blown fight would lead to her being forbidden to leave for the evening.

"Are you in a hurry, Ernst?" Máma asked with a smile, as he shoveled a mound of mashed potatoes into his mouth.

"I'm going to the Sokol," Ernst mumbled. "Gymnastics."

"What about your homework?"

"I did it this afternoon, Máma."

Ernst went out every evening, and not always to the Sokol, as he claimed. Last week, Lena had come upon him down by the river, smoking with friends. His movements were never subjected to the kind of scrutiny reserved for hers, even though he was four years younger.

"I'm going out with Eva," she said now, to piggyback on his announcement.

"Where?" Father said.

"Just out for a beer." She knew better than to tell the truth. He knew the reputation of the Café Slavia. "Eva needs cheering up."

"That's nice of you, dear," Máma said.

Father said, "You'd better be home by eleven."

"Tomorrow night," Máma announced, "I want us to observe Shabbat at dinner."

What? Where did this idea come from? But Lena didn't want to discuss that now; she had to leave.

The café was crowded, a buzz of excitement in the air. Lena and Eva elbowed their way through to the bar to order two pilsners. Peter waved them over to the table in the corner where he sat with Lotti. He kissed Lena and Eva on each cheek.

"Isn't the meeting going to start?" Eva said. She remained standing while Lena scooted next to Lotti on the bench.

"Sit down," Peter said. "They're always late. Finish your beer with us."

He was a few years older, in his midtwenties, with a prematurely receding hairline and short stature, not good-looking in the conventional sense but possessing a boundless energy, a disarming smile, and no shortage of female admirers.

Lena smiled at Lotti, who smiled back, blushing. Lena vaguely remembered her from the *Realgymnasium,* but Lotti had been in the year below her, so they'd had little direct contact. She sat with her hands in her lap, picking at a fingernail, glancing over at Eva and then Peter and back at Eva again.

"We met that German expatriate everyone's talking about," Lotti said. "He's very interesting. Otto something. What's his name, Peter?"

"Otto Eisenberg. He's supposed to be here."

"It does seem to be all anyone can talk about," Eva said.

"He was in Vienna until two weeks ago." Lotti turned to Lena. "He doesn't think Schuschnigg's last-minute efforts are going to appease Hitler."

Lotti's not as shy as she first appears, Lena thought. She could see why Peter was attracted to her. She had smooth skin, sparkling hazel eyes, and a charming dimple on each cheek when she smiled.

"There he is," Peter said.

A huddle of young men moved toward them through the crowd. Very much at the center of this group stood a tall, scrawny young man, with a shock of unruly dark hair and a coarsely shaven chin. He wore a rumpled tweed jacket and a wool scarf and carried a large notebook and a stack of pamphlets. His companions jostled for position at his sides, engaging him in discussion as they walked. A blond youth with very bad acne almost bumped into a waiter carrying a tray of empty glasses.

"But surely you agree that the socialist revolution has to occur first, in order to establish the correct conditions for the defeat of fascism," Lena heard the boy say.

Otto ignored the young man at his heels and led the procession into the meeting room. Peter stood and grabbed his beer. "Let's go," he said, jerking his head in the same direction.

Eva wanted to go to the ladies' room, and Lena felt obliged to accompany her. By the time they emerged, the meeting had already been called to order and it was difficult to find a seat. Lena could see Peter and Lotti up front, but she and Eva had to squeeze in behind the piano at the back. The first order of business was the strike at the brick factory, now in its second week, and the need for support on the picket lines, but Lena found it difficult to focus. She wanted to get another look at that Otto fellow, but she could not distinguish the back of his head from the dozens of others.

Soon the fighter from the International Brigade was introduced, to thunderous applause. He was tall and dark-haired, with one arm in a sling and an eye distorted from a swollen red scar across his eyebrow. He spoke in harrowing details of the intense fighting at Teruel; the sight of young mothers weeping over the bodies of children killed in a direct hit on a school; and a terrible scene in a village overrun by Franco's forces: the school teachers, the librarian, and the mayor singled out for execution and buried in a mass grave. Lena covered her mouth to stifle a moan.

But then he spoke of the courage and determination of the Spanish comrades. Their cause was just. The industrial and agricultural collectives continued to thrive. They remained defiant, true to their slogan: "*No pasaran.* They shall not pass." He raised his fist in salute.

"*No pasaran,*" the crowd responded. "*No pasaran.*" It gave Lena chills every time.

And then Otto rose and was introduced. She saw now that he had been seated up front. He gave a one-sided bear hug to the previous speaker, taking care to avoid his wounded arm, and launched into a fiery speech.

"Hitler is giving material aid to Franco while the Soviets are halfhearted in their support for the Republican side," he said in the clipped syntax of Hochdeutsch, High German.

His audience had no difficulty understanding him. Mostly self-identified hybrids like Lena, mostly Jewish, they had been raised bilingual. All of Lena's schooling had been conducted in German, while Czech was the vernacular at home.

"This is the forefront of the fight against fascism," Otto continued. "Only the Popular Front can succeed. Communists, socialists, Trotskyists, anarchists—we have to put aside our differences and remain united."

"He's not handsome at all," Eva whispered. "Quite funny-looking, in fact."

"Shh." Lena smiled. His face was gaunt, his ears huge, and his hair stuck up at a peculiar angle. He paced back and forth as he spoke and pounded his fist against his other palm, as if forcing the words out.

"Hitler will overrun Austria any day now. He will then be snapping at the heels of Prague. The unions and the Popular Front have to show the Beneš government here that we have the *strength* and *determination* to stand *firm* and *resist.*"

He must be hurting his hand, Lena thought. She joined the rest of the room in clapping and cheering and giving him a standing ovation. It was stirring rhetoric. But very scary. Could it really be true that Hitler would invade Austria? Czechoslovakia would be surrounded, with Austria to the south, Germany in the north.

She lingered after the meeting, finding a seat at Otto's table. Peter's friend Josef said, "Surely Britain and France would not tolerate such aggression."

"They've done little to stop Franco," Lena heard herself say.

Otto turned his gaze directly on her and she felt her face flush. "Exactly," he said. "We have to mobilize the masses to defeat fascism." She forced herself to maintain eye contact. His dark eyebrows and square jaw gave his face a distinguished demeanor. She saw he was older, maybe ten years older than Lena and most of her friends. "The Czech people must not repeat the mistakes made in Germany."

More people approached the table; someone had bought Otto a beer, and he reached across Lena to accept it, his arm brushing her shoulder. She caught a whiff of tobacco on the sleeve of his tweed jacket, sweet and pungent.

He was pressed for details about life in Berlin and his escape from the lion's den. He had hidden on a rooftop while the Gestapo hauled off two of his comrades; they had not been heard from since, presumed to have been deported to Dachau. He gave a tiny shudder, most likely imperceptible to anyone not seated close, but then changed the subject back to the next steps in political organizing.

"It will be essential to enlist the support of the unions and other progressive factions throughout Czechoslovakia," he said. "If Hitler grabs Austria, he will surely turn next to the Sudetenland." He tipped his glass and gulped down half the beer, leaving a thin line of froth on his upper lip. "Tell me about your organizing efforts. Have you been able to reach any of the German-speaking workers there? Are they unionized?"

Josef and Peter spoke of the difficulties, the anti-Czech sentiment in the region, the rise of the fascist elements, the small success they'd had the previous month in Vejprty. Otto listened intently, probed with more questions. He produced a pipe from his pocket and stuffed it with tobacco as he talked. More people pressed behind Lena to get closer, like children at the teacher's knee, she thought. She found herself wanting to listen to him all night, too.

Indeed, it was after midnight before she thought to check the time. The crowds were thinning out; only a few remained at the table. She plucked up the courage to ask Otto directly, "What exactly has brought you to Prague?"

He lowered his voice a notch and replied, as if speaking only to her, "I'm here working for the Spanish government, to establish an Economic Information Bureau. To enlist more support and investment from European nations."

She could not imagine anything more admirable: working for Spain by day, and at night offering his wisdom and leadership to the Popular Front in Prague.

But she had to drag herself away. She could only hope that her father would be asleep when she got home.

But Father was waiting up.

"What time do you call this?" he roared.

She tried to skirt down the hall to her room, but he blocked her passage, looming tall in front of her. He grabbed her coat lapels and drew her toward him, his eyes filled with fury. Lena tried to pull away, but he tightened his grip and for a moment she was afraid he might choke her.

"Stop!" she screamed. "Let me go!" Waking up the household was her only hope.

She pushed against his chest and jerked free. But he snatched her arm and slapped her hard across the face, knocking the breath from her. Lena was stunned. He stopped; he looked shocked, too. He'd not hit her like this since . . . when? Surely not since her primary-school days. There were constant restrictions and curfews, but not this.

"Jakob!" Máma ran from her room. "What are you doing?" She tugged at Father's arm.

"I told her to be home by eleven."

"Stop! She's not a baby," Máma pleaded. "She's nineteen."

"While she lives under my roof, she will abide by my rules," Father said.

Lena heard Sasha, woken by the commotion, crying. Lena brushed past Máma and ran to comfort her. Father would not follow her to Sasha's room. She threw herself on the floor next to the bed, stroking her sister's forehead.

"It's all right," she said. "Go back to sleep."

"Why was Father shouting?" Sasha asked.

"He's . . ." Lena stifled her own urge to weep. "He's just not himself these days," she said. "It's not your fault. Go back to sleep."

She sat until Sasha settled. Ernst must have heard the noise, too, but not a peep out of him, although Lena saw his light on when she returned to her room. She collapsed on her bed, furious and exhausted, her face throbbing. Yet she also felt an odd tingling of excitement from the evening's events that she couldn't quite explain to herself.

The following evening, Máma brought out the Shabbat candles, for the first time in years. But they did little to dispel the tension around the table. No one felt inclined to say prayers.

And on Saturday, Hitler marched into Austria, preempting the referendum vote. Prague's Wenceslas Square was filled with a huge demonstration in protest. But Lena was confined to the apartment all weekend, as punishment for having violated her curfew.

CHAPTER 3

PRAGUE, MAY 1938

Lena arranged to meet Eva for lunch on Střelecký Island now that the weather was finally warmer. She was free to take as long as she wished; Otto was off again, to an undisclosed destination, and would not be returning until the day after tomorrow. She was often on her own in the office but very content. It felt perfect: located on a narrow street, on the second floor above a used bookshop, close to a friendly café frequented by artists and radicals. The morning light filtered through the trees to brighten her desk as she worked. She typed up reports and answered the telephone and now had a thirty-page document Otto wanted translated from French into German. She felt competent in her tasks.

When Otto had first offered her the job in his Economic Information Bureau, she wasn't sure. She felt intimidated by him and nervous that she would not live up to his expectations. He needed a typist and a "general dog's-body," as he put it. The pay was less than she was earning at the textile office. And there was her father to deal with; of course he would not approve.

But Father was preoccupied with the news from Vienna. The day she prepared to tell him about her decision to change jobs, Frau Grünbaum burst into the room in a panic, quite incapable of focusing on Sasha's piano lesson. Her sister and brother-in-law were trapped in Austria.

"It's impossible, Mr. Kulka," she cried. "You would not believe what those Nazi brutes are doing. My poor brother-in-law, he is not in good health; he has the diabetes. But he was pulled like this, by the beard." She tugged at her own chin, jerking her head to the side. "He was forced to clean the pavement, on hands and knees, while the soldiers stood over him and laughed. They smashed the windows of all the Jewish businesses. My nephew, he is afraid he will be forced out of the university. They are trying to leave the country, but it is very difficult. You have to help them. Please, Mr. Kulka, you have always been so good to me."

Lena was unclear about what her father could do to assist, but he disappeared into his study to make telephone calls. When he emerged an hour later, she told him, "I am going to start a new job on Monday." He dismissed her with an impatient wave and left the apartment. She chose to interpret this as a nod of approval.

"Does he need to give his permission?" Otto asked the following day. His tone was not unkind. He smiled as he lit his pipe.

Lena blushed. They sat in a cafe in Malá Strana, three doors down from the small office space he had just secured. "No, I suppose not," she said, with a light laugh, and stared into her coffee cup.

"I'm very glad we'll be working together," he said. "But remember what I told you: the nature of the work is highly confidential." He reached across the table and took her chin gently in two fingers to bring her gaze up to meet his. His thick black hair, untamed by any oil, tumbled over his forehead, accentuating his bushy eyebrows. His jaw was cleanly shaven. "If anyone asks, you say we are working on economic aid for Spain. Nothing more."

Lena nodded. She understood that she had to be discreet. She did not understand exactly what he was doing. But she was helping Spain—that was good enough for her.

She had now been in the job six weeks. She sensed he was testing her. At first, she had not been permitted to touch the teleprinter that whirled in the back room, spewing out mounds of tape. The back room was where Otto retreated whenever Señor M. from the Spanish embassy visited.

She listened to the rumble of their voices behind the closed door, and then the señor would leave without glancing at her; she never knew his full name. There were others who came and went, mumbling their names incoherently, scuttling off without leaving a message if Otto was not there.

"What do you do all day?" Eva had asked more than once.

"Just type and answer the phone."

"Type what?"

"Reports. Economic reports."

She didn't say that the Condor Legion didn't sound economic. Nor did Heinkel He 51 fighters or Messerschmitt Bf 109s or Ju 52 bombers. Or that now that she was allowed to work directly from the teleprinter, she was processing reports from garrison towns and Luftwaffe bases inside Germany, information about squadrons fueling up and heading to Spain, communications penned by A-54 or D-14. When Eva came to pick her up one day at lunchtime, she quickly scooped up her work and locked it in her desk drawer. Now she made excuses and arranged to meet Eva elsewhere; it was safer that way.

Eva was already ensconced on a bench near a splendid display of chestnut trees; overladen with their white blooms, they draped over the river as if in a choreographed curtsy.

"How is Mr. Eisenberg today?" Eva asked, nibbling on a sweet bun.

"He is away on business, if you must know, ma'am." They had settled into a playful, teasing way of discussing Lena's work and her boss.

"Aren't you afraid he has another woman on the side?"

"Eva, stop. You know it's not like that."

"Come on—the two of you cooped up in that tiny office all day? You can't tell me there's nothing going on."

"We work together—that's all," Lena said, and then rummaged through her lunch bag because she was afraid she might blush. "Here, do you want one of these sandwiches? Adele always gives me far too much."

The truth was, Lena appreciated that Otto did not try to take advantage of her. It made him even nobler in her eyes. There had been some awkward moments. Sometimes she looked up from her desk and caught him staring at her, and she flushed and looked away. Sometimes she caught herself watching him as he focused intently on his reports, drawing on his pipe. And two days ago, she spun around from the filing cabinet just as he was rising from his desk, and they were suddenly face-to-face in the cramped quarters, only centimeters apart. She mumbled an apology and stepped to the right, but he stepped the same way, and then they both moved left, as if locked in a dance, and she could see dark tufts of hair on his chest where he had opened the top buttons of his shirt in the afternoon sunlight, and she could smell the warmth of him mingled with the familiar scent of his tobacco—and then she really did become flustered and she stepped backward and bumped into the filing cabinet while Otto laughed softly.

But Eva was saying something about her parents. "I can't believe it. They suddenly want to go to services. They've only ever attended on High Holidays before."

"As if that's going to stop Hitler," Lena said. "My mother's been trying to get us to observe Shabbat, but no one has much enthusiasm for it."

When Lena returned to the office, she was astonished to see Otto at his desk.

"I'm sorry," she said. "I went out for lunch. I thought you were gone until tomorrow."

He waved his hand in an odd flutter. "Doesn't matter, doesn't matter. But now, this is urgent. There are some new developments." He looked toward the back room. The door was ajar, and Lena caught a glimpse of two men she didn't recognize. "I may need you to stay late tonight to finish this up. I hope that's all right."

"The translation?" Lena said, pointing to the report she had started working on.

"No, no, that can wait."

The telephone rang, and Otto leaped to answer it.

"Yes, we have it," he said into the mouthpiece. "It's coming through now."

Lena stayed until after six o'clock, typing. Señor M. bustled in with another man from the Spanish embassy, and they huddled over the teleprinter in the back room. Otto made more telephone calls, turning his back to her and covering his mouth as he whispered clipped responses, and then darted back to the men. At one point, she heard a shout, an exclamation, followed by the door slamming shut. They emerged at intervals to hand her tape or handwritten notes for her to transcribe. Her job was just to type, not ask questions, but she recognized that this was different from anything she had been assigned before. Reports from Saxony described German troop movements around Olbernhau and Prina. Ten divisions, by one estimate, closing in on the Czech border. Lena gasped. She looked up and caught Otto's eye. He gave a stern nod.

"Is this true?" she said.

"Now you see, you really have to keep quiet," he said, tracing a line across her mouth with his fingertip, as if sealing her lips in silence.

She returned to her work, the sensation of his touch lingering like a footprint.

They closed up the office after seven. Señor M. scooped up the pages Lena had typed, sealed them in a large manila envelope and took off running.

"Let's get a drink," Otto said.

She assumed they would go, as usual, to the Café Slavia, but he steered her in the opposite direction, toward the castle, his hand on her waist. "We cannot talk about this with anyone," he said.

"What does it mean?" she asked.

"Hitler is pushing toward the Sudetenland and simultaneously stirring up resentment among the German-speaking population there. It is a very dangerous situation. As I predicted, he wants to march into the Sudetenland, just like he took over Austria."

"Surely he can't do that," Lena protested. "My father always talks about how important the region is; all our heavy industry is there."

"Of course. That's why Hitler wants it. And he knows the German population has been hard-hit with unemployment and is ripe for his propaganda."

"I know I shouldn't ask . . ." Lena hesitated. It had been an unspoken rule that she not probe for details, but now she could not help herself. "Where did this information come from today? How do you know that it's reliable?"

He took her hand. "You did important work today. But the less you know, the safer you are." His eyes burned into hers. "Let me just say this: there are comrades, brave comrades, who stay in Germany, and this is how they resist. They work on the railways, they live in small towns, they see things."

Otto chose a tiny restaurant off Loreta Square, where they drank beer and ordered bowls of goulash. He asked her about her family.

"How old is your brother?"

"Ernst is fifteen."

Otto nodded. "That's good. Too young to be called up. Is he involved in politics?"

"No." Lena rolled her eyes. "All he cares about are his stupid games or sneaking off to smoke with his friends. What about you? Where is your family?"

Otto shook his head, as if he wanted to dismiss the subject, but Lena insisted: "Tell me."

"My mother died when I was five. I hardly remember her. And my father died when I was twenty. Shortly after that, my brother joined the Hitler Youth. He was only fifteen, the same age as your brother now. He was so keen to be a little fascist. I have not seen him in years."

"So you have no one," Lena said. She sat across from him at a small table by the window. She dipped her spoon into the steaming bowl of stew.

"I have my comrades," he said. He reached for her hand. "And you. I'm very glad I have you with me here."

Lena felt her face flush, but she did not look away. He interlaced his fingers with hers and then caressed the inside of her arm with soft strokes of his fingertips, and she felt something melting below her belly button. And when they finished their meal and he said, "Come back to my place," she could not resist.

He led her to his apartment, just a room, really, on the top floor of a narrow building tucked behind the main railway station. He kissed her on the lips, softly at first but then urgently, pulling her close, steering her toward his bed under the eaves. He was sweet and gentle when she confessed she had never been with a man before, and afterward he cradled her in his arms. She watched his chest rise and fall as he snoozed. She yearned to stay all night, but she could not defy her father's curfew again. Not yet. He had relented a little, but he still expected her back by midnight.

The following morning when Lena walked to work, she saw the headline BENEŠ ORDERS 35 DIVISIONS TO GERMAN BORDER. She grabbed the newspaper and read the article, standing on the street corner. The Czech president was ordering a large-scale military mobilization, the report stated, "acting on information provided by an unidentified foreign embassy in Prague."

On Sunday there was to be a large demonstration in Wenceslas Square. The Popular Front called for a show of strength; socialists, communists, and Trotskyists would unite with the social democrats to urge the Beneš government to stand firm against Hitler. Battalions of armored vehicles drove through the city on their way to the northern border, cheered by people on the streets. Czech flags suddenly appeared in corner shops, and when Lena brought one home, Sasha paraded around the apartment, waving it high above her head.

Lena told no one about Otto's role in leaking the information about the German troop movements. The secret bubbled inside her and enhanced the excitement she felt about participating in the demonstration.

But on Saturday morning, Father said, "I forbid you to go."

"But you always talk of being a Czech patriot," Lena said. "This is a time to show our strength as a country."

"It is too dangerous. The Reds are blowing the whole situation out of proportion. I don't want you out on the streets."

Lena appealed to Máma, but she was no use. "Your father knows best," she said.

At the Café Slavia that evening, all discussion focused on the demonstration. The anarchists were going to join in. A journalist from an American newspaper was in town. Peter had talked to someone who said a British Labour Member of Parliament would be there. The world would see that Czechoslovakia was not like Austria, would not be wiped off the map without a fight.

Otto sat with his arm around Lena, making it clear to everyone that she was now his girlfriend. Lotti smiled in approval; Eva grinned. She was with the new man in her life, a fellow named Heinz. He had recently arrived in Prague from Budapest.

"What exactly is this little march going to achieve?" he said in a booming voice. He had a thick Hungarian accent. "Your president has already ordered the troops to the frontier, no?" He finished one cigarette and used it to light the next.

"This is not a little march," Peter said. "It's going to be huge."

"It's important for the masses to keep the pressure on the government," Otto said. "To show Beneš that he must not back down."

"I can't believe my father won't let me go," Lena said.

"Come anyway," Otto said. "How's he going to stop you?"

"You don't know my father. He'll lock me in my room, if necessary."

"So don't go home tonight," Otto said. "Come stay with me."

Lena blushed, and everyone laughed and raised their glasses to toast that suggestion.

Lena woke up in Otto's bed and made love with him again in the dawn light; she watched as he made coffee at the tiny stove in the corner, and then walked across the river with him hand-in-hand to join a massive demonstration of unity; she saw friends from school, from the café, even two women from the textile office. She thought this had to be the most exhilarating day of her life. By early evening, she was jubilant but exhausted, her feet sore and her cheeks sunburned. She wanted to relax, take a hot bath, maybe curl up and read to Sasha, then have an early night.

But the thought of home made her realize the repercussions she was sure to face. She hesitated after crossing the Bridge of Legions, her flat in sight, wincing at what might lie ahead. Perhaps Father would not be home. Perhaps, she tried to convince herself, he would be preoccupied and forget she had not returned last night. Perhaps Máma would have covered for her in some way, or perhaps . . . but she ran out of other possibilities, of ways to imagine this marvelous day not ending badly. She pressed her thumbs together and entered the apartment on tiptoe.

Father cornered her on the way to the bathroom. "You deliberately disobeyed me," he said through clenched teeth.

He took a swing at her. She tried to dodge, but not in time. He clipped her hard across the face. She dashed into the bathroom and locked the door. She saw her reflection in the glass: the left side of her face was inflamed, and blood dripped from her nostrils. She dabbed her nose with her handkerchief and gingerly touched her cheek and forehead. She was going to end up with a monstrous black eye.

Máma knocked on the bathroom door. "Are you all right?"

"What do you think?" Lena screamed. "I hate him. I'm never going to speak to him again."

Two weeks later, Otto told her the Economic Information Bureau was moving to Paris. It was a Thursday morning, and she stood at her desk, had not even had a chance to sit down yet, when he sprang the news. She felt the wind knocked out of her.

"Why?" she gasped.

"Madrid thinks it's no longer safe for us to stay in Prague," Otto said. "Sooner or later, Hitler will be here."

Lena collapsed into her chair. Her immediate thought was not her fear of Hitler arriving but that of Otto leaving—she would lose her job and her lover. Tears welled up; she turned her face away, unsure if she should let him see her cry. He came from behind and stooped to wrap his arms around her.

"Come with me to Paris," he said, kissing her ear.

Now she could not stop the tears. "How can I do that?" she said. "My parents will never let me."

"They may. You don't know if you don't ask."

"I'm not speaking to my father," Lena said.

"Ask your mother, then."

CHAPTER 4

UPPER WOLMINGHAM, SUSSEX, ENGLAND, FEBRUARY 1940

Otto hunched over the typewriter at the table by the window, trying to nail down his analysis of the final months of the Republican resistance in Barcelona. The *k* and *m* keys jammed together again. He cursed and carefully disentangled them, getting ink on his fingers. He became aware of a repetitive whining noise and something rubbing against his leg. Masaryk emitted a piercing meow: breakfast was long overdue. Otto didn't care for cats, but he had come to grudgingly accept the stray's presence in the cottage. He had referred to him only as "the cat" until the Czechs had arrived at Oak Tree Cottage three months earlier, and someone, probably Peter, had decided to name the cat after a national hero: Masaryk, their first president.

Looking up from his work, Otto gazed out through the diamond-shaped lattice panes fringed with lead, as he struggled to summarize the role of the Soviet secret police in the defeat of the revolutionaries. The condensation from the morning dew was now clearing, and he saw the milkman making his way up the village street, his bottles clanking in their crates. Today was Wednesday: he would be expecting his weekly payment.

"Masaryk, if you behave yourself, I'll give you the top of the milk," Otto said, as he rose and stretched his long limbs.

He searched for the earthenware jar where they stored their cash. In the kitchen, the deep stone sink with its single tap, the sole source of water in the cottage, was piled high with unwashed plates and cups from the previous night. The jar on the window-sill contained only one 10-shilling note and a pile of change. The others would receive their allowance from the Czech Refugee Trust Fund tomorrow, to restock the piggy bank. Otto's own funds were depleted, the small advance he'd received for his book long gone. The group shared their resources, paltry as they were. Luckily, they didn't have to pay rent.

He scooped up a handful of coins from the bottom of the jar and met the milkman at the front door.

"Morning, guv," the milkman chortled, clearly in a good mood. "What will it be today?"

"Two pints, please."

"Coming right up, sir. That'll make it three and ninepence ha'penny for the week."

When Otto had arrived in England, he'd been completely baf-fled by the ridiculous currency. But he could now distinguish the half crowns, the florins, the sixpenny and threepenny pieces, and the tiny farthings. He sifted through the coins in his hand. There was some satisfaction in giving the exact change, as if this consti-tuted a refusal to be defeated by the system.

Back in the kitchen, he reached for a saucer and poured off the rich cream topping for the cat at his feet. Upstairs, floorboards creaked. Otto braced himself for the onslaught; he knew he would get no more writing accomplished until the morning chaos had subsided. He heard the higher-pitched female tone that meant that Lotti and Peter were awake. The men allowed the couple the privilege of sleeping in the front bedroom upstairs, while they squeezed together in the tiny back room—but the thin walls offered little privacy.

Emil bounded into the living room, filling it with his adoles-cent energy. Barely eighteen, he was the youngest of the group and still inhabited his body as if it were on short-term rental, loaned for some special occasion but, unfortunately, three sizes too large.

"*Mein Gott*, Otto, it's freezing down here. Why didn't you light a fire?"

"I'm trying to save coal."

Emil scooped yesterday's ashes into the bucket and carried them outside. The back door led to a small garden, the outside toilet, and the coal shed. A blast of wind whipped the shed door back on its hinges, slamming it into the wall of the cottage with a loud thud. Emil returned with wood kindling and crouched in front of the fireplace.

"I'll do it," Otto said, edging him out of the way.

Otto prided himself on having acquired, through patient trial and error, the ability to create a perfect coal fire. It was quite different, he had discovered, from woodstoves. Besides, this fireplace had its own little quirks. Otto had lived here for five months before the others arrived, and felt he was the only one who understood this. He tore strips from yesterday's *Times* and interlaced them with the twiglets of oak to construct a pyramid, an infrastructure of support for a few strategically placed lumps of coal.

Emil was at his side with two cups and offered one to Otto. Otto wasn't fond of the ritual English cup of tea, but good coffee was impossible to find.

"Anything in this morning's post?" Emil asked.

"Nothing. But the second delivery should be here soon." Otto lit a match to the base of the fire.

"I can't believe how long it takes for letters to get here," Emil said.

Otto opened his mouth to say something but stopped himself. The boy eagerly anticipated the postman every day, waiting to hear from his older brother, Josef. Josef had been traveling with Peter, Emil, and Lotti the previous summer as they'd made the dangerous crossing from Czechoslovakia into Poland, but they had separated in Katowice. Josef had wanted to wait for his girlfriend to join him and had urged Emil to go ahead with the others; he had not been heard from since. Emil was still under the illusion that Josef would make it to England. Otto thought his chances slim and feared the worst, but Lotti made him promise not to voice these thoughts in front of Emil.

"*Ja, alles ist unterbrochen.* Everything's disrupted." A vague, fatuous statement—but a promise was a promise.

Otto didn't like to admit it, but he himself experienced an odd fluttering in his chest every time the postman approached. He was expecting a letter from Lena. She should have obtained her visa by now. He liked to pride himself on his objectivity. Being alone in the world allowed him to be free of illusions, with no need to gloss over danger. But he had to get Lena here. Yes, it would be nice to have the warmth of another body in the bed at night. He remembered her smooth, wide cheeks and bright blue eyes, her lithe tenderness. But it wasn't that. He was the one who had brought her to Paris; he had to get her out. He was convinced that Hitler was just waiting for warmer weather before launching his next attack, and he did not believe France would be safe.

Lotti came downstairs, heading for the fire with hands outstretched. Otto watched as she picked up Masaryk and held the cat between her breasts, nuzzling her chin against its neck. He followed the curves of her figure under her tight green pullover and wool skirt. She had a pretty face from this angle, with smooth skin and a slightly pointed chin. She closed her eyes and rocked the cat gently back and forth. Otto felt a stirring in his groin and forced himself to look away. Although they were a self-declared commune and shared just about everything else, there was no suggestion that Peter would share his girlfriend.

She went to the kitchen. "Anything come in the post?"

"Nothing yet."

He ran his fingers over the coarse stubble on his jaw. He should have shaved before anyone else was up; now he would have to wait for a chance to use the sink. He could hear Lotti running water and banging pots and realized he should have made a start on cleaning up, but she seemed to be doing it now.

"You should hear back from Lena soon, don't you think?" Lotti raised her voice over the noise.

"Yes. We'll have to see if she had any luck with the letter from Muriel's aunt."

Emil looked up from *The Times*. "Her word worked for you, didn't it?"

"It did, but she was there in person at the port in Newhaven—that's the thing."

Pure chance. Muriel was the one who had sponsored him, but she was sick that day, came down with a bad cold, couldn't make the journey. So she asked her aunt to meet Otto in her place. He still chuckled at the memory. Mrs. Courtney-Smithers: his first introduction to the realities of the English social-class system. All Otto knew was that some eccentric left-wing woman was going to be there to vouch for him. When he arrived at the immigration counter, he saw a regal-looking white-haired lady with a uniformed chauffeur at her side—not at all what he was expecting.

"Ma'am, how do you know this, er, this Mr. Eisenberg?" asked the officer, shuffling through Otto's papers.

"It's my niece who is sponsoring him."

"How does she know him?"

"I haven't the faintest idea."

The woman spoke as if that were an absurd question. She held her head erect and wore a jacket rimmed with fur. She must have been shorter than the officer, but in Otto's recollection she seemed to tower above him.

The officer hesitated. "Well, ma'am. Er ... hmm. Do you know anyone who could provide a reference for him?"

She gave him a long, cold stare and said in what was clearly, even to Otto's untrained ear, the haughtiest upper-class accent "Young man, surely my word is good enough."

Of course, that was before the start of the war. The latest plan to get Lena here had been Peter's idea: a letter from Mrs. Courtney-Smithers would have some influence, a visitor visa easier to come by.

"Can I get some help in here?" Lotti said.

Otto hauled himself up from the sofa. In the kitchen, Lotti handed him a dish towel and pointed at the clean plates draining on the counter. Sleeves rolled up to her elbows, she immersed her hands in the sink full of suds.

"Did you hear the weather forecast?" she said, handing a clean saucepan directly to Otto, as the counter was full. She leaned forward to peer at the sky above the garden hedge. For an instant, her breast brushed against his forearm.

"It's supposed to snow again later."

"I should wake Peter. Muriel asked him to fix her fence. The dog keeps getting out. Peter should get over there before the snow starts."

"I'll do it."

The prospect of getting out of the house was appealing. It would be nice to see Muriel, and he could take a bath there. And surely he could patch up a fence. Why should Peter do it and get all the credit?

Lotti regarded him with a look of amusement. "Take Emil with you, then, if you're going to work on the fence."

"I can do it."

"Take him anyway. He needs something to do."

"Who needs something to do?" Emil stooped in the doorway, with a mischievous lopsided grin.

Tomas's voice came from the living room. "You can help me with the flag badges. I want to beat last month's totals."

Emil rolled his eyes and grimaced. "Maybe later."

Tomas was an odd one. Short and surly, with thick, black-rimmed glasses, he often squirreled himself away in the corner, aloof from the others. Otto didn't remember him from Prague, although apparently, he had heard Otto speak at the Café Slavia. Tomas had appeared at the cottage a week after Peter and the others, forced, like all foreign refugees, to leave London soon after the outbreak of war. He was obsessed with making flag badges to raise money for the Czech Refugee Trust Fund, with ridiculous self-imposed targets he urged the others to embrace.

Emil peered into the bread bin and pulled out yesterday's half-eaten loaf. "I'm starving. Is there anything else to eat?"

"That's it for now. Take the ration books with you and buy more bread on the way back," Lotti said. "There's this jam from Mrs. Thompson next door. Blackcurrant."

Emil twisted his face in disgust. "I had some yesterday. It's too tart."

"Have plain bread, then. You'll survive."

Otto caught her eye, holding her gaze for a few seconds, pondering her words.

CHAPTER 5

SUSSEX, FEBRUARY 1940

Otto and Emil set off down the village street, passing a row of ancient redbrick cottages similar to their own, with warped rooflines and tiny windows, some with brightly colored front doors. Even in this dismal weather, it was hard not to appreciate the charm. Otto hadn't expected this. He'd welcomed the chance to focus on his writing, without distractions. It was important to get the word out, reflect on the devastating loss in Spain, analyze the fragmentation of the Left, and expose the failure of Britain and France to support the struggle against fascism. He'd landed here by chance—an opportunity to be sponsored, stay rent-free in a cottage, receive a modest advance—all arranged through International Brigade contacts. He hadn't given much thought to what it would mean to live in a country village. He'd been surprised to find it so picturesque.

Lena would love it. She liked this sort of thing. With a sudden rush of tenderness, he recalled their walks through the Jardin du Luxembourg, the way she drew his attention to various shrubs. Normally, he wasn't one to pay attention to such things, could never remember what they were called—but Lena knew not only their German names, but the French, too. Now, he imagined them strolling together past the village shop, as he pointed out this particularly attractive cottage, covered in thick ivy, or, once the weather warmed up, admiring the flowers in the front gardens.

Otto shot a quick glance at Emil, afraid these musings were transparent on his face. But Emil was kicking a small rock down the street, as if on a football field. As they passed the shop, Otto groaned at the sight of a stout, middle-aged woman carrying two large shopping bags and bustling straight toward them. This was the not-so-charming aspect of village life. Otto couldn't remember her name but recognized her as one of the most overbearing of the neighbors. There was no escape.

"Good morning, boys!" the woman boomed, falling into step beside them. "Not too bad today, is it?"

"No, very nice," Otto responded, and quickened his pace, but this was not enough to dissuade her from coming even closer.

"Still bitterly cold," she yelled, a few inches from his face. She always shouted, as if this would help compensate for his inadequate command of the English language. "And they say it's going to snow again later. That wind what we had last week was something terrible, wasn't it?"

The weather was always the favorite topic of conversation.

"You boys must be on your way to Mrs. Calder's," she continued in full cry. "How is she doing down there at The Hollow? I hardly see her these days. Mr. Adams still visiting, is he?"

"I really don't know," Otto said.

Second-favorite topic: Muriel's comings and goings. She was a natural subject for local gossip, totally eccentric in the eyes of the villagers: wealthy, radical in her political affiliations, unconventional in her behavior and tastes. Divorced. And openly having an affair with Alistair Adams, a London man.

"I think it's such a shame she had to move from the Manor House." Branson. That was her name: Mrs. Branson. She was forgetting to shout quite as loudly now that she was getting into her rhythm. "I don't think it's right. I bet she's upset about it."

"I think she understands this," Otto said. "Everyone has to make the sacrifice."

There was a lot of talk about the Manor House. The army had recently requisitioned it for use as officers' quarters. Otto knew that Muriel in fact appreciated the privacy of her new home, a much smaller but comfortable house at the far end of the village, tucked away from the eyes of the local gossips.

"Well, I hope the army takes good care of it. Such a grand house. And beautiful grounds. You know, my Derek worked for Mrs. Calder as a gardener before he signed up. Very good to him, she was. I don't care what anyone says—she's always very good to those what work for her."

They reached the square at the center of the village, bordered by the imposing manor on the right, with three military vehicles parked in front, and to the left the arched lychgate leading to the churchyard. Mrs. Branson turned down the hill, while Otto and Emil continued the short distance to Muriel's driveway. The tall hedgerows towered above them on both sides, lending a persistent dampness to the rough track. But the dankness lifted as the lane opened up into a clearing and the house itself came into view.

The dwelling was a two-story, timber-framed structure with an intriguing pattern of squares and rectangles created by the dark wood beams and the yellowing plaster, and two tall chimneys, one at each end of the house. The original building was one of the oldest in the village, dating from the fifteenth century, left in ruins until Muriel had restored and expanded it several years earlier. It had been envisioned as a summer house for visiting friends from London, but now it was to be her home for the duration of the war.

Muriel always insisted they were to dispense with the formality of knocking. Otto pushed open the heavy oak front door and called out to announce their arrival. Lancelot the dog came bounding up to greet them.

"Is that Otto?" came a voice from the back of the house.

"Yes, and Emil is here with me."

"Oh, good. Come in! I'll be there in a minute."

A roaring fire filled the huge stone fireplace in the living room. There were three overstuffed armchairs and a large crimson sofa, and in front of them an Oriental carpet in hues of deep blues, reds, and gold. One wall consisted entirely of a floor-to-ceiling bookshelf, filled with rows of faded brown volumes and thin orange-and-white-striped Penguin paperbacks.

"I am so glad you've come." Muriel beamed as she joined them. She was tall and large-boned, with a broad, angular face, in her early forties. Her skin was still smooth and her step light. She was wearing a tweed skirt and a man's woolen cardigan over a white blouse, no jewelry. "Ethel is just finishing cleaning upstairs. I'll ask her to make some tea in a moment." She spoke in English today, although she could just as easily converse in German or French.

She navigated her way across the room, one arm extended in front of her, and sat in a chair next to the fireplace. She coped so well in familiar surroundings that a casual observer might be unaware she was losing her eyesight. A covert inherited defect was playing havoc with her retinas, gradually covering them with opaque patches impervious to light. She'd naturally had access to all the best Harley Street experts over the years, but apparently nothing could be done. She was doomed to a slow, relentless deterioration into total darkness. Otto found it impossible not to admire her courage. A lesser woman might have retreated into self-pity or despair, but not Muriel.

"Any news from Lena?" she asked.

"Still waiting."

"Please let me know as soon as you hear," she said.

"I brought Emil over to help me work on that fence you wanted repaired," Otto said.

"Oh, gracious, I forgot about that. Thank you, yes, yes. I don't want to risk another confrontation with old Pritchard if Lancelot gets out again and bothers the cows. Perhaps you could do that first, and then we can talk. There's so much I want to discuss. We have to start planning the play."

"Are you still going to do the play this year?" Otto asked.

"Oh my goodness, yes. We continued all through the last war. We may end up a bit short of male actors, but we can substitute with women, if necessary. After all, Shakespeare did the opposite, so why not?" she chuckled.

The previous summer, just after Otto's arrival, it had been *King Lear*. The annual amateur dramatic production in the converted medieval barn on Muriel's aunt's property had been a tradition since the turn of the century.

"I shall need all of you to help," Muriel said. "I was thinking that *A Midsummer Night's Dream* might be more appropriate this year, considering the circumstances. Don't you agree?"

"I am sorry; I cannot help. My English it is not good," Emil said.

"That's no excuse!" Muriel laughed, a big, contagious laugh, large enough to fill any room. "You're doing very well with your English. We'll have plenty of small supporting roles. And anyway, I'll need you all to help with scenery and props."

Ethel served them tea and retreated to the kitchen. Otto was warm and comfortable sitting by the fire, the dog nestled at his feet. This tea tasted much better than the brew Emil had provided earlier. He was reluctant to move. But the sky was now completely overcast; it did indeed look as if it might snow.

"Come on, Emil," he said, draining his cup. "Let's look at that fence."

"You should find whatever tools you need in the shed," Muriel said. "I think there're some wooden stakes out there, too. Thank you so much. It's so nice of you."

The cold hit with a force that left Otto reeling. He pulled up his collar and stuffed his hands into his pockets. At the bottom of the garden, behind a cluster of small fruit trees, a two-meter stretch of the fence had keeled over, leaving a tangle of stakes and rotting slats. Emil surveyed the damage, pulling at a fence post that was off-kilter, giving the base a firm kick. "The post looks solid enough, don't you think?"

"I suppose so," Otto said.

The wind whipped across the expanse of open fields to the south. Otto held the shed door open as Emil rummaged through a wooden box. He selected a hammer, a screwdriver, a set of pliers, and a small glass jar containing screws and nails, then scooped up a bundle of wooden stakes. "That should work."

The boy seemed to know just what to do. Otto allowed Emil to direct him to hold this and pass him that, as he pulled the fence post into a vertical position, inserted four stakes across, and reinforced them with twine. Within ten minutes, it was in passable condition.

Otto smiled in admiration. "Where did you learn to do that?"

Emil shrugged. "Picked it up. Josef taught me a lot. He did

most of the work on our family's cabin in the Tyrols, fixing it up."
He flexed his fingers and held them to his mouth, blowing on them.
"Come on. Let's get inside and warm up."

One of the joys of coming to The Hollow was the opportunity
for a hot bath. It seemed only fair to let Emil go first. When it came to
his turn, Otto had to be quick, not take the long, hot soak he would
have liked, because Mrs. Courtney-Smithers and her chauffeur were
expected momentarily. Muriel's aunt Pippa was taking her on an
excursion into town. Muriel said this was of no consequence and that
Otto should bathe as long as he wished, but he didn't feel comfortable. Muriel had become much more than his sponsor; he considered
her a real friend. Her unorthodox views and boundless energy almost
made you forget she was upper-class. With the aunt, however, there
could be no mistake. Ever since that first journey from Newhaven in
the back of the Rolls-Royce, Otto always felt he had to sit up straight
and tuck in his elbows. He couldn't imagine emerging from the bathroom with wet hair while she was in the house.

As they prepared to leave Muriel said, "Promise me you will
all come over for supper tonight. Alistair isn't returning until the
weekend, so I shall absolutely depend on you for company."

They reached Oak Tree Cottage just as it started to snow. Tomas
had moved Otto's typewriter and papers onto the floor and spread
out his badge-making paraphernalia on the table by the window.
He held one of the buttons up close to his face and dabbed it with
a small brush, touching up the red paint. Peter and Lotti sat on the
sofa, her legs across his lap. She was darning socks; he was reading
the newspaper.

"How did it go?" Lotti asked.

"We fixed the fence," Otto said.

"You did?" Peter looked up in surprise.

"I should say, Emil fixed it."

"We're all invited for supper," Emil said.

"That's nice," Lotti said.

Otto picked up his typewriter and was trying to decide where
to perch, when he heard the clink of the letterbox and saw a thin

blue envelope plop onto the mat. He lunged for it, convinced it was from Lena. A quick glance, however, told him it was not. The envelope was covered in postage stamps from Lithuania, endorsements from the Red Cross in Geneva, Thomas Cook in Lisbon, and the final forwarding stamp from the Czech Refugee Office in London. It was hard to tell at first whom it was for.

"Emil," Otto said, finally locating his name, "it's for you. It must be from Josef."

Lotti grimaced, as if bracing for bad news, and lowered her feet to the floor. They all watched in silence as Emil opened it and withdrew one sheet of notepaper.

"It's dated Vilnius, the thirteenth of December, 1939—more than two months ago," he said.

"Look!" Peter said, peering over Emil's shoulder. "The dots and the comma! Remember?" He turned to Lotti. "The code we agreed to in Prague."

The opening greeting was followed by five dots and a large, exaggerated comma. The lines of text were widely spaced, written in Germanic cursive.

"There's a hidden message written with milk and lemon juice," he said.

"I see that," Emil said. "But let me read this part first." Emil scanned it quickly and then read out loud.

Dear Emil . . . . . ,
We have reached Lithuania, which is a beautiful country, and we are enjoying visiting our cousins. There is a magnificent castle overlooking the city, which reminds us of Prague. We have seen many splendid lakes. The weather has been bitterly cold. The boots that Papa bought me last winter have been a blessing, because there has been a lot of snow already. We have been playing cards, and my uncle is always winning, you will not be surprised to hear.

I hope you are well and behaving yourself without me to boss you around. Say hello to all the others from me.
Love from Josef

Emil was silent for a moment. Then he said, "We don't have any family in Lithuania."

"Let's see what he's really saying," Peter said.

He rummaged through a box on the bookshelf and retrieved a small iron. Otto didn't know they owned such a thing. Peter covered the letter with a handkerchief and carefully dabbed at it to heat the paper. It took a good ten minutes to reveal the other letter, the one that had eluded the censors, written between the lines of platitudes. Emil stood next to him, watching in silence. Beads of sweat formed on his upper lip, moistening the soft down of his fledgling mustache, a recent experiment. Tomas dipped his brush into the blue paint pot but then laid it down. They all waited, suspended in a capsule of anticipation.

Peter inspected the letter and handed it to Emil.

"This is in Czech," Emil said, looking at Otto. "I'll translate."

In Prague, Otto's social circle consisted entirely of bilingual Czechs who spoke German just as fluently, and to which they could easily revert in the company of non–Czech speakers. So he survived speaking only his native tongue, unable to decipher more than a few words of the mysteriously bundled Slav consonants, with their multiple hooks and accents. Now that they were in England, they continued to use German most of the time.

Emil read aloud:

We got arrested in Krakow. Finally released after much delay, but had to wait for K.; her release took longer. We found some contacts who gave us new documents. Tried to head north but can't get to England now, so we are turning east. Have to put faith in our Soviet brothers in spite of M-R. Be brave. Hope you are safe. I'll write more when I can.

There were a few moments of stunned silence. Then everyone began talking at once. "Why the hell are they going east?" "Why were they in Krakow?" "What does 'M-R' mean?"

"With the Nazis all over Poland now, they probably thought it was just too dangerous, so they had to go in the opposite direction," Otto said.

"'M-R' must mean 'Molotov-Ribbentrop,' the Hitler-Stalin pact," Peter said. "They're betting on it being safer in Russia than in any territory controlled by the Gestapo."

"How far east is Lithuania?" Lotti asked.

"Let's see." Tomas had erected a large map of Europe on the living room wall, above the sofa. Soft shades of pastel pinks, yellows, greens, and blues distinguished each nation from its neighbors, giving a beguiling illusion of tranquility. Only the lines of gray pins indicating the advance of the Third Reich betrayed the true condition of the continent. Tomas scrunched up his eyes close to the map, scanning the territory to the east of Poland, until he identified Vilnius. The others watched as he inserted a pin.

Except for Emil. He slumped in the armchair, staring blankly at the fire. Lotti reached out to rest a hand on his shoulder. He shrugged her off and made for the front door.

"Emil," she beseeched, as he let in a blast of cold air. Peter restrained her, quietly shaking his head.

Emil slammed the door behind him. Otto hesitated. He considered following Emil but instead picked up his typewriter and retreated upstairs. Perhaps he could get some work done up there. And divert his attention from a queasy anxiety in his chest. Of course Lena was not in the same dire straits as Josef. The Nazis were not in France. Yet. But he bitterly regretted having left her behind in Paris.

CHAPTER 6

PARIS, JANUARY 1939

It was too cold to sit in the flat. Lena had used the last of the *boulets* in the minuscule fireplace; they didn't give off much heat and left the room reeking of coal dust. She had a few twigs of kindling in the scuttle, but she should save these. Instead, she would walk to the library, cozy up in her favorite corner, and read all the newspapers.

A biting wind pummeled her back as she made her way down the street. On days like this, the 6th arrondissement kept its charms hidden under a thick mantle of gray. No one sauntered down the boulevards, admiring the shop windows, waving to passersby, or pausing to chat with those sipping *pastis* at the outdoor cafés. The city was hunkered down. Anyone who had to be out on the street scurried past, shoulders hunched against the elements. All of this exacerbated Lena's own bleak mood.

Today, Otto was closing the bureau. He had not wanted her to come with him.

"There is no need for you to be there," he'd said, setting his jaw in grim determination. Lena had hoped they could do this together, that she might be able to offer some solace.

Everyone was devastated over the loss in Spain: the fascists had won, the International Brigade had disbanded, the volunteer fighters had returned to their countries of origin. But Otto was taking the defeat harder than anyone. He shook his head and left without her.

Now, as she waited for the light to change, she felt a soft tap on her shoulder. "Lena! I thought it was you."

Marguerite looked up at her with a sparkling smile. She was tiny, the top of her blue beret barely reaching Lena's chin. Lena leaned down to receive a kiss on each cheek.

"When did you get back to Paris?" Lena asked.

"Sunday." Marguerite slipped her arm through Lena's as they crossed the street.

"How was it?"

Marguerite rolled her eyes and puffed out her lower lip. "*Mon Dieu . . .*" With her free hand, she dismissed the topic.

She had been in Toulouse, visiting her family, strictly observant Jews who disapproved of everything Parisian. Lena laughed and squeezed her arm. It was impossible not to be cheered by Marguerite's vibrant energy. They had met the previous summer when Lena had first arrived. They had worked together in the socialist movement, in the last-ditch efforts to persuade the French government to intervene in support of Spain. They had marched in the streets, sorted through donated boxes of food, and assembled packages to send off to the brave comrades holding out in Barcelona. Marguerite was studying French literature at the Sorbonne and working part-time, but in her spare moments she offered to show Lena around. While Otto worked long hours, they explored bustling street markets or tranquil gardens tucked away in surprising corners. They admired the artists displaying their wares on the Quai des Grands-Augustins or sat on a bench in the Jardin du Luxembourg and talked for hours. Those first few months in Paris were giddy, happy times.

"Otto is closing the bureau," Lena said now. "I have to find other work."

"I know a family who needs a part-time nanny," Marguerite said. "It's all the way over by the Place de Clichy, and only one day a week, but if they like you, they might give you more hours. I can introduce you tomorrow. Sophie is an easy child. You would just have to entertain her, take her to the park, cook her lunch, that sort of thing."

"But I'm completely useless in the kitchen," Lena confessed. "We always had a cook at home. My mother never taught me a thing."

"Just make noodles. She'll be happy. Follow the directions on the packet."

Lena laughed. "I suppose I can do that."

"Have you heard Eva's news?" Marguerite said. "She's coming next week!"

"Really?" Lena felt a pang of jealousy. Eva had written the month before that she was thinking of leaving Prague, but Lena hadn't known it was confirmed.

"I'm sure you'll hear from her soon."

Marguerite had been Eva's friend first. They had met as teenagers, when Eva visited her cousin in Normandy, and had remained pen pals ever since.

"I can't imagine how she's persuaded her parents to let her leave," Lena said. "They're far more conservative than mine, and Eva's their only child." Lena's mother had convinced her father that she might be in danger *if things got worse*, as she put it, because of Lena's *associations*. But Eva was less directly involved in politics.

"Eva says everyone knows there's nothing for young people now in Prague," Marguerite said.

Yes, now the threat was more menacing, it could surely no longer be denied. Four months earlier, Britain and France had betrayed Czechoslovakia at Munich, tossed her aside like a piece of rotten meat. Hitler had annexed the Sudetenland, just as Otto had predicted, and had nudged closer than ever to Prague.

"Will Eva stay with you?"

"No, she's coming with her boyfriend. A man named Heinz?" They had reached the Place du Panthéon. "I have to go," Marguerite said, checking her watch. "I have a lecture at eleven. But I'm sure I can get you that job. Meet me tomorrow night at Les Deux Magots. Eight o'clock. I'll take you to the Beaufils family."

She kissed Lena again and took off—like a spark that had flared to life and then died.

Lena wished they could have spent the whole morning together, and she wanted to hear more about what Eva had written.

But she felt uplifted by this potential employment. She was anxious about money, yes, but especially now, with Eva coming, she needed to reestablish her footing in Paris. She didn't want Eva to see her like this. She wanted to be lively, to show Eva her favorite spots.

Her letters to Eva last summer had been full of exuberance. Yes, she'd met Eva's friend Marguerite; she loved her and everything about Paris. She loved walking arm-in-arm with Otto through the streets of the Left Bank; she loved the bright cafés overflowing onto the cobbled streets, showering passersby with music and laughter; she loved the crêpe makers with their roadside carts, serving her favorite *citron-sucré*, sweet and sour and paper-thin crisp; she loved the days working with Otto and the evenings at Les Deux Magots with expatriates from Budapest, Berlin, Brno. She enveloped herself in the sounds of the French language, with its uvular trills and nasal diphthongs. She had never been so happy.

Of course, Lena read the newspapers. The ominous signs were on every page. But she pushed them to the back of her mind.

When Lena returned home in the early afternoon, she found Otto on the landing, struggling with a large box of papers. He smiled when he saw her.

"Thanks," he said, as Lena opened the door. He sounded cheerful. He leaned forward to kiss her on the lips.

"Everything all right?"

"Done. I cleared everything out. And I have a great idea. I'm going to write a book. The definitive history of the Spanish Civil War."

He seemed quite exuberant. She cleared space on the kitchen table for his box.

"It is so important to learn from the mistakes in Spain. We have to understand what happened. Oh, and here," he said, reaching into his coat pocket. "This was downstairs in the mailbox. A letter for you. From Eva."

Eva brought with her a firsthand account of the despair and disillusionment in Prague.

Everyone there believed war was inevitable, that the young should get out while they still could. Peter and Lotti—"Yes, they're still together; I can't believe it"—were making plans to go to England. Another friend of Eva's was trying to get a visa for America. Someone from her family's synagogue was applying to the Dominican Republic.

"How does my mother seem to you?" Lena asked. "How is Sasha? Did you see Ernst?" The questions tumbled out.

"Sasha is growing tall! She misses you. I caught only a glimpse of Ernst. He didn't say much. Your mother looks all right, a bit tired. She insisted I give you this."

Eva handed her a box of strawberry *koláče*: sweet and sticky and delicious. They ate half of them on the spot. Tucked deep into the box was a long letter. Máma had been writing every week, but short notes, full of inconsequential gossip. Somehow, the pastry box gave her permission to admit that they were afraid. They heard horror stories coming out of Germany and Austria about life under the Nazis. Thousands of Jewish businesses looted without police intervention, Jewish cemeteries desecrated, the German streets littered with the shattered glass of hundreds of synagogues on Kristallnacht.

The violence of it is inconceivable, Máma wrote. *Can you imagine? We always thought of the Germans as such a civilized people.* They had decided to leave, she said, to emigrate, perhaps to South America. They would send several trunks ahead to Paris. Father was making arrangements for storage.

"What does this mean?" Lena said. "How could my father just leave his business? Would they abandon the flat?"

"It's not easy," Eva said. "Some people are selling everything to pay for the visas and permits they need."

"What about your parents?"

"They can't leave my grandmother. She's too old to move."

Lena wrote to her mother, seeking details, but received no answers to her questions; the weekly letters resumed their superficial tone. For her birthday the next month, Máma sent a package. Lena ripped it open, hungry for more information, but it contained only a small book of Čapek poetry and a watercolor, painted by Sasha, that brought tears to her eyes.

CHAPTER 7

PARIS, 1939

Otto spent his days on research in the library at the Sorbonne, launching himself into his new endeavor with enthusiasm. He conducted interviews, gathered testimony, and reached out to everyone he knew to find a publisher to sponsor his book. In the evenings, people still flocked to his side in the café to listen to his analysis of current developments. He and Heinz often locked horns.

"Britain and France won't let Hitler invade Czechoslovakia," Heinz declared.

"I can't believe you still pin your hopes on Chamberlain and Deladier," Otto said. "They were both cheered as heroes on their return from Munich. They want to avoid war at any cost."

Tuesdays, Lena had her babysitting job. Marguerite was right: Sophie was a charming child, and unfazed by Lena's lack of culinary skills. Week after week, she sat at the kitchen table, swinging her legs in delight, spooning up noodles coated with butter and grated cheese.

On a chilly March morning, Lena had agreed to work an extra day at the Beaufils'. She allowed herself five more minutes under the covers while Otto shaved at the sink. He had the wireless on high volume. Then she heard the news. She screamed, jumped out of bed, clasping her hands to her mouth. Otto startled and cut himself, and cursed.

The Nazis had invaded Prague. The clipped words of the news broadcast stung like ice.

For months, they'd talked of its being inevitable, but that didn't lessen the impact.

Otto pulled her close, dabbing at his chin with a handkerchief. She rested her head on his chest, feeling the deep resonance of his voice as he talked, trying to calm her. They dressed and walked to the Métro and bought *Le Figaro*, standing outside the *tabac* in the bitter morning air, to read the whole story. Lena translated the parts Otto didn't understand. Later, a sight she would never forget: the *Paris-Soir* paper, tossed to the floor of a train on the Porte Dauphine line, a muddy footprint soiling the image of the tanks rumbling across the Vltava. The tears rolled down her cheeks.

She returned home that evening to more bad news. Otto had been summoned to the *préfecture* for questioning. His reputation made him an obvious target. For the second time in a month, he had to show his papers, answer questions about his political activity and his finances.

"They threatened to deport me back to Germany," he said.

"How could they?" Lena said. "You'd be arrested immediately."

"I am fully aware of that," he said.

"What are you going to do?"

"The situation in France is not good. There is mounting resentment against the refugees from Germany and Eastern Europe. And now, with the flood of migrants across the border from Spain, it's only going to get worse. I've been talking to some of our former International Brigade contacts. They're going to try to get me a visa for England."

"What about me?" Lena said. "Would I stay here on my own?"

"Let's see what happens with my application. I have to leave. I can't risk the French authorities deporting me. They're unlikely to bother you." It was true; his notoriety did not extend to her. "If I'm successful, we'll work out a way to get you there, too."

Máma's letters became even shorter, the tone terse and evasive. Lena found it impossible to read between the lines. Then, in May, Máma sent word that she was trying to get Sasha out alone. She enclosed a claim chit for a warehouse on the rue La Fayette; apparently, they had already shipped some belongings. She instructed Lena to go separate Sasha's clothing and books to prepare for her arrival.

Lena was bemused by the eight large trunks labeled with her family name, tightly packed with winter clothes, ornaments, silver candlesticks, a complete set of fine bone china and other knick-knacks, even the small Persian carpet from Father's study—and the antique rosewood box, inlaid with an intricate pattern of brass, in which Máma kept the family photographs.

As a child, Lena hated the annual visits to the photographer's studio to pose for those portraits: the stiff white frock she was made to wear, the ache in her cheeks from wearing a forced smile, the blinding flash. Sasha liked to look at these on occasion, giggling at the photographs of Lena when she was small. But Lena had not thought to bring any with her when she'd left.

Now, she fingered through the box. On the top, the photographs from the family holiday in Constanta, the date on the back: August 1935. Lena remembered the exhaustive preparations, the vast trunks packed for every possible contingency, the train ride down through Bucharest to the Black Sea. It was the last time they went away together as a family. She found a snapshot of Sasha squinting into the sun, carefree, innocent, fair curls framing her sweet face.

Lena picked up another photograph and chuckled. She and Máma walking across the Charles Bridge: they'd been to a bakery in the Old Town to get pastries for some special occasion and had run into their downstairs neighbor, Mr. Kopecký, out practicing with his brand-new Leica. He was so conceited and pompous with it, they thought him ridiculous. He caught them unawares, in full stride, Máma with her mouth open midsentence. The image had a natural quality that Lena much preferred to the formal portraits. They were wearing identical, calf-length woolen coats with wide lapels, pulled tight at the waist, their heads adorned with simple hats, and each clutching a white pastry box encircled with ribbon. Such a mundane errand. She had not been enthusiastic about accompanying Máma that day. Now she would have given anything to walk to the bakery with her.

Lena scooped up the photographs. She then dutifully sorted out Sasha's belongings, repacking and relabeling everything. Sasha's clothes seemed enormous; how she must have grown in the past year! Lena was excited at the prospect of seeing her again, holding her hand, listening to her incessant chatter. She had no idea how she would feed Sasha when she arrived, but she would manage somehow. She mentioned the plan to Mme. Beaufils, and little Sophie danced around the flat, announcing that she and Sasha would become best friends. Never mind that Sasha spoke no French and Sophie not a word of Czech, or that there was a three-year age difference between them. Sophie picked out one of her rag dolls, which, she declared, she would give to Sasha the moment she arrived.

Three weeks later, Otto announced that he had been sponsored to enter England. A wealthy widow living in the countryside south of London was willing to vouch for him, and he had received his visa. He would leave in a week.

"Come with me," he said. "Let's try to get you a visa, too. A visitor visa—that shouldn't be too hard."

"But I have to wait for Sasha," Lena said. "Máma is sending her to Paris."

"*Mein Schätzchen*," he said. "How is she going to do that?"

"I don't know. But I can't leave if there's a chance Sasha will arrive."

He opened his mouth, as if to say more, but then just quietly shook his head.

On his last night, they walked along the Seine in the warm evening air. She hooked her arm through his. He kissed her lightly on the forehead.

"I'll send for you as soon as I'm settled," he said.

Lena nodded. She wasn't going to mention Sasha again. But she couldn't help thinking that he spoke as if she were a trunk left in storage, like those her parents had sent.

"I'll work out a way to get you a visa."

"I don't see how," she said. "No one's going to sponsor *me* to write a book."

"I'll find people in England who can pull strings, I'm sure."

Lena missed him terribly in the days that followed, but she busied herself moving into Marguerite's flat in the rue Cassette. And, little by little, she discovered the joys of being on her own. She liked lying in bed in the morning, engrossed in a novel, without being criticized for her choice of reading material. She could spend hours window-shopping in the narrow streets of Montmartre, with no one tugging her to move on. For the first time in her life, she answered to no one—neither Father nor Otto telling her what to do.

She had very little money, but she made do. She sold the gray serge suit that Máma had insisted she purchase in Prague but that she'd never worn, and other superfluous items: two hats, three pairs of shoes, a brown leather handbag, an ugly gold bracelet she'd received for her sixteenth birthday. That would see her through a few weeks. Summer infused the city with a warm glow. In the evenings, she met up with Marguerite or Eva and sat in Les Deux Magots, making one drink last all night.

On a warm August afternoon, Lena ran into Heinz on the Boul'Mich.

"Well, well, well," he said, taking hold of her hand before she could stop him. "Look who's here! A wonderful sight to brighten the day."

He brought her hand up to his lips and, in an exaggerated pose of chivalry, kissed her fingertips. Lena was puzzled. He'd seen her only two nights earlier and had hardly noticed her. He'd sat with his arm around Eva but had spent most of the evening talking with a group of men at the next table.

Then she remembered: Eva was out of town. She was visiting her cousin in Normandy.

Lena pulled her hand away.

"Max, this is Lena," he said now, turning to his companion. "Lena's still pining for her lover boy who left for England two months ago. She won't let anyone else in her bed. Such a waste, don't you think?"

Lena looked up at him, squinting into the sunshine. He was handsome, no doubt about that, with dark eyelashes and an olive complexion, his black hair neatly oiled in place, and a short-sleeved white shirt, the cuffs rolled up almost to his shoulders, revealing bronzed, muscular forearms.

"*Ma chérie*, you really need to let your hair down," he said. "Now more than ever. We need to enjoy ourselves while we can. There's going to be a war."

She looked at him in surprise.

He smirked again. "Haven't you heard? Hitler's signed a non-aggression pact with Stalin. It was on the news just an hour ago, sweetheart. War is now a certainty."

Hitler and Stalin? How could that be? The communists had always been the staunchest enemies of the fascists.

"Yes, quite a shock. What will your Otto think about that, eh?"

"I don't know," Lena stammered. She wished she did. She wished she could turn to him for advice.

"But surely," she said, "no one wants war."

"Stalin has given Hitler the go-ahead to invade Poland. Britain and France will have to declare war." He seemed almost smug at the prospect.

"What's so special about Poland?" she said. "They didn't step in to rescue Czechoslovakia."

Heinz shrugged. "I'm only telling you what everyone's saying." He reached for her hand again. "Let's go for a drink later and have a full debate." He winked, and turned to his companion again. "Don't you just love a woman who knows how to argue?"

Lena shook her head; he really was insufferable. She stepped to the side. "Excuse me. I have to go."

When she arrived home, she found a letter from Otto. She opened it immediately, standing in the foyer, opposite Mme. Verbié's loge. Absurdly, for a moment, she imagined it might offer an interpretation of the day's events—but of course he had posted it a week ago. He again wrote how much he wanted her to join him in England. His last plan had fallen through; he'd tried to get her sponsored through International Brigade contacts. But now he had another idea: a work permit to enter as a domestic servant. He was making arrangements. Lena was to wait for further details.

She climbed the stairs to the fifth floor. Did she really want to go to England? What little she knew about the place was not very appealing: huge factories and smoking chimneys. London, maybe, but Otto was stuck in the middle of the countryside. It sounded dull. Yet she was flattered. He was going to great efforts on her behalf. And it was hard to be alone so much of the time. But she didn't want to get her hopes up. Everyone said it was difficult to get into England nowadays. And she had to wait for Sasha.

Ten days later, the Germans invaded Poland and the continent plunged into war. An impenetrable barrier of silence put an end to the letters from Prague. The trunks sat in the warehouse. Sophie still asked occasionally, "When is Sasha coming?"

Otto's scheme to get Lena a domestic work permit application fell through on a technicality with the paperwork; by the time she resubmitted, the regulations had changed and only applicants residing in Nazi-occupied territory were eligible. She tried for a temporary permit but couldn't prove she had enough money to support herself. Lena dreaded the repeated trips to the embassy with the hope that she couldn't suppress, the disappointment she couldn't dispel. The weather turned cold again. Money became tighter, her skirts looser.

The war didn't seem to amount to much. Poland got a beating, and there were skirmishes in Finland and, briefly, along the German–French border, but then everything stalled. *C'est le drôle de guerre*, everyone said. It's a phony war. They will negotiate a peace treaty soon.

Certainly, France wasn't in danger. The Maginot Line would hold firm.

But Otto kept urging Lena to leave. In the midst of winter, he wrote, in a buoyant mood, this plan was sure to work. An invitation for a visitor's visa. From someone very rich, very influential. He enclosed that letter from Mrs. Courtney-Smithers. *Just go back to the embassy and show them this letter,* he wrote.

CHAPTER 8

SUSSEX, FEBRUARY 1940

The Czechs received their weekly allowance, and Peter suggested a beer at the Fox and Hounds. Otto declined, hoping for a chance to finally do some writing. He hadn't had a moment's peace all day. But then Emil said he didn't feel like going, either. He'd been subdued ever since he'd received his brother's letter the day before, and now sat on the sofa, stabbing at the fire with morose pokes.

"Here, take a look at this," Otto said, tossing him a well-worn copy of *Homage to Catalonia*. "You'll like it."

Otto had skimmed through it again recently: a rather simplistic analysis of the conflicts between the anarchists and the socialists, but some insightful firsthand reports on the fighting in Spain. And the first section, with its description of the workers' republic in Barcelona, was truly uplifting. It might keep Emil distracted for a while.

Emil studied the back cover. "Oh, yes," he said, his face brightening. "Milton told me about this. George Orwell. Caused quite a stir."

"Yes. He had the audacity to question the Moscow Party line." Otto threaded a piece of paper into the typewriter.

Emil flipped through the pages. "This will be good for me. I need to read more in English. But it will take me a long time to get through it."

"I don't need it. It's Milton's copy. I'm sure you can keep it as long as you want."

"When is Milton coming down again?"

Muriel's son, Milton, was in his first year at Oxford. Rather naive, spoiled rotten, in Otto's opinion. But he and Emil were about the same age, and they'd become good friends over the Christmas holidays.

"In a couple of weeks, I think." Otto adjusted the alignment of the paper.

"Josef always wanted to go to Spain," Emil said. "Did you ever think about going?"

Otto turned to him in surprise. Of course, Emil was very young, and at the time, Otto had kept his position strictly secret. But he had always suspected that Peter knew the true nature of Otto's work for Spain, and he assumed Peter had told the others.

"I didn't go to Spain, but I worked for the Republican government."

"I thought you worked for an information bureau or something," Emil said.

"It was certainly a lot more than that." Surely, Emil didn't think he'd functioned as some sort of advice clerk. He had never taken fire, never had to kill, but his work hadn't been without risk. Otto shook his head in disbelief. When he first arrived in Prague, he was viewed as quite the hero, the one experienced in the struggle against fascism. He loved the thrill, the buzzing in his chest, whenever he held the attention of the whole room, loved seeing the admiration in people's eyes.

"Well, what *were* you doing?" Emil asked.

"I worked for the Republican intelligence service."

"You mean you were a secret agent?" Emil's eyes widened.

Otto smiled. "Yes. In a way." There was no longer any need to be furtive.

"What did you do, exactly?"

"Collected information on the support Hitler was giving to the Spanish fascists. Arms shipments, movement of planes, that sort of thing. Sifting through information we received from our contacts inside Germany."

"What did you do with the information?"

"We passed it on to officials in the Spanish embassy in Prague. They had people in direct contact with the War Office in Valencia. And then, later, we worked with the embassy in Paris."

"You were a spy!"

Otto laughed. Much of the work had been rather mundane. But there had been moments of real excitement. Especially when the troop movement crisis happened, in May '38.

"Damn! I've never met a spy before."

Two days later, Lena's letter arrived.

> It didn't work. They're not giving out any visitor visas anymore. They barely looked at that fancy letter you sent me. I need to wait for Sasha anyway. I'm . . .

Otto didn't read the rest. He slumped onto the sofa. Why had he allowed himself to believe that he would soon meet Lena off the boat? And why was she still harboring this ridiculous idea of her sister joining her? Did she not understand the peril she was in? Once there was fighting in France, it would be impossible to get Lena out. She was stuck in that miserable hole of a flat, with no one to help her. No, he had to get her out of there.

"Not good news, I assume," Tomas said, pushing his spectacles up his nose.

"What? No."

Otto went to the kitchen in search of a glass of water and looked out on the back garden. A blackbird sat on top of the moss-covered wall. A huge, impenetrable wall separated him from Lena. Even when fleeing from the Nazis, crossing the border at midnight, hidden under a tarpaulin in the back of a lorry, he'd not felt this powerless.

Peter stood in the doorway. "We'll just have to come up with something else."

"Like what? Your last clever idea didn't work out so well, did it?"

"I think we should go to the Czechs."

"What on earth are you talking about?" Otto pushed past him to return to the sofa.

"Emil gave me the idea," Peter said. "Yesterday he couldn't stop talking about your having been a spy. He's building it up in his mind as a very glamorous thing."

"What does that have to do with anything?"

"Is it really true?" Lotti said. "That you were a secret agent?"

"Sort of. Yes."

"My God! Peter, why didn't you tell me?"

Peter shrugged. "I thought it was obvious to everyone that Otto wasn't really interested in . . . what was it? Industrial development?"

"It was the Spanish Economic Information Bureau."

"Precisely."

"What about Lena?" Lotti asked. "Was she an agent, too?"

"No. She worked for me, she was my secretary, but she wasn't an agent. And officially, she wasn't supposed to know what was going on."

"I was thinking yesterday," Peter said, standing on the hearth, facing the room, "when Emil was going on and on: Back in May '38, there were rumors. . . . Wasn't it the Spanish embassy in Prague that tipped off the Czech government about the Nazi buildup on the Sudetenland border?"

"It was indeed."

"And where did they get that information?"

Otto nodded. He was impressed. "Very good. Yes, they got it from us. We got the reports from our contacts in Saxony and passed them to the Spanish embassy. They tipped off Beneš, and he ordered the Czech mobilization. Stopped Hitler in his tracks. For the time being." Yes, it had been a real triumph.

"Good heavens!" Lotti said. "You were responsible for that?"

"Well, yes, together with a lot of other people. Some of our sources inside Germany took great risks to get that information out. I dread to think about what has happened to them since then. Yes, it was splendid at the time, but it didn't achieve much in the long run, did it?"

"It bought a few extra months, allowed some people to get out who might not have otherwise," Peter said. "What I'm thinking is: How can we use that to our advantage now?"

"What on earth do you mean?"

"Use it for some leverage to get Lena out of Paris." Peter poked the few remaining coals in the grate.

"I don't see how that's going to work. The organization I worked for closed long ago. The Spanish government no longer exists. The Czech government no longer exists. We have no contact with anyone from those days. I don't see how any of it can be of use now."

"But President Beneš is here in London now."

"So?"

"He has the Czech National Council based here, trying to establish the government in exile. There're people at the Trust Fund Office who are associated with the council."

"What are you getting at?" Lotti said.

"Otto's agency gave the Czech government valuable information back in '38," Peter replied. "I'm sure we can persuade the Czech Council people here in London that Lena was a part of that operation and that they need to repay the favor."

"I don't see how a tiny group of exiled Czech bureaucrats can do much. I'm sure they're full of their own self-importance, but really . . ."

"They must have links with British officials here. There're people in powerful positions in this country who feel guilty about appeasement and Munich. It's time for them to make amends." Peter reached for his coat from the hook behind the front door. "Come on. Let's go."

"Where're you going?" Lotti said.

"Let's get out of the house. We can't afford to keep that fire burning all day."

"Where's Emil?" Lotti said.

"He went to The Hollow," Tomas said.

"I hope he's all right," Lotti said. "He seems so forlorn since he received Josef's letter."

"You baby him too much," Peter said. "He just needs time to

take it in. Come on everyone—we need fresh air. And we need to talk to Muriel."

Peter led the way across the recreation ground toward a stile between two tall hedges, with a sign indicating the public footpath. The stile was smooth and worn from years of use, the weathered wood of the lower cross-steps indented from the thousands of footsteps that had preceded them on this route. Peter swung his leg over, climbed down, and offered Lotti a hand. She laughed lightly as she landed in his arms. Otto caught himself staring as they embraced.

Their route stretched out through three long fields bordered by high hedgerows. A gentle incline in the terrain allowed a view of the woods beyond and, to the left, the rolling contours of the South Downs in the distance. Out of sight beyond them, but almost palpable in Otto's mind, lay the English Channel and the shores of France. And Lena.

"So, does Muriel know you were a spy?" Lotti said.

This was getting out of hand. Otto had never thought of himself as a *spy*, exactly. He was just passing on information that was important for the defense of the Spanish Republic. But, well, let them think that. It was odd to be talking about it openly after years of being secretive, but it couldn't do any harm now.

"I talked with her about the Sudetenland situation. When I first arrived. She knew I was involved with the movement in Spain when she sponsored me, so I told her about the bureau."

"Here's the plan," Peter said. "Otto and I will go to the Czech Council office tomorrow."

"Tomorrow's Sunday," Otto said.

"Monday, then." Peter was in full swing. "We'll concoct an elaborate story about Lena's playing a key role in the Sudetenland business."

They cut through the next field and picked up a narrow path that led to the driveway of Muriel's place at The Hollow. They found Emil in the living room, nestled in front of the fireplace, playing chess with Alistair.

"Come in, come in," Alistair effused. "How delightful to see you all. Emil is giving me a thrashing here."

Alistair was strikingly handsome, probably in his early fifties, well preserved, with a lively stride, a warm, jovial disposition, and always a beguiling smile. He wore his signature brightly colored bow tie; today's was a deep red with small blue dots, setting off his crisp white shirt and navy blue waistcoat. He gestured for them to sit.

"How are things in London?" Lotti asked.

"Frightfully dreary. The wretched blackout, and sandbags everywhere. One might just as well spend the weekend in the country. Not that the company isn't delightful down here, of course." He flashed that smile again. "What can I offer you?" He slipped effortlessly into the role of host, even though he generally visited only on weekends. Muriel joined them as they sat by the fire.

"Lena didn't get her visa," Otto said. "They're not giving out any visitor visas at all."

"Oh no," Muriel said. "I'm terribly sorry. Aunt Pippa's letter didn't help, then."

"No," Otto said. "We have to find another approach."

"Peter has a wonderful idea," Lotti said.

"Do you know how to reach the British intelligence service?" Otto asked Muriel. "We're thinking of using Lena's involvement with my bureau in Prague as a ploy to get her in."

"Hmm . . . that's an interesting idea, but I'm afraid I don't have any acquaintances in MI5. At least, not as far as I know," she chuckled.

"We're going to London to talk with the Czech Council," Peter said. "I'm sure we can convince them Lena was an important part of the bureau's work and needs to be brought to safety over here."

"It makes more sense to work with the British," Otto said. "They're the ones who will have to issue a visa."

Alistair appeared with a tray of wine glasses and a plate of crackers. "You need someone to put in a word at the Foreign Office," he said. "Muriel, surely some of your good Tory friends here in Sussex have useful connections."

"Most of them are busy trying to hide the fact that they so enthusiastically welcomed Ribbentrop into high society when he visited London before the war," Muriel snorted. "Lauded him for being staunchly anticommunist. But I could try to talk to Lady Charlotte, I suppose."

"Lady Charlotte?"

"McMahon's wife, over at Durfield Park. We used to avoid any discussion of politics, because we disagreed on just about everything. But it was Lady Charlotte who first approached me about sponsoring refugees. After Munich. She called on all the local gentry, I believe, but I don't think too many obliged."

"McMahon might give it a shot," Alistair said.

"What are they talking about?" Tomas turned to Otto, screwing up his nose.

"*Entschuldigung!*" Muriel said. She was fluent in German. "*Es tut mir leid.* I'm dreadfully sorry. Please forgive me. We're trying to decide who would have most influence at the Foreign Office."

Peter said, "I think we should go with my plan for an approach to the Czech Council."

"I have one hundred and seventy flag badges to give them," Tomas said. "If we all worked on them tonight and tomorrow, we could get to two hundred and fifty, I'm sure. That would impress them."

"Oh, for heaven's sake," Otto said.

"Well, it couldn't hurt," Muriel said with a smile. "We'll lean on the British, and you work on the Czechs."

Later, as they rose to leave, Alistair put an arm around Otto's shoulder. "As soon as Lena arrives, you have to bring her here to meet us right away. I simply have to see this girl. She must be something to be worth so much effort." He winked.

CHAPTER 9

LONDON, FEBRUARY 1940

Miss Marjorie Hubbock glanced at the clock on the wall above her desk. Quarter to three. She gave a ladylike cough in an attempt to attract the attention of the young woman at the opposite desk. Mrs. Perkins continued to work, jabbing at the keys much too aggressively. It was no wonder the keys kept getting jammed, a regular occurrence that had led to some undignified expressions of frustration earlier in the day. If Mrs. Perkins was not more careful, she was going to break her typewriter, and there would be no end of difficulties in getting a replacement.

"Ahem." Miss Hubbock coughed again. No response from the other desk. Finally, realizing that she would just have to be more explicit, she said, "Mrs. Perkins, do you see what time it is?"

Mrs. Perkins looked up at the clock. "Almost ten to three," she said, and returned to her typing.

Trying to control her exasperation, Miss Hubbock announced, "It's time to put the kettle on for afternoon tea."

"I have to finish this report for Mr. Watkins, Miss Hubbock. He needs it by the end of the day. Do you think you could possibly make the tea today?"

Miss Hubbock was rendered speechless. Mrs. Perkins was perhaps twenty years her junior and had been here for less than a year.

Miss Hubbock had been at the Foreign Office for the past twelve years, long before all these flighty young women had taken it into their heads to enter the workforce, and she held a very important position. Miss Hubbock was Senior Secretary to the Assistant Clerk, the Deputy Head, and the Assistant Director of the Special Operations Department, led by the Deputy Under Secretary of State, who in turn reported directly to the Permanent Under Secretary of State. Her responsibilities, the precise details of which she was of course not at liberty to divulge, included writing up confidential memos, recording the minutes of highly sensitive meetings, and handling all incoming telephone calls.

This last duty called for particular tact and skill. Naturally, one had to be polite at all times yet firmly resist pressure from callers who believed their particular concern should receive immediate priority. Just that morning, for example, she had had to field calls from the French attaché, the department heads at both the Ministry of Supply and the War Office, and a very persistent Mr. Lisicky, from the Czech Council, who had now called three times. But Mr. Lyndhurst and Mr. Watkins were much too busy to take any calls. They had to complete a detailed analysis of the situation in Finland, which the Prime Minister would need for a speech in the House of Commons tomorrow. Miss Hubbock had recorded each telephone message in her scrupulously neat handwriting, to be delivered at the end of the day.

Now, this young upstart was asking her to go and make the tea. On second thought, however, perhaps it was just as well. She had recently noticed that Mrs. Perkins, in spite of specific directions, persisted in pouring Mr. Lyndhurst's tea first, when Mr. Watkins preferred his tea on the weak side and Mr. Lyndhurst was more partial to a stronger brew. It just went to prove the old adage that if one wanted something done right, one had to do it oneself. With a sigh of resignation, Miss Hubbock rose from her desk and went to the lounge.

And so it was that while Miss Hubbock was otherwise occupied, the telephone rang again and was answered by Mrs. Perkins. The caller said he was Sir Somebody-or-Other and was most insistent on speaking with Mr. Lyndhurst immediately. He had a very posh accent, which made him difficult to dismiss, and as Mr. Lyndhurst was going to break for tea in a few moments anyway, Mrs. Perkins could see no harm in knocking on the door that led to the inner office where the gentlemen worked.

"Sorry to interrupt you, sir," she said, "but there is a Sir Rupert McManus, I think it is, on the phone, sir, who says he has to speak with you right away, sir."

"Sir Rupert? Oh, Sir Rupert McMahon," Mr. Lyndhurst said, coming into the front office. "All right, I'll talk to him. Where's Miss Hubbock?"

"She's making the tea, sir."

"Good heavens. I see. Right, then." He reached for the pile of messages sitting in his box and glanced through them. "Well, put him through, please, Mrs. Perkins."

He returned to his desk, leaving the door ajar. "Sir Rupert! How are you? What can I do for you? The Czechs? Oh, yes, I see that Mr. Lisicky has called a few times. Been frightfully busy working on a report for the PM, you know. I see, I see . . . Yes, quite . . . Quite so . . . Naturally . . . Well, I'll see what I can do . . . What's the name? . . . Can you spell that for me? Good gracious . . . I see . . . Yes, indeed . . . Quite so . . . Oh, not at all, not at all. Glad to oblige."

"What was that all about?" asked his colleague.

"It seems the Czechs have an agent in Paris they have to bring over. Vital to their work over here, apparently."

"Why's McMahon getting involved in that?"

"Oh, the Czechs have been having a go at him, it appears. Everyone's tripping over themselves being nice to the damn Czechs these days. Better let this one through to shut them up."

"What's this Czech chap's name?"

"Well, that's the darnedest thing. It's a girl."

CHAPTER 10

PARIS, MARCH 1940

Lena returned from the market carrying a baguette, a pear, and thirty grams of gruyère, the smallest piece the cheese man would sell. She immediately checked the letterboxes opposite Mme. Verbié's office. She had been anxiously awaiting more news since she had received a cryptic note from Otto, two days earlier.

> *Think we've found a way to get you here,* he'd written. *Wait for official notification. Don't ask too many questions. Just follow instructions.*

She saw it at once: protruding from the top-floor slot, a large white envelope, thick and opaque. It was addressed English-style to Miss Lena Kulkova, postmarked London SW1, and decorated with an official signet: a shield topped by a crown and flanked by a lion and a unicorn. She was about to open it right there opposite the concierge's loge, when she became aware of Mme. Verbié staring at her with blatant curiosity. She didn't understand what Otto meant about not asking questions, but maybe she should be discreet.

Lena took the stairs two steps at a time, and reached the top floor breathless from both the climb and nervous anticipation. Her heart raced. She took a few deep breaths to calm herself and then opened the envelope. She extracted a sheet of official stationery with the letterhead *The Foreign Office, King Charles Street, London SW1*.

Dear Miss Kulkova,
On behalf of His Majesty's government, I am pleased to
inform you that you have been invited to enter Great
Britain on a special permit, granted at the discretion of
the Foreign Office.

The necessary entry papers are enclosed with this
correspondence. They need to be endorsed at His Majesty's
embassy in Paris, which is located at 35 rue du Faubourg
St.-Honoré, in the 1ère arrondissement. The hours of
operation are Monday to Friday, 9:30 A.M. to 5:00 P.M.
No appointment is necessary.

I understand that time is of the essence. I have
therefore taken the liberty of making travel arrangements
on your behalf.

I am enclosing a ticket for the 10:30 A.M. flight from
Le Bourget on Sunday, 10 March. I trust you will find this
convenient.
Yours sincerely, Thomas Lyndhurst, Esq.
Assistant Director, Special Operations

What on earth did this mean? Lena looked inside the envelope
again. Indeed, there they were: an entry permit and a ticket to London,
sitting in her hands. She reread the letter carefully, unsure whether
her imperfect command of the English language had deceived her.
You have been invited to enter Great Britain on a special permit. How
had Otto managed this? She looked at the ticket. Le Bourget was the
airport—she knew that. An aeroplane ticket—it frightened her. Was
she going to have to pay for it? It must be very expensive.

She had to show this to someone and decide what to do. Marguerite would not be home until late. But Eva—yes, she would go
and find Eva.

Lena caught up with her as she was leaving her apartment with Heinz.
Lena wanted Eva to herself, but they ended up walking as a threesome
across the Jardin de Luxembourg, through the sadly neglected lawns
and flowerbeds, so faded from their former glory. Eva and Heinz

were engaged in animated discussion, something about a Hungarian writer they'd just met; Lena couldn't pay attention.

"You're very quiet, Lena," Eva said. "What's happened? Did you hear something from home?"

"No, nothing like that. I've . . ." Lena faltered, then blurted it all out: "Otto's somehow managed to get me an entry permit to England. I really don't understand how. It just arrived in a very fancy letter. With an aeroplane ticket to London."

"Good Lord!" Eva said. "A plane ticket?"

"Yes, for the tenth." She pulled the envelope out of her handbag. "Look at this. Do I have to pay for it?"

Heinz took the ticket, turned it over, inspecting it. "I'm pretty sure it's all paid for," he said.

"That's incredible," Eva said as they continued walking. "I suppose if anyone could do it, Otto could."

"You must be damn good in bed, sweetheart—that's all I can say." Heinz had his arm around Eva, but he winked at Lena over her head.

"So, are you going?" Eva asked.

Lena was about to say something about waiting for Sasha, but it suddenly felt ridiculous. Heinz would be scornful. Everyone told her a child could not travel on her own now, in wartime conditions. Instead, she heard herself say, "Well, yes, I suppose I am. I tried so many times to get into England; I don't see how I can turn this down now. It's not as though this special permit is transferable to anyone else. There're so many others trying to get in. . . ."

"Not anymore," Heinz said. "Why would anyone want to go there now? They say Hitler is going to attack London with his huge stockpiles of poison gas any day now."

"But Otto thinks—"

"Who cares what Otto thinks?"

"Oh, shh, Heinz," Eva said.

"Well, he was right about Barcelona, right about Munich. I trust his instincts in matters like this. He . . ." Lena felt a thickness in the back of her throat.

"You miss him, Lena. Why won't you admit it?" Eva said, with a gentle laugh.

"It's not just Otto. You know Peter and Lotti are over there now, too. I got a letter from Lotti last week. They're living in a commune, by the sounds of it. From each according to his ability, to each according to his needs. I like that. We have to hold on to our ideals, even in wartime." Lena linked her arm through Eva's. "It's just . . . I wish you could join us, Eva."

"Oh, don't worry about me."

"But I don't want to leave you here alone."

"I'm not alone." Eva in turn slipped her hand through Heinz's arm and pulled him closer to her again. "And Heinz is sure he's soon going to hear back from his cousin in Chicago." She looked up at Heinz. "If he does get a visa to America, I might go with him."

"How would you be able to do that?"

Now it was Eva's turn to blush. "Well, we've talked about getting married."

Lena looked at Heinz in surprise. He turned away, his eyes pulled toward the tight-fitting skirt and elegant legs of a passerby pursuing a poodle straining on its leash.

CHAPTER 11

PARIS, MARCH 1940

The following morning, Lena received more startling news: a letter from her father. At least, it was unmistakably his small, scratchy handwriting that traversed the page. But this ostensibly came from someone called Hans Weimer, and not from Prague but from Belgrade. It was one short page, dated the 12th of February, more than three weeks earlier.

> *Dear Lena,*
> *I am here in Belgrade with your brother. We spent some time in the mountains. The others stayed home. We are going to meet up with our old friend Schweik. You will remember him.*
> *Love,*
> *Father*

Lena stared at this in disbelief, trying to decipher it. Her father and Ernst had left Prague and fled over the mountains to Belgrade? Leaving Máma and Sasha behind? How could they do that? And why Belgrade? Presumably, they'd traveled through Slovakia and Hungary, avoiding Nazi-occupied Austria. She knew the Czech consulate in Belgrade was one of a handful that had refused to close after Hitler dismantled Czechoslovakia; it had stayed open in a gesture of defiance. *They can't be doing anything very useful,* she thought; *they probably have no funds.* But was that why her father had headed there?

Whenever Lena thought of her father, she felt nothing but anger. It was like an old jersey that she automatically slipped into without considering whether there could be anything more suitable to wear. She remembered the arguments, the beatings, the vow never to speak to him again. Yet now he and Ernst had made a clandestine escape from occupied Czechoslovakia. *We spent some time in the mountains.* This was a dangerous route—Lena understood that much. And even from Belgrade, he hadn't dared use his real name. The last she'd heard, her parents had been unable to envision anything but an officially sanctioned emigration, bringing all the trappings of a bourgeois lifestyle. None of that was possible now. Leaving over the mountains meant carrying nothing but the clothes on their backs, hiding by day, traveling at night. How could she not grudgingly admire him?

She showed the letter to Eva. She tracked her down that afternoon, for once without Heinz at her side. The weather was milder. They walked toward the river.

"It's hard to believe," Eva said. "My father would never do anything like that. What's this part about meeting up with Schweik?"

"I don't know. I can't make any sense of it."

Yet no sooner were the words out of her mouth than she suddenly got it, and simultaneously Eva did, too. They stopped on a traffic island in the middle of the street and in unison cried, "*Osudy dobrého vojáka Švejka!* The Adventures of the Good Soldier Schweik"—the famous fictional Czech soldier in the Austro-Hungarian army.

"That's it," Lena said. "*Our old friend Schweik. You will remember him.*"

"Oh my God!" Eva said. "They're going off to be soldiers. To join the army. But what's your father doing invoking the name of Schweik? He can't approve of his anarchistic beliefs."

"Not at all. But he knew I'd understand the reference." Lena said. "I can't believe I didn't get that right away. They must be trying to connect with the Free Czech Army."

"Yes, I think Belgrade is one of the places they're mobilizing."

"My father always was fiercely patriotic. Still, I never imagined he would do something like this. And Ernst just turned seventeen. Surely he's too young."

"They're probably not too fussy at this point."

"Come with me to the library," Lena said. "Let's see if any newspapers have reports on the Free Czech Army."

Eva looked at her watch. "I've got to go. I'm meeting Heinz at four o'clock."

So Lena went alone. *Le Figaro* had a short item on page five about a division mobilizing in Agde, in the South of France, with volunteers shipped in from recruitment centers in Belgrade and elsewhere. They were to be deployed with the French army, if needed. But they were short of uniforms, tanks, and ammunition and embroiled in negotiations with the French authorities for funds. Father had liked to boast about the efficient military back home, with its sophisticated weaponry, so impressive for a young nation. This venture sounded more like a Boy Scouts outing, pleading for additional tents and raincoats.

And Ernst: he was a child. When Lena had last seen him, he'd been a scrawny adolescent waiting for his growth spurt and a real reason to shave. Now he was heading for the South of France to be sent into an ill-equipped army. And Sasha and Máma were on their own in Prague. What was Father thinking, leaving them behind? What would Máma do for money? Lena had no idea—and no way to contact any of them.

She had never considered her family close-knit, but now they were all separated from each other, and it suddenly felt frightening. She knew that Máma would not send Sasha out now. Not now that she was on her own. And if Sasha was not going to appear in Paris, there was no reason for Lena to stay.

Lena looked again at the letter from Mr. Lyndhurst. So she was supposed to return to the embassy with this invitation and get it endorsed by the cheerless clerks she'd encountered so many times before. She broke into a grin at the prospect of waving it in their faces. She hoped they would feel suitably rebuked. It was almost four o'clock. If she splurged on a Métro ticket, she would get there before they closed.

She sprinted up the embassy steps, waving her letter in triumph at the entrance guard. He merely nodded and directed her to the long queue. Apparently, Mr. Lyndhurst of London SW1 was not empowered to exempt her from taking her place once again among the huddled masses. It was unbelievably crowded and stuffy. She inched forward at an excruciatingly slow pace, her excitement dissipating. Now she was annoyed that she had not brought anything to read and worried that they might close before her turn.

Finally, she was called to the counter, where she found herself indeed standing face-to-face with one of the familiar clerks. Lena beamed inanely at him and produced her letter with great flourish. But he displayed no glimmer of recognition. He studied the letter and the accompanying permit, stared at Lena, inspected her passport photograph, and looked at her again, back and forth several times, wordlessly. Lena realized she was holding her breath and that her stomach was growling; she hadn't eaten in hours. Suddenly, the official scooped up all the documents and disappeared through a heavy mahogany door behind him.

Lena felt exposed and self-conscious. She couldn't recall ever having seen a clerk leave the counter. She tried to breathe normally. She lowered her hands out of sight and tried to cross all her fingers, one over the other.

The clerk reappeared, accompanied by an older man, bald, with red, blotchy skin. This newcomer repeated the scrutiny of Lena and her paperwork, mumbled something inaudible, pointed to something on the permit, held it up to the light. Lena saw an elaborate watermark hidden beneath the surface, like an occult gem. She was suspended still in a moment of time as three pairs of eyes focused on this piece of paper. Finally, the bald man reached for his stamp and thumped his authorization onto the permit and her passport. He handed both back to Lena with a silent nod.

Was that it? She walked out in a daze; she had a visa for England! She laughed out loud at the unexpected turn of events, at the joy of it—and saw a chestnut man on the corner. The warm smell from the brazier was enticing; on impulse, Lena indulged in a small bag of nuts. She cracked one open and bit into the soft meat, almost burning her tongue.

"I've decided to go to England," she announced to Marguerite later that evening. "I've got a permit and an aeroplane ticket." She showed Marguerite the letter.

"Goodness!" Marguerite nodded in approval. "All right. We'd better start getting you ready. The tenth is this Sunday."

There was not much to do. Lena's life in Paris was compact and could easily be uprooted and fitted into one small suitcase. She had never flown before but assumed she would not be permitted to bring the massive trunk her mother had thought essential on her departure from Prague two years earlier. Most of its former contents had either worn out or been sold anyway. She spent the next three days giving away many of her remaining possessions, including the trunk itself. Most of her Czech and German books went to Eva, the French to Marguerite. After much deliberation, she decided to pack her complete set of *À la Recherche du Temps Perdu*; it was ridiculously heavy and bulky, but she loved Proust and thought it would be a way for a little bit of Paris to accompany her.

And the hideous gas mask from Mme. Verbié: it had been tossed aside and never used. People had long ceased carrying their masks with them; the mannequins in the shop windows on the Place Vendôme no longer sported masks decorated with colorful bows. Lena took the mask in and out of the suitcase several times, before finally wedging it next to the Proust. She didn't want Mme. Verbié to discover it discarded—and perhaps she might need it one day.

Her final day in Paris, Lena walked one last time along the banks of the Seine and through the Latin Quarter. The plane trees were showing tiny buds of green; spring flowers from Provence had arrived on the Quai aux Fleurs. In the rue Duhesme, two women still wrapped up in their winter wear—knitted bonnets, black overcoats, woolen stockings—called out a cheerful "*Bonjour, mademoiselle!*" Arms outstretched, hands reddened and cuticles torn, they proffered up their glistening carrots, plump leeks, and perfectly round cabbages, extolling their virtues with a barrage of superlatives. The work of yesterday, today, tomorrow: unchanging, except for the variation in produce with the seasons. She had seen these women many times before, but they probably did not remember her and certainly would not miss her. She smiled and bid them a silent adieu.

There were other farewells, so much harder: to the Beaufils and little Sophie, to Mme. Verbié—good people who had shown her so much kindness. Final hugs and handshakes, one last look deep into their eyes, a fervent hope that everything would turn out well.

And Eva and Marguerite: What if it *was* going to be dangerous to be in Paris?

"We'll be all right," Marguerite maintained. "If things take a turn for the worse, Eva can come with me to my uncle and aunt's place in the Gorges du Tarn. It's completely hidden away from the world; they grow all their own food. We can stay there until it settles down."

"It might be over soon, anyway," Eva said, flicking her hair over her shoulder. "They're saying this stalemate will end in a truce before long."

They were sitting in Les Deux Magots on her last night. The weather much milder, they were back on the terrace, and the accordion player had returned to the street corner. The distinctive smell of Gitanes wafted over the tables, the smoke hovering in thick layers in the amber light.

A group at the next table called out to the musician. He sauntered over, black beret askew, eyes red-rimmed. He gave a vaudeville bow and compressed the bellows, his sinewy hands plying the keyboard. Lena soon recognized the tune: "*Tout Va Très Bien, Madame la Marquise.*" It was an absurd ditty, the tale of a butler trying to reassure his mistress that everything is fine back home, when in fact it becomes clear that the gray mare is dead, the stables have burned to the ground, the castle is in ruins, and the Marquis has committed suicide. But "everything is fine," *tout va très bien*, went the catchy refrain. Lena loved it, and soon the melody reverberated from table to table.

"*Tout va très bien, Madame la Marquise. Tout va très bien, tout va très bien . . .*"

PART II

CHAPTER 12

ENGLAND, MARCH 1940

Lena looked up from her book. The vast expanse of the English Channel was all she could see, the white tops of the waves appearing as tiny specks thousands of feet below. She became aware of her left hand still clutching the upholstered armrest. The aeroplane appeared to be staying aloft, so perhaps she could relax her grip.

Craning her neck forward, she could see the engines out on the wing, the faint oscillation at the hubs the only hint of motion. If she understood the physics of it better, perhaps it would be easier to have confidence in this improbable venture: a huge, bird-shaped machine with fifteen passengers (and her suitcase, weighed down with the Proust volumes) lifting up into the sky and speeding north, purely on the strength of those propellers. Lena had watched with a mixture of fascination and terror as the giant blades stirred from their slumber on the ground. Faster and faster they whirled, like the roundabout in Letna Park that she and Ernst loved so much when they were little, going round and round until her mother sitting on the bench became a blur; faster and faster, until the blades moved so quickly they looked like the whizzing spokes of a bicycle wheel; and then suddenly vanishing altogether, becoming invisible, as the noise thundered through the cabin. This motion somehow allowed the plane to speed down the runway and, miraculously, lift up into the wide-open sky.

Peering ahead again, her cheek pressed up against the window curtain, Lena saw a line of chalky white bluffs fringed with green as the English coastline came into sight. A few wispy clouds floated just below. Once you got used to being up here, the view was spectacular.

"More coffee, mademoiselle?"

The steward was back, offering a silver pot balanced on a starched white towel. Lena declined. She had earlier accepted a crouton with pâté and was feeling slightly queasy.

"When are we expected to reach London?" she asked. She had no idea how long this flight would take.

"We shall be arriving at Croydon Airdrome in about forty-five minutes, mademoiselle," he replied, with a slight bow. "May I get you anything else?"

"Oh, no thank you."

Lena wasn't sure what to expect on her arrival. She had written Otto to say she was leaving on the tenth, but there had been no time for a reply. She presumed he would be there to meet her. She suddenly wondered what she would do if he were not. Well, she had his address; she could find her own way there, if necessary. She had traveled on her own to Le Bourget on the RER train, feeling quite adventurous. There had been talk of Eva and Marguerite accompanying her, but Marguerite had to work, and Eva had suddenly announced that she hated platform farewells and would say good-bye in the Place de la Contrascarpe.

"I don't think there's a platform at the airport," Lena protested.

"You know what I mean. Reminds me of those tearful partings at the station in Prague. The huge, unspoken fear of not knowing when or where we would meet again." Eva shuddered.

Lena nodded. She was still haunted by the look in Máma's eyes the day she left. So she and Eva took leave of each other instead in the bustling market square; a quick, tight hug, and then Eva disappeared into the crowd, leaving Lena with an empty space in front of her and a lump in her throat.

But once on the train, she felt her courage returning. The thought of seeing Otto again gave her that fluttering excitement that she'd felt when they were first lovers. She always marveled that he wanted her—he who was admired by so many, wiser by far. She closed her eyes and imagined the feel of his body next to hers, walking down the street, sitting together, lying in bed—and then opened her eyes in apprehension. Maybe it wouldn't be the same. Maybe she and Otto would be like strangers.

Just at that moment, the plane lurched, as if stumbling to the bottom of an air pocket, and her stomach heaved in fright. But then it stabilized and began to descend in a gentle controlled glide. In the gaps in the mist, Lena caught tantalizing glimpses of the English countryside, spread out like a patchwork quilt: verdant fields and woods, meandering rivers, small clusters of red-roofed buildings, a little oval lake reflecting a glint of sunlight. It was beautiful. Where were the dark Satanic mills of the England she knew from school textbooks? The lush greenness enfolded her in a welcoming embrace, dispelling her lingering doubts.

And now, safely back on terra firma, she found her welcoming committee: Otto, looking taller and thinner than she remembered, standing next to a gleaming counter, and behind him Peter, and there was Lotti, waving excitedly at her from across the spacious hall. Lena noticed them immediately, framed in a spotlight of sun from a huge skylight. Suddenly she had closed that gap and was in Otto's arms, her cheek pressed hard against his coarse jacket, taking in his warmth and his smell, so strange and yet so familiar. She looked up, and he grinned at her, his hair all askew; he rocked her gently in his arms, pulling the top of her head toward his lips. All the months of waiting and trying and failing and hoping and not hoping—all that was now compressed into the past.

"Lena, Lena, *mein Schätzchen*," Otto said. "You're here at last!"

"He's been like a dog with a bone, obsessed about getting you over here," Peter said with a laugh. He and Lotti embraced Lena, kissing her on both cheeks.

"I was worried for your safety," Otto said, pulling her toward him again.

"What was it like to fly in an aeroplane?" Lotti asked, as they made their way toward the exit.

"Terrifying and really wonderful. And so fast. It took no time at all."

"Well, *mein Schätzchen*, you're to continue your journey in style," Otto said. He ushered Lena through the heavy exit door. Peter carried her suitcase. "Muriel lent us the car for this auspicious occasion."

"This really is a special treat," Peter said. "Petrol is scarce. The old Bentley hasn't had a run for almost two weeks."

"We have to constantly remind Peter to drive on the left." Lotti laughed. "It's a little nerve-racking at times."

"Luckily, there's hardly any traffic," Otto said.

"And luckily, it's daylight," Lotti continued. "A few weeks ago, we went down to the South Coast for the day and came back at night. Headlights aren't allowed because of the blackout. Tomas was leaning out of the window, trying to light the way with a tiny hand-held torch."

Lena basked in her friends' jovial chatter. A wave of contented exhaustion swept over her. Of course this was the right place to be. For the first time in months, she could relax. She sank into the leather seat and leaned on Otto's shoulder, as he put his arm around her. He kissed her, on the mouth this time, the roughness of his chin brushing hers, their noses jostling in an awkward fumbling for the right position, until their lips discovered the remembered softness.

Peter was driving and Lotti was up front, saying something about having taken the wrong turn. Suddenly, Otto pulled away from Lena to peer forward.

"No, this is right. I remember we passed that pub, the Three Swans."

"We have to get back to the Oxted Road," Peter said.

"It's just up there on the right," Otto said.

"It's such a maze of little lanes and convoluted routes," Lotti said, "it's easy to get lost."

"It's beautiful. I couldn't believe how green it looked from the air." Lena turned to Otto. "You didn't tell me it was so beautiful."

"Wait until you see the village," Lotti said. "There're lovely walks in the fields and woods."

Lotti seemed bubbly and talkative, very different from the shy young thing Lena remembered from two years ago in Prague. She turned around to face Lena. Her eyes sparkled, and all the muscles of her face joined in a coordinated dance around the words as they tumbled out.

"Muriel is planning a party tonight," she continued. "Milton is down from Oxford, and Alistair will be there, perhaps with a couple of his London friends. It will be so much fun."

These names meant nothing to Lena. "I'm just so happy to see all of you." She squeezed Otto's hand. "What about Josef? Isn't he over here, too?"

"He never made it. He was arrested in Krakow. By the time he was released and managed to secure new documents, it was too late to leave through Poland. He's heading toward the USSR, we think."

"Oh no!"

"His brother, Emil, is with us. Do you remember him? He's really upset about Josef," Lotti said. "He doesn't like to talk about it much."

"He received a letter from him—from Vilnius, of all places," Peter said.

"I just had an extraordinary letter from my father," Lena said, leaning forward into the gap between the seats. "He and Ernst escaped from Prague and reached Belgrade. It sounds as if they're trying to reach the Free Czech Army unit in Agde, in the South of France."

"Your father?" Peter exclaimed. "That cantankerous scoundrel?"

"I know. It's hard to believe."

"Sounds somewhat foolish," Otto said.

"Sounds very brave," Lotti said

"How did you get out?" Lena asked. "When did you leave? It was after the invasion, wasn't it?"

She was hungry for news. The letters she'd received over the past year had, of necessity, been vague and circumspect. Now, safe in a motorcar meandering along leafy English lanes, she could finally hear firsthand what had happened when the Nazis rolled into Prague a year earlier—the previous March.

"Yes. Almost immediately, the Gestapo started arresting people who'd been involved in the movement," Peter said. "We had to move from house to house, sleeping in a different place every night. And there was the curfew. You couldn't be out on the streets after 11:00 P.M. Suddenly, about two weeks later, they started accepting applications for exit permits at Gestapo headquarters. The queue stretched around the block; we were there all night and into the next day."

"Peter's father kept us supplied with coffee and sandwiches so we wouldn't lose our place in the line," Lotti said.

"People were coming and going, rumors flying," Peter said. He looked at Lena in the rearview mirror, his eyes sparkling. "We heard that you couldn't get an exit permit unless you had a train ticket," he continued. "And you could only buy a train ticket with foreign currency, which of course no one had. Then someone said Thomas Cook was selling tickets for Czech *koruna*, so my father rushed over there for us, but they were sold out. That's when we ran into Josef and Emil, who told us of a place near the Silesian border where you could get smuggled into Poland."

"It was really scary," Lotti said. "We had to cross through the woods at night. I still have nightmares about it."

"Has anyone heard from Prague since the war started?" Lena said.

"Very little. Lotti had a letter from her aunt," Peter said. "Through Portugal. And then my grandmother wrote to me in October."

"Did she say anything at all about my mother?" Lena asked. "I haven't heard a word."

"No, nothing about anyone in particular. It was mostly about food shortages, long queues for bread, that sort of thing."

"I'm really worried. I can't imagine how she's coping now that my father's left."

"She'll be all right," Lotti said. "It's not easy, but she won't be in danger. The Nazis were only going after people who'd been active in politics."

The journey progressed through small towns and villages, the lanes becoming increasingly narrow and banked on either side by tall, thick hedges. Dappled sunlight danced on the road ahead. It was so pretty. Lena leaned on Otto's shoulder and tried to banish her anxiety about Prague.

Oddly, it was not until Lotti announced that they were approaching Upper Wolmingham that Lena thought to ask, "How on earth did you manage to get that special permit for me from the Foreign Office?"

Otto chuckled. "*Mein Schätzchen*, you've been brought over here in order to continue your vital duties on behalf of the Czech secret service."

"We made up such a good story about your crucial role in the discovery of the Nazi buildup in Sudetenland, we almost believed it ourselves," Peter said.

"There it is." Lotti pointed at a row of redbrick cottages as they drove down a quaint village street. "Oak Tree Cottage."

"Which one?"

"Next to the butcher's shop. With the faded yellow door."

"Aren't we stopping?"

"We have to return the car to Muriel," Peter said. "And announce the safe arrival of our precious cargo from Paris."

He maneuvered the Bentley down a narrow, bumpy lane; overhanging tree branches scraped the roof and windows as they passed. They tumbled out, and Lena found herself in front of a more substantial house than those on the village street.

She was more interested in learning further details of Josef's arrest in Krakow, and Peter and Lotti's journey across Poland, than in seeing a lot of new faces. But half a dozen new faces were sitting around a dining room table, finishing off lunch. A tall, gray-haired man leaped up to greet them immediately, extending a long arm and a charming smile, introducing himself as Alistair, kissing Lena on both cheeks and slapping Otto on the back with a chuckle. A large, rust-colored dog bounded underfoot. Two young men and a couple in their thirties smiled politely, and at the head of the table was a woman Lena assumed must be Muriel. She did not get up, but her face flushed with pleasure.

"Lena, my dear, welcome to England," she said. "We've heard so much about you. We're simply delighted to have you here."

"Thank you so much." Lena tried to pronounce *th* correctly, but it still came out sounding more like *zsank you.*

"How is Paris? How are the French coping with the war? They don't have a blackout on the Champs-Élysées, do they?" asked one of the young men, sitting immediately to Muriel's left. He had a bright, fresh demeanor and short wavy hair; he looked about eighteen. His broad cheeks and angular jaw bore a striking resemblance to Muriel's.

"No, just for a few days—I think last September—but not since then," Lena replied.

"Of course not," declared the woman at the other end of the table. "The French are far more sensible about this sort of thing, aren't they? I don't suppose they have food rationing, either?"

"No, there was some talk of it, but nothing yet."

"We all have a wretched little ration book now," Alistair said. "Such a nuisance."

"Rationing is a much fairer system of distribution when food is scarce," retorted the young man whom Lena took to be Muriel's son. "Surely you're not taking the Tory position that the wealthy should be allowed to hoard as much as they want."

"Believe me, Milton, the wealthy will find a way around rationing." Alistair turned back to Lena. "Meat rationing goes into effect here tomorrow. As you can see, we're making the most of it here today while we still can."

There was a huge, much-depleted joint of roast beef in the center of the table, along with various bowls of vegetable remnants. Lena caught a whiff of the meat and realized she was very hungry.

"I say, can I offer you anything to drink?" Muriel said. "Or eat? You have had lunch, I presume? We've rather made pigs of ourselves here, I think, but I'm sure we could put together something."

Lotti quickly replied, "Oh, no, we don't want to impose. We just wanted to say hello as we dropped off the car. Lena hasn't even seen Oak Tree Cottage yet, and Emil and Tomas are waiting for us."

"Well, we're looking forward to seeing you all back here tonight," Muriel said, rising to approach the visitors, still crowded around the doorway. Lena noticed with surprise that she walked with one arm extended in front of her and that her eyes roamed in unfocused, random movements. Otto reached out to take hold of her arm and guided her toward them.

She clasped Lena's left hand in both of hers. "I do hope you'll be happy here, my dear. We can't offer much compared with the delights of Paris, but we'll do our best to provide some diversion."

"Thank you so much," she said again.

As they walked back up the driveway, Lena said to Otto, "You didn't tell me Muriel is blind."

"Oh, didn't I? I suppose that's because after a while, you just don't notice."

Oak Tree Cottage was smaller and more primitive than Lena had imagined, but she was charmed by the low ceilings, the crooked beams that traversed the walls, and the lattice-patterned windows. There was a fire in the grate and a sweet little cat curled up on the hearth, and in the kitchen a pot of hot soup. It was not roast beef, but it was warm and filling and accompanied by a delicious, crusty brown bread.

As they ate, the conversation returned to the exchange of news about all their mutual friends and acquaintances.

"Do you remember Gustav?" Peter said. "I ran into him a few weeks ago at the Czech refugee office in London. He jumped from a moving train near the Dutch border to avoid being shunted back into Germany. He's living somewhere near Birmingham."

"Tell her about Hilde," Lotti said.

"Oh God, yes, poor thing." Peter chuckled. "Hilde Spitzova. We met up with her in Poland, near Katowice. She was smuggled across the border under a pile of manure in a ramshackle wagon and still reeked two weeks later." He screwed up his face, as if he could still smell her now. "But she made it, I believe. We heard she got a domestic-worker permit and is somewhere in Essex."

Amazing exploits, probably exaggerated, but utterly satisfying nevertheless; Lena felt drunk on the camaraderie. It was as if they were describing an exciting new motion picture, except this was real—ordinary young people caught up in extraordinary times. But the news wasn't all good. A friend of Peter's had made it to the Polish border but hadn't been heard from since. And Lena became aware of Emil sitting in silence next to her, head buried in his soup. She hadn't known him well back in Prague. Josef was more in their group, Emil a couple of years younger but the spitting image of his brother.

"I'm so sorry to hear about Josef," she said.

"Yes, it's ironic," he said, a quiver in his lower lip. "It was Josef's idea for us to try to reach England."

"What did he say in his letter?"

He shrugged. "By the time he was released and had new papers, the war had started. He couldn't make it through Poland."

Lena gave his hand a gentle squeeze. "He'll be all right. He's very resourceful."

Emil nodded. He gave Lena a grateful smile and helped himself to another slice of bread. "Tomas should tell you the story of how he got an exit permit," Lotti said, looking over to the table by the window.

Tomas seemed odd. Lena hadn't known him in Prague, either. After wolfing down his soup, he'd retreated to the window, where he was bent over little pots of paint and some sort of buttons. But he looked up now, as if suddenly coming to life, and said, "I managed to get an invitation from a long-lost aunt in Dubrovnik."

"The clerk at Gestapo HQ didn't know how to spell *Yugoslavia*," Lotti said, with a shrill laugh.

"I said I didn't know, either. Trying to sound as helpful as possible, I suggested she just put *ins Ausland* instead."

"*Ins Ausland!*" Lotti said, giggling again. "Abroad! Can you believe it?"

"So that's what she did," Tomas said. "And I duly hopped on a train to England. I suppose if she knew how to spell, I wouldn't be sitting here."

Lena laughed, too. "Who would have thought any of us would be here, in this little village in England?" she mused.

"Thank goodness you've now joined us," Otto said, taking her hand and raising it to his lips. As if on cue, Lotti and Peter jumped up from the table, clearing plates.

"We're going for a walk," Lotti announced, pulling Emil out of his seat. "Come on." She glared at Tomas.

"What?"

"Lena needs to get settled in." And with a bundling of scarves and jackets, they were out the door, leaving Lena and Otto alone in the cottage. Lena laughed, felt herself blushing. Otto led her up the creaky staircase to the front bedroom and pulled her onto the bed.

CHAPTER 13

SUSSEX, APRIL 1940

After Lena's arrival in the household, the sleeping arrangements called for some flexibility. The two couples took turns using the front bedroom, alternating with sleeping in the living room, with a camp stretcher shoved next to the sofa, reinforced by suitcases placed underneath to support the extra weight. They shared the cold tap in the kitchen as the only place to attend to basic hygiene. In spite of the cramped conditions and her uncertainty about the future, in spite of her ever-present worry about her family, Lena felt happier than she had in a long time. In her reflection in the mirror, she saw the color returning to her cheeks. She loved waking up with Otto next to her. She nestled into the cocoon of his embrace and the close-knit companionship of the group. She grew fond of Masaryk the cat; he often chose her lap. It was a sheltered bubble, bound to rupture sooner or later, but Lena was powerless over the timetable and just about everything else, so she was determined to enjoy it while it lasted.

The savage winter had yielded to a glorious spring. Hundreds of tiny leaf buds decked the trees around the churchyard and the square; daffodils, crocuses, primroses, and tulips gleamed in front gardens. The surrounding woods were alive with fresh new growth. It was green, green, green.

The back garden at Oak Tree Cottage was transformed. When Lena arrived, it was merely a cold void to dash through on the way to the coal shed or the outhouse; now it became much-needed extra living space. Peter and Emil raked away dead leaves and cut back overgrown brambles to create a sheltered den that trapped the sun. A wobbly table was procured from Muriel, and a few wooden crates served as seats.

There was still the blackout to contend with, and rationing for a few items, like butter, bacon, sugar, and now meat, but otherwise it was hard to believe this was wartime. The early introduction of "summer time" meant long hours of evening daylight before the blackout screens had to be applied. There were complaints in the village about the dark mornings, but the inhabitants of Oak Tree Cottage were rarely awake early enough to notice. They stayed up late reading, talking, listening to music on the gramophone, or playing charades. Peter, of course, was a natural master of miming, but Tomas, too, had a surprising talent: his impersonation of Neville Chamberlain made Lena laugh until her stomach ached.

Otto spent the days writing, churning out pages at a furious rate and with an apparent renewed sense of purpose. Lena sat and watched him hunched over the typewriter, chewing on his lower lip as he concentrated on his work. It was new, this chewing habit, but she found it endearing. She was trying to focus on the hem of a fine silk dress: sewing work that Lotti had taken on to supplement the group's meager income. Lena was no seamstress but felt obliged to contribute. She had applied for her allowance from the Czech Refugee Trust Fund, but it had not come through yet.

Lotti did most of the cooking, putting together delicious soups and stews on the little primus stove.

"Did you learn to cook at home?" Lena asked.

"My mother showed me some things. We could afford only a part-time cook, so she did most of it herself. What about you?"

"My mother never did anything," Lena said. "We always had a cook. Did your mother keep a kosher kitchen?"

"She went to the kosher butcher, of course, but beyond that, no," replied Lotti. "She always thought the two-sets-of-everything idea was ridiculous. Can you imagine trying to do that in this kitchen?" She laughed.

As beautiful as the spring was, it brought with it the potential end of the stalemate in the war. Otto believed that Hitler had been just biding his time, waiting for better weather, before he launched a new offensive in the West.

"It will be ferocious," Otto said.

"But the Germans have lost their earlier advantage," Tomas said. "The French and British have been building up their defenses."

"*The Times* says the blockade of Germany is beginning to bite," Lotti said. "Hitler will soon be forced into a truce."

Otto said nothing more, chewing on his lip. In bed late at night, after he made love to her, Lena asked, "What's going to happen, Otto? Are we going to be all right? Will France withstand an onslaught? Will the people in Paris be safe?"

"I don't know, *mein Schätzchen*; I don't know," he said, as she lay in the crook of his arm. It was dark as ebony in the room, the blackout screens preventing even a chink of moonlight from illuminating his face. She didn't ask those questions during the daylight hours, when she would have had to look into his eyes.

In the evenings, they often wandered down to The Hollow. They were always made to feel welcome; they took baths, sampled cowslip wine and local beers, listened to the large collection of classical music, or heard Muriel sing and play the piano. She had a repertoire of traditional Sussex folk songs and a beautiful voice, strong and resonant. And she was pursuing plans for the production of *A Midsummer Night's Dream*. The whole village was expected to participate. She persuaded Tomas and Lotti to create a forest backdrop from a combination of dried leaves and twigs, scraps of green and brown velvet, and a papier-mâché cliff face.

Milton spent more time in the village, having resigned from Oxford at the end of the Hilary Term. He saw no point, he declared, in reading history in an ivory tower when momentous events were unfolding before his eyes.

"I'll probably be called up to start making history myself any day now," he said.

Muriel engaged him in gentle banter about his changing views;

two terms at Oxford had apparently caused him to abandon his pacifist, anti-imperialist stance that he would have nothing to do with this war.

"It's the war that's changed, Maman," he said. "We have to defeat fascism."

His relaxed way of talking with his mother fascinated Lena. When alone, they spoke French, a practice they continued if Lena was the only other person present. She found it hard to imagine such intimacy with a parent and viewed their relationship with a mixture of curiosity and envy. Milton was almost twenty, but he seemed immature. He'd apparently led a sheltered childhood, educated by French and German governesses, before attending an exclusive private day school nearby. His brief foray to Oxford had been his first time away from home.

He loved to spend time with the Oak Tree Cottage refugees, and they enjoyed his company. One day, he proposed an excursion to Brighton on the South Coast. They took the train from the station down the hill in Bigglesmeade, and then changed for the main line at Lewes. After weeks in the country, Lena loved sampling the joys of urban living. They wandered through Kemptown and the Lanes, past charming shops, tearooms, and pubs, and then for miles along the promenade, past the piers, heading west toward Hove. The sun was shining, but a bracing sea breeze coated everything with a taste of salt. Lena was enthralled; she had been to the sea only once before, on that holiday to Constanta with her family.

But where was the soft golden sand she recalled from the Black Sea, the sand that you could squiggle your toes into, run on barefoot? What was that in its place, stretching ahead in an endless line of gray?

"It's a pebble beach." Milton let out an easy, gentle laugh. "Shingle, stones," he explained.

"You don't have sand on the beaches in England?"

"Yes, in some places. Farther west, at Chichester. And in Devon and Cornwall. But here we have pebbles."

They climbed down a set of stone steps. The pebbles felt hard and painful underfoot, but up close, their gray was far from monolithic. There was pale gray, dark gray, blue-gray, green-gray, mingled with some tan and white and yellow; some of the stones were striped, some speckled black and white, all jumbled in a random assortment.

At the water's edge, the surf tumbled in rhythmic motion, to and fro. Each retreat of the waves drew a mass of pebbles away from the shore, then back with a thundering roar. The group stood shoulder to shoulder, mesmerized by the power of the sea. Lena tried to focus on the course of one particular pebble, light gray with distinctive black spots, as it was churned back and forth, but she lost sight of it in the undertow.

On an impulse, they went to the Odeon in Kemptown to see *Gone with the Wind* and emerged late into the moonless night, missing the last train out of Lewes. They had to walk back to Upper Wolmingham along dark lanes meandering through sleeping villages.

When they woke late the next day, it was to the news that Hitler had made his move. The Germans had invaded Denmark and Norway. It had taken them just as long to walk home from Lewes as it took the Wehrmacht to conquer Denmark.

CHAPTER 14

SUSSEX, MAY 1940

For months, the map of Europe tacked to the wall above the sofa had been largely ignored. The colors were faded, the top edge sagged in the center, and the lower right corner flapped in the breeze every time the front door opened. It was like the ugly wallpaper Otto remembered from his grandfather's house in Bavaria: after a while, you didn't notice it, even though you walked past it several times a day.

But now, the map became the center of attention.

At the clink of the letterbox announcing the arrival of *The Times*, Otto jumped up, wanting to be the first to scan the headlines. "What did I tell you?" he said.

He knew he shouldn't sound so smug. But really—so much for all that nonsense about a quick truce, or the blockade forcing Hitler to his knees.

"Let me see." Tomas grabbed the newspaper and walked over to the map. Armed with a fresh supply of gray pins from the village shop, he had assumed responsibility for meticulously documenting the advance of the Wehrmacht.

"What's the latest?" Emil asked, coming down the stairs.

"Doesn't look good. A German division has broken through, deeper into France. I'm trying to find St. Quentin." Tomas peered through his thick glasses, scouring the northeastern corner of France, a pin poised in his right hand.

"How can this be happening so quickly?" Emil said. "It's unbelievable. Norway, Belgium, Holland overrun. Now the French border breached."

"There it is." Tomas inserted the pin and wrote the date in black ink.

"They'll be in Paris in no time," Otto said.

"My God, Otto," Lena said. "There's no need to sound so gleeful. What about all those friends of ours in Paris? They must be terrified."

"They should have escaped while they could."

"I can't believe you're saying that. You know how hard it was for me to get a visa."

"Let's not write off the French defenses just like that," Lotti said.

"And the British Expeditionary Force has made a big push across the River Dyle," Lena said. "They're sending a full armored division into Belgium."

Otto shook his head. He couldn't believe how inept the English military appeared to be. How had they ever built an empire on which the sun never set? He looked again at Tomas's map. It was hard to shake off the image of a rising tide and an ever-shrinking piece of dry land, on which they were stranded.

But he saw no point in succumbing to panic. "If you'll excuse me," he said, returning to his typewriter, "I really have to get back to work."

He wanted to focus on his writing. Events were running away from him; this new war was escalating, and he'd not yet completed his analysis of the last war—the war in Spain. He was getting bogged down trying to analyze the conflicts between the revolutionary factions in Madrid.

"What are we going to do if the Germans cross the Channel?" Lena said, her voice rising. "Can we hide out in this village?"

"I don't want to run anymore," Emil said. "I want to stay and fight. I'm going to sign up for that new Local Defense Volunteers force."

Otto could not restrain himself. "That's just for the English," he said. "They're not going to let us join."

"We've got to do something," Peter said. "I can't stand listening to the news, feeling useless, just waiting for the Nazis to arrive."

Peter went to London to see if the Czech Council had any update on a Czech regiment forming in England. He had not returned by late afternoon. The others went to The Hollow for the evening: Churchill was giving a big speech, and Muriel said they should listen together. And see Milton before he left for army training camp; he was being drafted into the anti-aircraft artillery.

They found Muriel and Alistair on the back terrace, drinking cocktails; Milton was said to be upstairs packing. The new Prime Minister's speech was not due for another hour, so they relaxed in the evening warmth, enjoying the view of the South Downs. Lena identified Venus, twinkling in the western sky. Alistair brought out the gramophone. The melodic notes of the *Pastoral Symphony* filled the air.

"Oh, lovely," said Lena. "I love this piece, especially the last movement."

"I suppose it's still all right to play Beethoven!" Alistair chuckled, handing her a very large glass of sherry. "I hope no one will accuse me of treason."

"So, what's Churchill going to say?" Otto asked.

"Stirring words for the masses, I suppose," Alistair replied. "Stiff upper lip, all that sort of thing."

"I can't believe we're hanging on that man's every word." Muriel sneered. "Has everyone forgotten how reactionary he is?"

"I don't know much about him," Lena said.

"He threatened to shoot the miners who went on strike in twenty-six. He said, 'Send those rats back down their holes.'"

"We're a lot better off with him than with that idiot Chamberlain," Alistair said. "If they'd listened to Churchill five years ago, we wouldn't be in the frightful pickle we're in now."

"This whole thing is simply beastly," Muriel said. "I just cannot believe we're going through this again. Milton's leaving in a couple of days, you know. I'm thankful that he's not being posted abroad, but I absolutely hate it. We lost so many last time. Three-quarters of the men I danced with at my coming-out ball were killed in the trenches. And that was supposed to be the war to end all wars."

"But that war was completely different," Milton said, jumping into the conversation as soon as he joined them. "That was an imperialist squabble between the great powers. This war is about the struggle against fascism."

"I envy you, Milton," Emil said. "I wish I could join the fight."

"You see, it's not so different from 1914. Somehow, they always get the young men excited to become cannon fodder," Muriel said.

"I do think things are different this time around," Alistair said. "On that, Milton and I are in agreement, for once. We can't just lie down and let Hitler walk all over us. You know what is really upsetting Muriel, don't you?" he continued, winking at Lena. "She's finally realized that she's not going to be able to do the play this year. We were supposed to begin rehearsals for *A Midsummer Night's Dream* next week, but Puck and Lysander are in France, and all the fairies are in a panic about a pending invasion and quite incapable of learning their lines. I've finally persuaded her to abandon the idea."

Milton passed around cheese and crackers and the last of a jar of olives Muriel had brought back from France before the war. Alistair refilled everyone's glasses, and Lena began to feel tipsy.

"These olives are a treat." She bit into the firm, salty flesh. "*Měl bys to zkusit,*" she said, turning to Emil. "You ought to try one."

He puckered his lips and shook his head. "*Ne, díky.*"

Lena laughed, basking in the mingling of languages as the conversation glided from English to German to Czech and back to English again. It moved like a symphony, the wind instruments coming in there, the violins here: intelligent discourse among friends. She wanted to cling to this moment. Men were being sent off to the front, the Nazis were within shouting distance, and she still had no word from Máma, but she was here with Otto and a group of like-minded souls in this green and pleasant land, and she felt oddly happy.

Churchill came on the radio and promised nothing but blood, toil, tears, and sweat. Lena, however, felt the promise of something else: a home away from home in this newly adopted country; a new family to stand in for hers, which was scattered and fragmented; a sanctuary in these scary times.

CHAPTER 15

SUSSEX, MAY–JUNE 1940

Peter returned late at night, when the residents of Upper Wolmingham were sequestered behind their blackout curtains. At Oak Tree Cottage, everyone was awake, waiting. Lena and Otto sat on the sofa, reading. Lotti was darning, Emil and Tomas played chess. They were all occupied yet also keeping one ear open for Peter's return. They were like eager parents waiting to hear every detail of the first day of kindergarten.

But when the door eventually swung open, Peter looked pale and exhausted, his face drained. He sank onto the sofa and closed his eyes.

"What happened?" Lotti said. "Peter, what's the matter?"

"It's getting nasty out there," he replied after a moment or two. "Look at this."

He drew from his pocket a rolled-up copy of the *Daily Mail*. He spread it open and smoothed out the wrinkles. The headline screamed, INTERN THE LOT.

"What does this mean?" Lena said.

"*Internieren, gefangen nehmen.* Intern, imprison."

"What?"

"All enemy aliens. In case they're acting as spies for the invaders, ready to welcome parachute troops with open arms. Everyone's in a panic about a so-called 'fifth column.' As soon as they hear your accent, they think you might be German. A respectable elderly woman screamed at me on the train. I had to move to another carriage."

"That's ridiculous!" Lotti said. "Why would we want to—"

"This doesn't apply to us," Tomas said, trying to read the entire article. "It's just enemy aliens. Germans and Austrians."

"But Otto . . ." Peter said.

"That's absurd. He's been wanted by the Gestapo for years."

"I'm afraid that's a subtlety that's likely to be lost on the *Daily Mail* and its readers," Peter said.

Everyone in the village seemed on edge. In the shop, two women walked out as soon as Lena entered, as if afraid of contamination. The shopkeeper remained cordial while collecting the ration coupons, but it was hard to ignore the anti-alien crusade conducted by the tabloids displayed on the shelf behind her.

"It's hard to believe," Lena said when she returned. "They used to be so friendly."

On Saturday evening, Emil and Tomas set off for the Fox and Hounds for a pint of beer but returned five minutes later.

"The barman refused to serve us."

Mrs. Thompson next door went out of her way to assure them that she was not swept along by this wave of public opinion. She had a bumper crop of rhubarb. Every day she knocked on the door with another bundle.

"I said to Mr. Thompson last night, I said, 'No, this ain't right.' He said I should be careful about coming over here, but I told him, 'This don't apply to *my* foreigners, it don't.'"

"Thank you very much," Lena said, accepting the stringy pink stalks. She wasn't sure what to do with them. You had to stew them for hours and add lots of sugar to make them palatable—and they'd already used all their sugar rations.

"No, I said to Mr. Thompson, I said, 'They had to run away from Hitler, they did. Don't make no sense for them to turn round and help him, now, do it?' I said, 'Stands to reason that none of you's going to let Hitler walk in the door.'"

Lena welcomed Mrs. Thompson's kindness, although she guiltily discarded the rhubarb over the back fence.

The news from France continued to flood in, terrifying. Tomas traced the Maginot Line onto the map from a diagram in *The Times*, but it turned out to be more like a sieve than a barricade; Panzer divisions poured deep into the heart of the country. Lena, Peter, and Lotti took the bus to Haywards Heath to see the same ridiculous Charlie Chan picture three times, just to be able to see the newsreel shown with it. There was something compelling about seeing the images on the screen, always the irrational hope that perhaps the news would be better there than in the newspaper. Instead, there was the announcer's astounding ability to make the frantic evacuation of Dunkirk by the British sound like a great military victory. Yes, it was moving to see the flotilla of small fishing vessels coming to the aid of the British navy, to pluck over three hundred thousand soldiers out from Rommel's reach within three days.

"But it's a full-scale retreat, for heaven's sake," Peter said. "They've left behind all their tanks and artillery and guns."

Now there was nothing between England and the Wehrmacht except a thin blue line of sea.

The following week: more terrifying images, another exodus. The roads south from Paris jammed with cars, bicycles, carts, trucks, and horse-drawn traps, piled high with suitcases, furniture, mattresses, pets. Tired, anxious faces jostled in the crowds. Lena's eyes flickered over the screen, searching the throng absurdly, desperately, for Eva or Marguerite.

Constable Bilson pushed down harder on the pedals and bent over the handlebars to try to get more leverage. His heart pounded in his chest. The hill up to Upper Wolmingham seemed steeper than ever in this heat. He should have waited for the cooler part of the day, or, better yet, put this whole thing off until tomorrow morning.

But the chief inspector from Lewes had insisted: he needed a report today. Something about the bigwigs from London, they'd been onto him. Wasn't right, in Fred Bilson's opinion. They should come and do their own dirty work. This was way over his head. Constable Bilson was patriotic enough and wanted to do his bit to help, of course he did. But they shouldn't be asking him to do this.

"Just go and look them over," the chief inspector had said. "See if you can find anything suspicious. Check their papers, that sort of thing."

It wasn't that simple. These weren't just any aliens. They belonged to Mrs. Muriel Calder, and Constable Bilson wasn't about to pick a quarrel with her. She had her peculiar ways, mind, there was no getting away from that. There were those who didn't approve of her at all, what with her getting divorced and all her peculiar visitors—strange London types. And, well, yes, a fair share of foreigners. You never knew who was coming and going, especially now she was down at The Hollow. But she was the Lady of the Manor, and she had always been good to the villagers. It was Mrs. Calder who had built the nurses' cottage opposite the school, paid for everything, she did; all the Bilson children received their inoculations there, free of charge. You couldn't argue with that. No, Constable Bilson didn't want to get into any sort of bother with Mrs. Calder.

He made it to the top of the hill and turned to the right, relaxing into the gentle glide down the village street, feeling his heartbeat return to normal. There was Oak Tree Cottage, a few hundred yards ahead. As he was passing the village shop, however, a booming greeting startled him and almost caused him to teeter out of control.

"Constable Bilson! Just the chap I want to see!" Colonel Knowles from Romley Place emerged from the shop. He strode right into the path of the policeman's bicycle. His portly frame was encased in a tight white suit that had obviously fitted him better when it was purchased; the jacket's single button strained to cover his protruding belly.

"I say, Constable, what are you fellows doing about those aliens living right here in our midst?"

"Aliens, Colonel?"

"Don't be evasive with me, Constable. You know who I'm talking about: those damn Bolsheviks staying somewhere in this village, in one of the Calder woman's cottages. I don't know which of these wretched hovels it is, but I know you do."

"We're following all the correct procedures, sir. I can assure you of that."

"Procedures, my foot! Intern the lot, that's what they're saying, and I couldn't agree more. Can't be too careful about this sort of thing, you know. We're on our own now, Constable. We're better off this way, if you ask me. No more damn Allies to pamper. But we have to weed out the fifth column, Constable, or they'll be shooting us in the back when the Germans attack. Haven't you received instructions to round them up?"

Bilson wanted to end this unpleasant conversation as quickly as possible.

"As a matter of fact, sir, I'm on my way there right now," he said. "The chief inspector has asked for a report this afternoon, so if you will excuse me . . ."

"Chief Inspector Montgomery? Over at Lewes? Oh, splendid, splendid. I'll give him a ring on the telephone. Good day, Constable."

Bilson now had a sour taste in his mouth and a heavy weight sitting somewhere between his shoulder blades. He approached Oak Tree Cottage and dismounted, propping his bicycle against the hedge next to the dilapidated wooden gate. In three short steps he reached the front door and knocked loudly, boldly. *Just get this over with*, he thought. *Check their papers and get out of here, tell Montgomery everything is in order. Then finish the paperwork down at the station and call it a day.*

The door was opened by a young woman, not beautiful but quite pretty, with bright blue eyes and a fresh complexion. He was taken aback. Of course, there were girls here, too, but he had somehow forgotten that, imagined he would be dealing with just the men.

"Afternoon, miss." He gave a little bow. "Constable Bilson from the Bigglesmeade Police Station. I need to check all your passports and immigration papers, if you don't mind. Shouldn't take long. May I come in?"

She opened the door wider, and he crossed the threshold, delving into his uniform pocket to retrieve his notebook. "You must be . . ."

"Lena Kulkova."

"Ah, yes. Right you are. All your friends here today, are they?"

"Yes, we are in the garden. A moment, please."

She had a soft, lilting accent. She walked through the tiny house to the kitchen and the back door beyond. Constable Bilson looked around the living room. On the table by the window were a typewriter and a pile of books. He picked up one from the top of the pile. *Hmm* . . . It was in foreign. No telling what it was about, but it stood to reason they would have foreign books. Couldn't be too much harm in that.

He turned as he heard voices from the garden.

And that was when he saw it. Tacked up on the wall above the sofa, in broad daylight, was a large map of Europe, with pins and black lines and arrows drawn all over it, numbers and dates, the sevens with that funny line through the stem, and other strange names he could not decipher. Code words, no doubt. A stone-cold chill ran right through him.

CHAPTER 16

SUSSEX, JUNE 1940

Lena was sleeping when the first pounding on the door vibrated through the house—asleep finally after a fretful night, enveloped in a vivid dream. She was walking with Sasha through a park, warm and green, crowded with throngs of people, being pushed forward, carried along with the swell, holding on tight to Sasha's hand, fearful of losing her. Suddenly, there was a loud bang behind her. Lena looked around—and felt Sasha's hand slip from hers. She sat up with a cry. Lotti stood at the bedroom door, a sheet wrapped around her, a bundle of clothes tucked under one arm.

"Lena, Otto, get up! There're policemen downstairs, lots of them."

Otto was already up, standing by the window, peering down at the street below. He was deathly pale.

"You have to come down, both of you," Lotti continued. "They want to see everyone's papers. Can I get dressed in here?"

Lena threw on some clothes and followed Lotti downstairs. The living room was overtaken with large brown suits and trilby hats filling the tiny space.

"But the village policeman, he came two days ago and he looked at everything," Peter was saying. "Did he not tell you this?"

"Oh, he told us, all right. Come on—we need everyone down here right now, with all the passports."

Peter dismantled the camp bed and shoved the bedding behind the sofa in an attempt to clear some space. Even so, the room remained very crowded with the six residents, in varying degrees of dishevelment, and the four neatly groomed plainclothes police officers. They tried not to bump into each other as the officers scanned papers, scrutinized faces, searched through books, upended sofa cushions. Otto's typewriter was turned upside down, the keys individually inspected, the pad of blotting paper from the desk lifted up to the light. The tallest officer, who had an aquiline nose and the air of being in charge, pointed at some obscure black splotches on the paper and mumbled to one of his colleagues. Another started rummaging through the shelves in the kitchen.

What were they looking for? Lena was desperate to visit the lavatory. When it was clear that the visitors were not going to leave anytime soon, she had to excuse herself and explain her need to use the outhouse. One of the policemen insisted on following her and stood guard outside while she relieved herself. When she emerged, Lena saw that she had forgotten to bring in the laundry the night before. After the argument, it had completely slipped her mind. Two short-sleeved shirts of Otto's, her pale blue cotton dress, a couple of towels, and assorted undergarments remained pinned on the line, damp now from the morning dew.

"Wide yee no fairtch in yer togs last nite, den?"

This appeared to be a question directed at her. The policeman's tone was firm but not unkind, and as she looked into his face for the first time, she saw that he was younger than the other officers, in his midtwenties, she guessed, with chubby cheeks and prominent ears. Lena could not understand a single word. Was he speaking English?

"I beg your pardon?"

"Yer tings 'ere." He gestured toward the laundry. The words came out a bit more slowly, but they sounded so different from the English spoken by either Muriel and her friends or the village people. "Did yee leef them oop as soom kinda signell, den?"

Lena was baffled. She glanced up at the sky and saw that it was going to be another sunny day. "I think they will dry soon," she said, hoping that was an appropriate response.

Back in the cottage, the officers stood around the table in the living room, looking at the map they had removed from the wall. They were pointing at the annotations scribbled over the Ardennes.

"Of course not!" Peter yelled. "This was all from the BBC. See, the wireless there? The BBC. Or *The Times*." He pointed a shaking finger at the radio in the corner and picked up yesterday's paper, which had slid to the floor and which he now waved in anger, dangerously close to that long, pointed nose on the chief officer.

"Shh, Peter," Lotti said at his elbow, speaking softly in Czech. "*Mluvte tiše*. It's not going to do any good to get angry with them."

"Speak English, please." The chief officer pointed to the map again. "Whose writing is this?"

Everyone looked around for Tomas, but he had just stepped out. Lena had started a trend to obey the call of nature, keeping the young officer with the strange accent busy on escort duty.

"It's Tomas," said Peter. "He's outside now."

"He's the German, is he?" asked the officer in charge, shuffling through his collection of passports.

"German? No, he's Czech."

"So who's the German? Otto Essenberg—is that right?"

"I'm Otto Eisenberg." Otto was standing in the corner, as if trying to keep a low profile. He looked pale and gaunt, his hair disheveled, a black lock sticking up above his right ear, lending an almost comical air to his appearance. He was still in his pajamas; they hung loosely on his thin shoulders, the faded gray-and-white-striped fabric fraying at the cuffs. He stole a glance at Lena. The memory of the previous night lingered between them, as bitter as the taste of the rhubarb.

"Mr. Iceberg, are you aware of the new regulations regarding enemy aliens? You are not permitted to own a bicycle, a radio, or a map."

"He doesn't," Peter said. "The radio is mine, and the map—"

"But I was given clearance," Otto said, speaking at the same time, "when I arrived. You can see it in the papers there, with my passport."

"I'm afraid all that is irrelevant now, sir. We can no longer afford to take risks in the protected areas."

"Protected areas?" Otto said.

"The risk of invasion, Mr. Iceberger. We cannot allow any alien elements to be in a position to give support to the enemy."

"But that's ridiculous!" Peter cried.

"There must be some mistake," Lena heard herself say, surprised at her boldness. "Otto is a prominent anti-Nazi. He was—"

"We want to fight the Nazis more than anyone," Emil said.

The police inspector held up his hand as if he were stopping traffic. "Enough!" he bellowed. "I have not come to hear a three-ring circus. I am addressing Mr. Iceberger here, and I will thank the rest of you to remain silent. Mr. Iceberger—"

"Eisenberg," Otto corrected him.

"Yes, well, Mr. Eisenberg, it's my duty to inform you that you are being taken into custody. You may pack one small suitcase. Be ready to depart in five minutes."

Lena followed Otto upstairs, hoping for a few minutes alone. But one of the policemen clambered up the creaky stairs behind her and stood watching from the doorway. Otto pulled his suitcase out from under the bed and began throwing in clothes, without folding them and without making eye contact.

"Otto," she pleaded, "I'm sorry about last night."

"Not now, Lena," he replied. He turned his back to get dressed, then continued packing in silence. When he was finished, the policeman led Otto away, closed the door, and motioned to Lena for her to stay behind. She sank onto the bed. The sheets lay in a crumpled mess, a soft indentation marking the spot where Otto had been lying only an hour before. She stared at it without stirring until she heard the front door open. From the small window, she saw Otto climbing into the backseat of the car, flanked by the officers. For the first time, she became aware of a crowd gathered in the street below. Otto did not look up.

The previous night, after supper, the others had all gone for an evening stroll, but Lena had stayed behind with Otto, welcoming some time alone.

She heated water for washing while he cleared the dishes outside. She watched him from the kitchen window as he stood in the last strand of sunlight, his forearms bronzed from his hours spent writing outside. She remembered when she'd first heard him speak, at the Café Slavia. She knew he must miss all that: the frenetic activity, the meetings, the cheers, the standing ovations.

Lena smiled as he circled the table outside, ducking to clear the clothes that still hung on the line. He brought such an intense concentration to anything he did, even such a mundane domestic task as this, chewing slightly at one corner of his lip. He gathered up the assortment of chipped plates, bowls, and tea-stained mugs into a precarious pile that wobbled as he approached the back door.

"Careful with that," Lena said, going to meet him. "Here, let me take something."

"I've got it," he said, adding his chin to the equation at the top of the pile for extra stability.

"We can't afford to replace any dishes," she said, meaning to sound lighthearted.

"I'm not going to break anything. And I'm quite aware of the state of our finances. All those visits to the cinema, the bus fares . . . There's hardly enough to feed us until the end of the week."

"We'll manage somehow. Lotti's been sewing all day; that'll bring in a few shillings." Lena poured the warm water into the sink. "We had to go see those newsreels."

"I don't see why. Just read *The Times*. It's all there."

"I had to see those scenes for myself. Paris, the fall of France . . . It's unbelievable. I can't imagine where Eva is. Or Marguerite."

"The Gestapo is probably busy rounding them all up."

"My God, Otto!" Lena gripped the rough rim of the sink. "Why do you always have to assume the worst?"

"Because terrible things are happening."

"But we can't just give up hope. I can't go through this thinking the worst will happen to all those we've left behind. I have to hope things will turn out all right in the end." She lowered the plates into the water. "We have to have faith."

"What? Are you getting religious all of a sudden?" Otto sneered. He stood leaning against the back door, arms across his chest.

"I'm not talking about praying—just keeping hope alive, keeping positive," Lena said. "We have to." The sun slipped behind the hedge, and it became quite dark in the kitchen. "You always used to say that we must fight until the end, never give up. Doesn't that mean believing that we will survive?"

Otto didn't answer. Lena finished the dishes in silence, ruminating on the conversation. She could not let it go; it was a sore she couldn't help poking, an itch that had to be scratched. She picked up a towel to dry her hands and followed him to his desk by the window.

"What about here, Otto?" she said. His attention was already focused on his typewriter, but she continued. "Don't you think things are looking better here, with the new government and everything? And all the precautions the British are taking against invasion, the road blockades and removing all the road signs? Isn't that a good thing? Compared with that panic in France?"

"I hardly think the Panzer tanks are going to be stymied by a few bits of barbed wire," Otto replied, without looking up. "And who's to say the British won't panic, too, when the time comes?"

"My God, Otto, what's happening to you?" Her voice trembled. "You've changed so much. I feel as though I hardly know you. It's hard to be with you when you're like this."

"You don't have to stay if you're not happy here," he said, turning to her, his eyes cold and hard. "No one's holding you prisoner against your will."

"I thought you wanted me here." She reflexively took a step backward. "Why did you go to so much trouble to get me out of Paris?"

"I felt responsible for you. I brought you to Paris, and I felt I should get you out."

Lena rubbed her hands in the towel, although they were bone dry already. "I thought you wanted me here," she repeated. "I thought you loved me."

But immediately she knew she should not have uttered those words. She wished she could pull them back.

"This is not the right time to be swayed by emotions, Lena," Otto said, rolling a fresh sheet of paper into the typewriter. "We need to be clear, calm, and objective."

Lena retreated upstairs and lay on the bed, trying to read.

Muriel had given her a copy of *Jane Eyre*, but she couldn't concentrate. The letters swam before her on the page in a jumbled maze; she read the same sentence over and over, like a needle stuck on a gramophone record. She heard the others return, the sound of laughter, the pop of a cork being pulled from a bottle, the clink of glasses. They must have procured some cowslip wine from The Hollow.

Why didn't she go back downstairs? Perhaps Otto would soften toward her, would be more cheerful with the others around. Instead, she wallowed in loneliness. She had thought she would find some shelter here in England. And, she told herself, it had been comforting to be with Otto, to lie in his arms again, like finding refuge after a storm. Only the day before yesterday, they'd walked down to The Hollow and climbed into the big bathtub together. He had taken the uncomfortable end, where the water taps were, and she'd leaned back in the warm suds, stroking the dark hairs on his chest with her wrinkled feet. He'd kissed her toes, making her giggly with tickles.

How had things gone so wrong? Why was this knot of anger and hurt twisting together in her gut, pulling her down as if into a bottomless pit? How was she going to stay in this cottage when Otto was being so cold to her? But where else could she go? She knew no one else in England.

She switched off the light and lay listening to the rumble of voices downstairs. When Otto crept into bed hours later, she pretended to be asleep. He did not reach out to touch her.

CHAPTER 17

SUSSEX, JUNE 1940

Lotti entered the bedroom and gave Lena a long hug. "Come down," she said, taking Lena by the hand. "We have to work out what to do next. They didn't even tell us where they were taking him. Did they say anything to you?"

Lena shook her head. "No, not a word." She hadn't thought to ask. They joined the others in the living room.

"It's outrageous. They can't possibly get away with this," Peter said. "Come on. We have to go to Muriel's, let her know, have her start working on his release."

Lotti looked at her watch. "It's very early still."

"Lena," Tomas said, "I'm so sorry about the map. It never occurred to me . . ." "It's not your fault," Lena said. She looked around the room. "Where *is* the map?"

"They took it with them."

She shook her head. "That's so stupid. I mean, they can't possibly think . . ."

"If it hadn't been the map, they would have found something else," Peter said. "They were trying to make a fuss about the washing

on the line outside. Said something ridiculous about it being a sig-
nal for German parachutists."

"That's absurd," Lena said. "The policeman was pointing to it,
but I couldn't make any sense out of what he was saying."

"There isn't any sense in it," Peter said.

"Otto's been here longer than any of us," Emil said. "He escaped
from Germany to get away from this sort of thing. Don't they understand that?" He paced up and down the living room, clenching his
fists and gritting his teeth. "They won't let us join the fight against
fascism. They arrest someone like Otto, who has the best anti-Nazi
credentials of anyone. What are they thinking?" he shouted.

"Emil, calm down," Lotti said.

"I'm not going to calm down until there's something to be
calm about. Did you see that damn village policeman standing out
there, looking so pleased with himself?"

"I thought he looked rather embarrassed, actually," Tomas said.

"Come on—he was the one who started all this." Emil towered
over Tomas, blocking his access to the kitchen. "I feel like going to
his pathetic little police station and hurling rocks through the window. That will give him something to talk about."

"What good will that do, exactly?" Tomas said. He pushed his
spectacles up the bridge of his nose. "Then you'll get arrested, too."

"I didn't say I would get caught. I'll go—"

"That's so stupid."

"Stop it, you two," Lotti pleaded.

"Otto has been dragged off," Emil shouted. "He might as well
have stayed behind and waited for the Gestapo."

"Come on," Peter said. "Let's not blow things out of proportion. That was not the SS. They were not brutal. They didn't come in
the dead of night. And there has to be some sort of appeal process."

Lena tried to ignore the cacophony and gather her thoughts.
She had been so upset with Otto last night—and now this. He had
probably been in a bad mood, perhaps preoccupied because he'd
suspected he might get arrested. He had said nothing, probably
hadn't want to worry her. Now she had to do everything she could
to get him released.

"Wait," she said, turning to Peter now. "I'm trying to think—you know how you and Otto got me that special permit? That story about my being a Czech agent?"

"Yes," Peter said, grinning. "Your vital role in the discovery of the German buildup on the Czech border in '38."

"Otto had much more to do with that than I did," Lena said. "I was just the lowly office worker. Whatever you did for me ought to work for Otto."

"You're right," Peter said. He looked at her with a glow of admiration. "Perhaps we should pay another visit to the Czech Council in London."

"We should go tell Muriel what's happened," said Lotti.

Muriel's house was unlocked, as usual. Peter called out to announce their arrival, but no one responded. They wandered through the living room into the dining room and the kitchen beyond. The back door was wide open, the sun streaming in.

"Hello!" Lotti called, leading the way out to the terrace. "Anybody home?"

Lena heard footsteps inside. She ran back into the house and almost collided not with Muriel but with Milton at the foot of the stairs. He looked bleary-eyed and was dressed in a burgundy silk dressing gown drawn tight at the waist. He jumped back, startled, catching himself on the bottom step.

"Good Lord," he said. "What are you doing here?"

"What?" Lena was equally surprised; he was supposed to be at army training.

"I do beg your pardon; how frightfully rude of me. You must excuse me." He smoothed his hair into place. "I've just woken up. Nothing like sleeping in a decent bed after a month on a hard, narrow bunk. I simply couldn't rouse myself any earlier. I say, are you all right? You look a bit peaked, if you don't mind my saying so."

"I have to find Muriel. Something terrible has happened. Otto's been arrested."

"What in heaven?"

"It's the enemy-alien thing. We thought he was going to be all right . . ." Her thoughts were running too fast for her English to keep apace, so she broke into French. "*Mais enfin, le gendarme* from the village was snooping around a couple of days ago, and then this morning they came en masse and took him away."

"That's preposterous!"

"Milton!" Peter came in from the terrace with Lotti. "You're back so soon?"

"Yes, three days' leave before I'm sent off to a ridiculous anti-aircraft unit. It's so—well, more on that later. Lena has just told me about Otto. I can't believe it."

"I know," Peter said.

"Did they have a warrant? Did they read him his rights? Did they say where they were taking him? They can't just drag someone off like that in this country, you know."

"There were four of them, plainclothes officers," Peter said. "They certainly acted as though they could do whatever they wanted. It seemed Otto had no choice but to go along with them."

"Yes, I suppose it did," Milton replied. "Well, we just have to secure his release as soon as possible. Where's Mother?"

"We were hoping you would know that," Lena said.

"I vaguely remember now. I was still half asleep, but I think she knocked on my door and said something about going over to see Aunt Pippa. She and Alistair have probably walked over the fields to The Grange. I'll give her a ring."

He reached for the telephone on the table at the foot of the stairs and lifted the receiver. "Hello, Operator? Yes, good morning. Bigglesmeade thirty-three, please."

There appeared to be a protracted response at the other end of the line.

"I see. . . . Really? . . . When was that? . . . All right, then. Thank you." Milton returned the receiver to its cradle. "I'm afraid Mother has left; we've missed her. She's gone to see Lady Charlotte, for some reason. And she won't have reached Durfield Park yet."

"You learned all that from talking to the operator?" Lotti said.

"Oh, yes," Milton replied with a grin. "She's always a wealth of information."

There was nothing to do but wait. Milton suggested a pot of tea. He invited them into the kitchen and put the kettle on to boil.

"So, how's life in the army?" Peter said.

"The food is terrible; the conditions are awful," Milton replied. "But, of course, one expects all that. It wouldn't be so bad if one felt one were achieving anything useful. But so far the training has been a joke. There aren't enough rifles to go around, so they have us practicing with broomsticks! I'm being sent off to an anti-aircraft unit in Portsmouth next week. I've no idea if I'm going to be given any real ammunition."

"That's incredible," Peter said. "I thought they were going full steam ahead with war production."

"Yes, I know," Milton said, pulling a large teapot from the shelf above the sink. "They canceled the Whitsun holiday, and Bevin brought in the sixty-hour workweek and all that. But they've a lot of catching up to do, it seems. All those years of appeasement and refusing to see what was going on in Germany, and that idiot Chamberlain saying just a couple of months ago that Hitler's missed the bus. It appears the Tories did nothing to prepare even after the outbreak of war. From what I've seen of the army these past few weeks, we'd better hope there's no invasion anytime soon."

"Don't say that!" Lena said, too loudly. "This country is the last hope. I can't believe that Britain will cave without a fight."

"I certainly hope not," Milton said. "And I want to do my part. But I want to join a fight I can believe in. With real weapons. And not just that 'defend your country' balderdash—a progressive fight, a fight against fascism. We have to be fighting for a new kind of society."

Lotti rescued the teapot, which sat frozen in Milton's hands, and gathered together cups. "That's all very well," Lena said. "But that option is a luxury no longer possible in Prague or Paris."

The current issue of the *New Statesman* lay open on the table. "Did you see this?" Milton said, pointing to a full-page article. "Trotsky has written a new manifesto on the war. He claims there would be no difference between victory for the old colonial powers Britain and France and victory for the new imperialists Hitler and Mussolini." He picked up a pencil and started to doodle on the page, tracing loops around the *T* in *Trotsky* in the headline. "We have to fight for a workers' revolution," he continued. "Not for saving bourgeois democracy."

"Trotsky is safely hidden away in Mexico," Lena said, feeling her pulse quickening. "If he were in Prague right now, talking about workers' revolution, he would be locked up. We have friends and family there. Their lives may be in danger." Her voice became shaky.

Milton turned to her with a warm, sincere look. "I'm sorry, I . . ."

Taking some courage from his apology, she continued, "Defeating the Nazis has to be the most important thing right now."

"Of course. I didn't mean to imply . . ." Lena met his gaze, noticing for the first time the rich, deep brown of his eyes. There was an intensity there, and it took her by surprise. She felt the color rise to her cheeks.

Peter said, "We seem to be forgetting that Otto has been arrested here in this country."

Lena blushed even more, realizing she had momentarily lost sight of that.

"Precisely," Milton said. "Why should we fight for an establishment that does something like that?"

The sounds of energetic panting and footsteps on the terrace interrupted them. Lancelot bounded toward them, tail wagging, mouth drooling; Alistair was not far behind.

Milton told Alistair, "The Special Branch invaded Oak Tree Cottage and arrested Otto."

"What?"

"We've got to get Mother and Aunt Pippa working for his release," Milton said.

"I'm afraid your aunt Pippa is a bit distracted by a crisis of her own right now," Alistair said. "She's gone over to Lady Charlotte's to commiserate."

"What happened?"

"The whole household is in an uproar because another chambermaid left to work at the new aircraft factory in Eastbourne," Alistair said. "That leaves only the chauffeur, the cook, and one parlor maid. Dear Mrs. Courtney-Smithers is beside herself. Cook could never be prevailed upon to make the beds, yet it is a task that, apparently, one person alone cannot possibly accomplish. She's considering a complaint to Churchill himself."

"Oh, for heaven's sake," Lena said, and then suddenly stopped herself and looked from Alistair to Milton, blushing again. "Sorry, I didn't mean . . ."

"No, you're quite right." Milton laughed. "It's absurd."

CHAPTER 18

SUSSEX, JUNE 1940

M uriel spent hours on the telephone. She started with Constable Bilson. He was incoherent, stumbling over himself in apology, full of deferential references to everything she had ever done for him and his family, until finally he disclosed that it was Detective Chief Inspector Montgomery at Lewes who had ordered Otto's arrest. Montgomery himself was impossible to reach; he was in a meeting, he was at lunch, he was out in the field. His deputy, an Inspector Norris, quite understood Muriel's concern—yes, it was quite correct, ma'am, that the Home Office directive did allow for individual discretion in the handling of aliens, but no, ma'am, he really couldn't say what factors had been taken into consideration in this case, he was not at liberty to divulge, blah, blah. Muriel slammed down the receiver and groaned.

After lunch, Norris was also unavailable, but a Sergeant Wiggins, more readily intimidated by an upper-class accent, was persuaded to reveal that there had been complaints about the inhabitants of Oak Tree Cottage from some quarters, quite fancy people, they were, as he understood it, and that certain evidence had been seized at the property. The poor fellow was then treated to a barrage of righteous indignation and a treatise on Tory appeasement that was quite over his head. He retreated in search of higher authority, which brought an Inspector Westlake to the phone. He was with the uniformed branch.

"It's being handled by CID, ma'am," he informed Muriel. "They never tell us what's going on."

"Surely you must know where they have taken my tenant," Muriel replied. She tried another line of inquiry. "I simply need to find out where he is and what the visiting procedures are."

"It's all very hush-hush," he said, "due to the sensitive nature of the situation."

"I quite understand, Inspector," Muriel said. "I have my own reasons for needing to contact him, also of a somewhat delicate nature." She had no idea what he might think she meant by this, but she sensed it was having some effect, so she continued: "It involves a young lady. As I say, it's a delicate matter and has no bearing on the reason for his arrest. I would be most grateful if you could let me know where I might be able to locate him."

"This is quite irregular, ma'am."

"Of course. Discretion is paramount, Inspector. You can rest assured—"

"I believe he may have been taken to the Lingfield Racecourse, ma'am. As a temporary measure, you understand."

"Thank you, Inspector," Muriel said. It wasn't much, but it was a start.

Muriel took Otto's arrest as a personal affront. He had been the original refugee at Oak Tree Cottage, her first protégé. It took tremendous courage for a German to stand up and resist the Nazis. She felt a natural affinity for anyone willing to cast himself in the role of outsider. She felt like an outcast herself. Not that she would ever claim to have exposed herself to the same danger, but she knew something of being ostracized. As the only heir to one of the largest landowners in the county, she had inherited the Manor House and its constellation of cottages just after the Great War. But, to the consternation of the local gentry, she had not fulfilled the role of Lady of the Manor with the dignity they expected. To this day, Aunt Pippa was shocked that Muriel answered the door herself when visitors called, instead of having a servant admit them. And then there was the problem of her church attendance—or lack of it. The designated front-row pew at St. Augustine's was conspicuously empty every Sunday. To top it all, Muriel publicly supported dangerous causes, such as the striking miners of Wales or Mr. Gandhi in India, and entertained an eclectic collection of artists, writers, and actors from London. Altogether, she was considered an embarrassment and was excluded from most social events.

None of this bothered Muriel. She laughed it off and entertained her dinner guests with anecdotes of being snubbed by stuffy old Mrs. Rees-Jones or pompous Colonel Knowles. But now this sergeant at the Lewes police station had hinted that someone with influence had reported the group at Oak Tree Cottage as potentially dangerous, and Muriel was furious. They hadn't been able to touch the Czechs, of course—they were protected as refugees—but they had taken Otto. It was outrageous, a deliberate personal attack. She was determined to find out who was responsible and secure Otto's release. When Alistair returned, she would ask him if they had enough petrol to drive to Lingfield. Perhaps if they simply showed up at the racecourse, they could make some headway.

The phone rang, sending her back to the table in the hallway. "Muriel! Thank goodness!"

"Hello, Aunt Pippa."

"What on earth have you been doing? The telephone has been engaged for hours."

"I've been trying to find out where they've taken Otto and who has the authority to release him. I'm not getting very far with the Lewes police. I may need your help."

"My dear, *I* need *your* help."

"Someone reported him to the authorities. I have to find out who. Has Lady Charlotte said anything?" Muriel rubbed the knots of tension in the back of her neck.

"She's no help. She herself is worried she's going to lose her chauffeur."

"What? I mean about Otto."

"Listen, dear, Cook tells me the oldest Bilson girl is now of an age to go into service. Can you find out if she is prepared to start here as a chambermaid?"

Peter thought Muriel was getting nowhere and that they should try their luck at the Czech Council offices. He suggested Lena accompany him. She tingled with excitement as she boarded the train—but then immediately felt a pang of guilt. Otto was interned somewhere, and here she was, enjoying the prospect of a trip to London. She had been to the capital only once since her arrival in England, three months earlier. She'd applied to the Czech Trust Fund for the refugee allowance that the others received, but had been turned down: she'd left Prague too soon, before the occupation. She had not been back to London since. She thought it might be awkward to be alone with Peter, but he seemed completely at ease, so Lena decided to relax and enjoy herself.

There I go again, she thought, forgetting that her main purpose was to work on Otto's release. She tried to imagine what he was doing, how he was coping with his confinement. They had no definitive information about where he was. Muriel had been unable to confirm either that he was at the temporary internment camp at Lingfield or where he might be if he'd been moved. At least the police had allowed him to pack his typewriter. Was he able to do some writing? How was his mood? Was he despondent or philosophical? She had no barometer for his current state of mind. She felt more disconnected from him now than she had when they'd been separated by the English Channel.

She watched the green fields speeding by. It had been lonely sleeping without Otto on the sofa. It had been lonely sleeping next to him the night before too, but she pushed that thought out of her mind.

"I should write to Otto and send it to that place in Lingfield anyway," she blurted out to Peter, sitting across from her. "I should have thought of that earlier and asked Muriel for the address."

"Let's see how much progress we make today."

The train stopped at a small station. The door of the compartment opened, and a middle-aged couple entered. They took seats by the corridor, the man lifting two suitcases into the overhead luggage rack. The woman wore a freshly pressed summer frock and matching white shoes, handbag, and gloves. She nodded a friendly greeting to Lena and Peter.

"Good morning. Lovely day again, isn't it?"

Lena nodded and smiled. The man opened up the *Daily Mail*. The headline: HUNDREDS MORE INTERNED. Lena glanced at Peter. There could be no more conversation, certainly not in Czech or German, nor in heavily accented English. She pulled *Jane Eyre* out of her handbag.

CHAPTER 19

LONDON, JUNE 1940

Peter said it was a short walk from Victoria to the Czech Council offices. He had lived in London for five months when he'd first arrived in England, and he led the way with confidence up Grosvenor Gardens, toward a maze of smaller streets. At every turn, there was some new wonder. Tall white facades glistened in the bright morning sun. The famous red double-decker buses swerved round the street corners, as handsome young men—boys, really—hung off the center pole on the rear platform. Streets full of life, the picture of normality for any capital city, with people calmly going about their daily business. But there were shrill reminders that these were not normal times: piles of sandbags or barbed-wire barricades around buildings, workmen removing the railings surrounding the gardens at Eaton Square. They needed the metal, Peter said, for tanks.

They reached Wilton Crescent. From a terraced row of identical five-story buildings, Peter selected one and guided Lena through the unlocked door. There was no identifying placard at the entrance, as far as she could see, but on the second floor was a door with a small brass sign indicating, in Czech and English, Czech National Council.

Inside, it was surprisingly busy. Two desks opposite the entrance each sported a young woman with a typewriter, one talking on the phone in fluent English. An open door behind them revealed another office, where several middle-aged men spoke loudly in Czech. To the right were a row of chairs beneath a window and five or six people waiting patiently for attention. The window was half open, and a grimy lace curtain fluttered in the breeze, but this did little to dispel the pungent odor of too many hot summer bodies. Outside, Lena could see the gray brick backs of the buildings from the neighboring block, and below, in each garden, the rounded, grass-covered humps of the Anderson bomb shelters that she had read about in *The Times*. They looked much smaller than she'd imagined.

Peter did most of the talking. He sounded very convincing: a prominent German anti-Nazi who had performed vital espionage work for the Beneš government in '38 had now been interned by the British. Peter asked to speak to a Mr. Lisicky, who, he seemed to think, would have the most influence, but he was nowhere to be found, so Peter had to content himself with a series of more minor officials.

They listened politely but appeared preoccupied with more pressing concerns. From snippets of conversations from the back room, Lena gathered that negotiations with the British Foreign Office over the recognition of the Beneš government in exile were at a critical juncture. And they were very excited about a recent cable announcing the imminent arrival of the Free Czech Army on British soil.

Lena jumped up when she overheard this and approached the desk.

"*Promiňte*," she said to one of the women. "Did I hear something about the Czech Army coming here?"

"*Ano, slečno*," the woman said with a smile. She was pretty, with beautiful, shiny black hair and cheerful eyes.

A short, balding man in his fifties, standing behind her, added, "Yes, President Beneš finalized a deal with the Foreign Office last week. They'll be arriving in British merchant navy vessels any day now. A few have already reached Liverpool."

"My father and brother made it out of Prague a few months ago. They wrote from Belgrade. I think they're trying to join the Army. If they joined in Belgrade, would they be coming here?"

That would be incredible. Lena felt light-headed in the thick air. She wiped her hand across her forehead, which was moist with sweat. She felt a gentle hand on her shoulder; Peter was at her side.

"They were lucky to reach Belgrade," the official continued, blowing smoke high over their heads. "We lost many good patriots who were arrested in Hungary. They're still imprisoned there."

"But if they did make it to Belgrade?" Peter said.

"The Czech consulate in Belgrade stayed loyal and has been assisting in the mobilization. If they made it there, they were probably shipped to Agde, in the South of France."

"And if they reached Agde?" Lena asked. This man was rationing out information, one answer at a time.

"All our forces in Agde will be brought to Britain by the end of next week," he replied, and turned his back.

"Where? London?"

But he was gone into the rear office, closing the door behind him.

"They'll be at Cholmondeley Park, near Cheshire," said the receptionist at the desk. "That's in the north of England, near Liverpool. We're setting up an army base there." She smiled at Lena.

"Can I get a message to them? They don't even know I'm in England."

"Let me find out," the woman said. She returned several minutes later with an address written on a piece of paper. Handing it to Lena, she said, "You can write to them there." She smiled again. "Your father and brother are real heroes. You must be very proud of them."

Peter turned to Lena. "Well done," he said with a smile.

Father a hero? It just didn't fit. It was about as plausible as a cotton shirt in winter or woolen mittens on a warm June day. But Lena's heart fluttered at the thought of his being in this country, of hearing news of Máma and Sasha. How was Máma supposed to manage on her own? How had she agreed to let Ernst leave? She looked at the piece of paper in her hand: the first possibility in months of contact with her family. She slipped it into the pocket of her dress.

They waited two more hours, but Lisicky's whereabouts were either unknown or not to be divulged. Nothing more could be achieved sitting there; Peter and Lena had to content themselves with leaving a detailed message for him and trusting that the friendly receptionist might put in a good word for a hero's daughter.

They emerged into bright sunshine and walked to Hyde Park. Office workers and shop girls sauntered out for their lunch break or sat in small groups on the banks of the Serpentine. People-watching had been a delicious pastime back in Prague and Paris, and here again was a kaleidoscope of humanity: young women with boyish bob haircuts, elderly couples walking arm in arm, women with infants and toddlers—so there *were* still children in London—and fellow refugees. Lena heard Dutch, Flemish, and Polish. Here in the wide-open space of the park, at least, there appeared to be no repercussions from speaking in tongues other than English. And there were soldiers everywhere, milling in twos and threes, in uniforms of brown and khaki and gray and blue. There were officers in kilts and women, even, in khaki skirts; men with NEW ZEALAND or SOUTH AFRICA emblazoned on their shoulder tabs; and others, with complexions of golden brown or gleaming ebony. Clearly, Britain was calling in reinforcements from all corners of the Dominions.

Lena recalled her conversation with Otto the night before his arrest, only two nights ago—though it seemed so much longer—when he had scoffed at the notion that the British could hold out against the Nazis.

"Don't you think it's encouraging to see so many troops everywhere?" she asked Peter now. "The English seem prepared to defend this island."

"I agree," Peter said. "You do get that feeling."

Why had Otto been so dismissive? She had always respected his opinion; he was so often right. But she refused to believe that the Nazis could invade England without meeting any resistance. Everywhere around her, she sensed a quiet determination to stand firm, to defy whatever unknown terror might be in store. Lena wanted to honor and embrace that.

"This is Speakers' Corner," Peter said. "Always an interesting scene."

They watched as a young man harangued the small audience

with calls for a negotiated settlement with Hitler. A square-faced woman with her hair pulled tight in a bun handed out broadsheets from something called the Peace Pledge Union; "Stop the War," they proclaimed. Some people heckled the orator, but it appeared very good-natured. There was laughter, and jokes that Lena could not completely understand, something about inviting Hitler over for a cup of tea, and then further repartee about not wasting precious sugar rations on him.

"Extraordinary, these English," Lena said, smiling at the odd combination of quiet resolve, gentle tolerance, and dry humor. It was difficult to reconcile this with the hysterical anti-alien sensationalism of recent headlines.

"Yes, it's interesting how political dissent is clearly still tolerated," said Peter, as they moved on to Oxford Street. "Do you want to hop on a bus, or shall we continue walking?"

"How far is it?"

They were making their way to the Refugee Committee's office in Bloomsbury. A visit there was de rigueur—a chance to hear news, rumors, and gossip from Prague.

"Two or three kilometers, I think."

"I'm happy to walk," Lena said.

Would she ever get to know London the way she knew Prague or Paris, with that intimacy that came from hours of walking, exploring hidden corners and claiming them as one's own? She tried to register all the landmarks and the names of the streets, but Peter was walking much faster than she would have preferred, and as her feet raced to keep up with him, her mind sped on its own trajectory. Lena's first glimpses of Selfridges, Regent Street, and Tottenham Court Road mingled with visions of Otto sitting in a tiny cell, cramped and distraught, cut off from the world, and Father and Ernst on their way to an army camp in England, having survived unimaginable ordeals.

Lena faced with trepidation the thought of seeing her father. After the furious arguments back home, she had vowed never to speak to him again. Clearly, the old rules of engagement no longer applied, but what would replace them? What would it be like to confront him once more—here, in this country?

At the Refugee Office, they ran into a fellow Peter had known during his military service in Bohemia. They exchanged greetings and news. He had heard from a family member in Prague, but the letter had been heavily censored, whole sentences obliterated. What could be gleaned was nothing but gloom: hints about severe food shortages and strict curfews for Jews. A group of Polish refugees he'd met reported having heard dreadful stories about Jews in Lódź being sealed off in a ghetto.

"A ghetto?" Peter said.

"Yes, cut off from the outside world and subjected to forced labor."

Lena had a sudden flash of memory: her grandmother describing the pogroms of her childhood.

"The accounts are probably wildly exaggerated," Peter's friend said. "You know how the Poles are—you can never believe anything they say."

Yes, it couldn't be happening all over again.

The Refugee Office itself had little information to offer: vague hints about a resistance movement developing in Prague, but nothing substantial, and no news at all to bring back to Emil about anyone who had escaped toward the East, as Josef had done last winter. It was all disappointing and demoralizing.

Sensing their deflation, the woman at the desk, a matronly sort who was bustling about, tidying papers and pamphlets, picked up a notice about a concert to be held that evening at Wigmore Hall.

"It's a fund-raiser for the committee. They're playing Dvořák and Smetana. I can give you two free tickets. Go on, enjoy yourselves."

She gave Lena a conspiratorial wink that made Lena realize she assumed Lena and Peter were lovers. Luckily, Peter was oblivious to this female innuendo.

"Would you like to?" he asked.

Lena looked down at her plain cotton dress. "Like this?"

"You'll be fine like that, dear," the woman said. "One good thing about wartime: as long as it's clean, it'll do." She chuckled. "This is not a formal affair. It starts at six thirty, so that everyone can get home before blackout time."

"Should give us time to make the last train," Peter said. "Shall we go?"

"Why not?"

An evening concert: it sounded quite delightful, so civilized. The perfect antidote to the frustrations of the day.

Lena sank deep into the plush maroon seat, easing her feet out of her shoes and allowing the tension to ooze out of her back and shoulders. She was pleasantly exhausted. They had walked for hours, getting lost in the narrow streets around Covent Garden, making a wrong turn at Piccadilly Circus, and finally traipsing all the way up Bond Street to reach the concert hall just in time. The auditorium was three-quarters full, and they were seated toward the rear. As far as she could tell from this position, the woman from the Refugee Office had been correct: the backs of heads and shoulders revealed a wide variety of styles and formality. Sprinkled among the few sequined gowns and shiny black coats were women without hats and men without jackets.

After a few mercifully short speeches thanking them for their support and urging additional donations for the Trust Fund, the music started with Dvořák's *Carnival Overture*. Lena remembered now she considered it rather too jarring for her taste. What she really wanted to hear was the program's finale: Smetana's *Ma Vlast, My Country*. She loved especially the second movement, the melodic depiction of the Vltava flowing through Prague, the repeating motifs, and the final, triumphant crescendo portraying the heroic legends of those who rescued Bohemia in its darkest hour.

In the short pause before it started, Peter whispered, "Did we tell you that on the night the Nazis marched into Prague, we had tickets for the symphony? Those cheap standing-room-only tickets we used to get. My parents couldn't understand how we would want to go to a concert on a night like that. But we did, and so did hundreds of others. The place was packed. And they abandoned the planned program in favor of *Ma Vlast*. They performed it from memory, no music. Everyone was on their feet."

From the opening chords of the harp in *Vyšehrad* to the culminating march in the final poem, *Blaník*, Lena's eyes were moist, her throat parched. She felt tugged back to Prague by a deep longing, an aching homesickness she had not felt since she'd left. She could not yield to this; she must remain strong. When the culminating applause brought the whole audience to its feet, Lena remained seated to compose herself. She brushed off Peter's solicitous inquiry with a vague wave, staring ahead as people turned to leave the hall.

If she had not been sitting like that, if she, too, had turned to leave as soon as the applause died down, she might easily have missed her. As it was, when her eyes first alighted on that familiar face, Lena did not immediately recognize what she was seeing. A trick of the mind, it must be, a phantom conjured up by the music of her homeland. Or a mere coincidence. After all, there can be only so many possible juxtapositions of features; no single visage can be truly unique. Those deep-brown eyes and high cheekbones, the full lips and the pointed chin, even that little mole on the upper lip, must surely coexist in another face, in another land.

But then those eyes met hers and lit up in excitement. Those lips opened wide in astonishment.

"Eva!" Lena cried.

CHAPTER 20

LONDON, JUNE 1940

There stood Eva, thinner than when they'd parted in the Place de la Contrascarpe three months earlier but unmistakably in front of Lena, stepping into the row of seats to clear the aisle, leaning forward now to kiss her on both cheeks.

"What are you doing here?" Lena managed to say. "How did you get to England?"

"I arrived two days ago, via the South of France. I left Paris with the masses, in *l'exode.*" She turned to kiss Peter and flashed him a flirtatious smile. "This is amazing. Half of Prague seems to be here."

"South of France?" Lena said, as they made their way to the foyer. Peter was a few steps ahead of them.

Eva turned to Lena and said, "So, you're with Peter now?" She gave a quick, brittle laugh. "I always said he and Lotti wouldn't last."

"What? No, no. They're still together," Lena said. She hoped to goodness Peter couldn't hear them. She clutched at Eva's arm to slow her down, pull her in toward her. "How did you get here from France?"

"I came on a ship full of Czech soldiers. Well, not a ship, exactly—a coal freighter, filthy dirty; we had to sleep on the floor in the coal dust. But we got here." As they rejoined Peter outside the concert hall, Eva added, "And guess what?"

"What?"

"Your brother was on the ship."

"Ernst? That's incredible." Lena turned to Peter. "Eva came from France. On one of those ships they told us about at the council offices."

"How many soldiers were there?" Peter said. "Where did you land in England?"

"What did Ernst say?" Lena said at the same time. "How did he look?"

"I didn't talk to him much. There were hundreds of troops. I only realized it was him just before we docked at Liverpool. I hardly recognized him. He's grown half a meter, and he was in uniform. I remembered to tell him you're in England now. He had no idea, of course."

"Did he say anything about my father?" asked Lena.

Peter looked nervously at his watch. "We have to get to Victoria for the last train. Let's walk to the Tube." He pointed in the same direction in which everyone else was walking.

The throng swept them toward Oxford Street. Lena kept hold of Eva's elbow, but strangers bumped them constantly and it was hard to complete sentences.

"Did Ernst say anything about how they got to France?" Lena said.

"No," Eva said. "I told you, I hardly talked to him. It was all very chaotic."

 "Where's Marguerite?" Lena asked

"I don't know. I lost track of her."

"What do you mean?"

"Oh, it's a long story. But she made it out of Paris. Just in time."

"You haven't heard from her since?" Lena asked in dismay.

"No."

They had to dodge to avoid a knot of inebriated young men in uniform emerging from a pub, staggering up the street arm in arm, singing lustily. Lena and Eva were trapped behind the spectacle. Eva seemed unable to take her eyes off them. They were tall and blond and would obviously be very handsome once they sobered up.

When she finally returned her attention to Lena, she asked, "So, where's Otto? Isn't he with you?"

They had reached Oxford Circus and come to a standstill at the top of the Tube steps.

Peter looked at his watch again. There was no time to explain anything.

"Come with us, Eva," Lena pleaded. "Come with us to the station, so we can talk more."

"I have to get back to my hostel," Eva said. "I'll never find it unless I stick to the one route I know."

"Peter can tell you the way," Lena said. "He knows London very well."

"No, I think I'd better go back now."

"Promise you'll come down to Sussex soon. I have to hear everything. Peter, give Eva the directions. Do you have any paper?"

After a few scribbled notes on the back of an envelope and a quick wave as Peter practically dragged Lena into the Underground, Eva was gone again, almost as quickly as she'd appeared.

The train rumbled back to Sussex, the rhythm of the wheels thrumming a gentle lullaby. Indeed, Peter soon dozed off, his head cocked against the window frame, his mouth open, the lower lip quivering slightly with each intake of breath. They were alone in the compartment; this last train was eerily quiet.

An all-encompassing fatigue enveloped Lena, but she could not sleep. She stared out at the fading light of the long summer evening. She could just discern her reflection in the grimy window. She automatically raised her hands to rearrange her hair back behind its clips as she tried to piece together the puzzle. Eva seemed different somehow. Was it Lena's imagination, or had she been evasive? Why wouldn't she come with them to Victoria so they could talk more? They could have told her how to get back. Eva wasn't usually timid about finding her way around. She didn't seem herself. Shaken, perhaps, by whatever she had gone through escaping from Paris. She'd said nothing about Heinz. And what had she meant about Marguerite? It was maddening to have to wait for more details.

At least Eva was safely out of France. And Lena would surely be able to see her again soon. And Ernst, too, by the sounds of it. Amazing that he and Eva had been on the same ship! It was hard to imagine Ernst in uniform. The brother she used to fight and squabble with when they were little, who had then become very distant in recent years. Lena hardly knew him anymore. She fingered the piece of paper in her dress pocket: the address of the Czech army base. She would write to Ernst tomorrow.

And she should try to find out how to write to Otto. Her thoughts returned to him with a pang of guilt. She had hardly thought of him all evening, not since the first stirrings of the music. The excitement over the news about the Czech army had overshadowed the fact that they had made no progress in securing Otto's freedom. Should she have stayed longer at the Czech Council office? That girl at the desk had been friendly. Perhaps Lena could have persuaded her to do more. *I'm just no good at this*, she thought. Otto had somehow managed to get her a visa for England—but that was the thing about Otto. He was so persuasive. She hadn't been able to get the council people to really listen to her. Lena looked across at Peter. He had been so confident that morning. But he hadn't been successful, either.

Lena looked out the window at the huddled houses, the amorphous shadows where diligent citizens were applying their blackout shades to assuage the watchful local wardens. A gibbous moon rose in the east, as if to mock their efforts: any bomber flying overhead tonight would have no difficulty locating its target. How odd that the beautiful lunar glow could be something to fear. Were bombs really going to rain down on them? Would Lena ever find it within herself to be brave in the face of such an onslaught? She thought of the Londoners she had seen that day, and what she had gleaned of their quiet, solid resolve. Why had Otto said you needed to be free of emotion at times like these? Those Londoners seemed brave and ready for anything, but couples still strode arm-in-arm, still loved and needed each other.

Peter gave a soft snore, and his head jolted forward. He woke with a startled expression. Kicking off his shoes, he spread out full length on the seat. "Wake me up when we get to Bigglesmeade," he said, curling over onto his side.

The movement reminded Lena of Otto, of him curled up behind her in bed, his arm around her stomach, his knees tucked behind hers. Caught off guard, she felt tears well up. Where was he? It would be some comfort just to know where he was tonight.

The conductor opened the door to the compartment. He glanced at Peter sprawled out on the seat, looked as though he was about to offer a reprimand, but then thought better of it.

"Tired him out, have you?" He gave a gentle laugh. "Lower the blinds, love. It's blackout time."

Lena took one more look outside. The moon was even brighter now in the growing darkness. This same moon would be gazing down on Otto, wherever he was, and on Ernst, in England now, it seemed, and on Prague, too, on Máma and Sasha. She stared up at the silver orb, with its beguiling smile, and banished it behind the shade.

CHAPTER 21

LINGFIELD RACECOURSE, SURREY, JUNE 1940

It was the nights that Otto dreaded the most. He had lost count of how many he'd spent in this cell. It wasn't even a cell, exactly, but an improvised version, in the racetrack stables, reeking of horse manure, with a hard concrete floor, no furniture, hot and stuffy. It wasn't too bad during the day, when he could wander around, but at night it was unbearable. Noises traveled easily between stalls: the sounds of snoring and coughing, and incessant chatter, speculation and squabbling.

It was worse than listening to Emil and Tomas arguing, or Peter carrying on as if he knew the answer to everything. It called for the same strategy: Otto refused to get embroiled in these conversations. Even that morning, when he'd seen Lorenz Schönmann perched on a bale of hay, eating porridge and waving him over, Otto had been evasive, brushing off Lorenz's questions about everything he'd done since Prague, not wanting to go into all that, not wanting to confront how much things had changed, how much he had changed. Lorenz had heard Otto was working on a book about Spain, but Otto didn't want to talk about that, either. He had his typewriter with him, but he was beginning to think he might never finish the book.

Perhaps Lena was right: he was changing, becoming a stranger even to himself. When he was with her, he felt forced to counterbalance her hopelessly naive optimism. He needed to point out the reality of the situation; it was a mantle he wrapped himself in to create a buffer, but he had thought he could shrug it off anytime. Now he wasn't so sure.

Otto felt a heavy inertia he did not recognize. In earlier days, he would have been organizing, lining up alliances, plotting the best strategy for when the Nazis arrived. He watched from afar as some of his fellow inmates took steps along those lines—well, not that, exactly, but there was an advisory committee negotiating ways to improve life in the camp, and the musicians were organizing a concert, whereas he, Otto Eisenberg, sat on the sidelines.

Being arrested had shaken him. He had thought he would be protected by Muriel's influence. When the French authorities had been on the verge of scooping him up, she had come to his rescue with an entry permit for England. Surely she could keep him out of the clutches of the British police. The pounding on the cottage door so early in the morning, the heavy footsteps following him upstairs as he went to pack, the thick shoulders squeezing either side of him in the back of the car as they carted him off—just to recall these events made his heart hammer at his throat.

He remembered another pounding at a door, this one in the dead of night, long ago in Berlin, when he'd seen the storm troopers in the street below, had climbed out onto the roof and hidden in the nook behind the chimney, watching in horror as Rudolf and Max, good comrades, were dragged off. Never to be seen again. Presumed to be in Dachau.

Another roll call. Unbelievable. That morning, they had counted 893 men filing onto the grandstand and filing out again. Next time it was 882, then 897. None of these numbers seemed to satisfy. The commandant, who had a ludicrous white handlebar mustache, repeatedly shuffled through his papers, trying to resolve the discrepancy. Two uniformed police officers joined the debate, gesturing to the group of new arrivals on the far side of the arena. One of them removed his helmet and scratched his head in what could have been a pose from a Laurel and Hardy routine.

"*Mein Gott!* Look at them!" said Schmidt, the man paired up with Otto in the stalls. "They can't get anything right. They need a good lesson in Aryan efficiency."

Otto refused to speak to him, but Schmidt—who used only his last name—stuck to him like a leech, following Otto around during roll call, in the lines for food, even out to the latrines, talking nonstop.

"When the Wehrmacht arrive, they'll show them how to run this place," he continued.

That day there had been at least fifty new arrivals: men of all ages, some young and brisk, others stiff with arthritis. One dark-haired youth, his eyes darting with fear, had appeared at Otto's stall that afternoon, just before this latest roll call announcement. He clutched a small rucksack and his allocated bale of straw. Otto moved his own *paillasse* farther into the corner to make room for him, showing him how to smooth out the makeshift straw mattress. The boy was tall and lanky, fifteen at most. He certainly didn't look like a Nazi sympathizer, looked Jewish, in fact, though Otto was reluctant to ask. But the boy appeared so frightened, Otto had to say something.

"*Wie heisst du?* What's your name?"

"Karl. Karl Weiss."

"*Bist du allein?* Are you alone? No family?"

"*Mein Vater . . . Sprechen Sie Englisch?* Do you speak English?"

"Yes. You don't speak German?"

"No, not really. My father is German, but I've lived here since I was a baby." Otto thought he might burst into tears. "My father was picked up a week ago. I don't know if he's here. We never found out where he was taken."

"Put your things over there," Otto said, pointing to one corner of the stall. "Schmidt, get up, for heaven's sake. Make some room for the boy."

There were shouts from the far end of the stables; a posse of army officers strode through, rallying everyone out again for the roll call.

"Come on . . . Karl, did you say your name was? Perhaps you'll see your father out in the arena."

As they traipsed outside again, the rumors were flying. A group was to be shipped off tomorrow, destination: Australia, if one self-appointed expert was to be believed.

"Not a bad option," he declared in a grating Bavarian accent. "Hitler won't be able to reach us there."

Australia? Otto was broadsided by a wave of panic. Could he really be deported to the other side of the world, with no chance to communicate with anyone? He might never see Lena again. He knew he'd been too harsh with her that last night in the cottage. He should have apologized. Once he'd recovered from the shock of his arrest, he'd assumed it was temporary, that somehow his release would be arranged, that they would be together again, soon. Suddenly, he missed her, wanted her. Funny how a feeling could creep up on you like that. Like when you have been writing for hours and suddenly realize you are hungry. How would she manage without him? If only he could write to her. It was always easier to put things in writing. But no one was allowed any letters, in or out.

Yet maybe he was right to tell Lena not to be swayed by emotions. You had to keep your wits about you in times like these. To survive, it had to be every man for himself. If he hadn't climbed out onto that Berlin roof, if he had stayed behind to help Rudolf and Max, what would that have achieved? He had saved himself then, and he had to save himself now. Perhaps the Bavarian was right: being dispatched to the Antipodes would certainly put him out of the Gestapo's range. Tomas had friends who had been waiting for Australian visas for months. It could be viewed as a very desirable destination.

Major Mustache was shifting through his papers while the sergeant fussed with a megaphone.

"Testing. Testing. One, two, three, testing."

The volume alternately boomed and fizzled as everyone shuffled forward into the collecting ring, where one would normally have expected to see horses paraded before a race. Dozens of guards stood by, armed with fixed bayonets. New barricades of barbed wire now surrounded the arena.

"Gentlemen, may I have your attention, please?"

There was an ear-piercing squeak of feedback, which startled the commandant so much that he jerked backward and stepped on the toes of the officer standing behind him. The ever-present Schmidt, on Otto's right, muttered his disgust. The boy Karl, on Otto's left, rotated his head and shoulders in sweeping circles as he searched for his father.

Up front, there was more fiddling with the megaphone. Finally, the sergeant adjusted something and the show was back on.

"Ahem. Yes. Gentlemen, as I was saying," the commandant resumed. "I am here to inform you that a group of one hundred internees will be departing forthwith to another location. I regret to say that I am not permitted to reveal your ultimate destination at this juncture. When I call your name, please proceed to collect your belongings and reassemble at the far side of the arena. You will be departing within the hour. Everyone else, please remain where you are. Thank you."

A rumble swept through the crowd.

"In an hour? I thought it was tomorrow," shouted one man to Otto's left.

"Quiet!" roared the sergeant.

The commandant shuffled through his papers again. He needed two hands for this, so the megaphone was back with the sergeant, who held it in place just above the mustache.

Names were called out, one by one, and checked off as they left the ring. Adolf Ackermann, Georg Adler, Gustav Beuer. It seemed to be alphabetical. Otto held his breath after the *D*s, chewing on the corner of his lower lip. If he believed in God, he might have prayed. But he wouldn't have known what to pray for. Was it better to be selected or not? The names continued, but the order now appeared completely random: there was a Regner, a Moser . . . and then Hans Schmidt. Schmidt elbowed his way forward, turning to Otto with a solemn look on his face.

"*Auf Wiedersehen, mein Freund*," he said softly.

The group selected was getting larger, almost eighty, Otto judged. They were assembling on the other side of the grandstand. If there were to be only a hundred, his odds of being included were now pretty low. Something perverse made him want to be picked now, as though it were a much-sought-after prize. Perhaps it was better to get out of here, to leave this continent and escape the Nazis.

A young man named Kurt Guttmann was called forward, a pimply-faced youth with spectacles and trousers that were several centimeters too short. Another one who could not be much older than sixteen. It was ridiculous to be locking up children like this. What were they thinking? It was almost as bad as the Nazis rounding up youngsters for the Hitler-*Jugend* brigades, goose-stepping across playgrounds. His own brother, Hans, had rushed off to join their ranks at a tender age.

"Otto Eisenberg."

Otto was jolted out of his ruminations and froze. He couldn't move. "Otto Eisenberg," the commandant repeated, more loudly.

Otto stepped forward, his legs heavy as lead. So he was to go after all. He would be sent away from Europe and its rotten failed democracies, away from its botched revolutions and burgeoning dictatorships, away from the advancing Panzer divisions. He would no longer have to constantly look over his shoulder. He could start a completely new life, raising kangaroos or whatever it was they did down there.

"Erich Weiss."

"Dad!"

A scream came from where Otto had been standing. He turned to see the boy Karl run into the arms of a stocky man approaching from the far side of the crowd. Everyone watched as father gripped son in a bear hug. Karl was sobbing.

"Please, let me take my boy with me," the father said, choking back tears. "I can't leave without my boy."

Karl looked in the direction of the army officers, and his gaze landed on Otto. Their eyes locked.

"For heaven's sake," the commandant said, thrusting the sheets of paper into the sergeant's hands. "Do you think I'm running a family reunion here?"

"We have our one hundred men, sir," the sergeant said. "You recall they were most particular about that, sir."

"He can take my place," Otto heard himself say. "Let the boy have my place; let him go with his father."

Hours later, the moon rose over the grandstand and cast bright shadows through the stables. Somewhere in the distance, a violinist played something that sounded like Mozart. It was much quieter tonight; the mood had turned somber. Otto relished the privacy of a stall to himself.

CHAPTER 22

SUSSEX, JULY 1940

It rained during the night. Not a hard rain, but a steady pitter-patter on the awning over the front door. Lena slept lightly. Each time she turned over, she opened her eyes and tried to make out the shapes of the familiar objects in the room—the fireplace, the table by the window, the worn armchair—but it was too dark. Yet even if she couldn't see the details, Lena felt comfortable here in the living room. She finally had a room of her own. In the week since Otto's arrest, she had slept downstairs every night. After the others tucked themselves into bed in the two rooms upstairs, she sat in the armchair, cradling a last cup of tea in her own little space. She could keep the light on as long as she wished. She didn't have to fight for the covers. And she could jump up as soon as she awoke or lie daydreaming, whichever she preferred.

Of course, she worried about Otto every day. But she was getting used to being alone, and rather shamefully enjoying it. She felt as though she had elbow room after being cramped in a tight box. It was naughty to feel this way, especially as she had not been more successful in securing Otto's release. They had achieved nothing since her and Peter's trip to London, nearly a week prior.

Perhaps the new day would bring some good news. Muriel had sent Alistair to meet with someone in the Home Office. He was to spend the night at his club in the West End and return before lunch.

Lena willed herself to remain optimistic. It was incredible that someone with such staunch anti-Nazi credentials could be locked up as an enemy alien. They should be looking to Otto for advice, not arresting him. The authorities would surely recognize that if they heard the full story.

The rain appeared to have stopped. All was quiet upstairs. She opted for an early-morning walk before noise and chatter overtook the living room.

Outside, tiny raindrops glistened on each blade of grass, each leaf. Billowy cumulus clouds piled up behind the church spire, moving east quickly, in shifting formations. Lena squinted at them, shielding her eyes from the sun. She remembered a game she and Ernst had played when they were small, lying on their backs on the hill behind their *babička*'s summer house, watching the clouds between the treetops, creating stories based on the faces or animals they imagined there.

But Ernst was no longer a little boy gazing at clouds. He was a grown man in uniform, stationed at an army base in the north of England. Lena had just received a letter from him. He expected Father to join him any day now, in one of the final shiploads evacuated from the South of France. And he had enclosed a permit for Lena to come and visit, to stay overnight in the officers' guest quarters. Peter was encouraging her to go; he and Alistair pored over the map, located Cholmondeley Park, and debated whether Crewe or Chester would be the closest train station.

"I'm sure you could hitchhike from Chester without any problem," Peter said. "There must be lorries going to and from the base all the time. I could come with you, if you'd like."

"No," Lotti said, rather too quickly, glancing from Peter to Lena and then back again. "I'm sure Lena wants time alone with her family."

"Yes, I would prefer to go on my own."

She didn't want to jeopardize her friendship with Lotti, especially as there had been no further word from Eva. She needed the closeness of one solid female friendship at least.

"But I have to wait until Otto's been released," she continued. "I can't leave here not even knowing where he is."

Opposite the church, a footpath took off to the right; they often took this route through the fields to The Hollow. Soon she was swishing through the pasture, ankle deep in wet grass. She saw a flash of movement at the far side of the field: a large, russet-colored dog romping toward her, tail flailing high in delight. Bringing up the rear, a man approached from the direction of The Hollow. It must be Alistair, out walking Lancelot. Was he back from London so soon? What news did he have?

She waved in his direction, and he waved back. As they approached each other, however, she saw that the gait was too lively to be Alistair, the build too slim. It was Milton, running now to catch up with the dog, who was upon her, jumping up to greet her, drooling on her skirt.

"I thought you were Alistair," she said.

He laughed. "You sound disappointed."

"No. Sorry. It's just . . . I was hoping Alistair might have some news about Otto."

"Of course. I understand," Milton said. "Down, boy!" He grabbed Lancelot by the collar. "Actually, Alistair called a few minutes ago. He's taking the nine o'clock train. He sounded quite optimistic, said he met with someone in Whitehall, but I couldn't catch the details. It was a bad connection." He continued walking in the direction from which he had come; Lena retraced her steps, without discussion, to accompany him. "We'll find out soon enough."

They reached a large oak tree, where the path forked. "I'm heading over to Copley Woods to stretch my legs," Milton said. "Would you like to accompany me? Then we could go back to wait for Alistair. Mother was hoping you would join us for lunch."

"Yes, thank you. I would like that." Her feet were drenched, but she didn't care. "It's such a beautiful morning."

They walked on in silence. "So, you're back on leave?" she asked after a while.

"Just twenty-four hours. I'm fortunate to be based so close."

"Where are you now?"

"In Portsmouth. It's on the coast, not too far from here."

"And how . . . I mean, how does it seem to you now?" Lena asked tentatively.

"I feel a bit more useful. We've been setting up anti-aircraft bunkers, a whole network of underground rooms. The big guns arrive next week. Of course, I'm not supposed to say anything. Sworn to secrecy and all that." He grinned.

"I won't say a word."

They climbed over a gate and headed into a small wood, dark and shady after the bright sun. Lancelot scooted under the lowest bar and scampered ahead. Moisture dripped from the trees. Milton led them down a steep, narrow path.

"Watch your step here," he said. "I heard that your father and brother were arriving soon with the Free Czech Army. Have you heard any more from them?"

"Yes, they're in Chess-heer, is that how you say it? Near Chester."

"Cheshire?"

"Yes, that's it," Lena said. "At least, my brother is, and my father will arrive any day now. My brother has invited me to go visit them."

"You must go, of course," Milton replied. He motioned for her to go ahead now that the terrain was flatter.

"I'm not sure. It depends on what happens with Otto."

"But you must go to see them, hear news of your mother and Sasha. It's been so long since you've heard from them. You will learn something at least about what life is like in Prague now."

Lena stopped and looked at him in amazement. He understood. He even remembered her sister's name.

"Yes," she said. "That's it. I will go, of course."

They extended their walk to the village of Elminghurst, returning on a narrow, winding lane past several farmhouses and the quarry. Alistair was already there when they reached The Hollow.

"Lena, my dear." He beamed at her. "I'm so glad to see you. I think we're making some progress. Eleanor Rathbone has been creating a stink in the House about this whole internment business, and the Home Secretary is clearly on the defensive."

"But did you find out anything specific about Otto?" Milton asked.

"I'm getting to that," Alistair replied. He gestured for Lena to take a seat. "I met with a senior official at the Home Office. I explained all the extenuating circumstances." He stole a sideways glance at her. "I hope I didn't overstep the bounds of my mission, my dear."

"I'm sorry?" Lena was perplexed.

"I took the liberty of going into some detail about your situation," Alistair said. "I said Otto's girlfriend . . . ahem"—he paused, gave a little cough—"or, rather, his *fiancée*, was a Czech Jew with a father and brother in the Free Czech Army. That seemed to impress him. You know how one has only to mention Czechoslovakia and Munich in Whitehall these days to have them falling over themselves to make amends."

He looked from Lena to Milton and back to Lena again, then looked at his long fingers splayed out on his lap. "Anyway, ahem, the Home Office chap implied that Otto's release could be arranged. That is, ahem, providing he were to marry you immediately."

CHAPTER 23

SUSSEX, JULY 1940

"We must remember to buy fuel for the primus stove," Lotti said. She stood at the mirror at the foot of the stairs, rearranging her curls for the third time, pivoting to inspect her profile. Lena came down, wearing a simple white blouse and a gray skirt, together with a pale blue jacket borrowed from Muriel.

"Are you sure you don't want to wear the hat?" Lotti said. "It would bring out the blue in your eyes."

"No, I don't want the hat." Lena laughed. "I wish you'd stop fussing about what I'm wearing."

Actually, she wished that she and Otto could go off and do this on their own, but they were obliged to bring two witnesses. Peter and Lotti had seemed like the obvious choice, but now Lena wished they'd asked Tomas and Emil instead. Lotti was being entirely too exuberant about the whole thing.

"It's early-closing day," Peter called out from the kitchen, where he was working on the breakfast dishes. "We'll have to do any shopping beforehand. Everything will be closed after lunch."

"Where's Otto?" Lena said.

"I sent him off to borrow a tie from Alistair," Lotti said.

"Oh, for heaven's sake," Lena said, looking at her watch. "We need to go."

"We can meet him at the bus stop," Lotti said, checking her reflection one more time. Lena averted her eyes from the glass. Earlier, Lotti had tried to put some life into Lena's thin, straight hair. This had involved a lot of pulling and twisting and dozens of hairpins, and it was now very uncomfortable. Lena feared that if she caught another glimpse of it, she might be tempted to pull it all apart.

Peter steered them toward the front door. "Let's hope Otto doesn't get cold feet," he said, winking at Lena.

Tomas, reading on the sofa, lowered *The Times* onto his lap. "He doesn't have much choice in the matter, does he?" he said. "It's either this or off to camp on the Isle of Man."

"Come on. Let's go," Lotti said. She glared at Tomas. "There's a party tonight at Muriel's, but *you* don't deserve an invitation. Though, of course, knowing you, you'd never miss a chance for a free drink."

Tomas laughed. "Fuel bottle!" he called out after them. Peter grabbed the large glass jar from the table.

They caught up with Otto at the bus stop. He sauntered toward them wearing not only a navy-blue tie but also a crisp linen jacket he must have borrowed from either Alistair or Milton. It was a bit short in the sleeves, but he looked quite dashing. Lotti must have done something with his hair, too, because it was more compliant than usual, neatly parted and lightly oiled into place. Just behind him came Milton; he carried a small bouquet of flowers, a delicate lilac bloom surrounded by Queen Anne's lace, which he presented to Lena.

"Flowers for the blushing bride," he said, with a small bow.

And indeed she was blushing. Darn it, she could feel the color rising to her cheeks. "Thank you," she murmured.

"A small gesture," Milton said. He turned to Otto. "I hope all goes well. I'm frightfully sorry—I can't join you for the party tonight. I'm due back on base this afternoon."

He gave a cheery wave. Lena watched him retreat across the green, sorry that he wouldn't be there this evening. He always added a spark of fun.

Otto leaned over to kiss Lena on the cheek, and she smiled. He had been more outwardly affectionate since his release the previous week. He didn't talk much about his experiences at the racetrack. He had once mentioned a young boy he had befriended, but he'd been vague when Lena had pressed for more details. Yet something in Otto had shifted.

He turned to Peter now and said, "Did you bring the newspaper? I haven't had a chance to read it yet."

"Tomas has it. He always takes forever. He reads every word."

"I saw a headline about internees being shipped off to Canada and Australia. I wanted to read that."

"Yes," Peter said. "They're saying it's only the confirmed Nazis who are being deported overseas."

"That's not true," Otto said. His mouth was set in a hard line. They all waited, expecting more, but he looked at his watch and said, "What time is the bus due?"

The register office was across from the town hall. They had to get the fuel for the stove first, and Lena was afraid they might be late; there was a queue in the hardware shop. They hurried up the High Street, Peter carrying the refilled bottle and Lena still holding the flowers. Another party emerged as the group from Upper Wolmingham arrived: a very young bride, surely no more than sixteen, in a white cotton dress, wobbling on high-heeled shoes and clutching the arm of a soldier in army uniform. A group of middle-aged women dabbed at moist eyes and threw pink rose petals over the newlyweds, who posed for photographs. Lena and the others waited politely to the side.

"Rose petals!" Lotti said, stooping to pick up a handful. "That's a nice idea."

The office was narrow but bright and airy, with sunlight streaming in from two large windows. In front of the windows, a long table faced several rows of plain wooden seats, evidently intended for family and friends. Their little group made the room conspicuously empty. Lena felt a flash of nostalgia for fantasies she'd held years ago for a very different type of wedding day. Máma didn't even know she was getting married. And this didn't feel like happily ever after. What was it going to mean, really, for her and

Otto? They hadn't talked about it at all until last night, and then only briefly.

"Thank you for doing this, Lena," he'd said as they lay together in the darkness. By tacit agreement, she and Otto had taken the upstairs bedroom every night since his release. She would have preferred to talk with the light on, but he turned it off before rolling on top of her for lovemaking.

"It's the least I can do," she said. She wouldn't be here were it not for Otto. She wrapped her legs around him the way he liked, stroking the backs of his calves with her feet.

"You know, I don't expect a traditional marriage or anything," he said.

Of course not. She knew that. Marriage was nothing—a bourgeois institution, they always said. In all their political discussions. A bourgeois institution.

"I'm just happy there was a way to get you out of that place," she said.

She held him in the darkness. Otto would get the piece of paper he needed to keep him free. This wedding was purely an expedient procedure.

Now, the registrar appeared through a side door. He was a diminutive, soft-spoken man of about fifty, with a receding hairline and thin-rimmed spectacles. He introduced himself, shaking hands and gesturing for them to advance to the table. He nodded and beamed at Lena and Otto as they signed in, presented their identity cards, and completed the necessary paperwork. His right eye twitched as he supervised the process. Lena dutifully wrote her name as Kulkova, and then her father's name, Jakob Kulka. She hesitated at the next box: father's occupation. What should she put? He was no longer in the carbon-paper business, obviously. He was in the army, but she didn't know his rank. She wrote simply: *soldier.*

The registrar adjusted his spectacles and reviewed their entries. "Ahem. There must be some mistake," he said, with a little cough. "Your name and your father's, they do not match."

"Yes," Lena said. "Kulka, Kulkova, it's the same. Kulkova is the female."

"But they have to be the same name." The right eye twitched rapidly.

"But it *is* the same," Lena replied.

He shook his head and looked again at the names in front of him. He reexamined Lena's identity card. "I think we'll have to change his name to Kulkova in order for this to be valid," he said, rubbing his hand through what was left of his hair. "I can't have a discrepancy in the official records."

"That's absurd!" Peter protested. "That's like calling him Mrs. Kulka. His name isn't Kulkova; it's Kulka. This is the Czech custom. The woman takes her father's name with *-ova* added to it."

"This is most irregular," the registrar muttered, ignoring Peter. "I don't know if I can do this." For a moment, Lena thought the whole thing might get derailed on this technicality, but then he turned to Otto to ask, "Are you in agreement with this, sir?"

"Yes, of course."

"Well, this is a new one, I have to say. Kulka, Kulkova," he repeated. He shook his head again, adjusted his spectacles, and stared at the form. "I suppose I can let it go this once." Then he looked up and added, "But I can't make a habit of it."

A habit of it? Was this meant as a warning that he wasn't going to marry any more Czechs? Lena's mouth jerked as a spasm of giggles prepared to erupt. She bit the inside of her cheek in an effort to keep a straight face and forced herself not to catch Peter's eye. They stood in silence as the registrar completed the ledger.

"And these are your witnesses, sir?" he asked Otto.

"Yes."

The registrar turned to Peter for the first time, and his eyes fell on the bottle of purple methylated spirits cradled carefully in his hands.

"What, may I ask, is that?" he said.

"It's fuel," Peter said.

"I beg your pardon?"

"Another Czech custom," Peter said, holding up the bottle, as if to offer a toast.

This time there could be no holding back. The laughter burst out of Lena, propelling a glob of spittle onto the registrar's shiny black jacket. It rested there on his lapel throughout the proceedings, like a third witness.

She didn't tell Otto about the telegram until after they returned home, piece of paper duly in hand: Mr. and Mrs. Eisenberg. She joined him outside on the wooden bench under the kitchen window.

"My father's arrived in England," she said. He seemed to be having difficulty getting his pipe to stay lit; he was poking and puffing away and didn't look at her. "I'm going to go to Cheshire to visit him and Ernst."

"I thought you were never going to speak to your father again."

"That was before . . ."

"Before what?" He removed the pipe from his mouth.

"What do you mean, 'before what'?" She spread her arms wide in front of her, palms up. "Before Blitzkrieg, the fall of Paris, an imminent invasion, the Free Czech Army—all that."

"Have you forgotten how he wouldn't let you out for days at a time? How he beat you? Gave you a huge black eye and bruises all over your arms? His behavior was disgusting. He's a reactionary capitalist, isn't he? That's what you always said."

Why were they arguing? It wasn't what she wanted, especially not right before tonight's party, where she knew they would be the center of attention, in spite of all her efforts to downplay things.

She put her hand on his thigh and gently flicked away a few stray strands of tobacco. "Yes, he beat me, and yes, I said I would never speak to him again, but things have changed. He's my father, and he's done a brave thing, escaping to join the army. I want to go see him. I want to hear from him how my mother and sister are coping, or at least how they were when he left. I'm sure there're things he cannot put into letters." Her thoughts fell into place as she spoke, like pieces of a puzzle assembling before her eyes.

Otto looked as though he were about to offer another counterargument, but instead he gave a quick shrug and said, "All right. I'm sorry. You go. But I hope you don't expect me to go with you."

"No, I want to go by myself." Lena added, "When I get back,

perhaps we could go away together for a couple of days. Just the two of us."

"Perhaps."

But, realistically, where could they go? How could they afford it? She'd had to borrow money from Muriel for the train ticket to Cheshire.

They sat in silence, until Lena said, "Don't you ever wonder about your brother, where he is and what he's doing? You never talk about him."

"What's there to say? He's a Nazi." He fiddled with the pipe again, lit another match. "I have no interest in hearing from him. For all I know, he's in northern France, preparing to invade. I'm sure he would shoot me if he had the chance."

"You can't really believe that."

"Lena, Hans and I are nothing to each other—nothing. We haven't spoken in years. He's a fascist. It was probably he who denounced me to the Gestapo in Berlin the night Rudolf and Max were arrested." He looked over toward the privet hedge, but his focus was obviously far away. "Family isn't always the most important thing, you know."

CHAPTER 24

CHESHIRE, JULY 1940

The train took Lena from London to Crewe and then on to the little market town of Nantwich. What was it about a train journey that was so alluring? The endless track, with its open possibilities; the fleeting views of different slices of life captured in a single moment; the billowing, sooty-smelling clouds of steam; the *clickety-clack* of the wheels; the mingling of diverse passengers and voices and accents—it all excited her. Traversing the backbone of the country was like exploring the body of a new lover. She saw green fields, rolling hills, and small, redbrick towns. And the not so picturesque: grimy, crowded, terraced slums blackened with soot, and tall factory chimneys belching out smoke. The stations were crowded with young men in military uniform, heaving large duffel bags and smoking cigarettes, going to or from leave, she supposed.

She read a little but mostly stared out the window or exchanged brief glances with her compartment companions as they came and left. No one engaged her in conversation until Birmingham, when a young woman her own age joined the train. She was a redhead with pale, freckled skin and an unusual outfit: dark corduroy breeches, long wool socks, and sturdy brown shoes, together with a beige shirt, a green tie, and a hat with some sort of badge. As she took her seat opposite Lena, she removed the hat and shook her hair free from its bun. She offered a friendly smile.

"Phew! It's hot," she said. "I love this uniform, but it's a bit warm for this weather." She fanned herself with the hat and smiled at Lena, who could not stop staring at her. "Where are you traveling to?"

"Cheshire."

Lena had been practicing the pronunciation and thought she had perfected it. But that one word produced the response "Oh, where're you from?"

"Czechoslovakia," Lena said.

"My goodness, you're so brave," her companion replied. "You know all about invasion, don't you? You must know what to expect, unlike us."

"Not really." The idea surprised Lena. "I left before the Nazis arrived. But my family was there. My father and brother escaped, and they're in the army now, in this country. I'm going to see them."

"I just admire you people so much. I'm Jane, by the way. Jane Gaskell." She extended her hand and took Lena's in a surprisingly firm shake. "Would you like a sandwich?" She rummaged in her large handbag and produced a wax-paper bundle containing four neatly stacked cheese sandwiches oozing some kind of brown sauce. "My mum seems to think I'll starve unless she sends me off with enough food for a week."

The freckles flickered on her cheekbones as she spoke. She took a hefty bite out of one sandwich and offered the pile to Lena.

"Where are you going?" asked Lena.

"Reaseheath Agricultural College in Nantwich. One month of training before my assignment. Don't know where they'll post me yet."

"Post you?"

"Women's Land Army," Jane replied, pointing to the initials WLA on her green tie. "I have to do something for the war effort. But I can't stand the thought of being cooped up in an office or a munitions factory. This way, I'll be out in the fresh air." She leaned forward in her seat to add, "And I'm going to be earning forty-eight shillings a week, plus room and board."

Lena accepted a sandwich and discovered Branston pickle. She learned about the WLA and childhood summers spent on an uncle's farm in Devon and arguments with parents who were convinced that a girl's moral fiber would be undermined by going far from home to work in the fields. Lena laughed with a stranger and shared her sense of adventure as they both embarked on journeys into uncharted territory. And she knew this conversation would never have happened if she had traveled with Otto or any of the others. This experience was all hers. She did not have to filter it through anyone else's commentary. She was on her own out here in the world, traveling through England to a Czech army base. To face her father again after all this time. She could do this. Other young women were doing extraordinary things; she could, too.

In Nantwich, she inquired about the route to Cholmondeley Park. At first, no one understood her.

"Chol-mond-er-lee Park," she said, reading from her brother's letter.

"You must be wanting *Chumley* Park, love," said the woman in the newsagents on the High Street. "Where the army base is? Yes. That's how we says it, love. *Chumley*." She turned and shouted to an unseen person in the back room, "Stan! When's the Ramsey lad making his run up to Chumley? Young lady 'ere needs a lift."

A portly man emerged, dressed in a tweed jacket and cap, cigarette perched in the corner of his mouth. He gave Lena a quick nod and then engaged the woman behind the counter in a rapid exchange that Lena could barely follow. He spoke in one of those incomprehensible accents; to make matters worse, he mumbled around the cigarette, which dangled like a loose tooth. But when a young boy was summoned from the inner recesses and sent on an errand, Lena was given to understand that travel arrangements were being made on her behalf and that she was to stay put.

She browsed the racks of magazines, amused at the articles exhorting women to do their patriotic duty by maintaining all their efforts to look attractive. After several minutes, the door swung open with a clang of the bell, and in bounced the boy, with a young man in tow.

"There you are, Jim," the shopkeeper said. "Got a young lady 'ere needs you to take 'er out to Chumley."

The young man threw nervous, furtive glances at Lena and shuffled from one foot to the other.

"Go on, Jim," the woman said. "She ain't got all day."

"Thank you very much," Lena said, moving toward him with a smile to the rescue. "It's very kind of you."

He nodded and took her overnight bag. Without a word, he led her up the main street to the Post Office, where he motioned for her to wait while he went inside. Lena was once again left wondering what was happening, but he quickly reappeared, carrying a large canvas sack of letters, and approached a motorcycle leaning against the side of the building. A motorcycle! Good heavens!

Moments later, she was riding astride a motorcycle for the first time in her life, her valise installed behind her in a pannier, one arm around the waist of a silent stranger; the wind billowed her hair, as she tried to wedge her skirt down with her free hand to maintain some sort of decency. They sped past the rest of the town and into the countryside. The air was chilly now on her arms, and her teeth began to chatter. She was nervous and excited and slightly nauseous.

What was she going to say to Father? After she had sworn never to speak to him again, after he had beaten her a few weeks before she'd left Prague, she'd crept around the flat, peeking around corners to avoid bumping into him in the hall, maintaining a stony silence at the dinner table. She had never dreamed then that she would travel the length of a foreign country to seek him out.

The motorcycle banked around a curve, and the army base came into view. Lena was astonished. She had expected tents: Ernst had written that they were sleeping under canvas. But here, spread out across a huge meadow, were hundreds of small, pointed tents that reminded her of pictures she had seen of American Indian tepees. They were nestled in groups throughout the field and under the trees at the perimeter. But what really surprised Lena was the castle—there really was no other word for it. The imposing structure dominated the scene from its perch atop a rise to the right. There were three tall towers with turrets and narrow windows and a lake in front; all that was missing was a moat and drawbridge and knights in shining armor. The stone walls glowed in the afternoon sun, and from the largest tower flew the British and Czech flags side by side, their matching red, white, and blue colors flapping in the breeze. Standing firm together.

She dismounted at the gate and presented her identity card,

together with the letter and invitation from Ernst. The young guard saluted her.

"*Vítám vás, slečno.* Welcome, miss," he said. "Please wait here."

The guard lifted up the telephone in his little cubicle and waved the motorcyclist on to complete his delivery. Lena shivered. It was cool in the shade of the trees lining the driveway, and she pulled her cardigan out of her bag. As she crouched to readjust the clasp, she heard the crunching of gravel and a shout, and looked up to see a gangly young man in uniform, all arms and legs, running up the drive toward her. Could this be Ernst? And then he was upon her, towering above her, hugging her, pulling her against his rough army tunic, with a laugh two octaves lower than when she had last heard it, flinging his head back and losing his cap. He laughed again and stooped to retrieve it, and picked up her valise.

"You made it! How was your journey? Did you have trouble finding it? How are you? It's so good to see you!" he babbled, giving her no chance to answer. "Come to the officers' quarters. That's where Father is. He's a lieutenant colonel, you know."

"Goodness!" Lena had no sense of where a lieutenant colonel stood in the order of things, but it sounded impressive. "What about you?" she asked. "What's your rank?"

"I'm just a lowly private," Ernst said. "I was lucky they let me sign up at all. You're supposed to be eighteen. But Father talked them into it when we got to Belgrade."

Lena had so many questions; she didn't know where to start. So much had happened in the two years since she had last seen him.

"Are you all right?" she managed.

"Yes." He smiled. "I'm all right. Things are a lot better now that we're here. It was terrible in France, a real fiasco."

He led her up to a two-story building behind the big house. There were soldiers everywhere, all looking alike, with broad Slav faces, shorn hair, peaked caps, and green tunics. They huddled in groups, leaning on mud-splattered army vehicles, smoking, talking; some whistled as she passed.

"*Dobrý den!*" called out one, raising his cap in salute. "*Moc dobrý!*" said another. "Very beautiful!"

The Czech language: the comforting sounds of home. Lena laughed, very conscious of being the lone female in this man's world. Ernst opened the door and motioned for her to enter. The room was large, full of tables and officers, smoky and noisy but stunned into silence at her appearance.

She saw Father immediately; his back was to the entrance, but she recognized his prematurely bald scalp, with its rim of cropped, dark hair, and his strong, broad shoulders. He gave a startled, almost embarrassed look as he turned and his eyes fell upon her. He approached with a smile and reached out to hold her upper arm. This was as close as they would come to an embrace, Lena knew.

"Lena," he said, with surprising warmth in his voice. "I'm so glad to see you. I was very relieved to know you left Paris before the invasion."

He led her to a table, called for someone to bring drinks. Three officers, who had been studying a map at the other end of the table, nodded to Lena and withdrew in silence, taking the map with them.

"Father," Lena said, leaning forward, her fingers interlaced in front of her. She suddenly remembered the thin gold band on her finger and hastily covered it with the other hand. She wasn't sure it was real gold. They had found it in a pawnshop in Lewes; Otto thought they should avoid rousing any suspicions about the legitimacy of their marriage. But she didn't want Father to see it until she was ready to give him the news. "Tell me about Máma and Sasha," she said. "Where are they? How will they manage on their own?"

"They're still in the flat. I made arrangements. There is some money. The Nazis confiscated the business, but . . ." He gave a little shrug after his hallmark trailing *but*, which was both strange and familiar at the same time. "Your uncle Victor is going to keep an eye on them."

"Why couldn't you have brought them with you?" Lena asked.

"Your sister would never have made the journey," Father said. He looked around, scanning the room for something.

"What do you mean?" Lena said, her voice rising in alarm. "What's the matter with her?"

"Nothing's the matter with her, Lena," he said, turning back to her. "She's nine years old." He started to use the sharp, patronizing tone she knew only too well.

"Ten," Lena said.

"What?"

"She's ten."

"Right," he said. "Last month . . . her birthday." He looked at Lena and softened. "We considered it, us all going together, but . . ." He shook his head. "It was just as well. We had no idea how dangerous the border crossings would be."

"So, how is she? What is she doing?" Lena said.

"She's going to school. There's not much food, but . . ." He gave that shrug again. "She'll be all right. No one's going to bother them. They'll just lie low until this is all over."

I should ask him about himself, she thought, and asked, "How are you, Father?" She looked at him full-on now and took in his face. There were wrinkles at his temples and a crease in the center of his brow, a new weariness she had not noticed before. "Tell me about your journey."

"We made it," he said. "We had a close call crossing into Hungary, but . . ." He looked around for the drinks. "You must be thirsty, Lena," he said, waving to someone across the room.

Ernst said, "We had to run for it, under fire."

Lena turned quickly to her brother. For an instant, she thought he must be joking or exaggerating, like when he used to embellish some playground adventure or classroom prank. But she saw he was deadly serious.

"It was terrifying," he added. "We had to crawl through the mud to dodge the bullets."

"Oh my God," Lena said.

A young officer arrived with three cool glasses of blackcurrant squash. Lena had tried this drink once before at Muriel's and not cared for it, but now it tasted sweet and delicious; she was indeed thirsty. They sipped in silence for a few moments.

Lena said, "Then what happened?"

She listened intently as they described the arduous journey: not knowing whom to trust, whom to bribe; the days without food, the nights without sleep; the rigmarole of paperwork at the embassy in Belgrade; the arrival in France and the total chaos in Agde.

"Ernst was sent off to the front in the first batch," Father said. "To face the might of the German army, with no training, nothing. And I, an experienced soldier, was kept behind in camp."

"Luckily for me, if not for France," Ernst said, "we were soon met by the French army in rapid retreat, and so we all turned around and ran with them. Right back to the coast."

"Everything's different now that we're here," Father said. "Things are much more serious. We're getting new weapons. And President Beneš is coming to inspect us next week. We will make him proud." He lifted his shoulders and puffed out his chest, as though standing on parade already.

Lena looked around at the other officers in the room. A few were her father's age, but most much younger. She saw him through their eyes and knew that he must command respect. Those very qualities that she had come to fear—his tenacity, his brute strength, his rigid self-assurance—would all bode well for him here.

"You did the right thing coming here, Lena," he was saying. Lena was unsure whether he meant coming to this country, coming to Cheshire, or both. Before she could ask, he continued, "I need you to do something for me: I want you to write to your mother and tell her we've arrived safely."

"How would I do that?" Lena said. "I thought there was no way of getting letters to Czechoslovakia."

"Thomas Cook is taking correspondence through Portugal," he replied. "You can send a letter through the London office."

"Why don't *you* write to her?"

"It would be far too dangerous for her to receive anything from the army base here. It would attract too much attention. Everything out of here is heavily censored and covered with official authorization stamps." He glanced over his shoulder and lowered his voice. "Write to her, saying you have seen us. Don't say anything about the army. I just want her to know we made it."

How could she not do as he asked? It wasn't simply a newfound willingness to do something he asked of her—she, too, wanted Máma to know that they'd arrived. That they were all here, in England. Safe, for the time being. Now that she knew there was a way to get a letter through to Prague, it seemed simple enough. She would write to her mother.

But it was a decision that would come to haunt her in the years ahead.

CHAPTER 25

CHESHIRE, JULY 1940

D inner was held in the castle's great hall, a cavernous room with a massive stone fireplace at one end and swords and shields decorated with coats of arms displayed along the walls. Lena was seated opposite her father and next to Ernst, who squirmed with excitement at being permitted to join them in the officers' quarters. On her other side, to her immediate left, was a handsome young captain from Brno. There must have been fifty seated at the long, narrow table. The vast space echoed with voices and laughter and the scraping of cutlery on plates. Lena looked across at her father and saw her reflection in the long mirror on the opposite wall. She looked anomalous in her light blue cotton dress, sitting in a sea of army tunics. But there was color in her cheeks; she had caught some sun in the recent fine weather. Before dinner, she had freshened up in the cloakroom, and her hair was behaving itself; she looked presentable.

At first, she exchanged pleasantries with the captain. He asked her about her departure from Czechoslovakia and the time she had spent in Paris.

"I loved Paris," she said. "I was reluctant to leave. Good thing I did, of course."

"What did you like best about Paris?" he asked with a smile.

He offered her more bread from a large pewter bowl. Father was deep in conversation with a gray-haired officer to his right, but he turned now to hear Lena's response.

"Oh, goodness, so much," she said. "The street markets, the cafés, the Left Bank. And the people. I really liked the people."

"Humph!" Father said from across the table. "They proved to be completely useless in the face of the Nazis. I've never seen such panic and disorganization."

"I hardly think—"

"Imbeciles!" he said. "They behaved like a nation of imbeciles."

"You can't blame the French for being overrun by the Blitzkrieg," Lena said. "Everyone has been overwhelmed: the Dutch, the Belgians. And the Czechs," she added.

"But France is a great power!" He was raising his voice now, attracting attention from several neighbors. Other conversations petered out. "It was that damn socialist government that destroyed them. Made them completely defenseless, undermined their morale. Spineless cowards."

"With all due respect, sir . . ." The gallant young officer at her side was trying to intervene, but Lena could see where this was headed.

"For heaven's sake, Bartoš," Father said, "you saw it with your own eyes. That's what socialism will do for you."

The arrival of the main course provided a brief distraction: two serving boys passed out plates of steaming goulash and mashed potatoes. It smelled good. Lena hoped this might lead to a change of subject.

But then Ernst jumped into the fray.

"Father's right about that," he said helping himself to a mass of potato. "The way they retreated in the face of the enemy. No leadership. The highest officers drove back to the coast as fast as their fancy cars could carry them, followed by the lower-ranking officers and then, behind them, the men on foot."

"Exactly," Father said, pointing at Lena with a forkful of meat. "No moral fiber."

"I would have thought, if anything, that demonstrates a failure to follow egalitarian principles," Lena said. Captain Bartoš turned to her with a startled expression; whether he was surprised she had answered back or surprised that she might have a sensible idea in her head, she couldn't say.

Father ignored her comment. "The Bolsheviks have shown their true colors now," he continued. "The Hitler-Stalin pact. Fascism and socialism. One and the same thing. I always said so."

She should change the subject. Or just keep quiet.

"Actually, at one time you said the best thing about fascism was that it would stop the spread of socialism," she heard herself say. "I see you've changed your tune."

His fist slammed the table, and Lena flinched.

"Damn it, girl!" he shouted. "I see you've lost none of your insolence. You should be ashamed of yourself. You will not speak to me like that!"

Now she *was* going to shut up. She swirled the goulash gravy into her mashed potatoes, but she had lost her appetite.

Captain Bartoš gave a little cough. "Did your father mention that President Beneš is coming here next week? The men are very excited."

Lena avoided eye contact with Father for the rest of the meal and tried to make small talk with Ernst. Inside, she was seething, reliving the argument in her head, running through all the counterpoints she could have offered if they had not been in such a public setting. Of course she and her friends had been stunned by the Hitler-Stalin pact. It made no sense. Coming on the heels of the revelations about the atrocities and show trials in the Soviet Union, it was completely demoralizing. But that didn't mean they should abandon their dreams of changing the world.

She recalled the slums she'd seen from the train coming through Birmingham, the rows of crumbling terraced housing, the grimy poverty. No one should have to live like that. There were plenty of resources to go around in this rich country. Just take a look at this place, the castle and its splendid grounds. It was fine as an army base, but the thought that in peacetime it would house just one family: what an outrage! Ernst had told her before dinner that Lord Somebody-or-Other who owned it was now confined to a mere ten rooms in the east wing. Ten rooms! What made him any better than the people who lived in the slums?

At one time, Lena had placed so much hope in the socialist system that the Bolsheviks were creating. It was incomprehensible that they were now allied with the Nazis, but Otto maintained it was a strategic move on Stalin's part, to buy more time. She hoped that was true. Not that Father would have accepted that argument. But she didn't want to fight with him in public. Angry as she was, it didn't seem right to insult him in front of his men.

She would have to find an opportunity to tell him she was married. Father had asked her nothing about her life in England, how she'd arrived here, whom she was with. And he still hadn't noticed her ring. She'd been hiding that finger as much as possible—tucking the left hand into her pocket or covering it with the right. Her identity card still had her maiden name, and she'd been presented to everyone as Miss Kulkova. But she would have to tell Father soon.

Captain Bartoš had noticed when they were first introduced, before dinner. Father stepped away to converse with another officer. Lena lifted her hand to chase a stray lock of hair, and she saw the captain's eyes rest on the ring. She was standing in the sunshine, and it must have caught the light. A look of confusion crossed his face.

"I beg your pardon," he said. "I thought I heard your father say you were Miss Kulkova." He kept his voice low; Lena didn't think anyone else had heard. She had no choice but to throw herself at his mercy.

"I haven't told my father yet," she whispered.

Captain Bartoš nodded and smiled.

They emerged after dinner and stood in a small group, taking in the view from the terrace. The lake shimmered in the evening glow; beyond lay the throng of tents. A fish flashed into sight, before disappearing again below the surface. To the left, a row of tall poplars cast long shadows across the gravel driveway circle.

"It's beautiful," Lena said. "Can we walk a little before it gets dark?"

"Yes, yes," Father said with a vague wave. "Go ahead. Ernst can show you around."

"Please, come with me," Lena said. "We need to talk."

"I don't see what else there is to say, Lena. You know we'll never see eye to eye on these matters."

"I'm not talking about politics. There are other things. . . ." She made a move toward the lake. "Can we go this way?"

He followed her down the driveway. Ernst, too. Their feet crunched on the gravel. They passed a green Bedford lorry stacked with crates; two young officers were inspecting the contents. Father peered inside.

"Good, good," he said, with a nod of approval. He turned to Lena. "Finally we're getting some decent weapons. At one time, our army was one of the best equipped in Europe. But we left it all for Hitler."

"Father," Lena said. She would just have to come right out with it. "I have to tell you something: I'm married."

"What?"

"I got married."

"When was this?"

"Oh . . . last week." She couldn't bring herself to say "two days ago."

"Last week? When you already knew I was coming over here?" His voice rose several decibels. "You couldn't have waited to ask my permission?"

"Father," she said, trying to keep calm. "I am twenty-one years old. I don't need your permission." She aimed for a path that led around the field containing the tents.

"Who's the lucky man?" Ernst asked.

"Otto," she said. "Otto Eisenberg."

"Not that communist you associated with in Prague," Father said. "What's he doing over here?"

"He's doing what everyone else is doing: running away from Hitler."

"He's German, isn't he?"

"Yes. He was almost arrested in Berlin in '33."

"Why on earth did you do this, Lena?" Father said. "This is not a good time to think about marriage, with the war and everything. You should have waited until you had discussed it with me."

"This can't be a good time to be married to a German," Ernst piped in.

Lena clenched her fists and dug her fingernails into her palms. She stopped. Father and Ernst continued for another two steps and then turned to look back at her. She was not going to put up with this. She had not come all this way to be insulted. She was a grown woman, and she deserved some respect.

"For your information, it was Otto who found a way to get me out of Paris just before the invasion," she said. She could feel her voice quivering. She was determined not to burst into tears. "And I married him because I love him," she heard herself say. "You could just wish me well, instead of always having to criticize everything I do."

"Yes, but . . . ," Ernst said.

He sounded just like Father. "Not you, too," she shouted.

Lena spun around and retraced her steps toward the officers' mess, where she feigned a headache and asked to retire early. She was shown to a small room with a cot and a washstand, right off the officers' meeting room. She lay awake, listening to the sounds of laughter next door, before exhaustion finally overtook her and drove her into a deep sleep.

The following morning, Ernst rode with her in the army lorry to take her back to the station. It was much cooler, and a haze hung over the valley. The lorry was noisy and creaky, the seat uncomfortable. Ernst chatted with the driver, a sergeant from Plzeň; Lena couldn't hear their conversation over the roar of the engine. She tried to remember how far it was into town. It had seemed close on the motorcycle the day before, but now it was taking forever.

She was glad that half her family was here in England. But she couldn't help feeling as if it was the wrong half. She was furious with Father, and the way Ernst had to agree with everything he said was pathetic. She understood their journey had thrown them together, but couldn't he see that Father was being unreasonable?

It was Máma and Sasha whom she missed most, now more than ever, with a raw craving. The arguments themselves conjured up memories of fights at home, of Máma's attempts to smooth things over, and Lena's retreat to Sasha's bedroom to cuddle her and read a bedtime story; she could almost smell Sasha's soft skin now, feel her leaning into her, hear her laughter. She thought of Máma and Sasha stuck in Prague, tried to imagine what their life was like. Máma would be worried about them all. Lena must try to get a letter to her, make inquiries about the Thomas Cook arrangement.

At the station, Ernst offered her a hand as she jumped down from the cab. They stood on the curb, half a meter apart. He rearranged the cap on his head.

"How long will you be based here?" she asked.

He shrugged. "Who knows?" Now he fiddled with the collar of his tunic. It was as if he were playing dress-up in a costume that didn't fit.

"I don't know when . . . if I could afford to come again," Lena said.

He nodded. "I understand."

"So." They seemed to have run out of things to say. "Take good care of yourself." She gave him a quick hug.

"You too."

She entered the station. She was ready to go home. Home? Yes, home to Upper Wolmingham. That was her home, for the time being, at least, a place where she could be herself and be among people who saw the world as she saw it. She had told her father that she loved Otto. Was that true? It had just tumbled out. Yet she and Otto, and Peter and all the others—they were all in this together. Otto an orphan, estranged from his brother, Peter an only child, his parents quite elderly already; there was no news from them. Lotti worried about her mother, who had been in poor health for many years. Emil was separated from his brother; no word from Josef since the letter from Lithuania. All they had now was each other. Otto was right about that. She had escaped Paris and he had escaped internment, and they had each other. And the beautiful village, and the warmth of Muriel's family. That was home.

Lena returned to Oak Tree Cottage four trains and many hours later. The evening was warm, the back door open to the sweet, still air. She could see the others in the back, but Otto was on the sofa, reading. He jumped up immediately and pulled her into a fierce, urgent hug that took her by surprise.

"How was your father?" he asked.

"Otto, what's wrong?" she said at the same time.

Otto picked up *The Times* and pointed to a headline: ARAN-DORA STAR TORPEDOED.

"I don't understand," Lena said.

"Read it."

Lena quickly scanned the page. The *Arandora Star*, loaded with 1,500 enemy aliens, internees being deported to Canada, had been struck by a German U-boat off the coast of Ireland. Seven hundred were confirmed drowned.

"I think people I knew from the racetrack were on that ship," Otto said. There was a tremulous quality to his voice that Lena had never heard before.

"What?"

"People were being sent off. No one knew where, but there were rumors."

Lena looked again at the article. "But it says here only confirmed Nazis were deported."

"I don't believe it. They were selecting people completely at random." He pulled her head onto his chest. "Remember that young boy I told you about? Karl was his name." He made a guttural sound in his throat, as if he were about to say more but the words were ambushed there. He ran his fingers through her hair. Lena yielded to a new wave of tenderness. Otto wasn't perfect, but he was here with her, and she didn't want to be alone. She looked up into his eyes. There was a new vulnerability in his face that perturbed Lena and charmed her at the same time.

"I could have been on that boat," he said, his voice choking. "They called me, but I gave my place to Karl so he could be with his father."

They went out for a walk in the indigo twilight, strolling hand in hand toward the recreation ground. The swallows—or were they bats?—swooped between the trees, the vibration of their wings a parting chorus for the fading day. Lena looked across the field to the woods beyond, to the distant spire of the church at Elminghurst peeking over the treetops. The view was familiar, but something in the landscape had shifted.

CHAPTER 26

SUSSEX, AUGUST 1940

Lena walked to the shop to get bread. She opened the door—and literally bumped into Eva. They both gave a startled cry.

"Eva! *Dobré nebesa!* What on earth are you doing here?"

"I was just asking directions to your house," Eva laughed. She adjusted a gray and mauve hat that was perched on her head at a jaunty angle.

"I thought you were coming tomorrow."

"I came a day early. To spend more time together," Eva said. "I hope that's all right."

"Yes. Yes, of course."

"You don't sound so sure."

"No, of course it's wonderful. You just took me by surprise." Lena wrapped her in a hug. "You look very smart." Eva's dress matched her hat, the material stiff and starchy, obviously brand new.

Eva gave a nonchalant shrug. "Oh, well, you know."

"How on earth could you afford a dress like that?"

"I met someone. He treated me."

"Eva, you're amazing. I don't know how you do it. I have to get some bread," Lena said, taking her by the arm.

"This village is very picturesque," Eva said. "It's like something out of a fairy tale."

Lena switched to English as she led the way back into the shop. "Later, I will show you everything."

But Eva continued in Czech. "*Už jsem to viděla.* I walked all the way from the station. I think I've seen most of what there is."

Lena laughed. "There's so much more! I have to show you the fields and the woods, and wait till you see Muriel's house! It's fifteenth-century, really charming."

Back at Oak Tree Cottage, Lena put the water on for tea. Otto sat outside in the garden with the newspaper, poring over the list of names of people lost on the *Arandora Star.* The others were out for a walk.

"I went to see my father and Ernst up in Cheshire at the Czech army base the week before last," Lena said. "My father hasn't changed one bit. He's still trying to tell me how to lead my life. We got into one argument after another."

"I'm not surprised."

"Have you heard anything from your family?"

"No, nothing," Eva said, as Lena fiddled with the primus stove, trying to turn up the flame. "So, tell me all about your wedding. How did Otto propose? Was it very romantic?"

Lena laughed lightly. "It wasn't quite like that. We more or less had to get married to keep Otto out of trouble with the authorities here. But we're happy. He's being very nice to me these days."

"He was certainly very keen to get you here."

"What about you and Heinz?" Lena said. "What happened with those plans to go to America?"

Eva took a deep breath. "I have no idea where Heinz is," she said. "He was arrested by the French police. About a month before the invasion."

"Oh my God. Why?"

"Initially on some sort of visa technicality, I believe. But then they discovered one of his schemes. You know, all that black-market stuff."

Lena carried a tray with a teapot, a bottle of milk, and two thick white mugs into the living room and set it on the floor in front of the sofa. She looked at Eva, waiting for more.

"To be honest," Eva said, "I lost touch with him just before he was arrested."

"What do you mean?"

"We had an argument. I went away for a couple of days to see my cousin in Normandy. I came home early."

Eva averted her eyes and picked up the cat, which was rubbing up against her ankles, and settled him on her lap.

"I came home and found Heinz with Marguerite," she said. "She was leaving his apartment, looking flustered and shocked to see me. I was livid. I said things I shouldn't have said, wouldn't listen to anything she was trying to tell me. I refused to speak to either of them again."

"Marguerite was with Heinz?"

"That's what I thought. But she wrote me a note, said it had all been a big misunderstanding. But I refused to see her. Until it was too late." Eva's hands began to tremble as she continued: "The Germans were advancing. I went to find her so we could leave Paris together. But she had already left."

"Where did she go?"

"I'm not sure. I suppose she was heading for her aunt and uncle's place in the South. That's what Mme. Verbié said. You remember your Mme. Verbié?"

"Yes, of course."

"She was very nice to me. By that time, it was difficult to get on any trains leaving the city. She found a neighbor to take me in his car. Squeezed me in with his wife and their three dogs and all their luggage. French Jews. I rode with them as far as Poitiers."

"What happened to Marguerite?"

"I don't know. It was utter chaos on the roads. There was no way to find her. In the end, I had to save myself and get south as fast as possible. I heard about the Czech army base at Agde, and that there were ships leaving from there for England, and I decided to go there."

A silence fell between them. Masaryk purred on.

"I feel so bad about this, Lena. I know you must hate me. Marguerite and I always said we would stick together. I let her down. I was being so stupid and stubborn. I just hope she's safe somewhere in the unoccupied zone."

Lena placed her arms around Eva and rocked her gently. The cat jumped off with a squawk. Lena said, "I don't blame you. You weren't to know it would turn out that way. Everything is shifting all the time. You can't have an ordinary argument anymore. When you're ready to smooth things over, the other person could have disappeared. Missing. Like so many."

The next morning, they woke up to a new decree from the Home Office that sent them into a frenzy. All foreign nationals, so-called "friendly" or not, were to be banished from the "sensitive areas" within forty miles of the south coast. They would all have to leave Upper Wolmingham.

There were to be no exceptions. The good news was that other restrictions were to be lifted. The refugees would be able to work. The powers that be finally realized it made no sense to keep them idle when factories were desperate. The Czech Refugee Office would assign them to employment in essential sectors and help locate housing in London. And the men would be permitted to join the Pioneer Corp, constructing bomb shelters. There were hints that even the British armed forces were a possibility.

Emil was ecstatic. He was determined to fly with the RAF. He fashioned paper planes out of newspaper and aimed them across the room, adding sound effects to simulate the drone of engines and the crashing of bombs.

"You could apply, too, Tomas," he said.

"Don't be absurd," Tomas said. "They'll never take me with my eyesight."

"Let's find out if we can train to be nurses," Lotti said.

"I could never do that," Lena said. "I'm far too squeamish." But she wasn't afraid of hard work and wanted to make a contribution. She wasn't sure she had any skills, though, except for typing. Perhaps they would need typists.

Otto was excited. "We'll join the ranks of the proletariat," he said. "That will be interesting."

Muriel had a small gathering that night, and although the mood was somber, Lena was determined to have a good time, and for Eva to enjoy it, too. She wanted to show Eva that she harbored no ill will over the events in Paris.

Alistair took Eva under his wing to introduce her to the other guests while Lena helped Muriel with final preparations in the kitchen.

"I can't believe you're all going to leave us," Muriel said.

"I know," Lena replied. "I've been here only a few months, but it feels like home." She was going to get tearful if she didn't change the subject. "My goodness, what are you cooking?"

"Rabbit stew," said Muriel. "Old Pritchard has rabbits all over his land and is happy to get rid of them. He gave me three this morning. Off rations, of course. I'm trying not to think of them as sweet little bunnies." She gingerly groped for the casserole lid with an oven glove. "I hope this will taste all right. It's rather an experiment."

"It smells wonderful." Lena said then added, "Is Milton coming tonight?"

"I don't think so," Muriel said. "He thought all leave would be canceled. They're on full alert this weekend. It's the anniversary of the start of the last war—perfect timing for the invasion, for Hitler's ultimate revenge. Moreover, it's the full moon."

"Do you think it really will be this weekend?" Lena asked. They might have been discussing a much-anticipated social event.

"Who knows? If not, there will be another set of theories about why next week is the obvious date."

Alistair stuck his head into the kitchen. "Do we have time for a game of charades before dinner?" he asked.

"No, it's just about ready," Muriel said.

Lena went in search of Eva. She found her out on the terrace, sitting on the low wall in a tête-à-tête with Emil. Lena admired the view, drinking it in for one last time. She felt something brush against her sleeve; Alistair stood next to her.

"It's spectacular at this time of evening, isn't it?" he said.

"Yes. I'm going to miss it."

"You'll enjoy London, my dear. It's a delightful place."

Lena looked into his kind face. "Isn't Hitler going to bomb it to smithers?" she asked.

Smithers? No, that wasn't the right word, was it?

Alistair's eyebrows knitted in confusion for a moment; then he smiled. "Smithereens? Let's hope not. We'll have to put our faith in Milton and his splendid anti-aircraft fellows. They'll do their damnedest to stop him."

PART III

CHAPTER 27

LONDON, FEBRUARY 1944

L ena hurried up the Gray's Inn Road, glancing over her shoulder every half block to see if a bus was coming. She'd hop on the number 17 if one came, but she wasn't going to stand and wait.

Lotti was coming to dinner, and Lena wanted to prepare something special. Lotti's note said she had some exciting news. Lena tried to guess. Word from home? There was always a hope, a twinge of excitement at the possibility, although there'd been none for years now. A promotion for Peter? Perhaps—he was doing well as a radio technician in the RAF. Or possibly Lotti was finally to be offered the chance to train as a full-fledged nurse at Barts, the hospital in Smithfield.

A blast of cold air barreled down from King's Cross. Still no sign of the bus. She turned down a side street in search of a more sheltered route, passing a heap of rubble where once a house had brimmed with life. On the next corner, she spotted a queue: the familiar orderly line of women in woolen coats and sturdy shoes, huddled together with shopping bags at the ready, patiently waiting their turn for whatever was being offered. The ubiquitous seductive queue, any queue—it was something she often joked about yet was unable to resist. This one, only about a dozen strong, was in front of a greengrocer's. Partially depleted boxes of root vegetables were arrayed outside.

"What's here?" she asked the woman at the end of the line.

"I dunno, love. Just got 'ere meself."

Lena moved forward to peek into the dimly lit shop. A bare lightbulb hung over the counter, where a tall, gray-haired man was measuring something into the steel pan on the scales. Two women made their exit. They proudly displayed their bounty.

"He's got onions," announced one. "Only one pound per person, but he gave me extra for me mum. She's stuck indoors with her legs playin' up."

Onions! That did sound good. Onions had been off rations and exempt from distribution control for several months, but Lena hadn't seen one in weeks. She looked at her watch. Nearly five thirty. She should be getting home. But an onion would be just the thing to spruce up the potatoes and tinned Spam she was planning for tonight. She hesitated, looked again at the queue; there were now three more people in line. One of these women caught her eye.

"You comin' in?" she asked Lena, gesturing for her to go ahead. "Go on—you was 'ere before me, love."

"Thank you so much."

Fifteen minutes later, Lena emerged with her own supply of four firm yellow onions, which she stuffed into the bottom of her handbag. A fine drizzle had set in; buffeted by the wind, it carried a surprising punch, and Lena was wet by the time she reached home. She was fumbling for her keys on the doorstep, trying to retrieve them from among the onions, when Mavis Perkins, from the downstairs flat, joined her and let them both in.

"Goodness, Lena," she said. "You're drenched. Did you end up walking all the way home again?"

"I did," Lena said. "And look what I found at a greengrocer's off Acton Street." She pulled out two of the onions and handed them to Mavis. "I would never have found these if I'd been on the bus. These are for you."

"No, I couldn't."

"Go on—I have two more."

Lena climbed up the two flights of stairs to her own flat. She never knew when to expect Otto, couldn't keep up with his constantly changing shifts at the factory. And she never knew what kind of mess might await her.

"Hello," she called out.

She was greeted by silence from the two small rooms: the combined kitchen–dining room–living room that opened immediately from the front door, and the bedroom beyond. The tweed jacket that Otto wore when not in his work overalls lay on the floor. Lena scooped it up and threw it onto the green armchair, one of the few items they'd rescued when they'd been bombed out of Essex Road the year before. Three books were also scattered on the floor; she found space for them on the brick-supported planks that housed their modest library. The rest of the furniture—the dining table and chairs, the sofa and the small sideboard—was all standard issue under the Utility Scheme.

The light was fading outside; she lifted the blackout shades into place over the kitchen window. Piled high in the sink were the breakfast dishes and more. Why did he never clean up? Was it really too much to ask?

Keeping her coat on until she could make a fire, she set to scrubbing and peeling six large white potatoes from the box under the sink. She put them on to boil and cut up the onions, and then turned her attention to the coal bucket on the hearth. There were no large lumps left, only cobbles and slack. She managed to get a small fire going, just enough to take the chill off for an hour or two. She fried the onions until they were translucent, with amber edges. The potatoes were bubbling away on the stove when she heard the knocking on the front door two floors below. She ran down the stairs and let Lotti in.

"It's lovely to see you," Lena said, taking her by the hand and leading her upstairs. "Dinner's almost ready."

"Mmm. Smells good. I'm starving."

They sat at the table, eating heartily, talking and laughing. They hadn't seen each other in a month, even though Lotti lived only two blocks away. She worked grueling hours as a nursing assistant at the hospital and liked to save her days off for when Peter came home on leave.

"How is Peter?"

"He's doing very well. He was excited because one of the pilots took him up on a training flight. It was the first time he'd been in an aeroplane. He spends all his time on the ground, working on the radios."

"That's very important work, I imagine."

"Yes, but he loved being up in the plane." Lotti's cheeks glowed with delight, as if she had been the one taking the joyride.

Then Lena remembered Lotti's note. "You said you have some exciting news," she said.

Lotti beamed. "Guess," she said.

"I've been trying to guess all day. I don't know. Tell me."

"I'm pregnant!"

"My goodness!"

Lena looked at her friend again. She knew there was something radiant about her. This was so different from the last time, three years ago, when she'd been despondent. Lena had stayed up all night with her then, easing her through the cramps. The pills had done their magic: the worst had been over by morning.

As if reading her mind, Lotti said, "I definitely want to keep it this time. Everything is different now. Peter has a steady income. We're winning the war. It's only a matter of time. It has to be over soon."

"That's wonderful." She leaned over to hug Lotti. "How are you feeling? Let me look at you."

Lotti laughed and blushed and placed her hand over her stomach, still perfectly flat. "I'm feeling great. A little sick first thing in the mornings, but otherwise fine."

"When are you due?"

"October."

"Are you going to keep working at the hospital?"

"As long as I can."

"You'll get extra clothing coupons and two eggs a week!" Lena said. "Plus all that extra milk."

Lotti laughed again. "I don't really like milk. But I suppose I'll have to fatten myself up."

Lotti's joy was infectious, and Lena was thrilled for her. But, goodness, this was certainly not something she wanted for herself. She recalled the scare she'd had the previous month, when her own cycle had been delayed. She was always so careful. She studied the leaflets from the Mothers' Clinic, where she'd obtained her diaphragm. It wasn't foolproof, she understood that, so she kept a vigilant eye on the calendar and stayed up late reading, or invented a headache or cramps, on those critical days in the middle of the month. She had no idea why she'd been so late. She'd been relieved to see the bright red stain on her undergarments again.

Lotti was saying something about a woman at work who was going to give her a crib. "That's nice," Lena said.

The front door slammed two floors below, and she heard the familiar sound of Otto bounding up the stairs. She flinched inside, a small, reflexive tightening. What mood would he be in tonight? The door to the flat flung open to reveal him in his overalls and coat and the workingman's cloth cap he had taken to wearing. It must have stopped raining, for he was dry. There were gray circles under his eyes and a dark shadow on his chin; his cheeks were gaunt, his skin pale. He looked from Lena to Lotti and back to Lena again.

"Yew! What's that smell?" he said. "Have you been cooking onions in here?"

"Yes," Lena said. "I was lucky to find some."

"I could smell them halfway up the stairs."

"Hello, Otto," Lotti said. "How are you?"

He recovered his manners. "Good, good. How are you? How's Peter?" He planted a light kiss on Lena's forehead.

"Did you eat?" Lena said.

"Yes, at work. Liver and onions."

"So you had onions, too."

"They always have onions in the canteen. I don't know why you bother with scraping together stuff to cook at home. Go to the British Restaurant. It's all off rations, and it's cheap." He picked up the empty Spam tin. "How much did you spend on this? You could have bought a full dinner for both of you for only one and six."

"Sometimes I just like to cook at home and not sit at those noisy tables. I wanted to talk to Lotti in peace." Lena tried to keep her voice light. She didn't want another argument. "Lotti has some good news."

But they were interrupted by the Warning, the terrible, shrill, undulating howl of the siren.

Lena cringed. "Not again." She jumped up and took the plates to the sink. She turned to Lotti. "There's a pile of blankets on the windowsill in the bedroom. I'll get the holdall."

Behind the sofa she kept a bag stocked with two torches and extra batteries, a book with a few photographs from home and her passport tucked inside, a pack of cards, and a thermos of warm tea, which she replenished every morning. Except this morning she had forgotten; the tea would be tepid at best. She was getting slack.

There had been no raids for almost two weeks. Every pause raised the possibility that Hitler had run out of bombs or run out of steam or realized his was a lost cause. Lena was tired of all this; everyone was. In 1940, they'd been fresh and well fed. Now they were worn out. In 1940, Lena had almost welcomed the blitz. It was terrifying, yes, but there was nothing quite like a bombing raid to give you a sense of belonging. A bomb didn't care what sort of accent you had or where you came from—and everyone knew it. Huddled in the Tube station for the long nights of bombardment, Lena found a home in London. And the blitz gave birth to the first glimmer of hope that the Nazis' advance could be stopped, that Britain would not cave in.

Now, three and a half years later, it was clear the war would be won. Every day brought more good news: British and American forces were nibbling away at the foot of Italy; the Russians had broken through the siege of Leningrad and were inching toward Poland. It was only a matter of time. Lena heard that everywhere: it was only a matter of time. As if one were waiting for the water to boil or the dough to rise or a rose to bloom; one just had to sit back and wait.

Why, then, did they have to still tolerate this misery?

"Come on. Let's go." Lena stood with Lotti at the door, ready to leave. Otto hesitated in the middle of the room.

"I'm not going," he said. "I'll stay here. I can't stand the thought of another evening in the bloody Anderson shelter."

"Don't be ridiculous. What will happen to you if an incendiary drops on the roof or we get a direct hit?"

"I'll be fine. You go on. Anyway, there's not room for us all with Lotti here, too."

"I'll go to the public shelter," Lotti said.

"No, no, please," Otto said. "You go ahead. If it gets really heavy, I'll hunker down in the cupboard under the stairs."

Outside, the rise and fall of the siren continued unabated, now accompanied by the distant rumble of the approaching planes. Lena grabbed Otto's arm.

"No, you won't. We're going to stay together. Let's go to the Tube. Quick!"

In the hallway on the ground floor, they ran into Mavis and their other downstairs neighbors, the Clarks; they were retreating from the back garden.

"The Anderson's waterlogged," Mr. Clark said. "All that heavy rain last week."

So they all traipsed into the street. The pitch-black night was punctured by beacons of light from handheld torches. A small crowd hurried in silence to the Underground station. The drone of the bombers was getting closer. To the south, the swooping bands of the searchlights cut through the night sky. Lena tried to quell a rising panic; she felt exposed out in the open. She hooked her arm through Otto's and grabbed Lotti with her other hand, trying to keep them all together as she quickened their pace.

"Come on."

"Lena, calm down. They're still a few miles off," Otto said. "The men at work say that if a bomb has your number on it, it's going to get you, no matter what."

"That's absurd."

Lena had heard that before. It was so stupid. She thought of Tomas, killed in one of the last big raids three years before. Would the huge chunk of shrapnel have found him, tracked him down, if he had reached the shelter in time? Of course not.

Mr. Clark, two steps behind them, tapped her on the shoulder. "There's a street shelter right here. Used it once before, we did." He shone his light at a huge *S* and an arrow whitewashed on the brick wall to their left. "Let's go in here."

"It's probably full," Otto said. But he offered no resistance as their group moved down the stone steps, through the heavy wooden doors, into the sudden brightness of two long rows of faces looking up at them.

"Evening, all," Mr. Clark said. "Mind if we join you?"

The warden jumped up from his post by the door, knocking his ARP helmet askew. "Come in, come in," he said, moving a box to the floor. A wave of bottoms shuffled along the benches to clear more space. "More the merrier, I always say."

CHAPTER 28

LONDON, FEBRUARY 1944

This was a nasty one. The bombardment continued for hours, frighteningly close, with a fierce intensity. Even down in the shelter, the ground shook. The whistling shriek of the bombs and the thundering explosions felt right overhead. Lena resisted the instinct to duck at each new crash. Lotti leaned on her shoulder, trying to snooze. A man with a harmonica had been leading the crowd in renditions of Vera Lynn tunes during the early part of the raid, but he must have grown fatigued, for that had died down. Across from her, on the opposite bench, Otto played a desultory game of cards with a man in his sixties who kept dropping his cards onto his lap. A child cried at the far end; Lena tried to read but couldn't concentrate.

She always thought of her mother during a raid. Whenever she pictured Máma and Sasha back in Prague, she had a dreadful, tugging knot deep in her stomach. She was afraid for them. There had been no direct reply to the letter Lena had written back in 1940, at her father's insistence. Her Aunt Elsa had written a short response in the spring of '41: a tersely worded, one-page aerogram that found its way from Prague to Lisbon to Thomas Cook in London. Aunt Elsa knew Lena and Ernst and her father were all together in England, so Lena's letter must have arrived. But Máma herself had not replied. She must have been too fearful. Had Lena's letter placed her in danger?

For the past year, there had been horrifying reports, outlandish rumors about the treatment of Jews by the Nazis. Executions and wholesale massacres. In the East. Mostly in the Baltic States and the Soviet Union. And in the ghettos in Poland. Nothing like that in Prague, thank goodness. But it was very worrying.

She wanted Máma to know she was being brave through these raids, that she knew what to do, that she was here with friends and with Otto. She wanted Máma to know she could be proud of her; that she was practically fluent in English now; that she had been promoted to assistant supervisor at the Food Office; that she could quickly grasp the regular changes in the food rationing regulations. She wanted to tell Máma about the English people, how accepting they were of all this rationing, what a fair and equitable system it was, with many working people eating more balanced diets than before the war. She wanted Máma to know how accepted she felt here; that she had a nice little flat—tiny, but perfectly fine for her needs; that she was learning to cook with whatever was available.

If only there was a way to reach her. But all she could do was wait and hope.

It was just after midnight when the all clear sounded. At least the bombing didn't go on all night, like it had in the blitz.

"That's it, ladies and gents," the warden said. "Time to go 'ome to your beds." He threw open the doors to the outside world. He chuckled. "Ain't it nice of Hitler to give us a chance to get a bit o' kip? Watch your step, now."

They went out into the night. The acrid smell of smoldering debris filled the air. Emergency vehicles screeched through the streets. They picked their way through streets littered with shrapnel fragments, broken glass, and spent anti-aircraft shells. A huge blaze lit up the sky in the direction of King's Cross; its orange-gray glow took the edge off the darkness. Even so, Lena was afraid of tripping into some unseen crater, and she clutched at Otto and Lotti, one on each side, as they progressed gingerly down the block. Lena caught her toe on a large piece of metal and stumbled.

"Ouch!" she cried. "There's debris everywhere."

"I thought it sounded close," Otto said.

But two blocks farther, Lotti's street was unscathed.

"Thank God," she said. "I couldn't face . . . Not now."

"I know," Lena said, hugging her on her doorstep. "Are you going to be all right?"

"Yes. I'm exhausted. I'll go straight to sleep. I'm on duty at seven A.M."

Lena and Otto made their way home.

"Please, please, let's hope our street didn't get hit," Lena said. She also couldn't endure being bombed out again. Of course, that was nothing compared with being injured—or worse. But she couldn't bear the thought of picking through the filth and dust, trying to retrieve whatever was salvageable, those endless trips to the town hall to file for rehousing or new furniture, the forms to fill out. Starting all over again—if they could even find something.

As they turned the corner into Donegal Street, Lena held her breath. But it looked as if all was well. Just a few broken windows across the street, and some tiles fallen off the roof. They had been spared. It was all so arbitrary. Lena didn't believe that nonsense about a bomb having your number on it. But how *was* one to make sense of it, who was hit and who wasn't, who survived and who perished? You did your best, you took sensible precautions, heeded the warnings—but that didn't always save you. Shelters weren't infallible.

Sometimes there was no escape. Some people—like Lena's friend, Sheila, at work—believed prayer could save you. But that didn't make sense to Lena, either. She had abandoned religion long ago. The events of the last few years had done nothing to tempt her back. If God was so powerful that he could heed your prayers, why couldn't he put a stop to all this? And what about those who died? Was she to think they had not prayed hard enough or well enough? That God had therefore punished them? If that were the case, this God seemed like a nasty piece of work.

No, Lena wasn't going to pray to a God she couldn't respect. But she pressed her thumbs and crossed her fingers, and when Sheila gave her a little wooden four-leaf clover for her birthday and explained it signified good luck, Lena was amused but touched. It came from Sheila's village near Belfast; it was smooth and painted bright green and fit snugly in her palm, and she saw no harm in keeping it—just in case. She tried to hold in her mind an image of the end of the war, and of being with Máma and Sasha. The song the people sang in the shelter reverberated through her head:

I know we'll meet again/ Some sunny day.

Ultimately, deep down, we all believe we will survive. How else to carry on? We all believe we are immortal, invincible, in spite of all the evidence to the contrary.

The following morning, Lena was startled awake by the sound of pounding on the front door. She grabbed her watch. It was seven thirty. Who on earth could it be at this hour?

She threw her overcoat over her pajamas. Otto was fast asleep, curled on his side, just his hair protruding from the covers. She had forgotten to ask what time he had to work this morning. She slipped on her shoes and went downstairs.

Lena opened the front door to the sight of Eva standing on the stoop, suitcase in hand. She looked haggard around the eyes, but her hair was carefully styled, as usual, and . . . was that lipstick? Where had she found that?

"Thank goodness! You're still here," she said breathlessly. "I was afraid you might have left for work."

Lena ushered her in and gave her a hug. "*Co je?*" she said. "What's wrong?"

"I was bombed out last night. Huge raids in Hackney. Like nothing we've seen in years."

"Yes, we were hit hard here, too." They started up the stairs.

"Oh, this is nothing compared with the Hackney Road. Whole streets knocked out. The East End always gets the worst of it."

Lena let it stand. This kind of one-upmanship was common at work; she didn't see the point. There was never any way to prove who suffered the most. The BBC was always vague on details: keep the enemy guessing was the rule.

"Let's have some tea," she said, once they reached the flat.

"Put your things down. You must be exhausted. Are you still with What's-His-Name? Your airman?"

"Martin?" Eva tossed her hair back over her shoulders and twisted her face into a sneer of disgust. "Pfft . . . Turned out he was married! Can you believe that? With a two-year-old and another baby on the way!" She peered into the bedroom, where Otto was beginning to stir. Lena walked over and closed the door.

"I did meet an American sergeant the other night," Eva continued. "He gave me some lipstick! The Americans seem to be able to get their hands on anything. You wouldn't believe the food they eat. Plenty of meat, chocolate, everything. And he's going to bring me nylon stockings when he next comes to London on leave."

"You're amazing," Lena said with a laugh.

"Listen, do you think I could stay with you for a while?"

"You're welcome to our sofa," Lena said. "Until you find something." She had to offer.

"Are you still working at the Food Office?"

"Yes." Lena looked at her watch. "I have to get ready to leave."

"Can you pick me up a new ration book? I lost mine somewhere."

"You know I can't do that."

"Can't you just put an extra book in your handbag as you walk out the door?"

"No! I can't. Sorry. Do you still have your ID card?"

"Yes, I have that."

"So take it to the town hall and get reregistered here." Lena checked her watch again. "Then go to the Food Office at King's Cross. The local grocer is Edwards, on Pentonville Road. Look, I have to get dressed. Are you hungry?"

"Starving."

"Help yourself. There's bread on the shelf. Just the usual National Wheatmeal, I'm afraid, but I do have some nice plum jam from the country. My neighbor Mavis has a sister-in-law in Devon. She sent up a batch for Christmas."

Lena went into the bedroom, closing the door behind her. Otto was beginning to stir. "Are you working today?" she asked him.

"Late shift."

"Eva's here. She was bombed out last night. She needs to stay here, sleep on the sofa, until she finds something else."

"That could take a while."

"I know. I might ask Mavis if Eva can stay with her."

Lena dressed, then went back to the kitchen and poured the tea while Eva chatted away about her American, who had the improbable name of Chuck. Lena was only half listening, her mind already on work—they were preparing the changeover to the new twelve-month ration book, and there was already mass confusion in the office.

Just as she was preparing to leave, Otto emerged, fully dressed.

"Look who's here," Eva said, with a huge smile, as if his presence were somehow a surprise. "It's good to see you, Otto."

Otto smiled and ran his eyes over Eva. Lena noticed for the first time that she was wearing a very tight black woolen jumper that dramatically highlighted her curves. Otto poured himself tea.

"I've got to go," Lena said, giving him a kiss. "See you tonight."

She closed the door of the flat behind her and paused on the landing. She had a brief, uneasy feeling about what might happen behind that door. Then she hurried down the stairs.

CHAPTER 29

LONDON, MARCH 1944

"You can leave that now," Bert yelled. He was standing on the other side of the assembly line, next to a row of filling machines. "Bring over the twenty-millimeter shells from C Block."

Otto pretended not to hear him. The clamor of the massive machines provided good cover: the loud *plumph* of the necking machine as it came down and closed the casing, the thump as the girls released the foot pedals, the background whine of the grinding wheel. He hated this petit bourgeois foreman ordering him around.

But Bert was next to him now, tapping on his shoulder, shouting in his ear. This time it was just "Get the twenties from C," with a jerk of his head.

Otto grunted. He lifted three more packets of filled shells and placed them in the wooden box on the bench. He preferred to load them as they came off the line. Now they would pile up. Especially with Marge and . . . what was that other one's name? They all looked alike in their full-length protective clothing and their covered hair. But they were quick workers. Marge was the fastest, and there would be two full boxes' worth by the time he returned. It didn't make sense to change to the 20 mm's so soon before lunch.

He pushed open the heavy steel door and stepped into the blinding sunlight. It had turned into a sunny day. He squinted in the bright light reflected off the roof of C Block, across the yard. You didn't get the smell over here so much; the clouds of soot belching out of the power shop behind Small Arms usually wafted in the opposite direction. Here, it was nice enough to sit for a while, enjoy the sun. But, of course, if he dallied too long, Bert would be out looking for him with his "get a move on, we ain't got all day," when that was precisely what they did have: all day.

He entered C Block, adjusting his eyes to the dim light inside, and loaded up a cart with crates of empty shell cases. Out on the yard again, he spotted Harry Robinson pushing a similar load toward A Block. Harry was a porter, too, but he worked in Caps and Detonators. Harry was also the shop steward, and the only person here whom Otto considered a friend.

"Meetin' Monday night, Otto," Harry shouted across to him. Otto waved back in acknowledgment.

"Gotta talk to you at dinner," Harry yelled as he retreated.

Yes, he'd want to talk about the union meeting. It was hard to organize in here. There were all the different shifts and days off. And then the fact that it was mostly women. You couldn't get them to attend meetings. They said they had to rush off after work to shop or collect the kids. And when they'd tried to hold the meetings at lunchtime, Bert had reported them to Mr. Spencer himself, and there had been a hell of a fuss.

Otto remembered his first day here, how he'd been excited to join the proletariat. In Berlin, he'd stood at the factory gates, handing out broadsheets; now he would be inside. But it hadn't turned out the way he'd imagined. He had come prepared with ideas about how to organize, but just doing the work of a porter was much harder than he had anticipated. Most of his efforts in the first few weeks had been focused on keeping up with the pace. Once he'd grown more accustomed to the routine and his body was stronger, he'd discovered most people were not interested in his political ideas. Or they pretended not to understand his accent.

He had spoken to Lena about this once; she'd said naturally anti-German sentiment made it difficult for him to be an effective organizer. But no one except for Harry knew he was German. They fell for the story that he was Polish. His name didn't sound Polish, of course, but that showed how ignorant they were, these English workers. Harry said that for most of them, foreigners were indistinguishable. "You're all wogs, far as they concerned," was how he put it.

No, it wasn't that Otto was German; that wasn't the problem. He just didn't speak English well enough. Only last month, he'd been trying to make a very important point about the management's proposal to introduce piece rate, but apparently he didn't pronounce it correctly—it came out sounding more like *peez rate*—and Arthur, that odious little man from Receiving, yelled out, "I ate me bloody peas for dinner, mate," and the whole room collapsed in laughter, and Otto lost his train of thought and someone changed the subject and that was that.

He propped the door open with one foot and maneuvered his trolley over the threshold. The grimy, acid smell of the workshop stung his nostrils. Marge and the other girl were packing the completed .303s into the boxes at the end of the line. This was strictly against the rules, but Bert was nowhere in sight. Otto pushed his load over to the corner and went to finish what was supposed to be his job.

"Thanks," he said to Marge, as he took a stack of packets from her. "Can't understand why he had us change just before lunch."

"I know, love," she shouted over the machine noise. "But it gives us a bit of break, don't it?"

She had that yellowing of the skin around her eyes that came with constant exposure to the cordite. Otto was grateful he didn't have to handle it directly himself.

"Anyways," she continued, "can't be fussy. Them Spitfires needs them all, don't they?"

The Spitfires: providing escort to the bombers that were pummeling Berlin and Hamburg and Dresden night after night. This was what Otto couldn't understand: Why hadn't the German proletariat risen up in rebellion against the Nazis by now? Hitler had promised them no casualties. They must be completely disillusioned. Why weren't the workers taking over factories like this one in Germany, seizing the arms, and joining forces with their comrades in the advancing Red Army?

He loaded the boxes of completed shells onto another trolley, collected the docket from the shelf, and pushed out into the sunshine again to transport this consignment over to the building known as Shop 73. Here, rows of identical boxes were stamped and cataloged and constantly guarded by military police officers, before being shipped off under cover of darkness. The workers weren't supposed to know that they were making ammunition for Spitfires, but it was common knowledge.

As Otto approached, he saw the officer on duty was one he did not recognize: tall and thin and with that unmistakable English upper-class way of holding his head at just the right angle to regard everyone else with a sneer. Otto hoped he could avoid having to speak. With the regulars, he no longer worried about his foreign accent; he had managed to blend into the scenery enough to be accepted. But he didn't like the look of this one.

Otto handed him the docket for inspection and then pretended that the wheel of his cart needed attention, as a way to avoid eye contact. He jiggled the cart and nudged the caster with his boot. Behind him, he was relieved to see Fred Wallace coming over from the Booster Shop, wheezing under the strain of his load. He had to be sixty, with terrible lungs. Otto helped with the last few yards.

"Cor blimey," he whistled through the large gap in his front teeth. "Thanks, mate." He tipped his cap to Otto and then to the officer. "Here you are, guv." He stopped to catch his breath. "Ten crates of the finest. Each one with a special message for Jerry: 'Get lost!'" He started to laugh, setting off another bout of wheezing, but he continued undeterred. "I says to the girls back there . . ."

Fred was garrulous enough for both of them. Otto got away without saying a word. He hated sneaking around like this. Peter and Emil didn't have to. They were full-fledged Allied servicemen, welcomed like heroes into the RAF—Emil a pilot, just as he'd dreamed about back in the village, and Peter a qualified radio engineer—just because they were Czech, not German. Even Tomas had been assigned to a Civil Defense Service unit in West Ham, until a bomb got him.

What did the Czechs know about fighting the Nazis? They weren't there on the night of the Reichstag fire. They didn't witness the unleashing of the Stormtroopers and the Nazi propaganda machine; they didn't live through the mass arrests. Same went for Lena. She was so full of herself now, ever since her promotion to assistant something, always showing off how much she knew about the latest rationing rules, how well she knew the language, wanting to speak English at home.

Perhaps he could catch Eva tonight after work, take her out for a drink before Lena got home. Last Tuesday they'd gone to the King's Head and talked for hours. She wasn't afraid to speak German in public, and she listened attentively to everything he said, and she had a pert little nose and a dimple in her cheek when she smiled.

CHAPTER 30

LONDON, MARCH 1944

Lena spread the last of the butter ration over her warm toast then piled on a generous portion of jam. This was the jam from Devon, with large pieces of fruit—delicious. There were still three jars left. It was such a delight to be extravagant with something. She scooped up a spoonful containing half a plum and took a huge bite. The jam was soft and slightly tart and perfectly offset by the crunchy toast. She chewed slowly and deliberately, closing her eyes for a moment to savor the flavors and textures.

Lena and Otto were having breakfast together, alone for the first time in two weeks. Eva had left for an early appointment at the local labor exchange. She had refused to go back to work when she'd been bombed out of her flat. She hated her job at the aircraft factory in Mile End and was hoping to get reassigned to something closer to home—home now being here, on Donegal Street, though after Monday she would move downstairs with Mavis.

Lena was looking forward to having her living room back and a semblance of peace and quiet. She'd tried to ignore Eva's things piled all over the floor, but no matter where she looked, there they were: the open bag next to the sofa, with a tumble of clothes spilling forth; the stack of papers on the floor by the bookcase; the brush with trailing long hairs on the mantel.

"The Second Front demonstration is this Sunday." Otto peeked over the top of the newspaper. "Do you want to go?"

"Yes. We should. We have to do something." Something to try to persuade the government to act. Huge demonstrations the previous year, a chorus of pressure from backbench MPs, newspaper editorials, dozens of broadsheets and pamphlets—and still no invasion across the Channel. "Is it in Trafalgar Square?"

"Yes, I believe so." Otto flipped through the newspaper, scanning the headlines. "I'll check with Harry at work. He'll know." He cleared his throat. "And tomorrow, Eva wants to try to salvage a few things from her place. I said I'd go over to Hackney to help her with that."

"Oh." Lena looked at him. He said no more. He opened the newspaper, avoiding eye contact with Lena, chewing the lower corner of his lip in that irritating way of his. *The Times* hovered like a barricade between them. A photograph in the center of the page facing her transfixed Lena: a huge cloud of ash bellowing out from the top of a mountain. VESUVIUS ERUPTS, read the headline. After decades of lying dormant, the volcano was spewing lava over Allied and Nazi forces alike. The image of that explosion would stay with her for hours.

The rally seemed smaller than last year's; nevertheless, the streets were beginning to fill. As they approached from the Strand, the crowd grew and filed slowly into Trafalgar Square. It was hard to make much headway through the congestion.

"Let's cut through this way." Otto pulled at Lena's elbow and steered her into a dead-end mews.

"That's not the way," she said.

"This is a short cut," he said.

"No, it isn't."

But it was. An alley took them to the next street over, which also led into the square. The crowd was just as thick here, however, filling the entire street. They were jostled by men and women, young and old, bundled up against the wind, inching forward as if on a pilgrimage.

There were men in work overalls or khaki uniforms or their Sunday best, or up from the country in their tweeds and flannels, and women with stout legs and sturdy shoes. Just in front of them now, a little to the right, a group of factory girls, they must be, wearing trousers even here in the streets, their hair cut short in the bobbed style, five of them, arms linked, laughing, the one on the end smoking a cigarette. Lena stared at this mannish camaraderie, this carefree audacity. It was so different from how the girls at her office behaved. She was friendly enough with them, but she hadn't convinced any of them to come to the demonstration. They'd murmured excuses about having to wash their hair or visit their aunts.

They came to a standstill. Lena perched on tiptoe, catching glimpses of the throng fanning out toward the fountains and the lions, a sea of banners and flags of every hue. She loved being part of this pulsing, throbbing mass, with feet tramping, shoulders rubbing, all united for a common cause. They moved forward again. She saw the *tricolore* of the Free French, and the Polish flag, and, yes, over there a Czech flag, and of course a mass of red: plain red flags and the red flags with the hammer and sickle of the Soviet Union.

The usual smorgasbord of groups and campaigns were well represented. The Communist Party was out in force, as usual. Freed now from the mind-boggling acrobatics it had to perform to justify the Hitler-Stalin pact—once the Germans invaded the USSR—the Party could now resume its more comfortable role as self-righteous leader of the fight against the Nazis. Buoyed by universal admiration for the heroics of the Soviet army, membership was soaring. Lena had been amused the previous year, at the height of the Red Army fever, to see that even bastions of free-market enterprise, such as Selfridges and John Lewis, flew the hammer and sickle in Oxford Street. Such incongruous displays of enthusiasm had abated somewhat, but the Party was actively recruiting. Otto was being aggressively courted by a shop steward at the factory. She could tell he was tempted.

"Look at the size of the CP contingent," he said now. "Given the success of the Soviet army, the Party will be well positioned to create revolution in every country in Europe."

"Yes, but what sort of revolution?" Lena asked. "The Soviets haven't created a true socialist society. All that manipulation of truth, the arbitrary justice, and the show trials—that's not what we want." She had just read *Darkness at Noon*, and it had horrified her.

"It's produced a better army than any other country, hasn't it?" He thought *Darkness at Noon* was greatly distorted. "They're defeating the Nazis because the people know they're fighting for their own homeland, not a country controlled by capitalists."

"But what about Spain? You were so angry at the Soviets for their ineffective support of the Republicans. And the attacks by the Soviet secret police on the revolutionaries in Barcelona. You said that was the main reason for the fascist victory."

"That was a different set of circumstances, Lena. The Red Army is saving the world now."

They quarreled about everything these days. He surely knew that she was partly right, and she knew that he was, but they pushed away from each other, staring at each other like boxers in opposite corners of the ring. She wanted to call a truce here in public. They were together just the two of them by default. Lotti had to work. Eva had disappeared early the previous morning, leaving Otto looking sheepish about the planned excursion to Hackney; then she had reappeared late at night, without any explanation. That morning, she'd claimed she had an upset stomach. And Mavis . . . well, Mavis said the demonstration wasn't her cup of tea, and, really, didn't Mr. Churchill know best? Otto was planning to meet up with some of the men from work, but when he and Lena reached Charing Cross, they were nowhere to be found.

"Let's try over there," he said, taking her hand and pointing toward the National Gallery. "We'll get a better view."

She supposed he took her hand because there was no other way to stay together. But it felt oddly cold and clammy. They had not been intimate in how long? A week? No—longer than that. And when they did make love, it felt mechanical and perfunctory, Otto thumping away while Lena let her mind wander and waited for him to finish.

She followed him now as he forged a pathway to the opposite side of the square. Lena caught a glimpse of a huge banner unfurled at the base of Nelson's column: TODAY THE SECOND FRONT; TOMORROW THE BUILDING OF SOCIALISM. Someone was making a speech from an improvised platform, but the loudspeaker was malfunctioning and the words were lost in the wind. A man in the crowd yelled, "Second Front now!" over and over, and others joined in so loudly that no one could hear the speaker up front.

They made their way to the steps of the National Gallery to gain higher ground. The Trotskyists had set up here—the Revolutionary Communist Party and its rival the Workers International League glaring at each other over their banners, each declaring END THE IMPERIAL-IST WAR—and the Common Wealth Party and the Miners' Federation with placards calling for full implementation of the Beveridge Report and health insurance for all, and the Peace Pledge Union advocating an end to the bombing of German cities, and a middle-aged woman in brown Utility tweed and hair pulled back in a tight bun carrying a sign: INDEPENDENCE FOR INDIA NOW. It all seemed good-natured, a hodgepodge of good intentions, but Lena couldn't help wondering how they were ever going to agree enough to get anything done.

"This will do," Otto said, staking out a spot with a good view of the square. A man adjusted the loudspeakers up front, and suddenly the amplification system crackled into action and the crowd cheered. The president of the Miners' Federation was introduced and spoke in ardent tones about the long-standing friendship between the miners and the Red Army.

"The Russians are smashing away at the Nazis, and we are still getting ready," he bellowed. "What is Churchill waiting for?"

The crowd roared in approval. There were more speeches along these lines, but Lena found her attention drifting. A woman in her forties, perhaps, stood to their left, coat drawn tight across a large bosom, her hand slipped through the arm of a boy of about fifteen, tall and lanky. Her son, obviously. Was her husband in the forces here or overseas? How she must hope and pray that the war would be over before her son was old enough to be called up, too.

Lena heard a man behind her say, "This will be interesting." She redirected her attention to the podium, where a diminutive man was preparing to speak. He seemed dapper and subdued, compared with his predecessors, and waited patiently as someone lowered the microphone for him.

"Who's that?" Lena asked Otto.

"Victor Gollancz."

"The publisher?"

"Yes. He's a writer, too."

Of course. She knew that. She had seen his Penguin paperback, published the year before, on the plight of the Jews in Nazi-occupied Europe, although she had not been able to read more than a few pages. It had made her sick to her stomach.

"Shh," said someone behind them.

You did have to strain to hear him: "Inconceivable inhumanity. The Nazis are pursuing a policy of deliberate extermination of the Jews throughout occupied Europe. As many as one million may have been exterminated already. The longer the delay in the Second Front, the more lives are in danger."

There was muted applause all around. He continued in this vein, but Lena could no longer hear him. She could hear nothing; everything was muffled, as if she were underwater. She was very cold all of a sudden—shivering, icy, black inside—and everything was spinning. And now she was hot, hot, burning up. She tried to loosen the scarf around her neck, but something was pulling her down, down, something heavy; round and round she went, as if she were being pulled into the drain of a bathtub, round and round, and she was afraid she was going to vomit, and her knees buckled, and then the next thing she knew, her cheek was pressed against something hard. It was a button. A button on a large bosom. The same bosom that belonged to the mother of the boy, it must be. The woman was clutching her arm on one side, and Otto had her on the other.

"Blimey, love. You all right?" the woman said. She turned to Otto. "You'd better find her somewhere to sit." She stroked Lena's shoulder. "There, there, dear. It's all right."

Lena felt the blood returning to her face, her head beginning to clear. What had happened? The woman whispered, "You're not in the family way, are you, love?"

Lena shook her head. "No, no. I'm so sorry, so sorry."

People stared at her. She felt like such a fool. They cleared a path as Otto led her to the edge of the square. He helped her perch on a concrete ledge.

"Are you all right?" he asked after a few minutes.

"Yes, I'm fine." And indeed she was. The spinning had stopped. All back to normal. "I'm so sorry. I don't know what came over me. Go back and listen. I'll be fine sitting here."

She wanted some breathing space, to sit with what she'd just heard. The information about the fate of the Jews under Hitler wasn't really new, but it was too much to take in. The rumors couldn't be true. It couldn't be that bad. So why was everyone nodding in approval, agreeing, as if this were one more political debating point? These were real people they were talking about. People like Máma and Sasha.

Otto said, "I think they're finishing."

People were beginning to disperse, but someone was still speaking; Lena heard intermittent cheers. She wished Otto would go back to the speeches, but he hovered above her. She stood and brushed off the seat of her coat.

"Are you sure you're all right?" he asked again.

"Yes. I said I'm fine."

"Let's walk around this way."

He steered her toward the far side, but a phalanx of policemen blocked their way, so they retraced their steps.

"Yoo-hoo! Otto! Lena!" Where was that coming from? "Up here!"

Perched on the roof of a bus stop were five young men, relishing their prime vantage point, legs dangling over the edge with glee. One of them was waving. Lena knew that face, but it took her a moment to place it out of context.

"Just a jiffy," he shouted. "I'm coming down."

The face disappeared from the roof and reemerged seconds later at eye level. It was Milton Calder. He shook hands enthusiastically.

"I thought it was you! How wonderful to see you. I say, isn't this a simply splendid affair?" He swung his arm in an effusive gesture over the square. "How have you been? How is everybody? My goodness, it's been so long."

It had been almost three years—years that he seemed to have

worn well. Milton had a new sturdiness about him. Not so much a physical change, although he was perhaps broader across the shoulders; rather, he had settled into his body more, as if he were more prepared to own it. He was wearing a tweed jacket with leather elbow patches, and a blue-and-green tartan scarf. His hair was longer than the army-regulation short back and sides he had sported when they'd last seen him, his wavy chestnut curls neatly parted on the left and oiled into place. He smiled in obvious pleasure at this surprise encounter.

"We have to find somewhere to catch up," he insisted. "I don't know about you, but I'm starving. Let's go to the Lyons Corner House. I love that place, don't you? Elegance for the common man." He flashed a big grin.

That warm, sparkling smile: Lena remembered it well.

CHAPTER 31

LONDON, MARCH 1944

They walked together up Charing Cross Road.

"Are you still at that place in the East End?" Milton asked Otto. "A munitions factory, wasn't it?"

"Yes. That's right. I'm involved with the union. The shop steward is very left wing."

"That's good. What about your writing? Are you still working on your book?" Lena was sandwiched between them, trying to keep up with their long strides.

"No. Events just moved ahead too fast. The Spanish war seems like distant history."

"But it's so important to understand its lessons for building socialism after the war is over," Milton said.

"Yes, perhaps. But, frankly, I don't have much—how you say?—strength for writing after a long day at the factory."

"No, I suppose not."

Milton turned now to Lena. "And what about you? You must be working, too."

"Yes. I'm at the Food Office."

"How interesting."

"If you ever have any questions about the points system, Lena's the one to ask," Otto said, his tone sarcastic, though he stared straight ahead, his face inscrutable.

Why does he have to belittle my work? Lena thought.

The teashop was bustling, crowded with women and couples and soldiers and families with young children. The waitresses in their crisp black-and-white uniforms dashed among the rows of tables with great efficiency, presenting menus emblazoned with the slogan FOOD IS A MUNITION OF WAR. DON'T WASTE IT! The high ceiling was covered with a ragged tarpaulin, stretched like a battered veil between the supporting pillars and remnants of art deco plasterwork.

"Is this the place that kept going right through the blitz?" Lena asked.

"Yes, that's right," Milton said. "A bomb took out the water supply, but they managed to keep serving."

They decided on sausage rolls and fish-paste sandwiches, along with a large pot of tea.

"So, what about you?" Lena asked Milton, once they had placed their order. "What have you been doing? Are you still in the army?"

"No, I'm not. Did you hear I was injured?"

"No!" Lena blurted out, rather too loudly. A couple at the next table turned to stare.

"Yes, back in '41. Our AA unit took a direct hit." He removed the serviette from his plate and spread it on his lap. "I was damn lucky. Got away with a messed-up foot. Some of the others . . ." He paused and gave a tiny shudder. "Some of the other chaps weren't so fortunate."

"I'm so sorry." She couldn't help looking down at his feet. She hadn't noticed him limping.

"Oh, I'm all right now," he said. "Made a full recovery. Just a few scars to show for it. But the army didn't want me back."

"Why ever not?" asked Otto.

"Purely political. I was deemed too dangerous, a radical stirring up trouble. All those bored soldiers with time on their hands. It's fine for the Workers' Educational Association to teach literacy. But political literacy, class-consciousness? No. The army didn't take too kindly to that." He laughed. He was no longer the charming but rather immature child that Lena remembered from three years earlier, but she could still see his playful side. "I became a convenient scapegoat," he said, with a grin.

The waitress arrived with a teapot, milk pitcher, and sugar bowl. "Thank you so much." He picked up the teapot. "Shall I?"

He poured the tea, carefully supporting the lid as he tilted the pot. Lena found herself staring at his hands. They seemed strong yet gentle, with a few fine hairs, long, slender fingers, and carefully trimmed nails. The middle finger of the left hand bore a scar, a jagged pink line extending over both knuckles.

"So, where are you now?" Otto asked.

"I'm working for Mass Observation."

"For what?" Lena asked.

"Mass Observation. The social research organization. Surveying everything from eating habits to public reaction to the conscription of women."

"You must know Mass Observation," Otto said. "It's quoted all the time in the newspapers."

"What do you do, exactly?" Lena asked.

"I pull together the information gathered from interviews, surveys, questionnaires, that sort of thing. I write it up in a report." He took large gulps of tea, draining his cup in one swoop, and reached for the pot to pour himself more. "The Ministry of Information is very interested in our findings." He smiled. "How to keep up morale and whatnot."

"That sounds interesting."

"It's marvelous. A real glimpse into public opinion." He turned to Otto. "Speaking of public opinion, do you listen to German radio at all? Can you get it on shortwave?"

"No," said Otto. He looked at Lena. "I've been tempted, but Lena doesn't think it wise for me to do that."

"No, I suppose not." He smiled. "I see your point. Well, it's very interesting, you know, quite an eye-opener." Lena recalled now that he spoke German surprisingly well, thanks to a German governess in his childhood. "One gets such a different picture than from the BBC. I heard Goebbels and Göring the other day, speaking at a rally in Berlin."

"I don't know how you can bear to listen to them," Lena said.

"But it's fascinating, especially if you read between the lines. They spend most of their time talking about the Bolsheviks. One gets the impression the Germans are terrified of the Russians but almost contemptuous of the British." He turned to Otto again. "Are you hearing anything about underground resistance inside the Reich?"

The sandwiches and sausage rolls arrived, served on white china plates. Lena helped herself to a roll and bit eagerly into the pastry. It was surprisingly tasty. She quickly reached for some stray pieces crumbling down her chin.

Otto said, "These days, I have no contacts inside Germany."

"Do you think there will ever be a workers' revolt against the Nazis?"

"That's a very good question." Otto's tone became more animated. "Why has there been no effective anti-Hitler movement in Germany? It can't be explained simply by the efficiency of the Gestapo or the indoctrination of the masses. Objectively, there must be something, some benefit for the German proletariat." He was holding a sandwich in one hand, waving it in midair as he spoke. Lena was afraid he was about to launch into a major speech, but he appeared to think better of it. He took a bite and paused to chew. "This will all end with the defeat of the Reich," he continued. "Then we'll see. Then conditions may be ripe for revolution."

"Will you go back after the war?" Milton asked.

"Yes, I will definitely go back."

Lena stared at him in amazement. This was the first she'd heard of this. Go back to Germany after the war? To live among people who had raised their arms in Nazi salute and cheered at the burning of books? Who had stood by as Jewish shops were vandalized and property confiscated? Did he think she was going to go with him? Didn't he think this was something they should discuss? How could he sit there and make such an announcement when they had not even talked about it?

Otto and Milton continued talking, planning the postwar socialist revolution, but she wasn't paying attention. She was astonished and angry. What was he thinking, coming out with a statement like that in front of someone they'd not seen in years? It must be obvious that she was taken aback. Was he trying to make her look foolish? Or was he making it clear that he didn't envision them having a future together?

She looked at the couple at the next table, now engrossed in tender conversation. They were both in uniform, he in air force blue, she in khaki. They leaned into each other, foreheads pressed together, fingers interlocked among the tea things. Lena knew she shouldn't stare, but she felt mesmerized by their obvious devotion. Had she and Otto ever been like that? Yes, of course they had. Those early days in Prague and Paris. She'd been enthralled by him—or at least by the thrill of walking into places on his arm, places where everyone knew him and knew that she was his girl. And when she had first come to England, hadn't they been happy together then? It seemed like they had. She had been relieved to be out of Paris, and he had been released from internment—and then they had clung to each other in the first, terrifying months of the blitz, because what else could you do but cling to the person you found yourself standing next to? But surely, it was more than that; they had been in love. She had many happy memories: walks in the fields in Sussex, sharing a bath at The Hollow, living in their tiny flat on Essex Road. What had happened to all that tenderness?

A month earlier, Lena and Lotti had gone to the cinema to see *For Whom the Bell Tolls*. What an amazing story—ordinary people displaying such courage against the fascists. Of course, Lena had read the book, but seeing it up there on the screen, Gary Cooper and Ingrid Bergman clinging to each other, she had felt something tugging inside her: she wanted to feel passion again, to feel the earth move. Was it her fault that she didn't have that anymore with Otto? Now she realized it was not. If he could talk about going back to Germany, everything had changed. There was no treasure, no secret stash of ardor that could be rekindled if only she were more persistent. This realization opened up a whole new vista, a lifting of a weight that had been dragging her down without her even being aware of it. If Otto was going back to Germany and she was not— and most certainly she was not—then what? She wasn't sure. But she viewed the prospect with a calm curiosity.

Milton was looking at her and must have asked her a question.

"I'm sorry?" she said. She leaned forward and cupped her ear with her hand, as if the noise was the reason she had not heard.

"I beg your pardon," he said. "I don't mean to pry. I just wondered if . . . I don't suppose you've heard anything from your family? In Czechoslovakia, I mean."

"No, I haven't."

"Lena doesn't like to talk about it," Otto said.

"It must be very difficult," Milton said, "terrible, not knowing. And all these horrific accounts of deportations. You must be so worried."

"Yes," she muttered.

"Of course, some people are saying the reports are wildly exaggerated," he continued. "But it's one of the strongest arguments for the Second Front, on humanitarian grounds alone. I thought Gollancz was very eloquent on the matter today, didn't you?"

Lena hesitated. Otto jumped in and said, "Anyone who bothered to read *Mein Kampf* could have predicted this years ago. The original version, that is, not the sanitized English translation. Hitler made it quite clear what his plans for the Jews of Europe were."

"The situation is not as bad in Czechoslovakia as it is in Poland or the East," Lena said. "I'm sure if they were in real danger, my mother would find a way to keep my sister safe, get her into hiding or something."

There was an image that often popped into her mind, as if on a motion-picture screen: Sasha sitting at an unfamiliar kitchen table, waiting for the war to be over and for Lena to come and fetch her.

"Yes, I'm sure she would try that," Milton said. He paused for a moment and then continued, "And your brother?"

"He's still in the Czech army. They're stationed somewhere in Suffolk. Getting very bored. Waiting, like everyone else. My father was demobbed last year and is living with another retired officer near the base."

Milton smiled. "Mother will be so glad to hear that I ran into you," he said. "I know she misses all of you."

Muriel: Lena missed her, too. She felt a pang of guilt for not having kept in touch. It had been difficult; she'd had so many changes of address in the past three years.

"How is Muriel?"

"She's well, thank you. Although she's practically blind now. But it doesn't seem to slow her down. She's busy with Women's Voluntary Service work, organizing clothing exchanges for children and knitting socks for the troops. Then, every few weeks, she goes on a rampage against Churchill. She was furious when he forced the defeat of equal pay for women teachers. She stopped collecting salvage for two weeks and insisted on at least ten inches of water in the bathtub, saying it was immaterial who wins the war. Then she got over it." Milton laughed. "That's Mother for you."

Lena smiled at the image of Muriel on a rampage. "I feel bad for not writing to her. I meant to several times, but . . ." Why *hadn't* she written?

"The post has been so disrupted anyway."

"How is the village?" Lena asked.

"Swarming with Canadians, but otherwise, much the same." His face had a way of lighting up as he spoke. "The army has ruined the rhododendrons on the Manor House grounds, but otherwise the village has come through unscathed so far." The smile suddenly drained from his face as he added, "East Grinstead wasn't so lucky. You may have heard: the cinema was bombed last summer, and over a hundred people died. Mostly children, watching *Hopalong Cassidy*. Some of them were children from the village."

Lena shook her head. She had not heard. How could such a tragedy have gone unnoticed? Another scene of devastation among so many. When would it ever end?

Milton checked his watch. "Good Lord, look at the time. I hate to end this delightful conversation on such a glum note. But I really must go."

"Are you still living in Upper Wolmingham?" Otto asked.

"No, I have a place here in town. A flat in Mecklenburgh Square. But I go down to Sussex quite often." He waved for the bill. "I say, why don't you come down for the weekend sometime? Mother would love to have you."

"Well," Otto said, "I don't know . . . My shifts . . ."

"That would be wonderful," Lena said at the same time. "I would love to see her again."

Milton pulled out a small diary from the inside breast pocket of his jacket and extracted the miniature pencil nestled in its spine. "Let's see. How about the thirty-first?"

"Yes," Lena said. She did not look at Otto. "That would be perfect."

"I'll check with Mother, but I'm sure that will be all right with her." He opened a page at the back of the diary and handed it and the pencil to Lena. "If you jot down your address, I'll drop you a line to confirm." He watched her as she wrote. "Donegal Street?"

"Off Pentonville Road," Lena said.

"Of course. Not too far from me." He smiled. "How delightful that we ran into each other." He rose from the table. "Well, I hope to see you on the thirty-first. I usually take the 6:15 from Victoria."

"Six fifteen is perfect," Lena said.

CHAPTER 32

LONDON, MARCH 1944

Sheila O'Neill put down her pen and stretched, opening and closing her fist. The knuckles on her right hand were red and swollen, and the fingers acted as if they had a mind of their own, twisting away from the thumb. She massaged them gently, coaxing them straight. It was always worse on damp days. She looked at the stack of ration books she had completed and the much larger pile still left to go and looked at the clock: 12:15. She usually took her lunch at twelve thirty. Just a few more.

Gladys Woodruff was hunched over her desk, dipping her pen into the inkwell, taking the next book from her stack. Gladys didn't reveal her age to anyone, but with a grandson who was almost grown, she had to be old enough to avoid registration if she wanted to. But she worked harder than any of them and had terrible posture to show for it. Sheila straightened her own shoulders, rolled her head in a gentle circling motion to try to relax her neck, and returned to work.

She was still on the Js. Ah—Jesus. How could there be so many Johnsons? She lowered the ruler to the next name on the list and carefully transcribed the information onto the cover of the new Ration Book Six. Name: Mrs. Eliza Johnson. Address: 37 Baldwins Gardens. National Registration number: OJA-6386-18. Then Sheila recorded the serial number of the ration book in the ledger: BJ 320517. You had to be so careful. One wrong digit, and there would be a discrepancy that could undermine the whole war effort, if Mrs. Manson was to be believed.

The door leading to the front reception area swung open, and Lena Eisenberg walked in, carrying a stack of papers. Lena always preferred that the girls call her by her first name, even though Mrs. Manson frowned on such chummy behavior.

"How is it out there?" Sheila said.

"Pandemonium."

Lena was always using big words. You wouldn't think she could be so clever, with her being a foreigner and all.

"Everyone's confused about the single sheet of counterfoils for meat, eggs, fats, and cheese. Amazing how a separate page of coupons for each food has become the natural order of things."

Sheila didn't know what to make of this remark. She herself was still confused about the new system, even though Mrs. Manson had explained it in detail at last week's staff meeting, drawing simulations of the new pages on the blackboard, with squeaky white chalk that had set her teeth on edge. But now, when Lena laughed lightly, she laughed, too, not wanting to have missed a joke.

Lena looked at the heap of books in front of Sheila. "Do you want to change after lunch? I can have Mildred come in here, and you can go to the front, if you like."

"All right, thank you," Sheila said. "To be sure, my hand's really cramping up bad today."

Mrs. Manson emerged from the back office, waving a sheet of paper. She wore her usual tweed suit and crumpled white blouse, her gray hair escaping in turmoil from the hairpins above her ears.

"Ah, Mrs. Eisenberg," she said. "There you are." She lifted the spectacles that dangled around her neck and placed them on the bridge of her nose. "New instructions from the ministry, ladies," she announced. Her eyeglasses were coated with dust. "The National Milk-Cocoa Scheme is to be expanded for all young workers under the age of eighteen, not just those in factories." She looked up, as if expecting a response.

"Let me see," Lena said.

"They're sending twenty-pound containers of milk-cocoa powder to be distributed directly from here," Mrs. Manson said. "I don't know where on earth we'll put them."

Lena took the paper out of Mrs. Manson's hand and examined it. "They don't say how many will be delivered."

"No, they wouldn't, would they?"

"My sister says no one drinks that stuff anyway," Sheila said.

"I can hardly believe that, Miss O'Neill," Mrs. Manson said. "It's very nutritious."

"We can be getting some space in the cupboards under the counter," Lena said.

She still had a queer way of saying things sometimes. When Lena had started here three years before, Sheila had thought she must be stupid because she couldn't speak well at all, worse than Sheila's little niece Brigit, who was only five years old at the time. Lena had a funny accent, yes, but it wasn't just that. Lena had a strange way of mixing up words and didn't know the meaning of simple things like *parsnips* or *pilchards*. And then there was that time—which they still laughed about together now—when Lena had said *confence milk*, instead of *condensed*.

No, you wouldn't know it to listen to her, but in fact Lena was very brainy. For starters, she was always reading—big fat books with tiny print and no pictures. And when Sheila was having a hell of a time trying to work the teleprinters, it was Lena who came to the rescue and helped her thread the perforated tape into the reader. Sheila liked her more than anyone in the office, even though she did speak funny—funny peculiar, not funny ha-ha. Now, of course, Lena was the assistant supervisor and helped everyone, knew more than Mrs. Manson herself, if truth be told.

Lena looked at the clock. "Why don't you go for lunch now, Sheila?"

"Lovely," Sheila said. "I'm going to run over to that fishmonger in Covent Garden. Mildred said the queue wasn't too bad yesterday. Mammy's mad for a taste of fish. Will I pick some up for you, if I can?"

"No, my husband hates fish," Lena said.

It was odd to hear her speak of her husband. She didn't mention him often. She had when she first worked here, but not now. Sheila knew that Lena's husband was foreign, too—had to be, with a name like Eisenberg—and that he was a lot older and worked in a munitions factory in the East End. When they were bombed out last year, he couldn't—or wouldn't—take any time off work, and Lena had to do everything on her own, just as if her husband were away. But beyond that, he was a mystery. He had never been to the office, and Lena had never showed Sheila a photograph.

Sheila grabbed her coat and walked through the front reception area to reach the street. The noise hit her as soon as she pushed through the door: women chatting and children running between their legs, and Sheila's colleagues handing out Ration Book Six and the special pages for orange juice and cod liver oil, and trying to explain all this in voices straining to be heard above the din. She noticed that the large banner over the waiting area had come loose at the top corner, its message, FAIR SHARES FOR ALL, partially obscured. She'd better mention this to Mrs. Manson after lunch; she wouldn't want the place looking slipshod.

As Sheila approached the front door, she saw a young man conspicuously out of place among the sea of housewives. He was fresh-faced and handsome in a cheerful sort of way, broad-shouldered, with bright eyes and a strong, confident mouth. He wore a plain Utility overcoat, but it was in good condition, set off by a well-pressed white shirt and navy blue tie, and carried with that subtle panache that could make some people stand out even with clothing so scarce. Well-off but not posh: Sheila had an eye for these things. He had removed his hat upon entering, and he held it up now in a saluting gesture as he walked toward her.

"I beg your pardon, miss," he said with a very charming smile. "Is this the office where Mrs. Eisenberg is employed?" He sounded posher than he looked. Very fancy accent.

"Yes, that's right." Should she not have said that? "She's not in some sort of trouble, is she, sir?"

This produced a hearty laugh. He opened his mouth wide to reveal perfectly straight white teeth.

"Goodness, no. I was just wondering whether she might be free to join me for lunch."

Well, this was intriguing. "I'll go fetch her." Then she remembered her training from her brief stint as a parlor maid before the war. "Who shall I say is calling, sir?"

He reached inside the breast pocket of his overcoat, retrieved a slim silver case, and produced a card.

"Milton Calder," he said.

CHAPTER 33

LONDON, MARCH 1944

Lena ushered Milton out onto the street. Taken aback by his unexpected appearance, she didn't want to engage him in conversation under the watchful eyes of the entire staff of the Food Office.

"I hope you'll forgive the intrusion," Milton said. "I was passing and thought perhaps you'd do me the honor of joining me for lunch."

"But how did you know where to find me?"

His eyes sparkled. "You probably don't have a lot of time. Will you permit me to take you somewhere special?"

"What?"

"The Myra Hess lunchtime concert at the National Gallery. Have you ever been?"

"No. But—"

"Shall we? We have to hurry."

He took her elbow and steered her toward the Strand. Perhaps she should have been cross at this presumption, but she couldn't help smiling.

"How did you know where to find me?" she asked again.

"Ah, true confessions. It did require a bit of research."

She couldn't help feeling flattered. "So you were not in fact 'just passing'?" she asked.

"Only in a manner of speaking." He broke into a mischievous smile.

They had to sidestep a pile of rubble in front of a shop. A middle-aged man in overalls was sweeping shattered glass from the pavement. Two other men were boarding up the windows with sheets of plywood; on one of these was painted, in uneven red lettering, *Business as Usual, Mr. Hitler.*

"Did you get any damage last night?" Milton asked.

"No, it was mostly east of us, I think."

Lena had spent the evening in the Anderson in the back garden, now serviceable again. Lena, Otto, Eva, and Mavis had made a foursome for whist. Otto was in a good mood, because he kept winning.

Milton hurried on at a speed that discouraged further conversation. Lena rarely strayed this far from the office at lunchtime and felt naughty for doing so now. It was one thing to pop out for a bit of shopping, but a concert? A total indulgence. She could see Trafalgar Square ahead, with the dome of the gallery coming into view. Why had Milton sought her out like this?

As if he had read her thoughts, he slowed down and said, "I feel I have to make amends; I'm afraid we have to postpone the plans for your visit to Sussex. I didn't want you to think I was giving you the brush-off, as they say. I was very much looking forward to it."

"Oh." Lena couldn't hide her disappointment. "What a shame."

She had been eagerly anticipating seeing Muriel and having an excursion into the country. And Otto had come around to the idea. She thought it might make him more cheerful.

"Unfortunately, I have to take fireguard duty this weekend," Milton continued. "Someone else was signed up, an older chap who lives two doors down, but he's taken ill, I'm afraid. I tried to find someone else to step in, but no one seems to be available. It's most regrettable, but there it is."

"Yes, of course."

"Mother was so looking forward to seeing you. I do hope we can find another time soon." Milton looked across the square. "I see there's quite a crowd already. I hope we can get a good seat."

People were assembled in front of the National Gallery, inching up the steps to enter the building. Lena and Milton fell behind three older women; ahead of them, at the top of the steps, stood a group of men who looked like American army officers, their boisterous voices echoing in the portico.

"I've started coming here quite regularly," Milton said. "It's simply marvelous. Now that most theaters and concert halls are closed and the wretched air raids are starting over again, London is so dreary at night. But this is a cultural oasis."

They shuffled into the foyer, where a row of women were collecting admission fees. Lena reached for her purse, but Milton gestured to stop her.

"My treat," he insisted.

Surely there could be no harm in his paying. He handed over two shillings and, with a hand at her back, steered her through the inner doors. Lena gazed up at the lofty ceiling. A stream of late-winter sunlight poured over the supporting columns and their ornate cornices.

"Magnificent, isn't it?" Milton said. "Even without the paintings, the building itself is a work of art."

"Thank goodness it hasn't been hit."

"Yes, like St Paul's. One can understand people believing that something seems to protect it." He smiled. "Are you terribly hungry? They do serve food here, sandwiches and whatnot. But perhaps we could wait until after the performance?"

"Yes, that would be fine."

The room to their left was functioning as a makeshift canteen. Through the open door came the sounds of teacups and cutlery echoing in a space too large, and the unmistakable smell of pea soup.

"This way," Milton said.

They climbed a short staircase and turned right, following the crowd and the signs to the Barry Rooms, number 36. The walls were bleak, with pale scars and abandoned descriptive plaques. Cobwebs wrapped around the colossal doorways between galleries. The cavernous rooms were unheated, like tombs.

"I wish I could have come here before they removed all the paintings. Where are they?" Lena asked.

"Hidden away in caves in Wales, out of the reach of the Luft-waffe." His hand was at her elbow again. "Here we are. Let's go over to the right."

They had reached a spacious room at the center of a cross-roads. More bare galleries stretched out in three directions from this hub; the fourth was blocked off by a huge golden curtain. In front of this stood a raised platform, about two feet high, support-ing a grand piano and a bench. Rows of wooden chairs spread out from there. The room was filling up. Most people filtered down the center aisle in search of seats, but Milton scooted to the side and found a prime spot in the third row.

Once seated, they fell into an uneasy silence. Lena looked up at another impressive domed ceiling, marveling at the intricate carv-ings on the supporting arches, and then over to an abandoned gilded picture frame with the artist's name, Turner, engraved at the base. She examined the coat collar of the woman in front of her, with its few specks of dandruff. Now that the rush of getting here was accom-plished, the awkwardness of the situation hit her with full force. How long was this going to last, and when would she get back to the office? Where was she going to make room for those tins of cocoa powder? And what on earth was she doing here with this man?

She would have to think of something to say. She remembered how interested she had been in learning more about his work.

"What are you surveying now?" she asked.

"I feel perhaps I owe you an apology," he said at the same time, their words bumping into each other in the space between them.

"What?" They both laughed. Lena waited for him to go first.

"I want to apologize if I appeared too intrusive last time."

"I don't think so."

"I feel I overstepped when I pressed you for details about your family."

"Oh, no . . ."

"No, I sensed your reluctance to discuss it, and I should not have persisted. I hope you'll forgive me."

Lena remembered now. That was after she had fainted, when Gollancz had spoken at the rally.

"It's all right. Otto thinks I'm ridiculously naive about all that." She stared at the folds of the gold curtain. "And I suppose he's right. But I can't give up hope. I have to believe that somehow my mother and sister will be all right."

"Of course you do."

Lena turned to him with a flush of gratitude. But further conversation was precluded by an outburst of applause as an imposing woman approached the piano. She was wearing a black skirt and jacket and a plain white blouse. Her face was strong and full, with the hint of a double chin, and husky eyebrows; her dark hair was smoothly parted in the center and coiled up to sit just above the ears. Lena wasn't sure exactly what she'd been expecting, but it wasn't this; someone petite and delicate, perhaps, more glamorous. This woman strode to the piano and took her seat.

There was no program, of course; precious paper could not be wasted. Lena tried to identify the piece: Beethoven? She always envied those people—dear Tomas had been one—who could immediately recognize any concerto or symphony from its opening bars. Dame Myra's right hand hovered over the keys, as the left traveled down the keyboard in a descending trill. The acoustics were surprisingly good. The melody eased a tightness Lena hadn't realized she was harboring. She needed more music in her life. Their secondhand gramophone and modest collection of records had been destroyed by the Essex Road bomb a year earlier.

Lena glanced at Milton; his eyes were closed, his face relaxed in a gentle smile of appreciation. He was right; this was such a good idea. Now that she knew of it, she would try to come again.

It was not a long performance. After two short pieces, it was over. But, in response to animated applause, Dame Myra nodded wordlessly and performed a brief encore, which Lena did recognize— Bach's *Joy of Man's Desiring*—played with great gusto, the pianist's hands crossing over each other in sweeping gestures, her shoulders bending into the notes. The audience was on its feet, swaying and humming, clapping loudly again at the end, calling out for more—but to no avail. The great diva retreated behind the gold curtain.

"Thank you so much, Milton. I really enjoyed that."

"Wonderful, isn't it?"

So wonderful that Lena allowed herself to linger for lunch—just for a while. After all, there had been two days last week when she'd hardly stopped all day; she'd nibbled on bread and cheese brought in from home, while trying to decipher the ministry's latest instructions on the new ration book. Now, she sat at a corner table with Milton and a large bowl of the pea soup. Her mind returned to their conversation before the music started.

"When my father and brother first arrived in this country, I went to see them at the army base."

It seemed easy to talk to Milton; she didn't feel the need to tiptoe around her words.

"I remember that. You were still in Upper Wolmingham at the time."

"Yes. My father was most insistent that I write to my mother and tell her they had arrived. He said he couldn't write himself, not from the army. So I wrote."

Lena put down her spoon. The soup had seemed like a good idea at first, and she had gulped down half a bowl, surprised at her hunger. But now it had lost its appeal.

"You worry that you should not have written?"

"Yes! I tried to be vague, of course. I didn't go into details. But I told her that I had seen them, that we were all in England."

"Do you know if she ever received the letter?"

"She must have. I had a letter from my aunt six months later. She knew that Father and Ernst had arrived. But my mother obviously did not dare write herself." Lena fell silent. She swallowed hard. She wasn't going to cry.

Milton said nothing. It was a soothing silence, not awkward. After a few moments, he said gently, "And you've heard nothing since?"

"Nothing. I worry terribly that I somehow exposed her to danger, drew unnecessary attention to her and Sasha. I can't bear to think of it."

Milton reached for her hand. "You mustn't blame yourself. I'm sure your mother was relieved to hear that you all arrived safely. She must have been worried. There's no way to know if there were any repercussions."

His hand rested on hers for only a moment. He withdrew it quickly and lifted his teacup.

Lena kept her eyes low, staring at the fingers that he'd touched.

"One still hears stories of children being hidden," Milton continued. "Kept safe from the Nazis."

"Yes! Exactly." Lena looked up. "That's what I say, but Otto . . ." No, she wasn't going to talk about Otto and what he thought. "When the war's over, I'm going to find her and bring her to live with me."

Lena watched Milton, wondering if he would scoff at this notion, as Otto had. But he simply nodded quietly.

"We have to hope for the best," he said after a moment, "and be optimistic about the future. After all, that's what drives us to be socialists, isn't it? Believing that things can be better, that man can be innately good and fair, given the right conditions, that we can build a more perfect world."

"Yes, I suppose so. I hadn't thought of it like that." What would Otto say to that? He seemed to have lost all his optimism.

"I think about this a great deal in my work," Milton continued, "traveling around the country, interviewing ordinary people. It's a marvel how much stock everyone's putting in the future, in things being better once the 'people's war' is over. They complain, of course, about the shortages and the queues and such. But now that they can see that we will win the war, there's a tremendous sense of anticipation. Of knowing things can never go back to how they were before." His voice was becoming more animated, but then he seemed to check himself and smiled. "Forgive me. I'm getting carried away."

"No. It's very interesting."

"Don't you think it was extraordinary that people queued for hours to buy the Beveridge Report?" He leaned forward over the table. "A three-hundred-page government paper. Over half a million copies sold."

"Yes." Lena smiled. "Even the girls at my office know all about it. They've read the summary, at least."

"Yes, now everyone's an advocate for social insurance and a

national health system. They've seen what government planning can do in wartime, and they want the same for peace."

"But isn't Churchill going to oppose it?"

"Of course. But that's one battle he's not going to win."

Milton grinned, unable to conceal his glee. He rested his hands on the table, fingers interlaced. Lena noticed again that jagged scar over the knuckles of his left hand.

"I've been going to Common Wealth meetings," he continued. "They're pulling together a coalition of the Left to push for full implementation of Beveridge now. And they're getting a lot of support. You saw, I'm sure, their incredible victory in the Eddisbury by-election. There's no turning back. People are not going to accept the old order of poverty, unemployment, lack of medical care. They know they deserve more."

Lena couldn't help smiling. His enthusiasm was infectious. She was reminded of the days of the Popular Front in Prague, before the war: the meetings, the rallies, working together for a common cause. It would be nice to feel part of a movement again.

"Yes, we certainly deserve something good to come of all this," she said.

Milton looked over her head. "It's getting late. I do hope I haven't detained you too long."

Lena had completely forgotten about the cocoa tins and cod-liver-oil pages lying a mile up the street. Now, in a mild panic, she looked at her watch. It was almost two o'clock! She jumped up. Mrs. Manson would be beside herself.

"I must go."

Milton helped her on with her coat.

"Thank you so much." She didn't want to appear ungrateful in her rush to leave. "I've had a wonderful time."

"The pleasure's all mine," he said, with a small bow. "I hope we can do this again sometime. And let's make plans for you to come to Upper Wolmingham next month. With any luck, we'll have better weather by then. Sussex is beautiful in the spring, as you know."

CHAPTER 34

LONDON, APRIL 1944

They planned a party on Saturday evening at Lena and Otto's place. Lotti came over after lunch to help Lena prepare. She had a recipe for a sponge cake made with dried eggs.

"But aren't you going to need butter or margarine?" Lena said. "I've used all mine."

"I swapped some sugar coupons for butter." Lotti delved into a canvas shopping bag and extracted a small cube wrapped in wax paper. "There's a girl at work with a very sweet tooth; she goes for anything that will get her more sugar."

"I hope it will work in this little oven. I've never tried to bake a cake in here."

Lena inspected the oven. A few black spots lay encrusted on the bottom shelf. She tried to scrape them off with a cloth.

"I'm excited that both Peter and Emil could get leave on the same weekend," Lotti said.

"I haven't seen Emil for ages."

"You'll hardly recognize him."

"I'm going to try to make dumplings and Czech cabbage." Lena checked her watch. She still needed to get to the shops. "And I think I have enough points for a can of sausage meat. It's not quite the same as goulash, but I just don't trust the meat at the butcher's. Mavis is convinced it's horse meat."

Lotti smoothed out the recipe, torn from a women's magazine, and started to reconstitute the dried eggs. She measured three table-spoons of powder from the packet she had brought with her and then counted out six tablespoons of water into a separate cup.

"The secret is to add the water a little at a time," she declared.

Outside, a steady rain fell, pounding against the windowpanes in powerful, frenzied gusts. The muck on the bottom of the oven was stubborn. Lena reached for a knife.

"What time is Otto getting home?"

"I don't know. His shifts are always changing."

"Don't they have Saturday afternoon off at the factory?"

"They work all hours. There's no end to the work of making bombs and bullets, I suppose." Lena scraped away at the oven. "At least, I assume that's what he does. He doesn't talk about it. He doesn't tell me much of anything these days."

"I'm sure he's not allowed to talk about his work at the factory."

"I don't mean just that," Lena said.

That would have to do for the oven. She scooped up the black fragments with a damp cloth and tossed them into the sink.

"Two weeks ago, we were talking to someone, and out of the blue he announced he's going to go back to Germany after the war. He hadn't said a word to me. I couldn't believe it. Going back to Germany!"

"I don't blame him for thinking about it," Lotti said. "I think about going back home all the time." Her hand drifted to the soft bulge at her belly. "Especially now."

Lotti's skirt was stretched taut, and as she reached for another spoon, Lena noticed the button at the back was undone, the waist-band gaping open a couple of inches.

"I hate the idea of my baby being born here, in a foreign coun-try. And my mother not even knowing she's going to be a grand-mother." Lotti beat the cake mixture vigorously.

"Did you try writing to your mother?"

"Yes, I wrote. Of course. But"—she sniffed and wiped her nose on her sleeve—"what do you suppose happens to all those letters? I imagine them piling up in some huge warehouse in Geneva or Lisbon or wherever it is they land."

"Perhaps the letters do get through but they just can't reply," Lena said softly.

"I don't know." Lotti's voice quivered.

Lena watched as she continued beating the mixture. Suddenly, Lotti slammed the bowl down on the counter so loudly Lena flinched.

"I'm so sick of this. I want to go home." She had tears in her eyes. "Do you think the war will be over before my baby is born?"

Lena put her arms around Lotti and felt her friend relax into the embrace. She didn't know what to say. Empty reassurances seemed pointless.

"I'm sorry," Lotti said, pulling away and wiping her nose on her sleeve again. "I'm so emotional these days. Forgive me."

"It's all right."

"No, it's selfish, really. Everyone's suffering. Everyone wants to go home."

They fell into silence. The rain slashed at the windows, unrelenting. From the sink, Lena looked out at the slate rooftops and the rows of chimneys. There was one spot where you could catch a glimpse of the spire of the church opposite King's Cross. Leaning forward, she could see the street below, people hurrying by, umbrellas bobbing as they went about their errands. The young man from the house next door, hobbling on his crutches, pulled his cap down around his ears. He'd lost a leg at Dunkirk, according to Mavis, yet he was always ready with a soft, gentle smile. An ordinary rainy London street, gray and grimy and nothing fancy, yet it was oddly comforting to Lena. She couldn't explain it to herself.

Lotti was scooping the batter into a cake pan. "I really don't think about going home," Lena said. "I do think about going back to get Sasha. But then I imagine bringing her to live with me here."

Lotti stared at Lena. "You want to stay here? And always be a foreigner? Always have people ask you all day long 'Where're you from?' Never really belong?"

"I don't feel that way. I do feel at home here. It would be wonderful to be here in peacetime, without having to worry about bombs or bread queues or blackout blinds. Doing ordinary things like going to art galleries or theaters."

"I think it will be wonderful to go home. Eat real Bratwurst. *Klobásy.* Wiener Schnitzel. Drink good coffee." Lotti grew more animated. "Walk across the Charles Bridge. Hear Czech spoken in the street. Be among our own kind."

"But the English people have been so kind and decent. And determined to carry on in spite of everything. Look how readily they accept rationing, everyone getting a fair share. You can bet back home they're all fighting and scheming about how to get more for themselves on the black market."

Lotti laughed. "There's plenty of black-market activity here, Lena. You just choose not to notice it." She picked up the cake tin, and Lena opened the oven door.

"Of course, there're always a few people breaking the rules. But I mean in general. The way people stand patiently in queues. In Prague, I'm sure everyone's pushing and shoving and trying to get more than the next person."

"We have no idea what's happening in Prague."

The oven door closed with a thud. Lotti's words hung between them like a thick fog. After a few moments of silence, Lena said, "I'll make some tea."

Lotti read *The Times* while Lena tidied the living room, picking up dirty cups and discarded clothing. There was a coating of dust over all horizontal surfaces.

"There seems to be no stopping the Russians," Lotti said from behind the newspaper. "The Red Army has retaken almost all of Ukraine."

"Still no Second Front."

"They'll have to make a move as soon as the weather improves, don't you think?"

Lena heard footsteps on the stairs leading up to the flat. Not Otto's big strides—a quicker, lighter step. There was a soft tapping at the door. Mavis, in raincoat and headscarf, held an offering in her right hand.

"Letter for you, by second post."

Lena's heart somersaulted, but she quickly saw this was no news from home; it was a small manila envelope with just a single brown stamp, postmarked London WC1.

"Thank you. You didn't need to bring it upstairs. Do you want to come in for a cup of tea? I have the kettle on."

"No, I can't stop. My mum's coming over in a bit. Oh, hello, Lotti. Didn't see you there. How you doing?" Mavis's face lit up with a huge smile. "Looks good, doesn't she?" she said to Lena. "How exciting to have a new baby coming along." She laughed. "Gives you something to look forward to, doesn't it?"

"Yes." Lena smiled. "It does."

"She's in a cheerful mood," Lotti said, after Lena closed the door.

"Mavis is a good soul," Lena said.

"Who's the letter from?"

"I don't know."

But Lena did have an inkling. The envelope was very thin, smaller than a postcard. Lena's name and address were typed with a well-worn ribbon. There seemed to be a problem with the *n* key, because it was consistently out of alignment. She looked at the postmark again. WC1? Yes, that would fit.

"Aren't you going to open it?" Lotti said, peeking over Lena's shoulder.

She could see no way to avoid opening it in front of Lotti. She found the letter opener on the table and extracted a tiny piece of paper, typed on both sides with the same faded ribbon.

She scanned it quickly and replaced it in the envelope. Lotti was staring at her intently. "Well?"

She would have to come out with it. "It's from Milton," she said, trying to sound nonchalant.

"Who?"

"Milton Calder. I told you we ran into him at the rally in Trafalgar Square." She stuffed the envelope into her skirt pocket and went in search of a rag for dusting.

"Why's he writing to you?"

"He invited us to go to Sussex, but he had to change plans at the last minute. So he wants to reschedule. In two weeks. That's all."

"Why would he write to you, and not to both you and Otto? Aren't you both going?"

"Oh, I don't know." Lena tried to wave the conversation to an end with a vague gesture with her rag, but she could feel her cheeks flushing.

"Lena, what are you doing?"

"Nothing." Lotti continued to stare at her. "*Nothing*," she repeated, with more emphasis. She almost said, *I'm dusting* but knew that would sound ridiculous.

"I hope you're not doing anything stupid, Lena. Otto's very fond of you. He doesn't always show it, I know that, but he really cares about you. You've been through so much together. You can't just toss that aside."

Lena sniffed. A sweet aroma emanated from the oven. "You'd better check the cake," she said.

CHAPTER 35

LONDON, APRIL 1944

Peter brought the gramophone from his place, along with two records of Czech music. He made space on the table in the corner, briskly turned the handle, and placed one of the records on the turntable. The beginning was scratchy, but then it cleared and the swinging notes of a gentle jazz melody filled the room.

"Oh my God!" Lena exclaimed. "Is this . . . ?" She picked up the record cover.

"Jaroslav Ježek." Peter beamed. "Remember?"

"Of course. Where on earth did you find this?"

"A little shop on Portobello Road."

"We have to dance to this," Lotti said, grabbing Peter and dragging him into the center of the room. "Otto, Lena, come on!"

Otto was trying to get the coals in the grate to light. "There's no room to dance in here," he said.

Lotti picked up one of the dining chairs and moved it to the corner. Peter pushed the table over to the kitchen area, and the armchair against the bedroom door.

"There's room. Come on!"

Peter and Lotti launched into a sort of modified polka with a touch of swing, with Peter adding some slapstick features of his own invention. Lena was unable to resist. She took Otto's hand and pulled him toward her. He had never been much of a dancer; as for Lena, her feet often behaved like a wayward two-year-old's, stumbling forward when they should go backward, moving fast when they should go slow. But she remembered once—in the back room of a place on the rue de Rennes—when they had twirled around the dance floor and had fun. He had his hand at her back now and swung her around, surprising her with his sudden vigor.

"Wasn't this the music those fellows used in the . . . What was it called?" Otto said. "The Liberated Theatre? What were their names?"

"The *Osvobozené Divadlo.*" Lotti shrieked with delight.

"Voskovec and Werich," Peter said, twirling Lotti around. "Their plays were so hilarious."

"And that motion picture," Lena said. "Remember that? *Hej Rup!* That scene with the industrialist and the unemployed laborer, it was so funny. Those hats . . ."

"And *Svět patří nám,*" Lotti said. "The world belongs to us."

"Whatever happened to those two?" Otto said.

He tried to spin Lena around under his arm, but she turned the wrong way and ended up bumping into the sofa. She fell onto the cushions in giggles.

"They got out," Peter said. "I read they're in New York now."

"Oh, good."

Was that a knock at the door? Lena hadn't heard the usual sound of the doorbell downstairs, or ascending footsteps. She jumped for the door, feeling dizzy for a moment. A tall young man in uniform was standing before her. She tipped her head and saw Emil smiling at her. He held a large brown bottle in each hand.

"Look at you!" she said, pulling him into a hug.

He wrapped her in a strong embrace. The bottles clanked together behind her, cold against her back. She looked up at him again: what a transformation from the gangly youth of the Oak Tree Cottage days. He filled out his uniform with a solid presence. His jaw was firmer; coarse stubble coated his chin. His baby-faced innocence was gone, but he smiled at her with genuine delight.

"*Jsem tak rád, že tě vidím,*" he said. "How lovely to see you." Another figure lurked behind him in the dimly lit hallway.

"I've brought Vladimír with me. I hope that's all right." He introduced his friend. "Flight Lieutenant Havel. He's in my squadron. We have to take the train back to base later tonight, so I hope you'll forgive our attire." His thumbs pointed to the lapels of his air force blues.

"You look very handsome," Lena said, smiling. "Come in, come in. Hello, Vladimír, welcome."

There were introductions, handshakes, hugs. Emil placed the bottles of beer on the table. Vladimír produced two more. Otto gathered glasses from the shelf. "Where're you from, Vladimír?" Peter said.

"Plzeň. But my family's originally from Prague."

"His brother was in Prague in '38," Emil said. "You remember Karl from *Die Tat*? Tall, dark hair, a beard."

"Of course. I can see the resemblance."

"Karl often talks about those days," said Vladimír, slipping into German. "I remember he much admired you, Otto. *Ich bin so froh, Sie endlich kennen zu lernen.* It's a privilege to meet you."

"Where's Eva?" Emil said. "Isn't she living with you now?"

"She's staying in the downstairs flat," Lena said. She watched Otto for his reaction, but he was back at the fireplace, poking the coals. "I invited her, but I don't know if she'll come. She's usually off chasing American servicemen."

She checked on the food. The cabbage was simmering on the back burner, just a splash of water in the bottom of the pot to prevent burning: perfect. But the dumplings: maybe this had not been such a great idea. They looked gray and heavy, barely afloat in the bubbling water, nothing like the *knedliky* of home. If they were a complete disaster, she could serve that extra loaf of bread instead.

The cheerful chatter continued behind her, Czech mingled with German, *Salz* and *pepř*, *chléb* and *Käse* intertwined as though inseparable, hard to tell them apart. Soothing background music, the languages of her childhood.

"Where is your brother now?" Otto was asking Vladimír. "Did he make it out?"

"Yes, we left together, through Poland, just before the start of the war." He helped Peter rearrange the furniture into its original configuration. "He's in the army, the Czech Brigade, based near Northampton."

Lena turned. "My brother's in the Czech Brigade, too."

"At Arthingworth?"

"Yes, that sounds right. He's coming to London on leave next weekend."

"Karl says they're all very bored. Nothing but endless maneuvers. Can't wait to see some action."

"Any hint of them making a move?" Peter asked.

"The rumor at work is that they're going to launch the invasion from Essex," Otto said. He was standing with his back to the fireplace, leaning against the mantel. Lena looked at him with surprise. Another thing he'd said nothing to her about. "A fellow at the factory has family living out near Harwich," he continued. "There's lots of activity down there. All very hush-hush. No one's allowed anywhere near the beach, but anyone can see they're building huge docks, launching pads or something. They're going to take the Nazis by surprise by landing in Holland."

Lena said, "It's not going to be much of a surprise if people keep talking about it."

"I heard they're going to land in Norway," Lotti said.

"Not with all those fjords," Emil said.

"They're not going to be able to pull off such a massive invasion from anywhere except Dover," Peter said. "They have to take the shortest route across the Channel."

"But that's exactly where the Nazis are expecting the attack," Otto said. "That's where they've fortified the most."

The beer was making experts of them all.

"Well, where are you boys bombing?" Lotti turned to Emil. "That should give us a clue." Everyone looked at Emil. He fell silent.

"It's all right," Lena said. "We know you can't tell us." He gave her a grateful smile.

"Anyway, they seem to be bombing everything these days," she continued, trying to shift to the kind of vague conversation you could have with anyone. "Sounds like the Germans are getting a pounding."

"One thing's for sure," Otto said. "When the invasion finally comes, we're the ones who're going to get a pounding." His eyes narrowed as they did when he was priming for an argument. "Hitler's not going to sit back and just take it. Things are going to be terrible here."

Lotti asked, "Are you talking about Hitler's secret weapon that we hear—"

Otto interrupted her. "The Nazis will surely launch a major attack, like nothing we've ever seen before." He gave the coals another poke, before adding, "It's curious how everyone is so desperate to see the Second Front but no one talks about the consequences."

"Anything to end the war," Lotti said. "That's what everyone wants."

"I think people are ready," Lena said. "No one's under any illusion that this final stage is going to be easy."

"On the contrary," Otto said. "Everyone's talking as if the war is practically over, whereas in fact the worst is yet to come."

"It can't be worse than the blitz," Vladimír said. "And the Luftwaffe is seriously depleted. Nothing like its former strength."

"I think it's going to be brutal. Massive casualties. Wait and see." Otto hurled out the words like a knight throwing down the gauntlet. There was another uneasy silence. No one jumped at the bait.

"Well, on that cheerful note," Lena said, "let's set the table for dinner. I think the food's ready."

She was barely able to control her irritation. Otto could never miss an opportunity to issue a dismal forecast about something. She drained the water from the *knedliky*, banging the saucepan down on the counter with far more noise than necessary, and pulled the casserole out of the oven. She hadn't been able to find sausage meat, canned or otherwise, so it was Spam again, but she'd used a recipe they'd distributed at the Food Office, layered it with beets and carrots. It looked all right. Smelled pretty good, in fact.

She suddenly remembered the letter from Milton, still sitting in her pocket. It tugged at her now like a warm current, pulling her toward something alarming and irresistible at the same time.

"Need some help?" Emil was at her side.

"Please. Bring the plates over. I think I'll serve from here."

"You made dumplings?" He put an arm around her waist and squeezed her with delight.

"I'm not sure how they'll taste. It might have been a mistake with this bread."

He laughed. "*Knedliky* with English National Wheatmeal: what a combination!"

"I tried to find white bread, but of course there was none."

There was a shortage of chairs, so Emil perched on the arm of the sofa and Peter stacked two wooden crates and a cushion to make a seat for himself. Everyone was hungry; they all ate with enthusiasm. Lena kept apologizing for the dumplings, which seemed stodgy to her, but no one was deterred. They were soon all gone. And the cabbage was delicious.

"What a relief after all that cabbage they serve the English way at work," Lotti said.

"Yes, on base, too!" Emil said. "Dreadful stuff. What do they do to it?"

"It's boiled for hours, until it's completely tasteless," Lotti said, with a laugh.

Vladimír chuckled, too. "And the carrots," he added.

"The English have no idea how to cook vegetables," Lotti said.

Lena waited for Otto to contradict her, but he did not. Finally, this was something they could all agree on.

She remembered Emil's brother, who had been arrested trying to get through Poland back in '39. While Peter and Otto were engaged in a loud debate about the Allied bombing of Berlin, Lena turned to him softly and asked, "Did you ever hear from Josef?"

"Yes!" He smiled. "He made it to the Soviet Union. I got a letter finally, a few months ago, from Kiev. He had obviously written others, but I never received them. He's with the Czech Brigade on the Eastern Front. Sweeping toward Germany now with the Red Army, I suppose."

"That's wonderful. You must be so relieved."

"Yes. I'm very proud of him." Emil reached across the table for more beer. "But, do you know what's strange?" He spoke quietly, close to Lena. "I fear more for him now I know he's at the front. When I had no idea where he was, I worried in a general sense, but it was a vague sort of anxiety. Now, I read about casualties on the Eastern Front and I'm afraid."

His frankness took Lena by surprise. It was like getting a sudden peek into someone's home through a crack in a curtain.

"But aren't you afraid for yourself whenever you go on a mission?"

"No, that's different. I'm too busy to be afraid."

She knew that couldn't be true. He took a swig of beer, and the crack in the curtain closed. Of course he was very brave; all the pilots were so brave. But she knew his unit must have taken heavy losses; he must think about his own vulnerability all the time. And he must have seen horrifying destruction from the air, destruction wrought by his own hand, which he also could not dwell on. *What terrible things we expect from these men*, she thought.

Lena cleared away the plates and brought over Lotti's cake—now transformed into a delicious-looking concoction, perfectly risen and golden and topped with canned peaches. *We carry on as if all this is normal*, she thought. *We do everyday things, like make the tea and find clean cups. The mundane normalcy: we have to cling to this.*

She thought of Ernst, too. If the assault really was coming soon, presumably the Czech Brigade would be in the thick of it. She was going to meet him for lunch in the West End the following Saturday. She had seen him only a few times over the past four years, and she had always felt disappointed, wanting an intimacy that wasn't there. But he was her brother, a tangible link to her fragmented family. What was Ernst feeling about the invasion? He liked to boast that President Beneš had assured them they would play a key role in the liberation of their country. Did he feel prepared? Or terrified? Would he ever tell her if he was? Since his safe arrival in England, she hadn't believed him to be in danger. But if he were to cross the Channel, if he were to be part of the attack, he would be in real peril. She knew she would be fearful for him. Just as Emil was for Josef.

Otto was probably right. Yes, they all wanted the Second Front, the invasion they had been advocating for months, years. But it would come at a price. A terrible price. Everything came with a price.

Emil and Vladimír left at nine o'clock to take the train from St. Pancras. Peter and Lotti lingered awhile. Peter and Otto finished off the beer. Peter put the Voskovec and Werich record on again, but the mood had shifted; no one felt inclined to dance this time. The dishes lay in the sink.

"We must help you clean up," Peter said. "Then we should go. I have an early start tomorrow."

"You can leave the dishes," Lena said.

"No, that's not fair."

Otto didn't stir, but Peter and Lotti set to work at the sink while Lena wiped the table. "When are you next on leave?" Lena asked.

"The sixteenth. If there's no Second Front, of course."

"You won't be going over with the invasion, will you?"

"No, but all leave will be canceled, I'm sure."

"Of course."

"I hear that all the time," Lotti said: "'if there's no Second Front . . . if there's no Second Front.' Everyone's holding their breath. Waiting."

The room was soon tidied, and Peter and Lotti gathered up their things. There was a lot to carry: the cake tin and extra plates they had brought over, plus two umbrellas and three bags of maternity clothes that Mavis had proudly presented just before the party, hand-me-downs from a woman next door to her mother. And the gramophone.

"Lotti, you shouldn't be carrying all that," Lena said. "Otto can walk over with you and give you a hand."

Otto relieved Lotti of the two largest bags and they departed, leaving Lena to herself. She sank into the sofa, kicked off her shoes, and reached into her pocket. She had been yearning for a moment of privacy to reread Milton's letter. She wondered if she had misread it in her haste when she'd opened it in front of Lotti. Perhaps its tone had been formal and perfunctory, or merely casual and friendly, and she had deluded herself, imagining an intimacy that had no basis in reality. She had been itching to read it again but postponing it, too, not wanting to be disappointed—yet she wasn't sure what she wanted the verdict to be. She took a deep breath and extracted the flimsy paper from the envelope.

Dear Lena,

Thank you so much for joining me for lunch at the National Gallery. I enjoyed myself immensely. The music was most agreeable, of course, but the presence of your company made it absolutely marvelous.

I very much hope that you can accompany me to Upper Wolmingham in a fortnight, for the weekend of the 13th–14th. Indeed, Mother is counting on it. I suppose it was presumptuous of me, but I assured her you would come, before ascertaining whether Otto's shifts could accommodate this arrangement.

Naturally, it would be most enjoyable to have both of you visit, but if he is unable to make it, I have to confess that the prospect of having your undivided attention is utterly delightful.

Does the 6:15 from Victoria on Friday still suit you?
Yours sincerely,
Milton

Lena stared at the faded type and the sunken *n*'s. What was he suggesting, exactly? Was this merely English politeness? Was she mistaken in thinking it was more than that?

There was certainly no mistaking the excitement in her chest at the thought of Milton's undivided attention.

Downstairs, the door slammed. Otto's footsteps were on the stairs. She slipped the letter into her pocket.

CHAPTER 36

LONDON, MAY 1944

Lena looked at her watch: eight thirty. Otto had said he would be home by nine, after his union meeting. She had to make a decision about next weekend. She had sent Milton a short note saying Friday the twelfth would be wonderful but had left it ambiguous whether she would be traveling alone or not. She had said nothing yet to Otto. He'd worked the late shift all week, and every night she was asleep, or pretending to be, when he slipped silently into bed beside her. She told herself she was waiting for the right moment.

The idea of going alone was tantalizing. Milton seemed to understand her and not feel the need to dispute everything she said. At work, whenever her mind drifted to the time he'd whisked her off to the National Gallery, she broke into a broad grin and Sheila said, "What's your little secret, then?" and Lena would blush and find an excuse to go into the back office.

She felt pulled toward Milton as if by an irresistible force.

But she had to resist. She couldn't go without Otto. Not to Upper Wolmingham. It seemed wrong, inconceivable.

She remembered those nights years ago, in the Café Slavia, when everyone had swarmed around Otto to hear his analysis of the situation in Sudetenland; when she alone had shared the secret of his role in discovering the Nazi troops' movements; how he'd clung to her in the darkness in Oak Tree Cottage, telling her about the boy who'd drowned on the *Arandora Star*. She thought of how he could still, when in a good mood, call her *mein Schätzchen* when she lay nestled on his shoulder. She thought of Lotti's words: *You have been through so much together. You can't just toss that aside.*

She heard the front door bang. He was home.

"How was the meeting?" Lena asked.

He threw his jacket onto the floor and sank into the armchair, sprawling his long legs out in front of him. He grunted but said nothing.

"How did the meeting go?" Lena asked again.

"Ugh. It's impossible to organize in that place." He looked over to the kitchen table. "Do you have any tea made?"

"I'll make some."

He'd brought home the *Evening Standard*; he picked it up now and hid behind the pages.

The only sounds in the room were the rustling of his newspaper and the water hissing in the kettle. The discussion waiting to happen hovered in the air.

"What shift are you working next week?" she asked.

"Same. Evenings. Days on Friday." He didn't look up. He was chewing on his lower lip again; she hated the way he did that.

"Will you have to work on Saturday?" If he had to work, his coming to Sussex would be a moot point.

"Don't know yet. They're piling on a lot of overtime." He returned to the newspaper. "See, this is what I was talking about." He poked his finger at a headline: LONDON: GET READY. "Hitler has a new type of bomb ready to launch as soon as the invasion starts."

That night, he seemed farther away than ever on the opposite side of the bed. He didn't call her *mein Schätzchen*. He hadn't called her that in a long time.

Ernst said he could be in London by noon, so Lena proposed meeting for lunch. She hadn't seen him in almost a year. She suggested the Lyons Corner House on Tottenham Court Road—the same place where she and Otto had gone with Milton on the day of the

Second Front demonstration. Now, Lena sat in the same section of the restaurant where they had eaten that day, waiting for Ernst. The waitresses bustled about as the lunchtime crowd filtered in.

From the next table, the sound of laughter: two couples, giddy and flirtatious, one woman brushing her hand against her escort's sleeve. Lena thought of Milton's face and gestures that day, his bright eyes, the fine hairs on the back of his hands as he poured the tea—vivid images seared in her memory.

She caught a whiff of sausages and mash from a plate that whisked by at nose level. Her stomach twisted in hunger. Otto had eaten the last remaining egg that morning and finished off the bread, leaving nothing for her. She'd intended to stop at the baker's on the way here, but the queue had been too long and she'd been afraid she would be late; now she was starving.

She was expecting Ernst to be in uniform and half raised her arm to wave to three different soldiers of similar build, before realizing they were not her brother. He was almost twenty minutes late. Was he lost? He didn't know London well. She should have included better directions. And she could have stopped for bread, after all.

"*Ty budeš tady.*" His voice was behind her. "There you are."

She jumped up to give him a hug. He was in mufti: brown trousers and a crumpled beige jacket, a white shirt and maroon necktie. His cheeks were flushed.

"Sorry, sorry," he gushed. "I missed my stop on the Tube. I was afraid you might give up on me."

"Of course not."

He sat opposite her. His hair was incredibly short, cut in the style of the American servicemen, flat across the top. His face was losing its boyish fullness, the cheekbones becoming more prominent, the eyes more deep-set. It was startling how much he was beginning to resemble Father. He smiled at her, relaxing now. He had a healthy glow; his forehead was slightly sunburned, with a speck of skin peeling on the bridge of his nose. Like her, he never tanned easily.

"So, how are you?" he asked, rubbing his hands together. "No more bombing in your area, I hope?"

"No. A few close calls, but we've had no damage."

"The raids have eased up a bit, haven't they?"

"A bit." She picked up the menu. "I think we should order." She looked around for the waitress. "There was heavy bombardment in the East End last week," she continued. "Near where Otto works."

"Ah, yes. Otto," Ernst said. "What does he do, again?"

"He works in a munitions factory."

"Really?" This seemed to surprise him. But he said no more.

The waitress arrived, and they ordered the same thing: sausages, mashed potatoes, and peas, with a pot of tea.

"How are things with you?" Lena said. "How is the new base?"

Ernst shrugged. "Much like the last one. The food's a bit better."

"And Father? How is he doing since his retirement? You wrote that he's still with you?"

"Nearby. They moved him and another retired officer to a village a few kilometers away." He ran a hand through his short-clipped hair, which bristled like a soft brush.

"Is he all right?"

"I don't know. He's difficult to talk to."

"You've only just noticed that?"

Ernst gave a thin smile. "I know you've been arguing with him for years. But he seems changed to me. Bitter, angry, resentful . . . I don't know."

"About what?"

"Take your pick: no one listens to him, nothing is run the way it should be, they more or less forced him into retirement." Ernst spread his hands wide, palms up: a gesture that looked like Father's. "He hates that he won't be part of the invasion, won't be there to defeat the Nazis."

Lena poured the tea and took a sip. "He hasn't heard anything from Máma, has he?" she asked.

"No. He would let you know if he had. He's not that bad."

"He must feel guilty about leaving Máma and Sasha behind."

Ernst gave her a sharp look. "There's no way Sasha could have made that journey. Or Máma, for that matter. You have no idea—"

"I mean before that. He shouldn't have waited so long, making their plans to emigrate. All those months they wasted, trying to make arrangements to bring the carpets and silver, or whatever it was they were doing."

"It wasn't like that."

"It was. The whole time I was in Paris, Máma would write saying they were working on this plan or that, or going to send Sasha out. You don't remember?"

"Of course. It wasn't that simple. The Nazis didn't make it easy for people to leave. There were complications at every turn."

"Sounds like they just left it too late."

"They were trying to do what seemed best at the time."

She let it rest. She didn't want to quarrel with him. Not now.

When the food arrived, they ate in silence for a while. The mashed potatoes were lumpy but tasty, and the sausages succulent; perhaps they even contained real meat. Ernst ate heartily, shoveling chunks into his mouth. Lena watched in amusement.

"All everyone's talking about here is the Second Front. What are you hearing?"

"We're kept guessing, like everyone else. Last week, we were confined to barracks for two days. No explanation. We all thought, *This is it—we're finally going.* But it was a false alarm."

"Are you afraid?"

"No," he said, too quickly. "It's what we've been training for. We want to get moving."

She wanted to say, *Be careful*, but it sounded so trite. "If . . . when . . ." She didn't know how to say it. The weight of terrible possibilities loomed in front of her—fears that refused to claim a voice. She stared over Ernst's head at the crowded room. A woman sat with two young daughters—were they twins?—ages twelve or thirteen, in matching blue frocks, the fabric stretched taut across tiny breast buds. An "awkward age," Máma always called it, neither child nor adult. Sasha would be about the same age now. It was hard to imagine.

"I often think . . ." Lena tried again. "I would like to have Sasha come and live with me here in England after the war is over."

"What makes you think she would want to do that?"

"She would love it here."

"She doesn't speak a word of English."

"She could learn fast enough."

"Well, we'll see." Ernst shrugged.

"Have you thought about what you'll do after the war?" Lena asked. "If your brigade ends up . . ." She hesitated. "Will you stay in Czechoslovakia?"

"I suppose. Why not? Try to get an apprenticeship or something." He shrugged again. "I don't think about it much. They say it could jinx you."

"I just . . ." She wanted to say more. But now she was afraid. Images of what could happen between here and Prague were too scary to contemplate. They fell into silence again.

Lena took another bite of sausage, but she couldn't finish all those potatoes, even though she'd been so hungry earlier. Ernst was still eating. He had worked his way through the sausages and peas and was now on the potatoes. She laughed.

"You eat just like you did when you were little," she said.

"What?" He looked taken aback. Now she had offended him.

"One thing at a time."

"I don't." He searched his plate, offered a few isolated peas as evidence.

"You do!" She laughed again. "Don't you remember the argument we used to have? I would always eat first the things I didn't like much, like carrots or peas, saving the good stuff for last. You said you should eat the best things first, because you never knew what might happen before the end of the meal." Lena shook her head. How odd that he should have said that; he was just a child. "Do you remember?"

Ernst nodded, suppressing a grin, his mouth full.

"It was a very serious debate. And then when Sasha got older, she declared that the most sensible solution was to eat one bite of everything in turn." She paused. "She was always so wise, from such an early age."

"I think I was right," said Ernst. "Now more than ever, it makes sense. You have to take what's in front of you. You may not get another chance."

When Lena returned home, Otto was sitting at the desk, combing over his old manuscript. He didn't look up.

"I'm going to Sussex next weekend," she blurted out, without preamble. Just like that, the words were out. She spoke in English.

"*Was hast du gesagt?*" He always responded in German.

"To see Muriel."

"That's nice, I must say," he said. "I thought we were both invited."

She was surprised he remembered Milton's original invitation—from the day of the rally. It had been weeks ago, and he'd never mentioned it again. "You said you had to work."

This wasn't exactly true, and she knew it. Half-truths: the room reverberated with them. She looked at their meager belongings, the trappings of their life together: the improvised lamp with the shade she had tried to patch, the dilapidated green armchair, their combined books sitting shoulder to shoulder on the shelf, her Austen and Brontë and the Proust she'd brought from Paris, his Marx and Engels. She often took comfort in these objects, in this little home of theirs, as if they could be the glue to hold them together. But it was a sham. These things could all disappear in a flash, under a pile of rubble, courtesy of the Luftwaffe.

"Actually, I want to go on my own," she heard herself say, holding his gaze. "I haven't been anywhere on my own in a long time."

He picked up his pipe and poked at the tobacco in the bowl. "It doesn't sound as if you're going on your own," he said. His voice was gray, like steel.

Lena steadied her breathing. She crossed her arms across her chest, preparing herself for battle. "I think it would do us good to have a couple of days apart," she said, keeping her focus resolutely on a spot above the mantelpiece.

"Fine. Suit yourself. I don't care."

He turned back to his manuscript. End of conversation.

Lena leaned against the sink, absentmindedly wiping the counter. That was it, then. She was going without him. Her stomach churned. Perhaps the sausages had been too rich after all.

CHAPTER 37

LONDON/SUSSEX, MAY 1944

Victoria Station was crowded. She should have expected it: Friday evening, the weather suddenly glorious, everyone happy to get out of London for the weekend. Where were they supposed to meet in this sea of people? She could see the ticket office ahead and edged in that direction; it seemed as good a spot as any. She pushed through the throng, clutching her holdall close to her chest, scanning the crowd for Milton. She couldn't see him anywhere. She decided to take her place at the end of the ticket queue.

A man emerged from the ticket office and created a handwritten announcement on the board outside. The news was passed down the line: the 6:20 to Canterbury was canceled. Someone behind her groaned; apparently, the 5:45 had been canceled, too. Lena kept her eyes on the board, as though she might miss something else if she looked away.

She and Otto had hardly spoken all week. They'd brushed past each other, the air thick with tension. Each morning when she'd left the flat, her jaw had been clenched so tight it ached. She wished she'd waited until the last minute before she'd told him she was going to Sussex. She'd searched for words that might smooth things over, but they'd all stuck in her throat. Perhaps she should have talked it over with him before making a decision. Was he truly upset, or was it true that, as he'd said, he didn't care? She couldn't tell. She reminded herself about the times he'd pulled away from *her* in the past, or made a fool of himself chasing after Eva. But she didn't like to hurt him. Perhaps she should call the whole thing off. She could just walk away now and go home.

"You're here!"

Milton stood before her, impossibly handsome, smiling, shamelessly thrilled to see her. "How clever of you to save a spot in the queue. I was terribly afraid we might miss each other when I saw the crush of people." He glanced around. "Is Otto . . ."

"No, I came alone."

"Marvelous."

His deep-brown eyes focused intensely on hers. He wore a linen jacket and open-necked white shirt, simple and casual yet with an unmistakable touch of elegance. He extended his hand toward her, and Lena realized he was offering to carry her luggage, which she was still clutching to her chest. She relaxed her grip and lowered it to her side.

"It's all right. I've got it," she said, and looked ahead to the announcement board again, to prove that she could take her eyes off him. "There's something up there about a train being canceled."

"The timetable is always somewhat arbitrary these days. But the six fifteen to Brighton is usually all right, for some reason."

"That's good."

"With the pleasure of your company, any delay will be incon-sequential."

She couldn't help laughing. And then blushing and look-ing away again. The queue was moving forward more rapidly. She reached for her purse, but Milton insisted on paying: two sec-ond-class returns to Bigglesmeade.

"Platform nine, sir."

He steered her off to the right, navigating through the crowd, dodging a cart piled high with luggage, skirting around a group of excited schoolchildren, swimming upstream through a swarm heading to the platforms at the other end of the station. Lena saw all this though a daze; more than anything, she was aware of a tingling sensation where his hand lay on her arm. They somehow found their way to the platform and, at Milton's suggestion, all the way to the front of the train to good seats, in a compartment to themselves, facing each other by the window.

"This is perfect," Milton said, lifting their luggage into the overhead rack. "I'm so glad to be getting out of London this weekend. It's going to be insufferably hot in town, I suspect." Other passengers were wending their way down the platform, peering in, searching for seats. "Obviously, everyone else has the same idea," he continued.

"I thought the government was trying to discourage people from traveling. Keep the railways free for the troops or something."

Milton grinned. "It's nice to see that the populace can still display some defiance, don't you think?"

Lena laughed. "I suppose so, yes."

"Of course, the coast is out of bounds. Restricted access. Did you notice the poster at the entrance to the station?"

She had not. She must have walked right past it.

"Just these past two weeks." He hung his linen jacket on the hook by the window. "One can't go beyond Burgess Hill without proof of residency."

"So where's everyone going?"

"Lewes, Canterbury, Midhurst. All those towns are advertising being 'not in the banned areas.' It's quite a boon for them."

"I suppose it can't be long, then," Lena said. "Before the invasion, I mean. If the coast is sealed off."

"No, it can't be long."

An elderly couple entered the compartment and settled into the seats by the door. The man tipped his hat at Lena and Milton; the woman smiled. Two middle-aged women followed with two teenage boys. The compartment was full now.

Lena hadn't ventured out of London in a long time. As the train chugged through the sprawling capital south of the Thames, she was shocked by the damage. You got used to it in your own neighborhood, no longer noticed the heaps of rubble, the exposed layers of flapping wallpaper and gaping fireplaces, the bizarre sight of half a bathtub or a truncated bed frame hanging precariously from a third story. Official reports of "incidents" elsewhere were kept vague. Now, it was terrible to see for oneself the extent of the ruins: rubble, flattened houses, blocks of flats shorn in two.

She averted her eyes. She couldn't take any more. And she was suddenly nervous at the prospect of seeing Muriel again.

"What did you tell Muriel about . . ." She lowered her voice. "Did you say Otto would be coming, too?"

"I told her I didn't know." He smiled. "Because I didn't."

"Whatever will she think?"

"Mother will be delighted to see you. And she's very broadminded. Surely you remember that about her."

Lena felt herself blushing again and looked out the window. The devastated urban landscape had given way to lush green fields.

There were a few telltale signs from the train: a glimpse of dark, amorphous shapes bunched next to a riverbank and, just south of Purley, a clear view of a convoy of lorries crossing a field. But it wasn't until Lena emerged from the station at Bigglesmeade that she understood the extent of the transformation of the countryside.

It was beautiful and green and filled with the sweet smell of honeysuckle and lilac, just as she remembered. But every possible tree had been called into service to provide cover for tanks and jeeps covered with olive tarpaulins. They lay camouflaged, huddled along the narrow lanes, forcing what little traffic there was—a farm tractor, a delivery van, even the villagers on bicycles—to navigate around these obstacles. There was no sign of the army itself. The vehicles lay dormant, like the toys of a sleeping giant.

"This is quite a sight," Lena said, as they walked up the hill to Upper Wolmingham.

"Yes, they're everywhere. They rumble through the lanes at night. In the morning, there are dozens more in new hiding places."

"Where are the men?"

"The officers are staying at the Manor House; the men camped out in Copley Woods. Canadians, mostly. Nice chaps. They spend a lot of time in the village." Milton smiled. "Mostly in the Fox and Hounds."

When they reached the central square of the village—bordered by the church, the Manor House, and the neat little cottages, their front gardens in full May bloom—the scene was so picturesque, it stung Lena's eyes. She thought of those few months at Oak Tree Cottage: the night when she first arrived, when Otto explained the rules of the commune, showed her the jar in the kitchen where they pooled their income, laughed about the rudimentary plumbing. It seemed a lifetime ago.

"The village hasn't changed much," Milton was saying. "Except for all that."

He nodded at a group of officers emerging from the Manor House, heading for the pub, laughing together. They were mostly absorbed in their own company, but one, a tall redhead, raised his hand to wave. Milton returned the gesture.

"As I say, they're not bad chaps. But they're totally ruining the Manor House and the grounds. Mother can't wait for this to be over so she can move back and get the place in decent shape again."

"Oh." This remark took Lena by surprise. She'd known Muriel only at The Hollow, where she seemed completely at home. "But it's so lovely at The Hollow."

"Yes, in a temporary sort of way. One never imagined it would go on this long."

They passed two more tanks, partially hidden under trees at the side of a house, before turning into the driveway leading to Muriel's place. Sunlight dappled the trees, and a soft carpet of wisteria petals lay underfoot. Lena imagined every day would be filled with delight if she lived here. She let out a sigh of contentment. Milton took her hand in his. His touch was strong yet tender, and thrilling. But as they reached the clearing in front of the house, Lena withdrew her hand.

Muriel was on the back terrace. She came toward them, one hand outstretched to feel her way. Lena moved forward into her embrace.

"Lena, my dear." She stroked Lena's hair, her touch compensating for what her eyes could not see. "How wonderful that you're here! How are you?" She led Lena back to the bench. "Come, sit beside me. I want to hear everything. Milton tells me you're working in the Food Office. Such important work."

Lena told her a little about the office, and Muriel listened attentively. Milton sat opposite them on the low terrace wall, his eyes on Lena. They were interrupted by Lancelot bounding up the steps, still full of energy but with soft gray hairs now surrounding his eyes and mouth. He was followed by Alistair, carrying a pair of gardening clippers and twine.

"I'm so sorry I missed your arrival," he said, setting down his paraphernalia and greeting Lena with a hearty handshake. "I was checking on the strawberries. You're just a bit too early, I fear. You'll have to come back and see us again in about three weeks."

"I haven't seen strawberries in years!" Lena laughed.

"You have to tell us everyone's news," Muriel said. "We worry so much about you being in London. We lost track of you. The last address I had for you was in Landsdowne Road, I believe."

"I'm sorry." Lena was glad Muriel could not see her blushing. "We had to leave because the landlady's daughter was bombed out, and then we were bombed out ourselves a few months later. It was difficult to keep in touch." This wasn't much of an excuse.

"Of course. I understand, dear." Muriel reached out with her hand, which Lena took in gratitude. "The post to and from London has been so erratic anyway. Tell me, how is everyone? How is Lotti?" Lena was grateful that, with perfect English tact, Muriel had not asked first about Otto.

"She's working as a nursing assistant at Barts. And she's pregnant. Due in October."

"How exciting."

"Supper's almost ready," Alistair said from the doorway. "We're having chicken. I hope that will be to your taste."

"We don't see much chicken in London," Milton said.

"We're fortunate. Old Hubbs down at Snaresbrook Farm keeps us well supplied."

"Let me get drinks," Alistair said. "The usual for you, Milton? Lena, what about you?"

It was almost like the old days, those enchanting summer evenings. Milton opened the gramophone and selected a Mozart concerto. The cowslip wine was soon buzzing through her veins. She caught the delicious aroma of roast chicken from the kitchen.

"Yes, I believe the strawberries are going to be rather successful this year," Alistair said. "But I'm afraid I utterly failed with the broad beans. Of course, before the war, one had gardeners to take care of all that sort of thing. But here we are, digging for victory." His eyes sparkled.

Lena smiled politely, but she was distracted by the conversation to her left.

"The ILP disgusts me more every day," she heard Milton say. "They're rejecting everything CW and the Labour Party are pushing for."

"What about the WIL and the PBI? Are they still going strong?" Muriel said.

Milton said something Lena didn't catch, and they both collapsed into peals of laughter. They seemed to be talking in their own private code.

"I see the Trotskyists are getting all the credit for the Tyneside strikes," Muriel said.

"Yes, much to the fury of the CP."

It wasn't so much that Lena couldn't follow the conversation. She'd read about the engineering strike and the threat to jail the strikers and had some understanding of the factions on the Left. And when Milton turned to include her in the discussion, she managed to say something semi-intelligent about the need for a united progressive front. But it seemed utterly unfair that Milton could have this kind of conversation with his mother; that he could be talking to his mother about *anything*, as if this were the simplest thing in the world. Perhaps that was why it had been difficult to write to Muriel. She wanted to be able to write to *her* mother, not to someone else's. Not that she could have this kind of conversation with Máma. They would have to steer clear of politics. But she'd be happy to talk about anything—even stupid things, like Mrs. Svobodova's curtains in the upstairs flat, or why Lena's handbag didn't match her shoes. It wouldn't matter—just to be able to see Máma and touch her and know that everything was all right, that would be enough.

Muriel, Alistair, Milton—they were all kind and generous and had the best political sympathies, but they didn't realize how lucky they were. Other families were torn apart. It wasn't their fault, they were not to blame, but they had everything; they had each other, together in the same country, they had a beautiful home, they had strawberries, real meat. This might be the "people's war," but some people were suffering a lot more than others.

Yet when they rose for dinner and she found Milton at her side, she looked into his eyes and the resentment melted away. "It's a different world here, isn't it?" he whispered in her ear. "Let's slip away after supper and go for a walk. There'll be plenty of daylight left."

CHAPTER 38

LONDON, MAY 1944

The lunch bell rang—a piercing noise that Otto would have found unbearable if it didn't signify a welcome respite. The workers spilled out of the workshops and headed for the washrooms to change out of overalls before eating. That was one union victory: the extra time allowed for changing and washing had eliminated a lot of the "tummy trouble" they used to get. Yes, the girls had been worked up about that, all right, had even threatened to strike.

Otto stood in the queue at the counter, waiting for his serving of buttered Spam and chips, scanning the crowd for Harry. He was hungry. He had missed breakfast. He'd worked overtime last night and had suddenly remembered as he turned into Donegal Street that Lena would be gone and there was probably no food at home. In a mild panic, he realized he had no idea where his ration book was or who they were registered with. But Lena had left his book on the kitchen table with a note giving directions to Edwards and Son on Pentonville Road. There had been no time to shop, however. This morning, he'd had only a cup of black tea and a few spoonfuls of plum jam scooped from the jar.

Harry waved him over to a table by the window.

"Wait till you 'ear this," he said in a conspiratorial half-whisper as Otto squeezed into the seat opposite him. "Had a drink with Dobson from the Branch Office last night. Gave me all the scoop on

Spencer, 'e did." Harry slurped his tea loudly. "You won't believe the profits they're rakin' in. Up more than ferr'ee percen' from last year."

It took a moment for Otto to catch his meaning. "What?"

"Yup. Ferr'ee percent, mate."

He must mean 30 percent. A 30 percent increase over last year's profits? That was scurrilous.

"And get this," Harry continued. "The men in the ROF filling factories make seven quid a week."

"The government factories are paying more?"

"Yeah. Took them for bleedin' ever to let us know that, didn't it?"

"What about the girls?"

"Same difference, mate. They get five smackers in the ROFs."

"Five what?"

"Sorry, mate. Five quid. Ten bob more than what they get 'ere."

Smackers, quid, bob: the English money was complicated enough without these slang words. And you didn't say *quids* or *bobs* even when it was clearly plural. He'd made himself a laughingstock with that mistake.

"Dobson's comin' over for the meetin' on Monday," Harry was saying. "Think you could get some of the girls in your section to come along?"

Otto said he'd try. Monday evening: Lena would be back, and he'd be glad of a good excuse not to be home. Not that he cared what she did. They'd been just going through the motions of staying together for months now. Years. If housing hadn't been impossible to find, he would have moved out long ago. He didn't find her attractive anymore. She was too strident, harsh. Still hopelessly naive about some things, but not in the endearing way she'd been in Paris, when she'd listened to his every word.

Perhaps Eva would be free tonight. They could go back to her place again. He remembered her shapely legs and the way she moved on top of him, and felt a quickening in his groin. But last week, she hadn't let him into her flat. She'd made an excuse about that stupid Mavis woman she lived with, was afraid she'd prattle to Lena. Later that night, he saw her leaving with her American boyfriend.

Harry waved to a man returning his tray to the shelves by the door, a young man with a marked limp, thin and scrawny-looking. Most of the women were making their way to the adjoining room, where *Workers' Playtime* was on the wireless. Otto could hear that nauseating "White Cliffs of Dover" song wafting over the airways.

"Mickey!" Harry shouted. "Over 'ere, mate."

The youngster waved back enthusiastically and scooted around the tables.

"This is Otto. The one I was tellin' you about." Harry turned to Otto. "Mickey 'ere has been coming to the Party meetin's." He beamed with pride.

"Next meeting on Wednesday—right, Mr. Robinson?"

"I keep tellin' you to call me Harry, son."

"Sorry. Harry." The boy grinned. "Comrade Harry."

Harry turned to Otto. "We have a lecture this week on the . . ." He pulled a leaflet from his rear pocket and unfolded it. He held it at arm's length and squinted at the print. "'The Class Struggle in the Nazi-occupied Territories'. Right up your alley, mate."

Harry was always trying to get him to CP meetings. Sometimes the prospect intrigued Otto. The communists were probably the only ones with the organization to create revolution in the aftermath of the war. He wondered who was giving this talk. He looked at the paper—no one he'd ever heard of. Otto couldn't imagine he'd have anything new to say. But having another excuse to be out in the evening was appealing.

"Did you hear the news this morning?" the boy said. "The Red Army has taken another town in the Ukraine. There's no stopping Uncle Joe! Won't be long before he's in Berlin!"

That was why Otto wouldn't go to the meeting: he had no stomach for the idolization of Stalin. One thing he was curious about, however: "What is the Party saying about the Second Front these days?" he asked Harry.

"Dunno, mate. Haven't heard a word."

It must be imminent, then, if the Party was quiet on the subject. The communists were the earliest and loudest in agitating for the invasion. If they were silent, Moscow must have received the word from Churchill.

Marge and the other girl waved to Otto as they passed by. You could see their figures when they weren't encased in the white overalls. That other girl was very attractive, with thick blond hair and a sassy sway in her walk. He must find out her name.

"Comrade Harry," Mickey was saying. "Did you read in the *Daily Worker* about the counterrevolutionary Trotskyists responsible for the Tyneside strikes?"

Otto opened his mouth to say something in protest but then stopped himself. What was the point? This was an ignorant youngster being taken in by the Party hacks, wasting their energy attacking the noncommunist Left. You couldn't have a serious political discussion with the likes of him—or Harry, for that matter, who was a good sort but hardly what you would call intellectual. He followed the Party line and was oblivious to the twists and turns that line took.

Otto yearned for the lively political discourse of the Berlin and Prague days. And even in Upper Wolmingham—those evenings with Peter and the group, and with Muriel and Milton—he missed all that. They hadn't always seen eye to eye, but it had been stimulating.

The work in here was mind-numbing; the war dragged on with endless monotony. He was surrounded by idiots. That was why he was so bad-tempered with Lena. He didn't mean to be—it just came out that way. He couldn't blame her for wanting to go off with Milton. Milton was young, charming, much better looking. And Milton had stirred up enough political trouble in the army to get himself kicked out—quite an achievement. Otto had to admire him for that. Of course Lena wanted to go to Sussex. He would like to see Muriel himself. He didn't know why he'd been so lukewarm about the idea. Yes, Muriel and Milton were firmly entrenched in the English upper class, but they had progressive views, and Otto owed his life to Muriel—he couldn't forget that.

The bell rang. The canteen echoed with the sounds of chairs scraping on the floor, plates clattering against each other, cutlery being thrown into the steel pot on the counter. Time to head back to the washrooms, to change into overalls again for the afternoon shift.

"See you later, mate." Harry patted Otto on the shoulder.

"It was nice to meet you, Mr., er, Otto, sir," chirped the boy.

Otto picked up another load of cordite boxes from C Block and returned to the shop.

Even before he pushed his cart through the door, he sensed the commotion. The girls weren't at their stations; they were huddled in the corner, some screaming and yelling, someone was sobbing, there was blood on the floor. Bert rushed over, pushing to get in the middle of things. A girl ran in front of him, carrying a wet cloth and a small metal box.

"What happened?"

"Doreen's gone and smashed her fingers in the cutting machine."

The circle parted like grass in the wind. In the center sat a girl, perched on an upended crate, deathly pale, quiet tears streaking down her cheeks. She bit down on her lower lip, both hands clenched in her lap. A bright red stain oozed across her overalls. Marge grabbed the first-aid box and pulled out bandages, shouted out instructions for the other girls to open this, hold up that.

"She's gonna need an ambulance, Bert," Marge said, without looking up. She added more layers, creating a massive fist of padding.

Doreen grimaced in pain.

A girl next to her was crying, "Oh my God. She lost at least three fingers in that machine."

"I think I'm going to pass out," someone else said.

Otto felt light-headed himself. On the floor next to the cutting machine lay something red, gelatinous, horribly digit-looking.

"Just calm down, calm down, the lot of you," Bert shouted. "For Christ's sake. Here, let me have a look."

"I always said that machine was going to get someone one of these days." This was from an older woman to Otto's right: Connie. Tiny, she stood barely to his shoulders, but she had a feisty streak. "They don't care. We ain't nothing to them." She spat out the words.

Bert tried to pull the wounded girl to her feet. Somehow she managed to stand. Marge supported her on the other side.

"Come on. That's enough gawking," Bert said. "Back to work."

There was a stunned silence.

"You've got to be kidding," Marge said.

"I'm not kidding. I said get back to work."

"Doreen's gonna need a doctor."

"What Doreen needs is to get back on that line. Back in the saddle, as they say. Come on. Jump to it." He clapped his hands and propelled Doreen forward.

"No!" Marge shouted. "No way, mister." She narrowed her eyes and looked over to Otto with such a fierce expression, he flinched. "Go and fetch Harry Robinson," she barked at him. "Come on, girls." She marched to the door, leading Doreen with her. "We . . . are . . . walking . . . out."

And that was what they did. Just like that. Bert was screaming and yelling for them to get back right now, but they ignored him and poured out into the yard. Otto beamed with pride. He ran over to Caps and Detonators to tell Harry Robinson, and Harry called for an ambulance.

CHAPTER 39

SUSSEX, MAY 1944

On Saturday, they went for a long walk across the fields to Elm-inghurst. Lena's arms tingled in the warm sunshine. Bright clusters of buttercups adorned the gateposts, as if they were smiling back at her. They talked comfortably and endlessly. Milton described his plans for the future. He was thinking of studying law.

"There's going to be a tremendous need for progressive lawyers in the postwar reconstruction," he said. "We're going to have to defend the nationalization of industry, build a whole new legal system, and support the education, health, and welfare services."

She loved his absolute faith in the possibility of change. They stood at the top of the Long Field, with its view of the South Downs. His grand plans seemed to match the sweeping vista.

"That will be something to look forward to. After all we've been through." Lena paused. "After all that's still to come."

"Yes." He paused, too. "I feel guilty that I won't be taking part in the invasion," he confessed. "So many will be risking their lives while I sit on the sidelines and cheer them on. That's why I have to be involved politically. I have to make a contribution."

He invited her to a meeting at Conway Hall the following week. He told her more about the Common Wealth Party platform. He asked her opinion, wanted to hear about the attitudes of the women she worked with. What did they think of the government? How would they vote in the next election?

"Do you think anyone is fooled by Churchill's feeble attempts to hop on the bandwagon and pretend he supports reform?" He picked up a thick twig and impersonated the prime minister puffing at his cigar, then lowered his voice to a Churchillian growl. "I suppose one will have to give the damn peasants something for fighting this war, just as long as we can go back to capitalism as it was in the good old days."

Lena laughed. Puffy white clouds danced across the sky.

They stopped for a beer at the Green Man, sitting at a tiny table under dark oak beams. He talked about the report he was working on for Mass Observation, on the need for state-sponsored nurseries for working mothers. He asked about the children of the women she worked with, who took care of them during the day.

Lena's mind felt alive, as though her brain cells were jumping for joy. But her body was feeling something else. A feeling she hardly dared name. She watched his hands as they cradled his beer glass. She saw that scar again, on the middle finger of his left hand. It was fainter now.

Milton behaved like a perfect gentleman, flattering and attentive. He placed his hand on her back as he guided her over the stream behind Snaresbrook Farm. He took her elbow as they walked down a steep, narrow path that led into the wood. A carpet of bluebells covered the ground, brilliant in the dappled sunlight.

"I'd forgotten the bluebells," Lena said. "They're spectacular."

"Yes. This is my favorite time of year."

They stood close, shoulder to shoulder, sharing this sight. And when they reached the kissing gate at the other end, he lingered, he on one side of the swinging barrier, she on the other. He looked into her eyes, and Lena held her breath—but then she looked away, overcome with nerves. He pecked her on the cheek, and the moment passed.

She wished she had not turned away. He would think she was brushing him off.

They enjoyed another evening at The Hollow, eating, drinking, talking, listening to music. It was warm enough to keep the windows open, delaying as long as possible the moment of turning on the lights and putting up the blackout shades. While Muriel sang some of her traditional Sussex folk songs in her rich, strong voice, Milton sat next to Lena on the sofa, his knee brushing against hers.

It was very late when Muriel and Alistair retired for the night. After Milton cleared the glasses, Lena said, "I've had a wonderful day. Thank you so much."

"The pleasure's all mine." He gave a little bow, almost in mock deference.

Lena laughed. She imagined throwing herself into his arms. But then she heard the sound of something dropping on the floor upstairs, and the soft, deep murmur of Alistair's voice, followed by Muriel's light laugh. Milton turned his head toward the sound. It seemed impossible to embrace with his mother's presence looming over the room.

He kissed her hand and bade her good night. Lena retreated to the attic guest room under the eaves. She lay in the narrow bed, in its smooth white sheets, astonished at the boldness of her body as it yearned to be with him. Yet she was also terrified at the prospect. Otto was the only man she'd ever been with. She was so familiar with the landscape of his body—the crook of his shoulder where her head nestled so perfectly, the wiry hair on his chest, his knobby knees. Recently, their lovemaking had seemed empty and mechanical. But it was comforting in its own way; she was used to it. She wasn't sure she would know what to do with anyone else.

Sleep did not come easily. She tried to quell the chatter in her head and the squirming of her legs, but at the moment when she felt perhaps she was sinking into the velvet comfort of oblivion, she jerked awake again, remembering Milton's shoulder rubbing against hers as they admired the view, and the urge she'd had to touch him. She tugged at the counterpane to loosen its grip at the foot of the bed. She could faintly discern the outline of the window behind the blackout shade, with a slim streak of moonlight seeping through. She thought guiltily of Otto lying at home alone.

She must have drifted off eventually. She overslept, missed breakfast. "Good for you," Muriel chuckled. "Must be all the fresh country air."

She seemed unperturbed by Lena's late appearance. Máma would have been cross; she always acted as if the flat were untidy if anyone was still in bed after 9:00 A.M.

"What can I get you, dear?" Muriel asked. She sat by the parlor window overlooking the terrace. She was arranging yellow roses in a small pewter vase. "Hubbs brought over some eggs this morning."

"Oh, no. Please don't go to any trouble. I'll just make myself a quick cup of tea." Lena was still stuffed from dinner.

"They say it's going to be even warmer today."

Lena couldn't take her eyes off the window, scouring the terrace and back garden for any sign of Milton. She longed to see him yet dreaded it, too, afraid that her yearnings of the previous night would be painted across her face.

"Milton walked back with Hubbs to look at the barn door. He'll be back soon. Hubbs is insisting it has to be replaced." Muriel moved to the terrace, carrying the roses, arranged just by touch into a perfectly symmetrical bouquet. "I don't know where he imagines we're going to get the materials. One simply can't get lumber anywhere these days."

Good heavens. Muriel owned the farm, too? Somehow Lena had not realized that.

"Feel free to take a bath, dear," Muriel said. "There's plenty of hot water."

Lena politely declined. Every time she used the toilet, she had to avert her eyes from the tub. She had such vivid memories of being there with Otto, stretching out together, scrubbing each other's backs.

She and Milton went for one last stroll before they took the train back to London. He walked ahead of her on the path that led back to the churchyard. He was not as tall as Otto but was broader across the shoulders, more solid. His muscles were supple under his shirt, and a patch of sweat seeped through below the collar. When it was just the two of them, it seemed simple to laugh and talk without worrying about the repercussions. But the repercussions were fast approaching, beginning on the other side of the churchyard, where they would bid farewell to Muriel and Alistair and return to London.

Lena recalled the uncomfortable scene at lunch. No one had mentioned Otto since she'd arrived. All this time. The longer this went on, the more embarrassing his absence from the conversation became. Finally, at lunch, Alistair asked after him, as if suddenly remembering a long-lost friend. Lena felt herself blushing and muttered something about his work. She probably sounded incoherent.

Thankfully, Muriel changed the subject. But soon the conversation turned to complaints about the old farmer who wanted to have the barn repaired.

"Doesn't he know there's a war going on?" Muriel grumbled.

A familiar refrain, but it seemed to have a hollow ring coming from her. Lena looked down at her plate, at a delicious rabbit stew, courtesy of this same farmer.

"We're all making sacrifices," Muriel continued. "After all, I've been unable to live in my own home for four years."

Lena found the tone disturbing. She had not remembered this from before. Had Muriel changed, or had Lena forgotten? She'd always known that Muriel was privileged. Why did it bother her now? Coming here was like stepping into a different world. Did she despise it or envy it? And how did Milton fit into it?

He rose to fetch the water jug from behind where Muriel and Alistair sat. They were outbidding each other in complaints about the cramped living conditions at The Hollow. Milton looked at her over their heads and rolled his eyes, and made a silent snapping gesture with his thumb and fingers, pantomiming their conversation. Lena had to concentrate on her roast potatoes to hide her amusement. Yet Milton did not protest or challenge them. When she thought of her tiny flat, or how Gladys from work was now living with her granddaughter and three nieces in a two-up-two-down, or the thousands of Londoners who had been bombed out and lost everything, she wanted to scream.

A heavy uneasiness settled in her chest. She'd pushed it aside for her walk with Milton, enjoying the green fields one more time.

But it came flooding back now as they returned to The Hollow. They collected their luggage and stood awkwardly in the doorway, saying good-bye.

Muriel was back to her cheerful self, and Lena thanked her profusely for a wonderful time, but the repeated invitations for her to return begged questions that hung in the air, unspoken, unanswered.

What was she doing with Milton? What did this all mean?

The train to London was crowded. They were lucky to find seats, packed in a compartment with three noisy young boys. There was no chance to talk. Milton gave up his seat at Croydon to a middle-aged woman with a bulging canvas bag. The fatigue from her restless night caught up with Lena, and she nodded off with the rhythmic rocking of the locomotive. Twice, her head jerked forward, snapping her awake.

On the Tube, Milton again invited her to join him on Friday for a meeting at Conway Hall. She said she would love to go. He smiled and said, "Splendid" in the way that made her melt. He got off at Russell Square, with a quick squeeze of her hand and a wave as the train pulled out of the station. She missed him as soon as she was in the tunnel.

Now, she was nervous about seeing Otto. How would he react to her return? Would they immediately argue? Had he found himself something to eat over the weekend?

She opened the door to the flat with trepidation. The room was empty, relatively tidy. There was a note for her on the table. A cheerful note from Otto. He hoped she'd had a nice weekend. He was sorry that he would be home late. The workers at the factory had walked out in a wildcat strike, and he was on the picket line.

CHAPTER 40

LONDON, MAY 1944

A week had never passed so slowly. Lena could not put Milton out of her mind. She thought of him when she first woke in the morning, with Otto far away on the other side of the bed. She thought of him as she walked to the Tube station, past the bombed-out wreckage on the corner of Killick Street, where the purple flowers of the firebrand willow herb sprouted idiotically from the depths of the rubble. She thought of him as she checked the eight-week reporting returns from the Holburn retailers, queued for butter and tea at the grocer's, and washed the dishes at the sink, gazing over the rooftops toward King's Cross.

Lena's thoughts fluttered back to Milton a hundred times a day, like a moth toward the light. Most of all, she remembered the view of his back as he walked ahead of her on the path through the woods, the feel of his shoulder against hers as they looked out over the rolling fields, the sight of his hands as he cradled the beer glass in the pub.

Why had she turned away as he'd been about to kiss her? Had he concluded she wasn't interested? Did she really have the courage to allow her feelings for him to run free? What if there was no way to reconcile their utterly different backgrounds? Or what if she just didn't want her life to become tangled and messy?

Otto seemed preoccupied with events at the factory. He stayed out late every night; they hardly saw each other. Lena spent the evenings alone. She wanted to tell him she was going to the meeting with Milton. Why sneak around, weaving a web of deception? Didn't he always say marriage was a bourgeois institution? Why should he care if she saw someone else? Yet, somehow, it didn't seem that simple.

Thursday evening, one more day until Friday; Lena could barely sit still. To calm herself, she took out her mending. There were socks to darn, her gray skirt was missing a button, and Otto's tweed jacket needed new elbow patches again. She made herself a cup of tea, turned on the wireless, and began to relax. There was something soothing about the repetitive motion of needle and thread, the firm pressure of the thimble against her fingertip, the sense of accomplishment when she could tie a final knot and trim off the thread, task completed.

And on the wireless, *It's That Man Again*, a favorite of everyone at work. It was difficult to follow Friday-morning conversation if she missed a week's episode. Lena laughed out loud at Mrs. Mopp and Colonel Chinstrap and their double entendres. She found herself distracted by some of the most salacious repartee, her mind wandering to a certain hillside in Sussex.

It was almost eight o'clock when she heard the front door slam and Otto's footsteps on the stairs. Her chest tightened.

"We won!" He stood in the doorway, a huge smile on his face. "The management, they give in. We'll be having a Joint Production Committee, like in the government ROF factories. Inspect all the machines for safety."

He strode across the room and helped himself to a glass of water, which he drank in huge gulps.

"And we all get more pay." He turned to face Lena. "My earnings will be seven quid a week."

She'd never heard him say *quid* before; it was always *pounds*, and always with a hint of contempt in his voice, as if he didn't approve of the currency of the realm. What's more, he was speaking in English.

"That's wonderful," she said.

Seven pounds: a lot more than she earned. His hair was disheveled, and there were dark shadows under his eyes. He sat in the armchair opposite her. "You won't believe how militant they were. They refused to go back until we got—how you say?—a commistment . . ."

"Commitment? *Eine Zusage?*"

"*Ja, ja. Eine Zusage.*" He reverted to German. "They agreed to slow down the line for all the cutting and necking machines. And Harry—now, he did a good job." He jumped to his feet. It was as if his enthusiasm could not be contained in a seated position. "Can I turn this off?" He switched off the wireless without waiting for a response. "Of course, Dobson and all those idiots from the Branch Office had to keep their distance," he continued, "with all strikes being illegal, blah, blah. Proved to be utterly spineless. Spineless." He spat out the words.

"Well, you won. That's marvelous."

"The workers really learned a lesson about the power of collective action." He looked directly at Lena for the first time since he'd entered and, with an almost imperceptible flinch, said, "How was your weekend in the country, by the way? You haven't told me anything about it. How is Muriel?"

"Well, you've been gone." Lena tried to keep her tone light. "Muriel is fine. She seems to be completely blind now. But she's otherwise well. It was lovely down there. They have so much food." She gave a light laugh and picked up her darning again, avoiding Otto's gaze.

"I suppose they're pretty much untouched by the war."

"Yes."

Lena remembered the rumblings of resentment she had felt in Sussex, but she didn't want to voice these to Otto. "But they're overrun with troops, gearing up for the invasion." A safe topic—he would be interested in this. "Everywhere tanks and army lorries, lying in wait."

"Ah. Interesting." He took out his pipe. "That means they're going to cross at Calais after all."

They fell into silence. Lena wished the wireless were still on. She concentrated on her darning, smoothing out the woolen lattice at the heel.

"I'm going to be out again tomorrow evening," he said finally. "We're all going out to celebrate."

"All right."

She breathed a quiet sigh of relief. No need, then, to mention her own plans. But a moment later she heard herself say, "I'm going out, too." She paused. He waited. She forced the words out. "Milton told me about a Common Wealth meeting. It sounds interesting."

"Common Wealth Party? Oh, for heaven's sake!"

Lena looked up at him in surprise. "Well, I . . ."

"They're just a tiny splinter group. What could they ever hope to achieve?"

"I just want to learn more about it."

Another silence. Then Otto said, "Suit yourself. But it's a waste of time, if you ask me."

At five thirty on Friday, Lena finished the retailers' ledger, gathered up her handbag and cardigan, and hurried through the lobby. Milton stood outside. He had just bought an *Evening Standard* from the boy on the corner, and his face lit up when he saw her. He looked relaxed yet elegant, his linen jacket falling smoothly from his shoulders, his open-necked shirt revealing sun-bronzed skin. In that moment, she knew there was no turning back. She didn't know what lay ahead, but she didn't care. It was as if she were poised at the top of a steep slope on her long wooden skis, high above Ždiar in the lofty Tatra Mountains, pausing for a moment before plunging forward.

She moved toward him, and he enfolded her lightly in his arms.

"How wonderful to see you again," he said. "I know a little place just around the corner from Red Lion Square. We could get a bite to eat, if you like."

Lena smiled. There was no need to talk. After hours scrunched over columns of numbers, she was delighted to throw back her shoulders, inhale the warm evening air, and stride arm in arm through the streets.

"Do you notice something different?" Milton asked, his tone more subdued.

Now that he mentioned it, there was something—a stillness in the air—in spite of this being central London. But she couldn't name it.

"There're no soldiers on the streets," he said. "The Americans: all gone. The pubs: empty."

"Oh my God."

"The proverbial calm before the storm, as it were."

Yes. The city was empty. This could mean only one thing: the invasion was imminent. Lena's gut twisted in fear. This was what they'd been waiting for, hoping for, for so long. But what if it failed? And what about Ernst? Would he embark with the first wave?

"It's exciting and awful at the same time," Milton said.

"Yes, exactly."

"I suppose your brother will be going over?"

"I believe so, yes."

"You must be worried about him." He faced her directly. "You know, we don't have to go to this meeting, if you would rather not. We could take a walk. It's a lovely evening."

It was. She was comfortable sleeveless; she held her cardigan in her free hand. "Tell me more about the meeting."

"Hugh Lawson will be there. He's the Common Wealth MP who won that sensational by-election in January, overturning a huge Tory majority. He's a great speaker."

"Can we go just for a little while?"

"Of course. We can sit at the back and leave whenever we want."

Forty people were already seated by the time they arrived; a dozen more hovered by a table covered with broadsheets and pamphlets. Lena did a quick survey: a mixed crowd of men and women in their late fifties or sixties, dressed in sensible Utility apparel; workingmen in overalls; young office girls; a few couples. The room rumbled with easy conversation. A man at the literature table waved to Milton; his right shirtsleeve dangled empty, tied in a knot just below where his elbow should have been.

An older man, completely bald, with a ruddy complexion, shook Milton's hand with vigor. Milton introduced her. Did he say "Mrs." or "Miss" Eisenberg? Lena wasn't sure. She hid her left hand behind her back to conceal her wedding ring. Why did she still wear it?

The bald man moved to the front of the room and called the meeting to order. He mumbled through some procedural matters about minutes and forthcoming meetings. He was barely audible from the back row. Lena looked at Milton, trying to catch his eye. Perhaps she could still take him up on the offer to go for a walk instead. But he was focused on a pamphlet he'd picked up from the literature table. She looked at his hands, lying gently on his lap, and his knee, almost touching hers.

The man up front seemed to pull himself together, as if snapping out of a trance. "Ahem. Yes, well," he said, raising his voice. "Enough of all that. I'm sure you haven't come to hear me go on and on." There were a few titters of polite laughter. "Ladies and gentlemen, without further ado, allow me to introduce our guest of honor, the Right Honorable member for Skipton, Mr. Hugh Lawson."

The room erupted into applause. A tall, imposing figure rose from the front row. Handsome in an unpretentious way, he was younger than Lena had expected, in his thirties, perhaps, with relaxed self-confidence. He wore a gray suit, in spite of the warmth of the evening.

"Thank you so much." He raised a hand to quiet the applause. "Thank you. I do appreciate your coming here on this beautiful evening. I'm sure you have more exciting things you could be doing." He smiled, and Lena could have sworn he looked directly at her. "But, my friends, we are at a critical moment in our country's history. Victory over the Nazis is now in sight. I believe we all understand that the invasion of the Continent will occur any day now. Of course, the war isn't over yet. We will have to endure retaliation, more raids, many more casualties. But the end is in sight."

He strode back and forth as he spoke. "That is precisely why it is so important for us to lay the groundwork for the postwar reconstruction we want to see." He stopped pacing and turned to face his audience square-on. "The Labour Party cannot provide the leadership on this. Its hands are tied by its coalition with the Tories in the National Government. And make no mistake: Churchill has made it clear he wants to return to full-blown capitalism after the war and roll back the progress we've made on a planned economy. Now is the time. Our soldiers returning home from the battlefields truly do deserve a 'land fit for heroes,' a nation with equality and justice for all."

As he continued to expound the platform, Lena found herself agreeing with everything: the need for decent work, fair pay, good education, and adequate housing and health care for everyone. If the government could organize a massive system of production and distribution for the war effort, it could do the same for peacetime.

Watching him hold the attention of the room, Lena was reminded of Otto in his heyday and the movement back in Prague, the sense of shared struggle, of devotion to something big and noble. The presentation went on for more than an hour, but Lena wasn't bored. There were questions from the audience, lively discussion. Milton raised his hand and asked a detailed question about levels of taxation, which drew a thoughtful response from the speaker.

As the meeting drew to a close and people rose to leave, Milton took Lena by the hand and led her out into the late-evening sunlight.

"That was interesting," she said.

"He's good, isn't he?" They were still holding hands. This time, she would not let go.

They walked on, the words flowing freely, their feet following with no regard to where they were headed, Milton's hand firm around hers.

"Are you a member of the Common Wealth Party?" Lena asked.

"No, but I'm considering it. They don't use the term *Party*, by the way. That's one appealing aspect. They consider it too restrictive, too reminiscent of the communists. The initials would even be the same: *CP*. So it's just *Common Wealth*: *CW*."

"Do you think they're big enough to achieve anything?"

She was playing devil's advocate here—she knew that. More precisely, Otto's advocate. It was hard to get his voice out of her head. It was Otto who had patiently explained to her the various factions in Barcelona and the history of the divisions in the socialist movement. Otto had taught her to distinguish short-term goals from long-term strategy. Eventually, by a process of osmosis, his knowledge had become hers, too. What did she—Lena by and of herself—what did she believe?

"It remains to be seen," Milton was saying. "Their by-election victories are certainly impressive. The Tories are rattled."

"What about the CP? Especially on the Continent. Don't you think the communists are going to be poised to seize control as the Red Army advances?"

"Perhaps, but I don't think we'll have the same conditions here."

It was different from her conversations with Otto. Milton's tone was tender, not argumentative. It was like floating in a gentle sea of ideas, not butting heads in conflict.

"Besides," he continued, "the CP won't have me."

"What do you mean?"

They were ambling through the back streets of Bloomsbury; Milton seemed to know where he was going. The streets were eerily quiet, as though the city were holding its breath.

"I dabbled briefly in the ILP during my Oxford days—and later, too." He hesitated for a moment. "So I'm considered persona non grata, as it were. The Party would accept me only if I were to provide a written 'confession' and break off all personal relations with any Trotskyists!" He laughed. "It's ludicrous. When they're opening the doors to any ordinary bourgeois with an ounce of vaguely progressive views!"

"That's absurd."

"Yes. It would be amusing were it not also tragic, a sad commentary on the state of the Left."

"I hate that sort of bickering. It won't get us anywhere." She didn't want the enthusiasm she'd felt at the meeting to be deflated so soon. "Can't there be a way to find common ground for the election and the postwar reconstruction?"

"Precisely. It will be crucial to have a united progressive front."

He came to a halt outside a three-story building in an imposing row; they had reached Mecklenburgh Square. The houses seemed to be struggling to retain their former dignity in the face of peeling paint and windows boarded with plywood. Milton let go of Lena's hand and looked at the ground-floor window.

"I'm afraid I've not paid attention to where we were walking," he said, with a sheepish laugh. "I seem to have led us back to my flat."

Lena felt her cheeks color. Could this really be an unintentional slip? It seemed unlikely. But he smiled at her, his face alight, and she realized she didn't care.

"Would you like to come in for a moment? I can't say I keep a full pantry, but I believe I can muster up the wherewithal for a cup of tea."

"All right."

His flat was larger than hers, with its own hallway directly inside the front door, and a small kitchen area, separate from the living room. It was sparsely furnished. The most striking feature was a large bookcase in the living room, stocked floor to ceiling. There were rows of historical biographies and volumes of political theory—Marx, Lenin, and Trotsky—as well as more recent contributions from Sartre, Orwell, J. B. Priestley, and George Bernard Shaw. But also poetry and drama: several volumes of Oscar Wilde, and Shakespeare, and a slim anthology of Keats. Lena idly browsed the shelves while Milton went into the kitchen.

When she thought about it later, Lena could not recall exactly what happened next. Or, rather, she remembered the *what* but not the *how*. He must have returned from the kitchen and encircled her from behind. She turned to face him, and he kissed her full on the lips, soft and moist, and there was a fumbling of clothes, and a moment later he was waltzing her backward to the bedroom, discarding garments en route. There was no way to stop. They stumbled onto the bed. He paused for a moment, raised on his elbows above her, his hands cupping her face.

"Is this . . . Is this all right?"

She wasn't sure if he meant all right to proceed, or to proceed without taking precautions, or to proceed in this position. But the answer was the same.

"Yes, yes." To all of the above. The words escaped in tiny gasps. She arched her hips to meet his.

CHAPTER 41

LONDON, JUNE 1944

The following Tuesday, Gladys Woodruff was the first with the news. She rushed in from the front office, flapping a stack of counterfoils in excitement.

"It's started."

For an instant, Lena was bewildered. What on earth was she talking about? The new cod-liver-oil counterfoils had already been introduced. Even Gladys could not be that confused.

But Gladys stood with her eyes wide as teacups, and then Lena knew what she meant. "They landed in Normandy early this morning. They say it's on the wireless."

Lena's hand flew to her mouth. Sheila jumped up, knocking her chair to the ground with a thud. Mrs. Manson emerged from her office. She had a wireless in there.

"Special bulletin coming up," she announced. "They're interrupting the usual program."

They stood in a circle around her desk. No one said a word. Mrs. Manson fiddled with the wireless, trying to eliminate the static. The BBC announcer intoned in a solemn voice that there was a special proclamation from Westminster. Mr. Churchill had just made a statement to the House. The first in a series of landings on the European continent had taken place, "on a scale far larger than anything that has been seen so far in the world."

Sheila crossed herself and muttered a prayer.

"Do you think this means the war will be over by Christmas?" asked Mildred.

"Praise be to the Lord, let's hope so," Sheila said.

"I wouldn't count on it, girls," Mrs. Manson said, switching off the wireless. "Now, back to work. We can't be slacking off now, not when our boys are crossing the Channel."

Lena tried to go back to her ledgers but couldn't concentrate. It felt surreal, finally, after all the years of waiting. She thought of the tanks rumbling through the lanes of Sussex, suddenly remembered the fresh-faced redhead she'd seen walking to the pub, one of thousands marching headlong into the melee. And Ernst. Where was he? She hadn't heard from him since their lunch together. And Máma. Dear Máma. Would she hear this news and know that help was on its way?

The whole world had turned upside down in the space of a few days. The Second Front had been launched at last and Lena had a new lover. She yearned to see Milton, to see him and hold him and to share this historic news with him. But he would not be back in London until the following week; he was on assignment in the Midlands. Perhaps Lotti would be home tonight. She couldn't bear the thought of another tense evening in the flat with Otto. They were living in a foggy no-man's-land. He came home late, and had slept on the sofa one night, but they hadn't talked; she hadn't explicitly told him she had slept with Milton, and he hadn't asked. But she knew he knew.

"Will I have to challenge Otto to a duel at daybreak?" Milton had said that first night as they lay in his bed. He was propped on his side, gently stroking her forearm with his fingertips.

He was joking, of course. But Lena would almost rather that than this stifling stalemate of silence.

The following week, Lena received a note from Lotti: she wanted to get together for dinner on Thursday. Lena had not yet told her about Milton. She had started to say something when she went over on D-Day, but then Lotti's neighbors, Wilma and Peggy, from across the street had come over, too, everyone wanting to listen to the BBC, since Lotti had the only functioning wireless, and they hadn't had a chance to talk more.

The truth was, she was nervous about Lotti's reaction. Lotti liked to talk about them all going back to Prague together after the war—she and Peter, Otto and Lena—and raising their families together. It was a picture Lena could never imagine herself fitting into, but she never challenged Lotti on this. Now, Lotti would see that she was throwing all that overboard.

But Lena really didn't care. Milton was returning to town later that night, and she couldn't wait to see him.

Lotti's note suggested meeting at six and going to the British Restaurant on Tottenham Court Road. Lena went to Lotti's straight from work.

"You're early!" Lotti greeted her, as they embraced. "Come in. I'm almost ready."

"I thought we could eat early and then go on to the News Cinema on Oxford Street."

"Yes, good idea. You know me, always ready to eat these days." Lotti was five months along, and seemed to be hungry all the time. "I have this terrible craving for sauerkraut, but I'm sure they won't have that anywhere!"

"But at least the portions will be huge at the restaurant," Lena said.

Lotti stepped back and looked Lena up and down. "You look very nice. My goodness, is that a new skirt?"

"Yes." Lena pirouetted, with her hands on her hips. The skirt was a delicate, pale blue with a soft sheen that glistened in the light from the window.

"It's lovely! How much was that?"

"Twelve points. I haven't bought any clothes in months, so I have plenty of coupons. It was three guineas. I got a frock, too. At Selfridges."

"It's even got pleats." Lotti fingered the material. "Goodness! What's the occasion?"

"Oh, nothing in particular."

"I'm so jealous! Just when those horrid restrictions are lifted and clothes are pretty again, I'm stuck with these ugly hand-me-downs." She pointed to her shapeless beige dress.

They laughed and walked arm in arm to the Tube. Lena started to tell Lotti about a woman at work who had confused Normandy with Norway. They were waiting to cross the street, and Lena was gesticulating with her hands to illustrate how she'd drawn a map of Europe for the poor girl, when Lotti suddenly noticed.

"What happened to your wedding ring?"

Lena halted midair, both hands outstretched. Then she turned to Lotti with a smile, linked arms with her again, and strode across the street.

"I took it off. I don't want to wear it anymore."

"What's going on?"

Lena did not respond. She continued walking, with a smile like a pancake spread across her face. She saw Lotti's eyes widen as the pieces slid into place.

"Lena Kulkova! Are you having an affair?"

"Don't you think you're making a mistake?" Lotti asked, as they left the restaurant, hurrying now, because they had talked so long. They were trying to make the seven thirty show. "Isn't this just a little infatuation?"

"I don't know what it is, but I can't remember when I felt this happy."

"You do look radiant," Lotti said.

As they turned into Oxford Street, they saw a huge queue at the cinema.

"Oh no! Look at that." Lotti said.

"I suppose everyone's eager for news on the progress in France," Lena said.

As they walked to the end of the line, she saw a familiar face in the crowd. "Eva!" she exclaimed. "How are you?"

And then stopped in her tracks, her smile frozen. Otto stood next to her. And Mavis, too.

Eva giggled nervously. Otto peered over everyone's heads, staring at the front of the queue.

Mavis broke the silence. "Hello, Lena. Lovely to see you, Lotti." She was the only one oblivious to the tension. "Fancy seeing you here! I'm just bumping into everyone this evening. I ran into Eva and Otto as they were leaving and invited myself along! You look wonderful, Lotti. Look at you! You're blooming! Here, come and join us. We can all go in together. That's it. Lovely!" Mavis pulled them into small talk as the queue shuffled forward.

"Isn't this *civilized?*" Otto said to no one in particular, curling his upper lip around the words.

They sat near the back, Lotti positioned between Lena and Otto, as the screen played dramatic footage from Normandy: a cloud of paratroopers descending like locusts onto French fields, tanks storming the beaches, the villages of Bayeux and Sainte-Mère-Église falling to British and American forces. The announcer praised their heroic efforts to the sound of stirring music. The audience cheered loudly, stamped their feet, whistled in appreciation. No one could resist being swept up by the spectacle.

But as the next feature was announced, Lena gripped Lotti's hand. "Oh my God! Look! Terezín!"

The people seated immediately in front turned in surprise. Otto jerked his head toward Lena in obvious disapproval.

The cursive script unfolded across the screen: the International Red Cross had paid a visit to Terezín, or Theresienstadt, as they called it, using the German name. The announcer's tone remained buoyant. The Red Cross, with representatives from the Danish government, had inspected conditions in the special town for Jews located just outside Prague. An idyllic city protecting them from the stresses of the war. The camera spanned the low concrete buildings. Young women tended a garden. Two bakers unloaded heaps of fresh bread from wood-fired ovens. In the cultural center, an orchestra rehearsal was in session.

Lena continued to grip Lotti's hand. She knew Lotti remembered Terezín well—it was a garrison town where Peter had done his military service, back in '36. They exchanged a brief, fearful glance. Was this where Máma and Sasha were now? And Lotti's Matka and Father and Babička? And Rosa, Rudi, and Max? All those left behind?

The camera swept past the orchestra to a stage where a group of costumed children were singing. Lena was riveted. Was Sasha there? She couldn't see very well; there were no close-up shots. And Sasha would be much older now, of course, almost grown. But there were some older children in the group, too. It was an opera, the announcer said, written and performed by the town's inhabitants. *Brundibár*, it was called: *The Bumblebee*.

They sat there, stunned, while the rest of the audience filed out. The lights came up to reveal a yellowish, smoke-filled haze.

"That didn't look so bad," Lotti said.

"Those terrible reports you hear must be grossly exaggerated," Lena said.

"You believe that balderdash?" Otto said. "It's obviously pure propaganda."

"What are you talking about?" Lena said. "That's from the Red Cross."

"You can't seriously think that's an accurate portrayal of a Nazi camp."

"But the cameras were there. You could see for yourself what it's like."

"They were clearly duped. It's a complete fraud."

"But the worst rumors have all been from Poland. The —"

"You really believe that Hitler is going to spare the Czech Jews?"

Lotti, sitting in the crossfire, sandwiched between them, tried to jump in as mediator: "Well, perhaps there's some truth—"

But Lena jumped up. "I'm sick and tired of you always being so damn pessimistic!" she shouted at Otto. "Always, every single time, you have to see the worst possibility. Why can't you just once say, 'Maybe it's going to be all right'? Would that be so terrible? Just once to allow people to keep a glimmer of hope alive? To refuse to accept that the only outcome is unimaginable horror?"

Lena turned on her heel.

"Lena!" Mavis wailed. "Where're you going?"

No one else needed to ask.

CHAPTER 42

LONDON, NOVEMBER 1944

"Are you sure you don't mind?" Lotti said.

"No, go on. Enjoy yourselves." Lena picked up the newspaper. She scanned the headline: CANADIANS CAPTURE ZEEBRUGGE.

"We won't stay long, I promise. He's just been fed and changed. He should sleep for a while."

Lena shooed Lotti and Peter out of the flat. "Go on. If you stand here and talk about it much longer, it will be time for the next feeding."

"We'll be at the Rose and Crown on the corner," Peter said, "if you need us for anything."

It was his last night of leave. He had been home for three days but was soon to depart for an overseas assignment.

"Go on," Lena said. "I'll see you later. Take your time."

Lotti cast a last, lingering look at the crib in the corner—fashioned from the bottom drawer of the chest of drawers, well-padded with small pillows and blankets. Almost as soon as the door closed behind them, Charles startled awake with a small cry, but then he gurgled and went back to sleep. Lena walked toward the crib and stared at the infant.

He had a wisp of brown hair in the center of his forehead, soft, chubby cheeks, and definitely Peter's chin. He was snuggled in several layers, warm and cozy. She gave the blanket at his feet an extra tuck for good measure and opened the newspaper. She flipped through the inside pages, searching for news about Czechoslovakia. Nothing. The RAF had sunk the battleship *Tirpitz* in a Norwegian fjord, and the Red Army had entered the suburbs of Budapest. All good news, but Lena could feel no elation. The Allies seemed to be stalled on the Western Front. France may have been liberated back in August, but the Germans were not conceding Belgium or Holland without a fight to the death. The Doodlebug rockets were still hammering London; the Nazi launching sites on the Continent were functioning with impunity.

She'd had enough. She wanted this to be over. Everywhere around her, there was an overwhelming sense of weariness. Gloom and weariness.

Charles stirred again, kicking his little legs under the blankets. A rivulet of drool escaped from his lower lip. Such sweet innocence, such a marvel, this new life perfectly formed, oblivious to all the death and destruction in the world, impervious to the lack of news about the fate of his grandparents or his aunts and uncles, unfazed by the latest devastation from flying bombs. Lena remembered Sasha as a baby: her rosy cheeks, the softness of her skin, that smell, almost sickly sweet.

Lena yearned for news from Prague. She'd received a letter from Ernst a few weeks earlier; the Czech Brigade was bogged down, besieging the port of Dunkirk. They were still in France! The Germans were refusing to surrender the city. So, after all this time, Ernst was still hundreds of miles from Prague. Perhaps Peter would get there first. He said he would be traveling to Czechoslovakia via a tortuous route—sailing through the Strait of Gibraltar—on assignment with the RAF and the Czech Ministry of Information, laying the groundwork for postwar Czech broadcasting services. She couldn't imagine how long his journey would take—he thought he would be gone for months—but perhaps he would be the first to reach home.

She realized it had been unrealistic—and Otto never missed an opportunity to point out how absurd she'd been—but somehow she'd imagined the Czech Brigade charging through with breakneck speed, and Ernst writing that he'd found Sasha. And Máma. Although Lena found it hard to picture Máma these days. When she looked at the photograph she had, of herself and Máma walking back from the bakery in Staré Město, she tried to imagine where Máma was, what she was doing now, but nothing came into focus. Mostly, she envisioned holding Sasha, having Sasha come live with her here in England.

She thought often of the newsreel they had seen of the Red Cross visit to Terezín, the grainy images of the children in the opera *Brundibár*, the conductor waving his arms in the air, the bright-eyed faces singing in earnest. Those children looked happy, well fed. She held on to this image with dogged determination.

The news from eastern Poland a few months earlier, after the Red Army liberation of Majdanek—and the discovery of a gruesome camp, a gigantic murder factory—was preposterous, impossible to accept. Many dismissed it as Soviet propaganda. Lena refused to believe it. But she could not shake a sickening, black fear.

Shivering at these thoughts, she put the kettle on for tea. She stood at the window, gazing out at the street. The blackout had officially ended two months earlier, and she could see a few isolated streetlights at the end of the road. It was queer to have no blackout screens. Lotti had no curtains to replace them, so Lena stared at the unfamiliar sight of her reflection in the glass. She felt oddly exposed and stepped away.

Lotti's flat was on the ground floor, so it lacked the view over the rooftops that Lena enjoyed from her own place. But it did have an extra bedroom—small, yet it would suffice. Could she be happy here? Peter had asked her earlier in the evening if she would move in with Lotti now that he was going overseas. It was no secret that her marriage to Otto was essentially over. Yet she stayed on at Donegal Street. She liked her flat. She kept hoping Otto would leave. He was gone most of the time, out with his friends from the factory, or often, she suspected, with Eva. By an unspoken agreement, when he did come home, he slept on the sofa.

"Tell him to leave, why don't you?" Sheila had said on more than one occasion.

"I can't do that. Where would he go?"

He wouldn't find anything else. As if to illustrate the point, the next day, Sheila's cousins in Croydon were bombed out, their house completely flattened by a Doodlebug. They moved in with Sheila and her mother and sister, squeezing a family of five into the tiny house.

"Move in with Prince Charming," Sheila also suggested.

Lena laughed. She enjoyed Sheila's gentle teasing. But Milton hadn't suggested that, and Lena wasn't ready to live with him. The following week, Milton's windows were blown out and the bathroom obliterated in a rocket attack, and he retreated to Sussex. Lena hadn't seen him for almost three weeks. Two weeks, five days, and nine and a half hours, to be precise.

The sirens wailed into action again, off to the east, toward Shoreditch, perhaps. No one paid them any attention anymore. What was the point? The buzz bombs came willy-nilly, at any time of day or night. There was nothing you could do about it.

The water boiled, and she made the tea—and then froze. Something—a prickling sensation, perhaps, at the back of her neck, as if all the tiny hairs were standing at attention, or a vague buzzing in her ears—something made her drop the cup on the table, spilling hot tea onto her wrist, and hurl herself toward the crib to grab the baby. Then there was an almighty flash of white light outside and a deafening roar, followed by a boom like an afterthought, an echo in the void. The whole building seemed to vibrate in anger. She heard screams coming from upstairs, the sound of crashing glass, the loud thud of a slamming door.

She landed on the floor, across the room, curled up in a ball, with Charles swaddled in her arms. He started to cry. Moving into a seated position, leaning against the wall, she separated the blankets to take a peek. He appeared unharmed. She rocked him gently, with her knees propped in front of her, trying to soothe him. She hummed a lullaby, to calm him, yes—but also to gain control of her teeth; the top row hammered against the bottom, and she could not make them stop. Her heart pounded in her chest. Across the room, two of the windows had fractured. In the crib, ten feet from where she sat, a huge shard of glass was propped vertically, like a spear.

Lena sat on the floor, stunned. Time passed. Two minutes?

Twenty? She became aware of shouts, noisy footsteps, crunched glass. The door flew open. Peter and Lotti stood before her. Lotti saw the broken glass in the crib and screamed. Peter took the baby from Lena's arms and helped her to her feet. She was still shaking.

"What the hell was that?" Lena said.

"An explosion of some sort."

"There was no warning, nothing."

"I know. We were in the pub," Peter said. "It wasn't a Doodle-bug. There was no engine noise. It came out of the blue."

"It has to be a flying rocket or something." Lena rubbed her arms, as if she needed to check that she was still in one piece.

"Oh my God," Lotti said, sobbing.

Peter pulled her in close. Charles started to cry in earnest now, his toothless gums circling a desperate wail.

"When on earth are they going to tell us what's going on?" Lena said. "All the rumors and ridiculous stories about gas explosions . . ."

"They were just talking about that in the pub," Peter said. "'Flying gas mains' was how the barman put it. Having quite a joke about it, they were."

"I don't see what's funny." Lotti glared at him and took Charles into her arms. "Look at that." She tilted her chin at the broken glass in the crib as she sat and unbuttoned her blouse to nurse.

Peter inspected the shattered windows. "I'll put up the black-out screens for now," he said. "In the morning, before I leave, I'll try to find some plywood." He stuck his neck out into the darkness. "I think it was a dud," he added. "It looks as though it exploded in midair, just before impact. They say the ones that hit the ground create a massive crater and wipe out the whole street."

"If that's a dud, I'd hate to see the real thing," Lotti said.

"Perhaps it was an act of sabotage," Lena said. "By a Polish slave laborer."

Peter extracted a glass remnant from the frame. "Whatever the reason, I think it saved us."

"*You* saved Charles," Lotti said to Lena. She rocked back and forth as she clutched him to her breast. "Thank goodness you were here. And that you were holding him."

"I don't . . . I really don't know how that happened."

"You have to move in here," Peter said. "I don't want Lotti living on her own with these things flying about."

Lena swept up the glass fragments. "It was quite by chance. . . . I can't explain. Something made me run and pick him up."

"A premonition," Lotti said.

"Except I don't believe in such things."

"Pure luck, then. Whatever it is, it makes me want you to stay."

"I know it's irrational," Peter said. "But I would feel better knowing you're here."

"Besides," Lotti said. "I feel guilty having the extra room when so many people are overcrowded. I would far rather have you live here than with some stranger."

"I suppose. But what about . . ." She wanted to ask something about Milton's staying over. Would Lotti approve?

"*Budeš tu jako doma*," Lotti said. "It would be your home. You would be free to do as you please." She looked Lena directly in the eye. "I mean that. I just want you to be happy."

Lena nodded in gratitude. "I could move in at the end of the week."

She walked the short distance back to her own flat, gingerly feeling her way around broken glass. The new streetlights at the end of the road had been shattered by the blast of the latest mysterious *Vergeltungswaffe* in Hitler's arsenal of revenge.

But Lena felt a flutter of excitement. She would have her own room at Lotti's: a new place to call home. Without having to tiptoe around Otto's moods. And, she thought to herself with a huge smile, a place to be with Milton when he was in town.

Five days later, Churchill officially announced that Britain had been under rocket attack for the past several weeks.

"Honest to God, I was beginning to think we were all crazy," Sheila said. "It's better now we know."

"Still not a word in the papers about where they're falling or nothing," Gladys said. They were gathered around the table in the lunchroom. "We heard them explosions yesterday evening, south of the river, great plumes of smoke."

"Poor buggers," Sheila said.

Gladys drew a sharp in-breath and pursed her lips in disapproval.

"Oops, sorry, Gladys. 'Scuse my French."

Gladys no longer insisted on being addressed as Mrs. Wood-ruff, but there were some standards she felt obliged to uphold.

"These rockets are beastly," Lena said. "They come out of nowhere."

"Better than the Doodlebugs, if you ask me. Ah Jesus—that waiting, holding your breath, seeing if it's going to cut out, then running to find somewhere to hide. The worrying on it is enough to kill you."

"I don't know," Lena said. "I'd rather get some warning."

"Not me," Sheila said.

"But that one last week"—Lena shuddered at the memory—"came out of the blue. I still don't know how I managed to grab Lotti's baby."

"I'd rather not know if it's going to hit me. Better to go quick." Sheila gave a little laugh.

A surreal conversation, Lena thought. "Anyway, it can't go on for much longer," she said. "The Allies have to get to the launching sites soon."

"Jesus, Mary, Joseph, I hope so." Sheila crossed herself. "I pray to the Lord Almighty that He'll keep us safe."

Lena wanted to say, *If the Lord was that Almighty, surely he could stop the damn things altogether.* But she didn't.

"When's you-know-who coming back, then?" Sheila said, after Gladys left the room. Lena's love life remained their little secret in the office.

"Tomorrow." Lena smiled. All that talk about rockets had shoved her excitement aside for a few minutes, but she longed to see Milton.

"Where's he going to stay, then?"

"He's bringing a workman up from the country to do repairs on his flat. I'm going to ask him to help me move into Lotti's."

"She doesn't mind, then, your friend? About him, I mean."

"No," Lena said. "She doesn't mind. She's getting used to the idea."

Sheila wiped the crumbs off the table. "And have you told *Mister* that you're moving out?"

"Not exactly. I'm going to tell him tonight."

Sheila gave her a skeptical look.

"I know. I will. I will."

Lena saw him at the top of the Tube steps as she emerged at Leicester Square. Milton wore a tartan scarf around his neck, his hands buried in his coat pockets, a rolled-up newspaper tucked under one arm. He unfurled as she approached and pulled her into a tight embrace. She inhaled the warmth of him, felt his freshly shaven cheek against hers.

"It's so good to be back," he said. He kissed her on the lips.

People jostled past. A large shopping bag bumped into her, buckling her right knee. Milton pulled away an inch and steered them over to the side, out of the flow of traffic, and then kissed her again, long and soft and moist.

"We should move from here, I suppose," he said a few minutes later. "Would you like to go to the theater? *Blithe Spirit* is still playing at the Duchess. Have you seen it?"

"No. I've heard it's very good." But it was not what she most wanted to do at that moment.

He pulled her close again, his hand in the small of her back. Their bodies pressed together. He groaned softly. "Oh my God. I wish my flat weren't in shambles."

"I suppose we could go . . ." She couldn't believe she was suggesting this. "Otto's working late all week. He won't be home until after ten."

They ran down the steps into the Underground and held hands all the way to King's Cross, sharing half a bar of chocolate that Milton found in his coat pocket, giggling like schoolchildren.

When they arrived at Donegal Street, Lena was relieved to see that the top floor was indeed dark. They crept up the stairs to avoid attracting attention from Mavis. She fumbled with the key, Milton kissing the back of her neck. Lena still half expected to see Otto lying in wait, but the flat was empty. She pulled Milton toward the bed, closing the bedroom door behind them, to provide a modicum of separation from the living room, the space that had become Otto's.

She reached for Milton hungrily, the brazen pleasure of it intensified by the tinge of danger.

When Otto returned much later, Milton was gone. He was staying the night at Alistair's club in the West End. Lena had washed herself at the sink but still feared that the smell of him lingered on her body. When she heard Otto come in, she emerged from the bedroom and stood in the doorway in her dressing gown, arms tight across her chest. Otto sat on the sofa, reading the evening paper, which Milton had left behind.

"I'm going to move out tomorrow," she said, without preamble.

He looked at her fleetingly and then turned back to the newspaper. "Moving in with Lover Boy?"

"No, I told you, Milton's place was bombed. Lotti's asked me to move into her flat. To be with her and the baby. Now that Peter's leaving."

Otto said nothing. He leafed through the pages.

"It will be better for both of us this way."

He did not respond. But she'd said what needed to be said. Sheila would be proud of her.

CHAPTER 43

LONDON, NOVEMBER–DECEMBER 1944

But on Monday morning, Sheila didn't show up for work. "She's been fighting off a cold," Gladys said.

"Her mum's been sick," Mildred said.

"Her hands have been playing up something awful."

"That'll be it, then."

Except that Sheila never took a day off, not even if her arthritis flared in anger. She couldn't afford to have her pay docked. And if she really couldn't make it, she would have sent a message; she would have sent someone to the pub or used the telephone box at the Tube station.

Lena couldn't stop worrying. Every half hour she gave herself an excuse to walk by Sheila's desk in the hope that she would have somehow slipped in. But her chair remained empty. Her mug rested next to the inkwell, her small wooden shamrock propped in the corner. Her thick navy cardigan, which she kept for chilly days, was draped over the chair. But no Sheila.

Just before lunchtime, Mrs. Manson emerged from her office, ashen-faced. "Mrs. Eisenberg, could you come in here, please?"

She closed the door behind her and stood at her desk, gripping the edge to steady herself.

"That was Miss O'Neill's cousin on the telephone. I'm afraid it's not good news." She collapsed into the seat with a thud. "Apparently, Lambeth was hit by a rocket attack early this morning. The young lady was hysterical, and I could barely understand her. She spoke in a thick Irish brogue. But I believe she said the entire street was demolished. They're still searching for survivors."

Lena reeled backward, scraping her ankle on the corner of the cabinet. She clasped her hands to her chest. She wasn't sure she'd be able to breathe.

"No . . ."

"I don't know how on earth I'm going to tell the girls," Mrs. Manson said. "I know some of them were awfully fond of her. She was somewhat uncouth, of course, but she was a good worker."

"Oh, my God." *Not Sheila. No. Please.*

"And we're so far behind with the butchers' accounts as it is."

Lena had to leave the room. "Excuse me."

"Thank you, Mrs. Eisenberg. I would be most grateful if you could tell the others for me."

Mrs. Manson sequestered herself in her office. Mildred fainted when she heard the news and had to be sent home. Gladys, red-eyed, kept the fort going up front. The afternoon passed in a blur. Lena kept thinking that Sheila would appear, bedraggled, perhaps, but joking about her lucky escape.

But she did not.

When Milton met Lena after work, she collapsed into his arms and sobbed. "Do you want to go down there and . . . look for her?" he said.

It was better than doing nothing. Better than imagining the worst.

She didn't know exactly where Sheila lived. Close to Lambeth North Tube station was all she knew. They emerged at a large crossroads and were pulled as if by a magnet toward Lambeth Road. They soon saw the commotion three hundred yards ahead: emergency vehicles; heaps of rubble; people with hollow expressions moving in slow motion; the WVS van dispensing cups of tea; crews loading stretchers into ambulances. The light was fading, but Lena thought she saw a row of bodies, covered in dark blankets, lined up on the ground.

They pushed through the crowd to the opposite corner and stopped in shock. A huge crater, fifteen feet deep and a hundred wide, had swallowed up the whole terrace of houses. It was ringed by a chaotic jumble of bricks and lumber and broken glass. Rescue workers clambered over a pile of rubble to the right. Water from burst pipes spewed into morose puddles, ignored in favor of more pressing priorities. The air was thick with dust. Lena drew her coat collar up over her nose. Her eyes began to burn.

Milton turned to a young boy, about fourteen years old. "Do you know where the O'Neills live?"

"O'Neills? Can't say I do, sir."

"You looking for the O'Neills?" This from another boy, older than the first, standing astride a bicycle, cigarette hanging from his lip. "Moira O'Neill?"

"I just know Sheila," Lena said. Her voice was hoarse. "It's a large family. . . ."

"Moira's over there, having tea." He pointed to the WVS van on the main road. A dozen women perched on a pile of rubble off to the side, teacups in hand.

After a few inquiries, Milton and Lena were face-to-face with a younger version of Sheila: the same blue eyes and auburn curls, same petite frame. She appeared to be about eighteen, hunched over, coat drawn tight across her chest. A streak of grime covered her right cheek. She looked up, and her silent eyes met Lena's. An older woman sat next to her, a protective arm around her shoulders.

"She's still looking for her family, love," this woman said, drawing on a cigarette. Two large curlers protruded from a paisley headscarf tied in a knot above her forehead.

"What happened?" Lena asked. A stupid question, perhaps, but she felt a compelling need for details.

"One of them V2s. Hit us at eight o'clock this morning. There was this blinding flash of light and a terrible roaring noise. Moira here had just left for work. She starts early, see. She was almost at the Tube but turned back when she heard the explosion. They just pulled out the lady what lived next door to her." She nodded over to the pile of corpses. "She didn't make it."

Another woman started wailing. The woman with the curlers continued, "What I don't understand is why they can't put a stop to it. The Russians are getting on fine. Why can't we?"

Lena sat and put her arm around Moira. "I'm so sorry," she said.

The girl looked up. "Ye must be Lena," she said. She pronounced it *Lairna*.

"How did you know?"

"I knew at once," Moira said. "Sheila spoke on ye all the time."

"She's a wonderful person," Lena said. "And tough. If anyone can make it out, she can." She gave Moira's shoulder a squeeze.

But when she turned her attention back to the rescue scene, another lifeless body was being pulled from the rubble.

They lay together on the bed in Lena's new room at Lotti's. She listened to the regular rhythm of Milton's heartbeat against her ear, the soothing gallop, replacing the need for words. He gently tugged at the eiderdown to pull it over her shoulders.

"I can't take it in." Lena wiped away fresh tears. "I can't believe she's gone." Milton stroked her arm under the covers. "It's so arbitrary."

"If only she'd left home a few minutes early. If only it had dropped a few minutes later. Or a mile farther south." Lena stopped herself. "But that's a terrible thing to say. It would have killed someone else."

They were silent again. The wind rattled outside.

"At least it was a V2. Must have been quick. She hated the Doodlebugs," Lena said. "How many areas have been hit like that?"

"There's no way to tell. The government is keeping it all under wraps. It's understandable, I suppose. They want to keep the Nazis guessing. But it's making people fear the worst."

"Just one rocket took out that whole street. And not a word about it on the news."

"They won't even allow obituaries to be published," Milton said. "I was in Epsom last week just after a rocket attack there. I spoke to a chap who'd lost both his sisters. He was told he couldn't place a death announcement in the local paper. That really does seem excessive. As if the Germans have spies scouring the *Croydon Advertiser*."

Milton's chest rose gently with each breath. She heard footsteps outside on the pavement and the mumbled conversation of passersby. Charles started to cry in the next room. Lena heard Lotti padding across the floor.

"It's so hard to believe," Lena said again. "Here I am, worrying all the time about Ernst being in danger, and about Máma and Sasha. And then it's the woman I sit next to at work who gets killed. It doesn't make sense."

He stroked her arm again, encircling her elbow with his fingertips. "When I was in the anti-aircraft unit in Portsmouth during the Battle of Britain . . ." Milton faltered. Lena looked up at him. "The man standing next to me was killed. Robert Bingham. He was from Bristol. One minute, he was handing me a shell to load into the gun. We'd been taking heavy fire all night, but we thought they'd passed over. All of a sudden, I heard a piercing whine . . ." He closed his eyes and winced. "It was horrible. A huge piece of shrapnel ripped him in two. Right in front of me. There was nothing we could do."

"Was that when you were wounded?"

"Yes. But I was lucky. It was nothing, really. I took a small wound in the foot. And here."

He extended the middle finger of his left hand. That jagged scar she'd first noticed a year earlier.

He hugged her close. "I often look at this scar and think of Bingham. I don't know why I survived and he didn't. There's no way to understand these things."

"Was that when the army wouldn't take you back?"

"Yes. I recovered fairly quickly, but it took six months for me to get medical clearance. Then they decided they were better off without me. I was told my 'revolutionary views' were incompatible with military service. Since then, they've more or less left me to my own devices. I get called into the Labour Exchange every couple of months, but they don't seem to know what to do with me. They're content to let me stay with Mass Observation."

His work: it would be taking him away again soon, no doubt.

"What are you going to be *observing* next?" she asked with a smile. She didn't want to sound as if she were making a fuss.

"I'll be staying put for a while. Hopefully, this fellow Jenkins will get my flat back into serviceable condition. I have to finish up the reports on the day nurseries in the Midlands."

He rolled over and kissed her. Lena clung to him.

The winter turned bitter. The coldest of the war, it was said. Lena and Lotti used their entire coal ration by the twenty-first of the month. An icy wind howled through the gaps around the windows. Lotti fretted about keeping Charles warm. Lena decided to go back to Donegal Street to see Mavis; the year before, Mavis had obtained peat logs through a man she knew at work. Black-market, probably, but they were desperate. And Lena remembered the extra blankets she'd left in the cupboard in her old flat, the ones they used to take into the shelter during raids. They could serve as insulation. Otto wouldn't be using them. He probably hadn't even noticed them.

She still had a key. She went early on Saturday morning, when she knew Mavis would be home and hoped Otto wouldn't.

"Lovely to see you, Lena. Come in, come in. I'm just putting the kettle on." Mavis was as cheerful as ever. "How's your new place, then? I do miss seeing you on the stairs. How's Lotti? Any news from Peter? And how's that bouncing baby boy? Getting big, I bet. My, hasn't the weather turned harsh? Our pipes froze two days ago. You'll never guess what I have." She paused to catch her breath. "Guess!"

Lena laughed. "I don't know. What?"

"Plum jam! From my sister-in-law. I remember how you like it, so I saved you a jar."

"That's so sweet of you, Mavis."

And yes, Mavis thought she could get hold of some peat logs early next week. She would give Lena a bit of coal to tide her over. No, no, she could spare it. She chatted on at a relentless pace—about the weather, and a new recipe for turnip pie, and the frost that had ruined Mr. Clark's cabbages in his allotment. It was only when Lena asked after Eva that Mavis stalled. "Eva? Oh . . . um . . . She's all right." She turned her back to tidy up.

"It's all right, Mavis. I know she and Otto are . . ."

"Well, she was always so partial to the Americans, wasn't she? They've mostly left now."

"I want to fetch something from the flat. She's not up there now, is she?" That would definitely be uncomfortable.

"No, she's at work. She's got a new job, in a butcher's shop on Upper Street."

Lena climbed the stairs and knocked, as if this weren't her flat—which it wasn't anymore. Otto opened the door and stared at her. He was unshaven and looked very thin.

"I want to pick up a few things." He stepped back to let her in. "How are you? Are you all right?" His trousers were bunched in folds under his waist belt. "Are you eating?"

"Yes, I'm eating, Lena. For God's sake."

"Sorry . . ."

The living room was a jumbled chaos of strewn clothes, over-flowing ashtrays, and discarded teacups. Lena stopped herself from picking up Otto's jacket, which lay on the floor. She averted her eyes from the unmade bed she glimpsed through the bedroom door. But she would have to go in there for the blankets.

"I'm sorry about your friend," Otto said, avoiding eye contact. "The one who was killed. Mavis told me."

"Yes. Thanks." She paused. "You were right about Hitler's revenge weapons. You said they would be ferocious."

Otto was right about many things. But not everything. Not everything. She had to remember that.

He shrugged. "The war will be over soon. A few more months, at most."

"Let's hope so."

"The Russians are doing well, aren't they?" Otto brightened. "Thrilling to watch."

"Yes." She was still standing. He hadn't invited her to sit. "Are you still thinking about going back to Germany after the war?"

"Yes." He took out his pipe. "With the Red Army advancing like this, Germany will be defeated, the conditions ripe for revolution."

He spoke the words, but he sounded fatigued and unconvinced, as if he had run out of steam. Where was the Otto who so passionately supported the International Brigade volunteers going to Spain, who held the room captive with fine speeches, who had plucked her out of her sheltered adolescence and promised to show her the future? He had vanished. Maybe he physically stood before her, but the Otto she remembered had disappeared—like Sheila had slipped away, leaving only a raw, gaping wound.

"As for this country," Otto continued, "*pfft.*" He spat in disgust. "How do you like what your Prime Minister is doing in Greece? Huh?"

"It's outrageous. And everyone's really angry about it." The British government was intervening in the civil war in Greece, providing military support for the right-wing factions against the Left. "We're all going to the demonstration next weekend." By *all*, Lena meant her and Milton and his Common Wealth friends.

"Are *we*? Well, isn't that nice?" Otto obviously knew whom she meant. "That scoundrel Churchill is going to be the big war hero in this country and win the election easily. You'll see. And then he'll annihilate the Left—just like he's doing to the antifascist partisans in Greece. His former allies."

"A lot of people in this country are determined to fight for progressive change."

"Are there indeed? What? You and your Lord of the Manor and his Common Wealth Party cronies? Sorry, but I don't think that will amount to much."

"Otto, please. I didn't come here to squabble."

He shrugged again. "Oh, I don't care. Do what you like." He turned away from her. "Get whatever it is you came for and leave me in peace."

CHAPTER 44

LONDON, 1945

On a late-January evening, Lena switched on the wireless for the six o'clock news. The announcer read the weather forecast, warning of more arctic winds and subfreezing temperatures. Milton's hair was ruffled, his shirt untucked, hastily redonned after their lovemaking earlier. He was leaving again in the morning, back to the Midlands, to collect journal entries from Mass Observation contributors. Lena tried to seal the image of him in her mind.

The chimes of Big Ben heralded the top of the hour. Lena held her breath, waiting, in that moment of suspense. The New Year had brought more shortages, more rocket attacks. What would the day's bulletin offer: a new breakthrough, a kernel of hope—or further setbacks, delays, and despair?

"Yesterday, in southern Poland, the Red Army liberated Auschwitz, an extermination camp on a scale unlike anything seen before. . . ."

Nothing had prepared her for this. The rumors, conjectures, doomsday predictions: easily pushed aside as wild exaggeration, sensationalist scaremongering. But now the crisp tones of BBC English described a scene of unimaginable horror: gas ovens, piles of corpses, storerooms stuffed with human hair, mounds of gold tooth fillings. Even the sanguine announcer could not banish all emotion from his voice.

Lena couldn't move; a black chill sank through to her bones.

There was more—the unbearable, unthinkable: "Emaciated survivors spoke of mass deportations of Jews from the far reaches of the Third Reich." Including Terezín.

The room began to spin, but Milton had his arms around her. He simply held her; he didn't try to search for words to smooth over the truth. They stood in silence. The BBC newsreader moved on—something about the capture of a Japanese airbase on Luzon. Hurried footsteps clambered down the hallway outside the flat, and the front door slammed in the wind.

When Lena tried to speak again, her mouth was parched, her words stuck together. "Máma must have found a way to get Sasha into hiding," she said. "With her fair hair and blue eyes, she wouldn't be seen as Jewish."

She waited for him to dismiss this as absurd. But he just stroked her hair and rocked her gently.

"We'll finish up those turnips tonight," Lotti said.

"I'm sick of turnips."

"I could find something to make them more interesting. We have enough points. A tin of tomatoes, perhaps?"

"Tomatoes and turnips?" Lena screwed up her nose. "Sounds like one of those disgusting English concoctions you always complain about."

"Spam?"

"Oh God, no. Not Spam again, please."

"Well, you think of something, then."

Lotti slammed down her cup. Charles, busy mastering the art of picking up a Farley's Rusk in clumsy fingers, startled in his high chair, flailing his arms. Lena picked up the biscuit and offered it to him. He grabbed it with a broad smile. Lotti, home with the baby now, did most of the shopping and cooking. Initially, Lena loved the idea. But some of Lotti's choices, and the monotony of endless potatoes and turnips, were grating on her nerves.

"I saw a recipe for mock roast pork, using breadcrumbs and nuts," Lena said. "It's supposed to taste like the real thing."

"If you can find any nuts."

Lena noticed a thin envelope in Lotti's hand. "What's that?"

"A letter from Peter."

"Why didn't you tell me? When did that arrive?"

"Yesterday. I haven't had a chance. You were out late last night, and this morning you've done nothing but complain about food."

"I'm sorry. I know I shouldn't." The anticipation of news from abroad made turnips irrelevant. "What does he say? Where is he?"

Lotti pulled out the letter. "Cairo. It's dated the tenth of February."

"That's what? Nearly two weeks ago. Does he say where they're headed next?" The Czech army was still stuck in Dunkirk. Perhaps Peter really would be the first to get word back from Prague. The thought was thrilling—but it filled her with dread. "What does he say?"

Lotti started to read. "My dearest Lotti—"

"He's writing in English?"

"We agreed that letters in English would make it through the censors more quickly." Lotti looked over to Lena and raised her eyebrows. "Shall I continue?"

"Yes, sorry. Go on."

Lotti resumed: "We reached Port Said yesterday. The Atlantic was rough, but as soon as we passed through the Strait of Gibraltar, conditions improved. We no longer need a full naval escort, and we are allowed to keep lights on at night. We unloaded our supplies onto lorries and have a day of rest before we proceed. You wouldn't believe the merchandise in the shops here! I saw fountain pens and wristwatches. We are heading up to . . ." Lotti paused. "That part is blacked out by the censor."

"The whole thing?"

"We are heading up to . . . to meet up with some Russian convoys. I don't know when I'll be able to write next. You can send post to the fourth place on the list I gave you.

"That's Tehran," Lotti said.

"Goodness! What else?"

"How is Charles getting on? What is his weight? What about

the rocket attacks? I take out the photograph of you and Charles every night and—"

"All right." Lena smiled and held up a hand. "You don't have to read all the personal sections. I don't mean to pry."

"He sends his regards to you. And Milton."

"So, if they're meeting up with the Russians, they'll probably move quickly. He could soon be in Prague."

"I know." Lotti gave a small shudder. "Heaven knows what he's going to find there."

The possibilities lurked, unvoiced, battling each other inside Lena's brain: a tiny kernel of hope struggling for air in a rising tide of despair.

Milton invited Lena to come to Sussex for the weekend. "Mother insists on seeing you again. She says I've been remiss in keeping you away so long."

The countryside was drab, cloaked in a gray blanket of winter. A bitter wind buffeted their walk from the station. By the time they reached the village square, a hard rain had set in.

But there was a warm welcome at The Hollow. The grate was piled high with logs, and the smell of freshly baked bread wafted from the kitchen. Muriel gave Lena an enthusiastic embrace.

"Lena, my dear," she said. "You've been in my thoughts a great deal recently. You must be so worried about your family."

"Yes." Tears welled up, catching Lena unawares. "I'm hoping for the best."

"Of course."

"My brother—or Peter—will be in Prague soon."

"Yes. You must let us know as soon as you hear from them." Muriel was content to leave it at that. Lena was relieved.

Lunch was a thick lentil soup and warm, crusty bread. Muriel wanted to know about Lotti's baby, Peter's journey, and Emil's next leave. Milton talked about the upcoming exhibition at the Tate on the future design of housing for the common man.

"Such a novel idea—they're proposing to build working-class

homes with indoor bathrooms," he said. "It's ironic how much Göring has done for slum clearance in this country."

"I think housing will be the key issue in the next election," Muriel said. "The Tories haven't offered any solutions."

"Everyone seems to think the Tories are going to dismantle the wartime coalition government and force a general election right after victory in Europe," Milton said, "with Churchill, the invincible war leader, as their trump card."

"Their only card," Muriel said. She turned to Lena. "What is your sense from the women you work with? Will they let the Tories mislead them again?"

"I don't know. I think people feel grateful to Churchill. On the other hand, they really hope for a better future for themselves. They don't want to have made all these sacrifices and then return to the old way of life."

"Interesting," Muriel said, nodding. "I hope you're right. But I'm afraid they can fool a lot of the people a lot of the time, as the saying goes."

"Abraham Lincoln." Milton smiled. "One of Mother's heroes. But there's such idealism about the new world after the war. It's all people talk about—when they're not talking about what they're going to eat next."

Lena laughed. "I'm going to eat more of that bread. The crust is wonderful."

And it was wonderful to feel so at home. There was none of the discomfort she had felt on her previous visit. After lunch, she sank into the big armchair in front of the fire and relaxed. Alistair returned from East Grinstead with amusing anecdotes about the pompous Colonel Knowles at the hospital board committee meeting. There was the promise of a walk in the woods later if the rain let up. While Muriel played the piano, Lena drank tea and Milton smiled at her from the other side of the hearth.

Later, when it was time for bed, without any comment or fanfare, she and Milton took the spare room, where a double bed had been made up. Milton pulled her onto him.

"I want you to stay with me here in England after the war," he whispered, cupping her face in his hands. He spoke with such tenderness.

"But I have to go and find Sasha." Lena's eyes filled with tears.

"Of course. But then bring her back here to live with us."

It was such an idyllic fantasy; Lena hardly dared speak, as if the notion were a fragile ornament that might shatter if touched. She nodded and closed her eyes to fight back the tears, burying her face against his chest. Their lovemaking was long and soft and delicious, like a sweet orange. Lena hoped the thick walls of the ancient house were soundproof.

When Lena returned home from work on Friday, Lotti announced, "I ran into Eva today on Pentonville Road."

"Eva?" Lena had not seen her in months.

"She wanted to know if you could meet her tonight in the Rose and Crown. She said something about receiving a letter from Paris. From someone she said you'd remember . . . Margarita?"

"Marguerite! Oh my God! When?"

"Seven thirty."

"I can't believe it. Marguerite!"

"Who is she?"

"My friend. You remember—I told you about her. She was Eva's friend first. But I lived with her in the rue Cassette. Eva lost touch with her in the chaos of the Nazi invasion, and we haven't heard from her since." Lena looked at her watch. "I have to go."

Lotti laughed. "Don't be ridiculous. You have over an hour. Let's eat. I tried that nut loaf again. I hope it tastes better this time."

It did. It was delicious, in fact, and Lena ate rapidly, partly out of nerves. For months, she realized, she'd been avoiding Eva; now she couldn't wait to see her. They'd had one awkward conversation back in September, soon after the liberation of France, when Lena had run into her and Otto in Regents Park. Lena had asked her then about writing to Marguerite, but Eva had said she had no idea how to reach her.

The Rose and Crown was full of noise and smoke. There was no sign of Eva. Lena bought herself a half of shandy and elbowed her way to a table in the corner. She had to ward off advances from three men, all drunk already, before Eva appeared, glass of Guinness in hand. She took a sip of her drink, leaving a coating of creamy foam on her lipstick.

"Did Lotti tell you? I heard from Marguerite."

"How did you find her?"

"She found me. She wrote to the Czech embassy, and they forwarded it on to the Czech Institute." Eva pulled a flimsy beige envelope out of her handbag. "It was sent to my old address and eventually on to me here. It took four months."

"Thank goodness she's all right. Where is she?"

"Back in Paris. She has quite a story. Here, you can read it. Your French is better than mine. I couldn't really understand all that stuff at the bottom of the second page."

It was unbelievable to see Marguerite's neat cursive, with the elaborate curly tails on the tips of the capital *M*s and *B*s. She was writing from an address in the tenth arrondissement. She had survived against all odds, with several narrow escapes. She'd fled Paris on a bicycle, crossing the line into the unoccupied zone with only one day to spare. She reached her aunt and uncle's farm near Millau, but two years later her whole family was deported; she got away by hiding in the orchard. During another raid, she lay concealed under the floorboards in a neighbor's house. Since liberation, she'd been trying to find her family. They had not yet returned from the East. She'd also been unable to find Heinz. She'd made inquiries: he'd last been heard of in Drancy in '42. But Marguerite was fine, beginning to regain weight, and applying to return to the Sorbonne in the autumn.

"She doesn't even mention the quarrel we had before I left," said Eva. "You know, when I thought she and Heinz . . ."

"I imagine that has faded in significance, in view of everything else she's been through."

"Yes, but still. What's all this about?" Eva pointed to the second page.

"*On ne reçoit pas la sagesse; il faut la découvrir soi-même,*" Lena read. "'We are not provided with wisdom; we must discover it for ourselves.' It's a quote from Proust, I think. *À la Recherche du Temps Perdu*. She's reflecting on the meaning of all the suffering she's witnessed."

"Ah. Well." Eva drained her glass. "Anyway, she's all right."

Yes, Marguerite was all right. It *was* possible to survive. A person could find a place to hide, conceal herself like a mussel in its shell. It was possible to elude capture against all odds, emerge unscathed into the light. There *was* hope. It wasn't foolish to believe that, to wish and hope and dream every single day, to pray. No, not pray, but hope more fervently than anyone had ever hoped for anything.

"Do you want to take Marguerite's address?"

"Oh, yes, please."

Lena made a note of it in her diary. They sat in silence, a veil of awkwardness lingering, intermingled with the smoke. Two men at the next table eyed them with interest. Eva threw them a flirtatious glance and, with a flick of her head, swirled her curls over her shoulder. Lena didn't want to stay here much longer. She took another sip of her drink; it was too bitter for her liking.

"How are you?" She turned to Eva. "Are you still working in that butcher's shop?"

"Yes. The boss is very strict about all the rules, but I do get extra meat now and then. The scraps no one else wants."

"And how's Otto?" Lena made an effort to sound nonchalant.

"He's all right. Working long hours, as usual."

"Does he still talk about going back to Germany after the war?"

"Yes. That's what he says. I don't know if they'll take him." Eva pulled out a pack of Players cigarettes. She offered one to Lena.

Lena shook her head. "What about you? Would you go with him?"

Eva snorted with laughter. "God, no. It's not that sort of a thing. Me and Otto, I mean. No. I don't really know what I'll do. My cousin—you remember her—used to live in Normandy. Her family made it out just before the invasion. Got to Lisbon and then on to Shanghai, of all places. They're now trying to get into America. She wants me to go, too."

Lena hadn't heard Eva speak of her cousin in years, but she didn't want to pursue the topic. There was something more important.

"I'm going to need a divorce from Otto before he leaves. Do you think he'll agree to cooperate?"

Eva shrugged. "You'd have to ask him."

"Obviously, either of us could sue for divorce on the basis of adultery," Lena continued. "The law was changed just before the war, I'm told. But there still has to be one guilty party, and we can't be seen to be colluding."

Eva looked puzzled.

"One of us has to pretend to be upset by the adultery of the other."

"I see you've studied this." Eva smirked.

Lena continued, undeterred. "And we have to prove the adultery. Name names."

"Has Milton proposed to you?" Greedy for gossip, Eva's eyes lit up.

"No. He can't propose to me if I'm still married to someone else, can he?" Eva was regarding her with a quizzical expression. "Well, we've talked about it. Just hypothetically. But I need Otto to agree for me to divorce him."

Eva tilted her head, blowing a circle of smoke over their heads. "You know, I can talk him into just about anything." She paused. "But what do I get out of this?"

"What do you mean?"

Eva lowered her voice. "I really need some extra clothing coupons."

For a moment, Lena thought she must have misheard. But there was no mistaking the look on Eva's face. Lena quietly shook her head, stood up, and left.

She heard Eva say to her back, "Just joking!"

But Lena had already committed to walking out.

CHAPTER 45

LONDON, MAY–JUNE 1945

Mrs. Manson closed the Food Office early. In an uncharacteristic gesture of goodwill, she announced at three thirty that they were done for the day. Or perhaps she was merely acknowledging that nothing more would be accomplished. No one could concentrate on ledgers or accounts. The whole city was on edge.

The Times had declared that morning, with a six-column headline, THE END OF THE WAR AT HAND. Gladys Woodruff's *Daily Mail* said, IT MAY BE TODAY.

Mrs. Manson had turned on the wireless for the one o'clock news, but there was no proclamation. "This suspense is dreadful," she said.

"Hard to get excited about it after all this time," Gladys said. "Not like last summer, when we thought it was going to finish so quick."

Nevertheless, at lunchtime she'd made an excursion to the tobacconist on Drury Lane and returned with three small Union Jacks. She gave one to Lena.

"They're going fast," she said. "Wouldn't do to be stuck without."

Lena took advantage of her early day to meet Milton at Euston. He was returning from Birmingham at four; she would surprise him. At the entrance to the station, people were already queuing around the block for the evening newspaper. An elderly woman had set up a makeshift stand under the central archway, selling twelve-inch strips of red, white, and blue ribbons. With a toothless grin, she demonstrated how these could be fashioned into a decorative hair tie. Red, white, and blue: the colors of the Czech flag also. Lena purchased two sets, one for herself and one for Lotti.

She made her way to platform four. The station seemed crowded for a Monday afternoon; the sun poured down from the high windows above the great hall. The scene was dotted with girls in colorful summer frocks and men in linen trousers and bright white shirts, like an Impressionist painting. A young woman also waiting for the Birmingham train had adorned her hair with three sets of the tricolored ribbons, in a very creative design, one bow at each temple and the third on the crown of her head. Lena wondered whom she was meeting. What private thoughts filled her head? Was she worrying about how to scrape together dinner tonight, or whether she would ever get rehoused? Or was she, like Lena, worrying every day about someone far away, excited and frightened as the end drew near?

The Czech Brigade was approaching Prague. Peter was getting close, too. There had been another letter from him, this one from Košice. His group was bartering its way across the continent—easy to do, he reported, equipped as they were with large bags of Lend-Lease white flour from America. The countryside was devastated and the roads congested with Russian and German tanks going in opposite directions. Nazi forces were retreating everywhere, in disorganized, unescorted chaos, their finely tuned war machine in tatters. But there was no hint of what might lie ahead in Prague. Rumors abounded, he said, but he had no reliable news.

The Euston concourse echoed with the hum of feet and voices, the screech of whistles, and the slammed doors of departing trains. Suddenly, a voice boomed over the loudspeaker: "Attention, please, ladies and gentlemen. Attention, please. Here is an important announcement."

The entire station halted in silence, with a collective sharp intake of breath. The pretty woman with the ribbons grabbed Lena's arm.

After what seemed like an interminable pause, the announcer continued: "The four-oh-nine for Nottingham will now depart from platform seven."

The crowd erupted with a groan of indignation and disappointment.

"This is tearing me nerves to shreds," the girl said, and then she laughed and withdrew her hand. "Ooh, sorry!"

The Birmingham train puffed its way into the station. Lena saw him as soon as he disembarked—tall, square-shouldered, confident in his stride. She ran to him. Milton lifted her into his arms and spun her around, almost knocking her into a couple of RAF airmen, who laughed.

"Is it official?" Milton asked.

"Nothing yet. But the office closed early. It's expected any moment."

They hurried, arm in arm, through the streets to Mecklenburgh Square and tumbled into bed. They emerged from the covers an hour later and turned on the wireless. They were just in time. The deep, gruff voice of the Prime Minister boomed over the airways.

"Yesterday morning, at 2:41 A.M., at General Eisenhower's headquarters in Rheims, France, the German High Command signed the act of unconditional surrender of all German land, sea, and air forces in Europe to the Allied Expeditionary Force and the Soviet High Command. Hostilities will officially end at one minute past midnight tonight, Tuesday, the eighth of May."

Lena was covered with goose bumps, standing in her underclothes. Milton wrapped her in a hug. They stared at the wireless, listening to Churchill's words.

It was over. No more bombs, no more rockets.

Outside, on the street, someone whooped in delight. Loud horns pierced the evening air.

Churchill went on to announce that the next two days were to be observed as public holidays: "Tomorrow, perhaps, we will think mainly of ourselves. On Wednesday, we will pay particular tribute to our heroic Russian comrades."

Milton laughed raucously at that. "Our heroic Russian comrades, indeed," he said. "We have to celebrate." He clasped her waist and lifted her feet off the ground. "Get dressed." He kissed her on the lips.

"Let's see if Lotti wants to come with us."

They collected Lotti and joined the throng in the streets, making their way to the West End. Milton carried Charles high on his shoulders. Lena walked between him and Lotti, an arm around each. Light flooded out through the open doorways of pubs and restaurants. The whole city was exuberant. The crowd took over the streets, stopped the buses, and some young boys clambered onto the roofs of the red double-deckers. People swarmed over the statues in Piccadilly Circus and the fountains of Trafalgar Square. Lena embraced the euphoria, the incredible relief, the sweetness of the moment. She felt she utterly belonged in this crowd. She'd shared the hardships; she understood the jubilation. She joined in the singing of "Knees Up Mother Brown" and "Take Me Back to Dear Old Blighty." In this mob, who would care if you didn't know all the words or couldn't carry the tune? On Shaftsbury Avenue, after they'd walked Lotti and Charles to the Tube, they came upon an impromptu bonfire, showering bright embers into the night sky. On the Embankment, the fireboats shot river water in wide arcs of delight and the floodlit Houses of Parliament blinked in the unfamiliar brightness.

Yet every now and then, Lena felt a twinge, a pull, the same nagging fear deep in her gut. She saw a poster in Trafalgar Square advertising the *Daily Express* exhibition on Regent Street: SEEING IS BELIEVING: IMAGES FROM BUCHENWALD AND BELSEN.

She turned her back, steering Milton away.

Two weeks later, the Coalition National Government was dissolved and a general election called for the fifth of July. Milton plunged into a whirlwind of political activity. With the coalition dissolved, he declared, the pragmatic course was to support the Labour Party as the only effective opposition to the Tories. He spent every evening at meetings, composing broadsheets, knocking on doors, putting up posters.

Lena felt too distracted to follow his exuberant reports. She briefly wondered if her work at the Food Office would continue but soon realized her job was secure. Anyone who believed rationing would cease with the end of the war in Europe was quickly disappointed. In fact, bacon and cooking-fat rations were reduced three weeks after V-E Day, and Lena had to deal with the usual confusion among the staff and the frustration of the customers.

Yes, life at work continued much as before, but Lena found it hard to focus. She was desperate for word from Prague. From Ernst, there had been only one cryptic telegram: *Arrived in Prague stop. Trying to find them stop.*

Nothing since. From Peter: nothing. Emil came over to the flat; he also had no news from his parents or from his brother, Josef. The Soviets were in control in Czechoslovakia, and new barriers to communication were quickly replacing the old.

Lena stayed home most evenings with Lotti. Partly, Milton was so busy, but mostly she needed to be with Lotti as they waited for news. Milton was sympathetic, but it just wasn't the same as being with someone who *knew*, who felt the same panic.

Then, one Thursday morning, just after Charles dumped a bowl of semolina from his high chair, Lena heard a *plop* on the front doormat and ran out to the hall. She found a letter for Lotti. Postmark: Exeter, Devon.

"Who do you know in Devon?"

"No one."

Lotti tore open the envelope. It contained a single sheet wrapped around a bundle, several pages thick, of a wider, coarser paper. As Lotti unfolded the package, Lena recognized the handwriting.

"It's from Peter!" Lotti cried.

Lotti glanced briefly at the cover sheet and passed it to Lena, before plunging into Peter's letter. Lena saw Lotti's hands shaking and had trouble controlling her own.

The cover letter was from a Lieutenant Wilson, who introduced himself as a British serviceman and prisoner of war, recently freed in Prague and flown back to England.

Please find the enclosed letter entrusted to me in Prague. I'm afraid your beautiful city is badly damaged, but your husband is in good health. It brings me great pleasure to be the bearer of this message. I hope, madam, it brings you some relief. . . .

Lena got no further, because Lotti wailed. She clasped her hand to her mouth and continued reading, eyes wide.

"What?"

Lena scooted her chair next to Lotti's, to read over her shoulder. As soon as Lotti finished one page, she passed it to Lena. They spoke not a word; Lotti intermittently gasped or moaned, and Lena heard strange, guttural noises that must have come from her own throat. The letter was long, six—no, seven—sheets. The words on the page, the first from Prague in years, swam before her; she blinked to clear her vision. She wanted to stop reading but couldn't. The writing got smaller and more scraggly as the letter progressed, as if Peter had been trying to finish it in a hurry, and Lena read faster and faster as she raced to the finish.

First the good news . . . Peter began. But there wasn't much good news. Lotti's mother was alive, still in Terezín, which was under quarantine now because of a typhus outbreak. She had somehow survived, but Lotti's father had succumbed two years ago. Peter's mother had also survived, had been with Lotti's there in Terezín, and had been released early, before the quarantine, because she was married to an "Aryan"; in fact, she had been deported only two months ago and was in relatively good health.

The rest of the news, my dearest, is almost all sad. . . . Peter's father had died of a heart attack just after his wife's deportation. All of Lotti's aunts and uncles who had stayed in Prague had perished; Lotti's neighbors the Buryáneks had not survived; the Steffels had all died in Auschwitz; there was no word yet about Gerta or Rosa or Max or Edit—all believed to have been deported to Lodž . . . The list went on and on.

And then the news Lena had been dreading for months, years:

Tell Lena I went to her parents' flat on Malostránské nábřeži. Strangers are living there. They would not open the door to me. The nice lady upstairs—I cannot remember her name, but Lena will know who I mean— told me that Lena's mother and the little girl were both deported to Terezín early on, in January '42. She showed me a postcard she received from Lena's mother two months after that. There has been no word since. It seems they were probably deported to the East later that year. There are still people returning; they arrive at the train station looking like walking skeletons—some are dead on arrival—but very few women or children among them. I've left notes on the bulletin boards of the offices of the National Council, but I have to say, it's a long shot. Tell Lena I am so sorry.

Lena and Lotti held on to each other in the London flat and sobbed. Lena's body shook so hard, she feared she would never be able to stop. The world was reduced to a wretched, gaping hole of pain deep in her belly.

It was a long time before either of them spoke.

"I have to go see my father," Lena said, wiping her face with her sleeve. The words took her by surprise.

CHAPTER 46

LONDON/AYLESBURY, JUNE 1945

Another surprise in the days that followed: she also wanted to see Otto. She sent him a note suggesting neutral territory, rather than the flat on Donegal Street. They met in Hyde Park on a Saturday afternoon and walked toward the Serpentine. The weather was bright but breezy, with stacks of cumulus clouds looming over the bandstand. Lena told Otto about Peter's letter.

"It turns out my mother and sister were both deported to Terezín—very early," she said. She had to pause to compose herself. "In January 1942. So long ago."

Otto said nothing. But it was a calm, accepting silence—not pregnant with criticism. She was grateful for that.

"I have to wonder if my writing that letter to my mother in the summer of 1940 placed her at increased risk. You remember? When my father really wanted me to contact her."

"There's no way to know. No sense in torturing yourself with that."

She nodded. She took a deep breath before continuing. "Peter said there're people still returning from the camps in the East. He's put up notices."

They had reached the water. Lena looked at Otto and stopped. He gazed back, not unkindly. In that moment, Lena knew: Máma and Sasha were dead. She knew it; she felt it with an absolute certainty.

After all the years of fooling herself. All the years of closing her eyes, blocking her ears, pushing the truth away, arguing with Otto, hating his pessimism. All those years when she'd been thinking of them and talking to Máma in her mind and wishing them safe, they'd been dead. All those birthdays of Sasha's when Lena had thought of her turning twelve, thirteen, fourteen; she had probably never made it past eleven.

She sat on a bench and buried her head in her hands and sobbed.

Otto sat next to her and placed a hand between her shoulder blades. "I'm sorry," he said.

A woman walked right in front of them, supervising two young children in the partition of bread for the ducks. Lena lifted her head and watched in silence until they moved on.

"You were right about so many things, Otto," she said at last, in a whisper.

He was silent for a while. Then he said, "I heard from my cousin in Berlin."

Cousin in Berlin? Lena stared at him in amazement. He'd never spoken of a cousin. "He told me my brother, Hans, was killed on the Eastern Front. At Kursk. Back in '43."

His voice was controlled, but Lena detected a hint of emotion below the surface. "So he also has been dead for . . . two years."

"Oh, Otto. I'm sorry. I . . . You didn't often speak of him."

"No." He was staring at the ground, scuffing the stones at his feet. "After he joined the Nazi Party, I didn't want to have anything to do with him." He picked up a pebble and tossed it into the water. "But he was my only brother. My only surviving family." He turned to her. "This cousin who wrote to me is a second or third cousin, or something, someone I barely know. I don't know how he tracked me down."

"What are your plans now? Are you going back?"

"I don't know." He shrugged. "Berlin is in ruins. Half the city is under American control. And I don't have a valid passport, of course. I'll have to see what happens."

He looked like a lost little boy. Lena had to fight off an urge to take him under her wing and protect him.

His upper body twitched, as if he, too, had felt that urge and wanted to brush it aside. He tossed another stone into the Serpentine.

"I understand you want a divorce."

Lena shot him a look of surprise.

"Eva told me."

"She did?"

"Yes. Didn't you tell her that?"

"Yes, I did."

"So, you're going to be the Lady of the Manor one day?"

"You know that's the last thing I want. I couldn't stand that."

Uncanny how he managed to zero in on the one thing that worried her.

"But you want to be with Milton?"

"Yes, I do. And I want to stay in England."

He nodded gently, staring at the water. "I hope you'll be happy, Lena. You deserve it. I'll do whatever you need for the divorce."

He lightly patted her arm and stood over her. With another quick nod, he left. Lena watched him retreat along the gravel path, his tall, lanky frame fading into the distance, his jacket tails flapping in the breeze. She fought off the impulse to run after him.

Milton said he would come with her to see her father in Aylesbury.

"But I haven't seen him in years. And he's very difficult. Very reactionary."

"He's your father. And you need to see him. I won't go if you really don't want me to, but I'd like to be with you. I'd like to meet him."

"At one time, I swore I would never speak to him again. But now . . ."

They took the train. Outside the station, arranged on opposite walls, they saw the posters of the National Government, featuring a huge photograph of Churchill, Let Him Finish the Job, and the Labour Party's response, We Organized for War. Now Let's Organize for Peace.

Milton bought a stack of the morning newspapers. "The *Daily Mirror* is throwing its full weight behind Labour," he said. "They've taken up the cause of the serviceman—the confusion about the service register, the slow pace of demobilization, the fact that so many have no homes to return to. Look at this!" He pointed to a headline over a photograph of a fatigued-looking soldier, helmet askew: VOTE FOR HIM. "They're galvanizing the women's vote—very shrewd."

Lena nodded quietly and fought back tears. He dropped the newspaper and put his arm around her. "I'm sorry. I'm being insensitive."

"No, no. That's good. I'm glad."

She *was* glad. It was important to look to the future—what else was there now? She reached for his hand and watched her reflection in the window as the train picked up speed through the battered city streets. Máma and Sasha had been dead for three years. Every morning she looked in the mirror and repeated this to herself, trying to let it sink in. *When did they die? Where? Were they together or apart? Did they suffocate in a gas oven, or did they die from starvation or disease?* Would she ever know? Did she want to know?

"I'm so angry with my father that he left them behind," she said. New, this anger, bubbling up through the layers of grief.

Yet when he opened the door of the dilapidated cottage he shared with another retired Czech officer, her anger wilted. He stood with shoulders hunched, a worn green cardigan sagging at his elbows. His eyes, cheeks, jowls had all drifted down with the force of gravity; he looked as if he were sinking into the ground. He had aged fifteen, twenty years.

"Father," Lena stammered. "How are you?"

He shrugged his shoulders and turned his palms upward—the familiar gesture, but a weakened version, despondent, rather than dismissive. He signaled for her to enter and looked out into the street.

"Where's that young man of yours?"

So he remembered that Lena was not coming alone.

"Milton is taking a walk. He will come later." Her words sounded stilted.

Father nodded and shuffled ahead of her down a narrow hallway, into a small kitchen. It faced a side alley and an adjoining cottage and was dimly lit, in spite of the brightness of the noon hour outside.

"So, you received my letter?" Lena said. The thought of it made her lower lip quiver.

He nodded again and sank into a chair at the table. He motioned for her to sit opposite him. He ran his hand across his bald scalp.

"This may sound harsh to you, Lena," he said, "but I resigned myself to this bad news some time ago."

Lena groaned and opened her mouth to respond, but he silenced her with a hand held high.

"Not when we left—that's not what I mean. I'm sure you're upset with me for leaving them in Prague. I understand that. But you have to believe me when I say I had no idea they would be in such danger." This sounded like a well-rehearsed speech. "We knew it wouldn't be easy," he continued. "That there would be shortages and the like. But we never imagined—"

"You could have left earlier. You could have left when I did, before the war. Plenty of people did. The Nebels left for the Dominican Republic, I remember. They got out. But no, you couldn't leave without all the silver and the carpets, all the trappings of your bourgeois life." Lena's voice grew more animated, her anger mounting— but then she looked at the gaunt old man sitting across from her and she couldn't do it. She couldn't maintain her rage. It wouldn't bring them back.

"I'm sorry," she said. "I shouldn't have said that."

"No, you're right. Knowing what we know now . . . we should have left. It was easy for you young people. You could pick up and go. And I'm very glad you did. But it's not so simple when you're older, more set in your ways." He fiddled with a white ceramic salt-shaker on the table, moving it in slow circles, tracing the pattern on the yellow oilcloth table cover.

"We did try," he continued. "We sent some things ahead to Paris, you remember. But we left it too late. And then we lost some time."

"What do you mean?"

"I was arrested."

"What? When?"

He looked up. "Soon after the Nazis arrived. Before the war started. You had to bribe people left and right to get anything: papers, foreign currency, and such. I paid someone who denounced me. Or maybe he was an agent provocateur. Who knows?" He shrugged. "But I was in jail for two months, and by the time I was released, it was too late. The war started and put an end to all that."

"This was *before* the war started? When Máma was still able to write to me?"

Father nodded.

"Why didn't she tell me?"

"Your mother probably didn't want you to worry."

Lena's eyes filled with tears. She reached across the table for his hands. He gave hers a gentle squeeze and tapped her forearm. "Let me make you some tea."

Above the cooker, four plates, bowls, and cups were neatly stacked on a shelf; next to that was another shelf, with two small saucepans and a frying pan. Large spots of mold darkened the wall above the counter. Lena wiped her eyes and watched him fill the kettle.

"What are you going to do, Father? Are you going back to Czechoslovakia?"

"No. There's nothing to go back for. The Czech army gives me a pension here. Not much, but it's something. Colonel Steiner and I will look for something better, a nicer place to live. He also lost his family." He turned to face her. "The English have been very decent to us. We must always remember this."

There was a knock at the door.

"That will be Milton," Lena said. "Shall I get it?"

"I can still answer the door in my own house, Lena. I'm not helpless, you know."

Lena couldn't help smiling as he shuffled back down the hall. She watched as Milton stood, filling the open doorway. The two men shook hands.

"Lieutenant Colonel Kulka," she heard Milton say. "I am honored to meet you. I am so sorry about your loss, sir."

CHAPTER 47

LONDON, JUNE–JULY 1945

Milton set a huge stack of the Sunday newspapers on the kitchen table. A front-page photograph showed Churchill waving to a crowd, left hand raised in a *V* for victory salute, right hand holding his signature cigar.

"Gladys, the older woman from my office, saw Churchill when he toured through Fulham last week," Lena said. "According to her, everyone was cheering wildly and shouting 'We love you, Winnie.'"

"Is she going to vote for him?"

"Well, no. That's the thing. She said she's voting Labour. She says we have to move forward now."

"Wonderful," Milton said. "You see, that's what the press just doesn't understand. People can still admire Churchill and be grateful to him, but he looks like a tired old man. And he's incapable of implementing the Beveridge Report and the reforms people want to see."

"Are you two talking about politics again?" Lotti laughed as she entered the kitchen, carrying Charles, and offered him to Lena, who sat him on her lap.

"This is the final week," Milton said. "We're going to Essex Road later, to hand out voter instruction leaflets. Why don't you come with us?"

"I'm a little busy." Lotti smiled. She was packing. In five days, she and Charles would be leaving for Prague. Peter had made arrangements for them to be on a repatriation flight, along with dozens of Czech RAF pilots. Emil would be on the same flight.

Charles reached for *The Sunday Times* and was intent on chewing the front page. Lena extracted the paper from his grip and offered him a rusk instead. She nuzzled her chin against the downy fuzz of his scalp. She kept thinking of what Peter had said, how he'd ended his letter, the last paragraph, which Lotti had reread out loud so many times: *We have to remember one thing above all else. All that matters is the new generation. Charles and his future siblings.*

Lena would miss Charles and Lotti. She understood why Lotti was leaving, why she and Peter wanted to be in Prague. Lotti was taking Charles to meet his grandmothers. But Lena was staying. Next week, she was to move into Milton's flat in Mecklenburgh Square.

"Look at this," Milton said. "Unbelievable. Instead of retracting his comment about the Gestapo, Churchill is repeating it. Gestapo in Britain If Socialists Win, Says PM. The Tories seem oblivious to the backlash this created."

"It's a terrible thing to say," Lena said. The mere mention of the Gestapo made her sick to her stomach. "That's not something that should be thrown around like a common insult."

"It put a lot of people off."

Lotti returned, carrying a stack of freshly laundered kitchen towels. "Don't get your hopes up too much," she said. "You're just going by what you see here in London. You don't know what the whole country is thinking. Yesterday in *The Times*—I did actually manage to read the paper yesterday—they predicted a Tory majority of seventy seats."

"We *have* to keep our hopes up," Milton said. "That's what it means to be progressive. There is no other possibility. We have to hope and work hard and get out the vote and believe that we can build a better world."

"Yes, of course," Lena said. *But*, she thought, *I've done nothing but hope for the past five years. For all the good it did.*

Lotti had been gone for almost three weeks now. Lena missed her dearly. But she focused on settling into the flat in Mecklenburgh Square. She relished living in just one place, instead of alternating between her flat and Milton's, carrying the next day's work things with her whenever she spent the night. She rearranged the furniture in the living room. She came upon a secondhand van Gogh sunflower print on Portobello Road and hung it in the kitchen. She found a nice piece of cod at the fishmonger's in Covent Garden; she baked it with a thinly sliced tomato, and it was very tasty—Milton said he'd had no idea she was such a good cook. He took her to see John Gielgud in *A Midsummer Night's Dream* at the Haymarket; they sat in the balcony and held hands. They spent lazy Sunday mornings in bed.

And now, today—finally—was the day for the election results. After three long weeks of waiting. Three weeks to tabulate the votes from servicemen overseas.

Milton was up at dawn. "The BBC is going to start announcing the results at eleven o'clock this morning," he said, pacing around the kitchen. "On the hour, every hour, as they come in." He checked his watch, although it was still very early: seven fifteen. "I was thinking of inviting the Bells over tonight to listen to the results together. Hopefully to celebrate." He grinned. "What do you think?"

"That would be nice." She enjoyed getting to know his friends; Simon and Tess were warm and welcoming. "But I don't know if we'll be celebrating," she said. "All the papers are predicting a Tory win."

At lunchtime, Milton appeared at the Food Office and announced to anyone who was interested that Labour had captured East Islington with a swing of 22 percent. They'd also captured St. Pancras and North Kensington. By early evening, the Labour gains came in torrents: Battersea, Barrow, Birkenhead, Mitcham, Mossley, Motherwell. Thirteen Conservative Cabinet ministers had lost their seats.

"This is incredible. It's a landslide," Milton said, back in the flat that evening, his voice choked with emotion. "This warrants something really special." He retrieved a dust-encrusted bottle from the back of the kitchen cabinet. "My grandfather's port from 1927. It survived the V2s."

While he was hunting for the corkscrew, there was a knock at the door. "I'll get it." Simon jumped to his feet.

He returned with a telegram. Milton opened it and looked at Lena with a huge grin. "It's from Mother." He laughed. "It's addressed to both of us."

It read: *You cannot fool all of the people all of the time.*

CHAPTER 48

LONDON, AUGUST 1945

The pubs and workingmen's clubs overflowed with jubilation. For the first time ever, there was a socialist government with a workable majority. Milton celebrated with glee. The flat was full of friends every night; two more bottles of Grandfather's port were called into service. The dreams rose sky-high: a national health service, a welfare state, nationalization of the banks, the mines, and the railways . . .

But, Lena thought, *the problems remain enormous. The housing crisis alone is overwhelming.*

A letter arrived from Lotti. She was reunited with Peter, and Charles was now able to pull himself into a standing position. Lotti's mother remained confined to Terezín because of the typhus quarantine, but she was reported to be in good health and Lotti hoped to see her soon. Emil had not yet been able to find his brother, Josef, who'd served with the Czech army on the Eastern front; sadly, he'd learned that his parents had been sent to Terezín in late '42 and had not survived.

The Adler family had all perished in Lodž; someone named Harry Feigl, whom Lena couldn't remember, had returned from Auschwitz but since died. Lena's Aunt Elsa and Uncle Victor were confirmed transported to Treblinka in 1943, where they must have perished. Even Great-Aunt Herta, who would have been almost ninety, for heaven's sake—did they have not an ounce of mercy?— had been deported to Terezín, where she had survived only a week. The Spitzer twins were missing, presumed dead.

Lena couldn't finish the letter. She didn't want to hear it. She couldn't let herself dwell on the fate of those who had stayed. She couldn't bear to think about what had happened to Máma and Sasha. She had to banish those thoughts, push them away into a deep cellar, behind a thick steel door.

She would never go back to Prague. She didn't want to think about Prague; she didn't want to talk about it. She turned her back and shoved as hard as she could against that door, digging in her heels, forcing it shut, until she heard it click.

EPILOGUE

ENGLAND, 2004

Oh, to be in England now that April's there. Well, here she is—with the weather obliging, for once. Sara stands at the French windows on a luminous emerald morning, surveying the lawn, with its border of well-trimmed shrubs. The gardener must be continuing his weekly visits, clipping the wisteria and snipping the hydrangea, keeping up appearances at all cost. As if nothing has changed.

"We could take a drive after lunch," she says to her mother, who sits in the winged armchair next to the fireplace.

She expects the suggestion to be welcomed with a smile, a visible relaxation of tension, perhaps. An outing in the car is the one thing Mum usually enjoys. Instead, she's fixated on the newspaper Sara spread in front of her.

"Oh dear," Mum says her voice rising. "Oh no." She points a blue-veined finger at the *Guardian* headline. "What am I supposed to do about this?"

"What do you mean?"

Sara can't hide her dismay. Just three months ago, on her last visit, the newspaper was still a reliable distraction.

"What am I supposed to do about this?" Mum asks again, a rising panic in her voice. Fifty dead and hundreds injured—mostly women and children—in the bombing of Fallujah, nineteen dead in Najaf—Iraq is a bloodbath.

"This is terrible, terrible." Mum shakes her head. "When will they ever stop?" She's wailing now, stabbing at the paper. "Nothing but fighting, fighting, fighting."

Sara has never seen her mother so upset. Mum has always been the one to maintain control, keep all feelings in check. She was disheartened last year during the buildup to the Iraq war. But not like this. Her father was upbeat, true to form, thrilled to see millions of young people filling the streets the world over, in massive antiwar demonstrations.

"Just look at that," he said, pointing at the television. "Who says they're just a bunch of juvenile delinquents? Gives you hope for the future."

"It's not going to do any good," Mum scoffed. "Bush and Blair will go ahead anyway."

Dad was dead before she could gloat that she'd been right—felled by a sudden heart attack the month before the invasion.

Sara removes the newspaper. She opts for a change of scenery now. A drive along leafy, green lanes. *We could even try lunch in a pub,* she thinks.

After ten minutes of fussing and coaxing, Mum is installed in the car. Sara starts the engine. "Shall we go to Upper Wolmingham? To the Fox and Hounds?"

"*Ja, ja.* That would be nice."

Sara doesn't usually notice her mother's accent, but she hears it now in that *ja*—her version of *yeah.* Growing up, she was always surprised when other kids asked, "Where's your mum from?"

Where's she from?

She's from here. She's from the kitchen, from the living room, from the bedroom at the other end of the long, creaky hallway. She's coming in from the garden with runner beans or peas. She's running the bath for Sara's little brother. She's baking a cake for the village fête. She blends into English country life like a chameleon.

But she *was* from somewhere else. And she has no family. It's just never discussed.

"We need to get gas," Sara says.

She knows she should say *petrol*. But she has been here only two days and the word sticks in her throat, sounds foreign to her now. In a few more days, it will roll out easily and she will talk about the *boot* and the *bonnet* and taking out the *rubbish*, not the *trash*.

Trash: rubbish. Gas: petrol. Tom-ay-to: tom-ah-to.

But she can't call the whole thing off. She straddles both sides of the pond: an aging mother on one continent, teenage daughter on the other.

She pulls into the gas station, silently converting liters into gallons and pounds into dollars: $7 or $8 per gallon, thereabouts. She will remember that next time someone complains about the price back home. The Ford Focus has a tiny tank, but it still sets her back £60—almost $100. Too late, she realizes she didn't need to fill up. Force of habit from the land of milk and honey and $2-per-gallon gas. She's the only one who drives this car now; half a tank would have been plenty.

The buttons on the machine are confusing. You have to pay inside, Sara remembers now. But before she figures that out, she seems to have selected the car-wash option for £3 on top. Well, what the hell. The car is filthy, anyway. Splattered in Sussex mud.

"Roll up your window."

Mum stares at her, uncomprehending.

Sara points her chin ahead. "We're going through the car wash."

She reaches across and turns the crank, awkward at this angle. No power windows.

Guiding the car into the tracks and shifting into neutral, she blinks to fight off fatigue. She's still jet-lagged, didn't sleep well last night.

The sharp burst of spray jolts her awake. The car jerks forward into the arms of the giant brushes. Soap envelops the windows and obscures the view as they're rocked gently forward. It's like being in a cave in a dark rain forest, sheltering from a storm.

Mum lets out a whoop of delight. "This is fun."

Sara sees her mother staring at the spectacle with childlike wonder, her eyes bright. She starts to laugh, and Sara laughs, too;

they both laugh loudly, until tears are rolling down Sara's cheeks. She wants to hold on to this moment, cherish the sheer joy of it, store it up as a bulwark in the face of what's to come.

Three months later, the heat wave breaks the day before Sara's arrival, leaving in its wake a cold and gloomy July like many she remembers from her childhood. The women's finals at Wimbledon are postponed yet again because of rain. She switches off the television and returns to the radio. She has discovered Classic FM on this trip: criticized by some as too lowbrow, featuring mainly the most popular movements of well-known symphonies and concertos. But really, what's so wrong with that? Mum seems to like it. The music soothes her. Earlier this afternoon, in one of her lucid moments, she recognized Beethoven's Sixth. So odd how she can retrieve the name of a symphony but not that of her granddaughter, and certainly not what time of day it is or who visited an hour ago.

Sara glances over at the bed. Mum is still sleeping. Her skin is stretched pale and taut over her cheekbones, her mouth strangely misshapen, gaping as if caught off-guard while it labors softly in the familiar task of taking the breath in and out, in and out, as it has for eighty-five years. Her hand lies exposed on top of the covers, its dry, wrinkled skin marked with irregular brown splotches and purple bruises from all the blood draws.

Sara is struggling to accept the deterioration since her last visit. She should have known from all the phone calls back and forth; in fact, the hospital bed in the living room and the wheelchair were her suggestions when she heard about the falls, the struggle to get up the stairs. But when she walked in the door yesterday, she was shocked.

"What time is it?" Suddenly, Mum's awake.

"Four o'clock."

"The middle of the night?"

"No, four o'clock in the afternoon."

"Four o'clock in the afternoon?" Her eyes dart around the room as she heaves herself upright. "I have to get up. I can't lie in bed all day."

Sara gently eases Mum out of bed. She used to be an inch or two taller than Sara, but now she barely reaches her shoulders. She stands before her like a tiny, frail sparrow and looks up with a smile.

"Thank you so much, dear. I'm sorry to be such a nuisance."

Sara settles her into the wheelchair. "Could you help me with more of the photographs?"

Yesterday, Sara unearthed a box from the back of the living room cupboard. She has never seen it before. Obviously an antique, it is beautifully crafted, from two different types of wood, one golden and the other a deep, rich red, rosewood, perhaps, and inlaid with an intricate pattern of brass around the edge. It's stuffed full of photographs. Those on top are familiar, although she has not looked at them in years: dozens of square black-and-white snapshots of her and Phil sitting on the beach, building sandcastles, exploring rock pools, piling sand on their father while he dozed. And the group shots from the large gatherings at Sara's grandmother's house, also from those early childhood years, carefully inscribed on the reverse in her mother's neat writing, with the date and subjects clearly designated *left to right*.

But yesterday, as Sara delved more deeply into the box, she uncovered other, much older photographs. She's never seen these before. And they are not identified.

"Who's this?" she asks. "Are these your parents?"

Sara knows almost nothing about Mum's family, almost nothing about her past. There was a grandfather, Mum's father—but he died when Sara was very young, and he wasn't mentioned much. And Uncle Ernst, she never met; he lived in Czechoslovakia, out of reach behind the Iron Curtain, until he died of a stroke in his fifties. Sara has heard occasional vague references to other family members who died in the war, but somehow she has always known this is a taboo subject. Something terrible happened, something too terrible to name.

"Let me see—where are my glasses?" Mum angles the photograph into the light. "Yes, that's right, that's right," she says, leaning forward to retrieve more from the box. One shows two women walking briskly in overcoats, carrying pastry boxes secured with string.

"Who's this? Is that you?" Sara asks. "Is that your mother?"

Mum leans back, dropping the photograph onto her lap and closing her eyes. Has she fallen asleep again? Sara continues to sift through the pile. A young girl on a beach, squinting into the sun, the date on the back: August 1935. Suddenly, Mum is awake again, leaning forward, reaching into the box.

"Oh my goodness, look at this one!" she says, her eyes brightening. "There we all are!"

"Let me see."

It's a faded three-by-five showing a group of young adults, six of them altogether, seated in a small, untidy garden with two sides of a brick dwelling angled behind them. No one is looking at the camera, each person engaged in some activity, either seated on straight-backed wooden chairs or standing around a table at the rear. Some are reading, one man is at a typewriter, and one of the women—there are two women—appears to be sewing. A black cat basks in the sunshine.

"Who are these people?"

"This was in Upper Wolmingham. Must have been soon after I arrived."

Sara looks into her mother's eyes. They look clear and focused now, and her voice is calm. Sara feels her own pulse quicken with nervous excitement. The haze has lifted; there is so much she wants to ask. She's afraid of saying the wrong thing, not knowing what might trigger the confusion again.

"Go on," she says, as gently as she can.

"I don't want to be cremated."

This comes out of the blue the following morning, as Sara helps her mother brush her teeth. She's in her wheelchair in the downstairs bathroom, in front of the sink.

"All right." Sara tries to keep her tone neutral, but she's surprised. Her father was cremated last year. So was Granny. Cremation has always been the progressive thing to do. "Why not?"

Mum returns to brushing her incisors in a broad, circular motion, round and round, as if stuck in a groove. Sara gently removes the toothbrush and offers her water for rinsing.

"Why don't you want to be cremated?"

"Because Hitler cremated my mother and sister."

Sara freezes. A memory comes rushing back to her from years ago, in San Francisco, after she had been there only a couple of years, maybe: the Jewish Film Festival. Funny how so many of her friends were Jewish. There was a film at the Roxie. Sara can't remember the title—something like *Generations Apart*. Sara was with Noreen and . . . what was the name of that woman who worked at Rainbow Grocery? They arrived late and squeezed into the back row. Sara can't recall much of the film itself, but it was about the sons and daughters of Holocaust survivors, and how they inherit their parents' grief. What Sara remembers most is her reaction. She couldn't stop crying. She sobbed and sobbed. Noreen put it down to Sara's feeling vulnerable because she and Alex had just made it through yet another big-fight-almost-breakup scene. But Sara felt there was something more. Something she couldn't pinpoint. They emerged from the theater, the fog rolled in with a vengeance, and Sara couldn't stop shaking the whole way home.

She looks at her mother now. Mum still holds the toothbrush, but she leans back, eyes closed. Sara remembers her mother's silences, the years of looking away, holding in tears, clamping down on any expression of emotion. "Don't cry," she always said. "There's nothing to cry about."

"Tell me what happened," Sara says now.

Mum sighs. "This is the thing: I don't know. I never knew what happened to them." She looks at Sara now and holds her gaze. "They have no grave, no date of death. That has always been the worst thing. Not knowing."

Sara walks into town to do errands. Karly, her sister-in-law, has come to relieve her, and she's glad for the break. She marvels at the patience of the caregiver, who does this full-time and is on a well-deserved vacation. The sky brightens as she walks up the hill; it's milder today. She unzips her jacket and quickens her stride, savoring the exertion. She enjoys this walk, enjoys the town, in fact, somewhat to her surprise. She didn't grow up here—her parents moved from The Hollow

many years after she left home, after Granny died—and she expected
to despise its all-white, small-town smugness. But now that she lives
in California, she's thrilled, in a guilty-pleasure sort of way, to be able
to walk to Marks and Sparks and Sainsbury's and buy chocolate bis-
cuits and tea, and whatever else takes her fancy, to bring back home.

As she reaches the pedestrian precinct, she checks her watch:
almost 4:00 P.M. It's 8:00 A.M. in California; Megan will be up soon.
She reaches into her pocket for her cell phones. Still nothing on her
English phone; she left a message earlier for Mum's doctor, wanting to talk to him about Mum's fluctuating levels of confusion. She
switches on her US phone, and immediately it buzzes to life. There's
a text message waiting. Sara pulls out her reading glasses.

OMG!!! It's all in capital letters. *I GOT THE PART!!!*

Sara's thrown into confusion and then plunged into guilt.
How could she have forgotten? Yesterday Megan was going to hear
whether she'd passed the audition. Sara should have called. But she
was exhausted and went to bed early, switching off her phone. Now,
she moves to the side, dodging a woman with a huge stroller, and
thumbs her response: *Fantastic!! So proud of you.*

She smiles broadly; she really is proud. The Berkeley Rep came
to the middle-school drama club to recruit extras for a new production. Sara thought it was a long shot. But Megan got accepted! That's
great. She can't remember what the show is called.

Her phone vibrates again. *Rehearsals start in three weeks. So I
don't have to do pottery camp, right?* ☺

Sara laughs. She insisted on some structure for the summer.
Megan wasn't keen on the pottery; Sara thought it sounded fun. She
texts another response. She's much slower at this than her daughter,
needless to say, but she still thinks she's pretty hip to be doing it at all.

Guess not. LOL. What's the name of the play again?

She goes into Boots. She needs more wipes and pads for Mum.
She finds them quickly and is standing in line to pay when the
phone buzzes back. Having to reach for her glasses each time makes
her considerably less hip.

Brundibár.

That's right. *Brundibár.*

"Next customer, please." The girl at the till is waiting for Sara to unload her basket. "Boots Advantage Card?"

Sara shakes her head no. *Brundibár*. It suddenly comes back to her. She clasps her hand to her mouth, stifling a strange grunting noise that's escaping from her throat. She can picture the book Megan brought home from the school library. Based on a children's opera originally performed in a Nazi concentration camp.

A Czech concentration camp. Terezín.

She gathers her purchases and stumbles outside. It was a children's book with beautiful illustrations. She wants to find a copy. She abandons her plans for Assam tea and cookies and heads for the bookshop at the far end of the mall. The book is there on a display table in the children's section, as if waiting for her: the glossy cover in yellow and pink, with a picture of the boy and girl with their milk pail. She strokes the dust jacket and clutches the book to her chest.

Back at the house, Mum is up in the wheelchair, looking perky. Karly has fixed her hair; they're drinking tea. Sara blurts out her news.

"Megan has a part in a show at the Berkeley Rep. In the chorus." She can hardly catch her breath. "They're doing *Brundibár*. The children's opera from Terezín."

Mum looks up, eyes wide. *"Brundibár?"*

"Do you know about it?"

"Of course I do."

Sara displays the book. "I found a copy in Waterstone's." She sits on the sofa. "Such beautiful illustrations." She hesitates. "How old was your sister? What was her name?" Sara can't believe she doesn't even know this.

"Sasha." The sound pierces the room. The three women hold it in silence for a few moments.

Sasha. Sara. Similar names.

Sara is the first to speak again. Softly, as if not to trample on a grave. "How old was she when she was in Terezín?"

"Eleven, maybe twelve." Mum's voice sounds thick. "She loved to sing."

Sara opens the book on her lap. "May I read it to you?"

Mum nods. Sara reads out loud, strong and clear. She reads

the story of Popicek and Aninku joining with the other children and animals to defeat the big, bad bully Brundibár, celebrating their victory over the tyrant.

"It's amazing that the Nazis allowed them to produce such an obvious allegory of resistance," Sara says.

"Tsk." Mum gives that familiar dismissive flick of her wrist. "The children were carted off to Auschwitz as soon as the show was over." She points at the book, her hand trembling. "Does your version have the very last page? The true ending?"

Indeed, there is another page, an epilogue Sara hasn't noticed, a last word from Brundibár himself. He's not done; he threatens to return. "*Nothing ever works out neatly/ Bullies don't give up completely.*"

When Sara looks up, tears are streaming down her mother's cheeks. She rushes over, crouching in front of the wheelchair.

"No," Mum says. "Nothing ever works out neatly. No matter how much you hope it will."

Sara takes her into her arms, and, for the first time she can remember, the two of them weep together.

ACKNOWLEDGMENTS

This novel would never have become a reality were it not for the early encouragement of Willa Rabinovitch, Junse Kim, Michelle Huneven, Robert Boswell, and Claire Burdett. I am deeply indebted to the ongoing support and feedback over the years from Susan L'Heureux, Martina Reaves, Ruth Hanham, Karen Hunt, Paul Davis, Richard Seeber, Linnea Chistiani, and Raleigh Ellison, and especially to David Schweidel, who constantly challenged me to improve my writing even if I wasn't prepared to accept all his suggestions. I am grateful to Pamela Feinsilber for detailed editorial advice in the revision process.

This is a work of fiction, but it relies heavily on the oral and written memoirs of my late parents, Vera and Jasper Ridley. In addition, I have shamelessly stolen a number of anecdotes from the memoir *Very Convenient Everywhere*, written by my parents' good friend, the late Richard Seligman, and used with kind permission of his son Peter. Another of my mother's friends from Prague, Fred Turnovsky, wrote a memoir entitled *Turnovsky: Fifty Years in New Zealand*, with early chapters which were very useful. I am also deeply indebted to my father's lifetime friend Christopher Small, who not only gave me valuable feedback on the manuscript in its early stages and corrected a number of anachronisms, but also gave me the long letters which my father had written to him during World War II, which provide extraordinary and unique insights into the political climate during the last two years of the war.

Other published works which I used extensively to educate myself about every facet of life during the period include: *The People's War* by Angus Calder; *London at War* by Philip Ziegler; *London 1945* by Maureen Waller; *Ten days to D-Day* by David Stafford; *The Twilight Years: Pairs in the 1930's* by William Wiser; *A Moveable Feast* by Ernest Hemingway; *The Spanish Civil War 1936-1939* by Paul Preston; *London War Notes 1939-1945* by Mollie Panter-Downes; *Ernie Pyle in England* by Ernie Pyle; *Continental Britons: Jewish Refugees from Nazi Europe* by Anthony Grenville; *Women in Wartime* by Jane Waller and Michael Vaughn-Rees; *The Internment of Aliens* by F. Lafitte. Also extremely valuable were the Mass Observation archives at the University of Sussex Special Collections Library; London's Imperial War Museum; and the BBC World War II People's Archives available on-line at http://www.bbc.co.uk/ww2peopleswar/categories/.

Jim Davies from the British Airways Archives and Museum at London's Heathrow Airport helped me understand details of air travel between Paris and London in 1940. Professor Igor Lukes from Boston University kindly met with me and provided interesting insights into the source of the rumors about Nazi troop movements on the Sudetenland border in May 1938, which we now know to be false, but which were taken seriously at the time. Marta Tomsky corrected the Czech and Ulrike Ganter and Birgit Zorb-Serizawa helped with the German.

I am very grateful to She Writes Press, especially Brooke Warner and Cait Levin, for believing in this work and giving it a chance to go out into the world, to Annie Tucker for her editorial expertise, and to Monica Clark and Reese Lichtenstein for assistance with proofreading.

And a million thanks to Judy and Abby who put up with so much and made it all possible.

ABOUT THE AUTHOR

Barbara Ridley was raised in England but has lived in California for more than thirty years. After a successful career as a nurse practitioner, which included publication in numerous professional journals, she is now focused on creative writing. Her work has appeared in literary journals, such as *The Writers Workshop Review, Still Crazy, Ars Medica, The Copperfield Review,* and *BLYNKT.* This is her first novel. Ridley lives in the San Francisco Bay Area with her partner and her dog, and has one adult daughter, of whom she is immensely proud. Find her online at www.barbararidley.com.

Author photo © Limor Inbar

SELECTED TITLES FROM SHE WRITES PRESS

She Writes Press is an independent publishing company founded to serve women writers everywhere. Visit us at www.shewritespress.com.

Even in Darkness by Barbara Stark-Nemon. $16.95, 978-1-63152-956-6. From privileged young German-Jewish woman to concentration camp refugee, Kläre Kohler navigates the horrors of war and—through unlikely sources—finds the strength, hope, and love she needs to survive.

All the Light There Was by Nancy Kricorian. $16.95, 978-1-63152-905-4. A lyrical, finely wrought tale of loyalty, love, and the many faces of resistance, told from the perspective of an Armenian girl living in Paris during the Nazi occupation of the 1940s.

An Address in Amsterdam by Mary Dingee Fillmore. $16.95, 978-1-63152-133-1. After facing relentless danger and escalating raids for 18 months, Rachel Klein—a well-behaved young Jewish woman who transformed herself into a courier for the underground when the Nazis invaded her country—persuades her parents to hide with her in a dank basement, where much is revealed.

The Sweetness by Sande Boritz Berger. $16.95, 978 1 63152-907-8. A compelling and powerful story of two girls—cousins living on separate continents—whose strikingly different lives are forever changed when the Nazis invade Vilna, Lithuania.

Portrait of a Woman in White by Susan Winkler. $16.95, 978-1-938314-83-4. When the Nazis steal a Matisse portrait from the eccentric, art-loving Rosenswigs, the Parisian family is thrust into the tumult of war and separation, their fates intertwined with that of their beloved portrait.

The Belief in Angels by J. Dylan Yates. $16.95, 978-1-938314-64-3. From the Majdonek death camp to a volatile hippie household on the East Coast, this narrative of tragedy, survival, and hope spans more than fifty years, from the 1920s to the 1970s.